The Infinite Woman

The Infinite Woman

EDISON MARSHALL

FARRAR, STRAUS AND COMPANY New York

To N. S. M. J.

". . . a maiden tall, young, slim-thighed, and strangely beautiful, the daughter of tameless Lilith."

from *Great Smith*

CONTENTS

BOOK I

INDIA

3

BOOK II

THE NOVICE

29

BOOK III

THE WORLDLY

125

BOOK IV

KRISHNA THE JOYOUS

209

BOOK V

THE DARK MOTHER

305

India

*W*HEN *the painter Ingres was about sixty-five years old and at the height of his powers—although he was to paint nobly for twenty more years—he received in his studio in Paris a young woman called one of the most beautiful of her times. She reminded him, he said, of the subject of his famous portrait, Mlle Rivière, and he would like to paint her in a similarly ornamental setting.*

"I don't think such a background would do for me," she replied, thinking of the rich velvets and embroideries of his masterpiece.

"Why not?" the master asked.

"I feel too close to the earth."

He appeared startled. "Then the earth must be very beautiful in your sight," he suggested.

"How did you know?"

"One with such visual beauty as you have can't fail to visualize beauty all about you. Each of us is a mirror to his own world. What scene would you choose?"

"I'd like to have you paint me nude in a harvest field. One whom I love very much would be pleased."

"He has a discerning eye, that person. Yes, it would tie up well— the autumn sky, the yellow sheaves, the sun on the stubble—a last brightness of the year in contrast with your brunette coloring." Then a smile curled his delicate lips. "But you know—I'll have to include an angel with a pointing finger."

"It would be nice to put in an angel, if you don't paint her as being too ethereal. She should be the kind to enjoy a bucket of ale with the harvesters. But what would her pointed finger mean?"

"In ancient symbolism, it means the presence of God."

3

"That's all right, too, I think. People have always felt the presence of God at the harvest."

"Will you sit for me, Lola?" the artist asked, his eyes alight.

"I'd be very grateful."

But circumstances prevented the sitting. No great painter ever portrayed her love for the earth and nearness to it, and harmony with it. If so, the sky should have had a dramatic array of clouds, betokening storms past and yet to come. The flight of geese overhead could suggest the wideness of her world and the boldness of her dreams. And not far from the angel with leveled finger should be shown another visitor to her scenes, a form equally beautiful whose finger was pointed down. Because of her beauty she was boon fellow to them both. . . .

There are signs and wonders on the great rivers of India, and if a lone goose passing high honked down at an alien child in her eighth year, the watching natives might well have touched their amulets. Called by the pretty name Lucia, and never wishing I was a little boy, still I would have recognized the sky-wanderer as my fellow adventuress. I did not yet know the word in English but knew its Hindustani equivalent. It meant one who seeks and finds treasures and will not turn back from danger.

My parents had brought me, like a four-year-old piece of baggage, from Ireland to Calcutta three rains before. But this time I accompanied Papa and Mamma, their fellow *voyageuse*—from Calcutta to Dinapore up the Ganges. They thought it the same as before, but I knew the difference. Papa, whose eyes ever glistened in his plain face, had told me without knowing he had done so.

"Larrikin, it's uncommon dangerous, a-going up river," he had said. "Drowned we may be in the deep waters, or murdered by heathens on the bank. But if we make Dinapore alive we'll live in a fine house, wi' bhoys and maidservants at beck and call, and you'll have a new dolly, and belike I'll win my jacket."

Papa meant that he would become a captain, which was much finer than being a lieutenant. "Larrikin" was his pet name for me.

4

It meant "little Lawrence" in the county where he had been raised, and the old folk there applied it to young scamps.

"I'm not 'fraid," I told him proudly.

"Then see you don't fret, or vex our pretty lady."

Our pretty lady was Mamma. I mustn't tag her about except when her face told me I could. When captain sahibs romped with me in our little bungalow, I could tell the very instant that Mamma's smile changed on her face, and it was time for me to go outdoors or to bed. On one occasion I had not heeded the sign. The Colonel Sahib was holding me on his lap, talking and laughing with me, and because Papa's face was so bright, I did not look at Mamma's smile changing and stiffening. Suddenly ashamed and afraid, I climbed down and ran off, and although Mamma never spoke of this badness, when the Colonel Sahib had gone she spanked me hard for something else I had done that day, and had completely forgotten.

Even when I was alone with Mamma and Papa, she did not want him to pet or play with me too long. Papa and I made it up, though, when she was away visiting.

All this was as it should be, I thought. It belonged with what was "good" as opposed to "bad"—the heaven and hell of childhood. It was the Law that Mamma should have her wishes in everything. But I felt sorry for Papa, instead of blaming him, when she scolded or shrieked at him because there was no money for her to spend. He had done something awfully bad a long time before. I did not know what "rose from the ranks" meant except that it was to blame for Mamma "marrying beneath" her and being fretted and vexed. The blood of a Spanish nobleman flowed in her veins, she said; and I felt sure she had been stolen by Gypsies from a castle in Spain. Her skin and eyes were dark enough, and all the princesses in the fairy tales had golden hair like hers.

We set out in river boats called budgerows, part of a great flotilla transporting the whole regiment. We stopped at cities with many towers and long bazaars, or put in at pretty villages to eat mangoes and drink coconut milk and peer at stone images of elephants, tigers, crocodiles, and strange gods. Often we saw wild elephants drinking at the river margin, and once a real tiger roared at us from a brushy island, and live crocodiles slept between their feastings on the mud reefs. But the gods whose forms were carved in stone did not show themselves even in the twilight. I was glad of that because they were so terrible.

Hardly an hour in the day were we out of sight of the smoke from rows of fires along both banks of the river. These were the burning ghats of the Hindus. Far and wide over the great river the things were floating down; and when I could not help but see one, I ran quickly and played hard. One night it seemed that morning broke in a red rush, and when I was wakened by shouting and ran out on the deck to look, it was a good thing that Papa had told me to be brave. It was as though the biggest burning ghat on all the river were setting fire to the flotilla. It proved to be the Colonel's boat, already a tower of flame, and three other boats were soon ablaze from the flying embers. The crackling roar of the great golden torches and the leaping shadows were Death's very voice and shape, I thought, and we would all go floating down in horrid blobs. . . .

But the boatmen strove mightily to bring our boat upwind, and while Mamma stood watching with her hands pressed against her forehead, Papa ran about stamping out firebrands falling on the deck. I saw one fall close to the cabin and I ran and picked it up and threw it in the water.

"None of our bhoys was burned up," Papa told me, when the last low flames had hissed and disappeared. "But some poor devils of natives ne'er need go to the ghats."

"I don't think that's fair," I answered.

"Ye're a queer little colleen, Larrikin. But the Ould Reaper will come for plenty o' us when he gets round to it. The bhoys in the band lost all their horns and drums and music, for which I'd almost trade the Colonel himself. 'Twill be fair dreary of evenings, without their blessed tunes."

I had loved the band music and had often danced to it all about the boat. Since the night a captain sahib had danced with me, Mamma had forbidden me to "show off" before company; but no one had stopped me from dancing with my shadow when she and Papa were visiting other boats, or in front of the native boatmen, who laughed and clapped their hands and gave me sugar cane and sweetmeats. I thought that the Old Reaper did not like music. He hated light feet and bright eyes and happy faces. Well, I hated him! If that would make him come for me soon, I hated him still. When, on the next evening, there was no music swelling and pealing across the water, I danced to a little tune running through my head.

"How old is the little memsahib?" a villager asked, when Manu and I went to shore with some boatmen to have a bent keel straightened.

"She has seen but seven rains," Manu replied. "If she were like most sahibs' children, that would count her hardly more than a baby. But in wit and learning, truly she is as a daughter of Hind who has seen seven suns."

"Will some sahib soon take her to wife?"

"Fool, the memsahibs may not marry until they have flowered. Then usually they keep company with youths of their own age or older for three, perhaps six years more, ere they are brought to lawful bed."

I knew most of the words, and because they were being applied to me, my mind groped for their whole meaning.

"What of unlawful beds?"

"God knows, and Shaitan guesses. But among them, few have the name of *harami*." The latter was a word I did not know.

"Manu, what does *harami* mean?" I asked, when the villager had walked on.

"It is one whose parents are not married to each other."

"I did not know it was possible."

"Truly it is," he instructed me gravely, "and thereby the unblessed one loses *izzat* (face) among his fellows—unless indeed the father is a great lord. At the worst, it is better than not being born at all."

"Is not to be born worse than to be dead?"

"The dead have breathed, worked and played, rested when they were tired, eaten when hungry, loved and been loved, and have wept and laughed. It may be—the gurus tell us so—that we are only visions flickering through the mind of Brahm, and when he ceases to dream, earth and heaven will pass away. Even so, I am glad that he dreamed of me—and of you, Laraka Memsahib."

His eyes always twinkled when he called me that, pretending that he was trying to say "Larrikin." In Hindustani Laraka was applied to a spitfire.

"It is commanded that you call me by my right name, in due respect to your mistress."

"By my gods, it is not Luch-cha?" Again he was teasing me, for although my first name was Lucia, Manu purposely slurred it to the Hindustani word meaning rogue. "I would not have listeners think you are a daughter of Shaitan."

"Then I will think up a new name—one that fits me like my skin—and it will be a secret between you and me."

In a few minutes I was taking great joy in watching the village blacksmith, a huge, brawny, bearded Punjabi, straighten the bent rudder. Sparks showered; his great hammer thundered; he handled the big piece of iron as though it were pine.

"He is strong as a god," I told Manu. "What is his name?"

"He is called merely Lohar, according to his trade."

It was the first time I had heard the Hindustani word for blacksmith, and I liked the sound of it.

"You may call me Lohar Memsahib."

Manu burst out laughing. "Little one, you will yet crack my ribs. Now if you were Russell Memsahib—" She, Major Russell's wife, was taller than Papa, and her coolies grunted when they lifted her palanquin.

"Russell Memsahib is big, but she is not strong like Lohar. She stood on the deck and yelled all the time the boats were burning."

Manu pulled his nose thoughtfully.

"Nay, I will not call you Lohar Memsahib—yet," he remarked. "I would not have my comrades fall down with laughing. But truly, baba, your spirit is stout for such a young one, the gift of Vishnu for all I know, for he provides for everyone's most bitter need."

T W O

AT Dinapore we did indeed live in a larger and better house than at Fort William. Although Papa had not yet won his jacket, servants were so cheap this far upcountry that he hired a groom for Mamma and a nurse for me, in addition to Manu, the cook, and the sweeper. It was still the least number serving any married couple on the station—Mamma told him so almost every day. We were little better than paupers compared to the Russells; and Captain Ferguson, although a bachelor, had twice as many in his stables alone, besides his own liveried palanquin coolies. What need did I have of a nurse? I would run just as wild. Why couldn't she have a maid in her place?

Truly, I neither needed nor wanted the weak-voiced, dim-eyed slut, and she became a lady's maid overnight. I wished, though, that I could have her job of combing Mamma's beautiful shining hair.

Izzat was almost as important as food or drink, and at eight I had learned how to gain some for myself. Wearing pretty clothes and keeping clean did not count as much as being made much of by the officers and men, and especially by the Colonel. I was too odd-looking to be called pretty, but I made every pooja (magic) that the natives taught me, so that I would become beautiful. I made the same prayer before a mirror as when pouring milk in a hand-molded mound of cow dung: "Let me be beautiful as Mamma!" It was more than desire and had nothing to do with vanity. I was aware of some deep-seated necessity . . .

When she and Papa entertained, Mamma sent me to the compound or to bed. I was forbidden to accompany my parents to the club or to family gatherings because I was "pert" and a "show-off." It was soon all too plain to me that Mamma did not like to have me near her even when she was alone. Sometimes it caused an actual ache in my chest, and there was always a little cloud over

9

every happiness. Yet I could not learn to be retiring and demure; truly I did not even try. The less she favored me, the harder I fought to win the favors of the very officers with whom she most frequently rode and danced. I could sing and dance well for one of my years, and could recite my experiences with natives—little adventures, ghost and animal stories, and the like—with a good deal of *élan*.

It so happened that Mamma became my ally in winning one heart's desire. When Papa had been ordered on a month-long mission into the Chota Nagpur, I begged to go with him. His protests that the road was long, rough, and possibly dangerous were stifled by Mamma's insistence that fever was a great deal less in the cool hills, and anyhow she couldn't look after me without Manu's help. In spite of Manu, I *ran wild*.

The issue settled, Papa rejoiced, and Manu's face shone. For part of the journey we put up at rest houses built by the John Company; farther on we slept in tents erected by our porters and camp boys. We saw wild elephants, bison bigger than the largest draft horses, and countless deer. Tigers killed and dragged away some of our bullocks, leopards murdered our dogs; and the chattering of monkeys was no more alien to our ears than the languages of the hillmen; and to me their faces were beautiful and strange. They had never before seen a *chota* (little) memsahib, and brought me delightful gifts.

Then among a tribe of what Manu called *haqir* (debased) Hindus, I had an experience which possibly had never come to any sahib or memsahib in Indian history. They would not have allowed an older alien on the scene; and if Papa had been in camp instead of away for the night conferring with a village headman, he would have been horrified at the thought of my going there. His confidence in Manu was well placed in matters within Papa's imagination. But there were other matters of which Manu's opinions would raise his hair.

Our head porter had asked Manu to go with him to a nearby temple, to see some pooja. Manu had refused, on the ground that he must stand guard over me. Out of respect for his izzat I did not interrupt the conversation, and when the porter had gone out, I had no need to voice the wish thrilling my heart.

"Wah, your eyes are like rush lights," he told me. "But you need not shine them at me, Laraka Memsahib, because if I did what they bid me, the sahib would beat me until I wetted my breech-clout."

"The sahib need never know," I answered.

"Yea, you can keep a secret, as I learned when you caught me in a shame. But, Laraka, although I know not its nature, this tonight will be mighty pooja which my eyes dread to look upon."

"I told you my name is not Laraka. It is Memsahib Lohar."

"And I told you you are still too little for its great weight. Still, the temple is but half a kos from here, and if you are slain I will be also, and so need not behold the sahib's wrath—" Manu thrust a finger under his turban and scratched thoughtfully.

"Why should they slay us, Manu? You shall ask them if the pooja is forbidden—"

"Religion is like arrack, little one. A small amount of it warms the heart; too much inflames the brain. There be danger, truly, but we will face it, as together we faced the raging tiger in the pit. Sit on my shoulder and we will go."

The temple was in a grove at the outskirts of the village. There the villagers were too excited to look at me twice. When Manu asked a white-robed guru if my presence was permitted on this holy ground, he gave me a dreamy smile.

"Tonight we do what is well in our god's sight," he replied. "Thereby our fields will be blessed and bear heavy crops. Bid the white child look well."

So far the scene was much the same as at a low-caste wedding. Drums were beaten and fifes blown; and the people surged about carrying torches, eating, drinking, and shouting; a few danced wildly and a guru fell in a fit. But when some other gurus began to sweep and sprinkle the ground in front of an image of the goddess Kali, there was no sound but their murmurings and the low hum of the flames. Then out of the temple came a young man and a young woman, wearing white robes and wreathed and girdled with flowers. They moved stiffly, and I would have thought they had eaten bhang except for the expression on their faces. I had never seen its like before and would never fail to recognize it thereafter. In Hindustani the word was *khushi*. In English it was rapture.

They knelt before the goddess, and two priests brought what seemed to be toy swords. Instead they were made of ironwood, worked to razor-like sharpness. Each made one quick movement in front of the kneeling figures at the level of their throats. Instantly the bodies toppled backward under the guru's hands. Then they lay side by side under two leaping fountains, brilliant crimson in the torchlight.

I threw my arms about Manu's neck, but did not avert my eyes until the jets sank low and then disappeared.

"We will go now, Manu," I told him.

"Wah!" he muttered, as though waking from deep sleep. "Yea, let us go quickly."

When I had got into bed, he brought me a wooden cup half-full of pleasant-smelling liquid.

"It be a little arrack, mixed with coconut juice and flavored with spice," he told me. "Drink it, chota memsahib, and you will sleep deeply with pleasant dreams."

"I need no medicine, for I am already drowsy," I answered. Actually my heart was thudding like a tom-tom, and the back of my neck tingled. "But if it tastes good—"

"The *burra* (great) memsahib—Memsahib Lohar—will relish the taste," he broke in, his eyes gleaming.

His lips were curled in a smile of love, not in jest.

"The thing they did was wicked," I told Manu. "If their god is pleased, she's a wicked god."

"There be many wicked gods," he answered, wiping his face.

"I will not make offering to her, and I hate her."

"God alone knows what you will do before you go to the burning ghat. I love you and tremble with fear."

"I will not be afraid of her. If I am afraid, no one shall know. But I will not take the name Lohar, for it is a man's name."

"It be true," Manu murmured.

"I will take a pretty name, something like Lohar but—"

"What of Lobiya?" he asked anxiously. "It is very good to eat."

"I think Lola is pretty, though I know not what it means. Yea, I shall be called Lola. Do you think it will be a lucky name?"

"Were the two we saw decked in flowers lucky? Is the tigress lucky in her wicked beauty? Heed not my words, Lola Memsahib! The *diwani* (madness) is upon me tonight. But this I know. Whether your kismet be good or evil, you will look it in the face."

THREE

*M*OST of the people living in the hills did not worship Kali or any Hindu god. All they had in their place were good or bad spirits called bhuts, who lived in the bodies of animals, in the rivers and lakes and forests, and especially in trees. Their usual way of driving off the bad ones and welcoming the good ones was to hold a big feast of deer and wild-pig meat and to drink palm toddy until even the little children danced with joy. As for cutting their own tribespeople's throats to please them, they would not dream of anything so wicked.

But among the Hindu gods was one who delighted my heart. The more that Manu told me about him, the more I wanted him for my own.

His name was Krishna and his business was herding cattle. He carried some kind of flute, on which he was always playing lively tunes that set the people to dancing. He encouraged the young men and the girls to get off together and make love, and it made him angry when a father sold his daughter to a mean old gray-beard. He himself had fallen in love with a girl named Râdhâ—Manu was not sure whether she was just a very beautiful mortal or a goddess born in mortal form. In any case he often played and romped with the village girls watching cattle, and for this he was greatly beloved by the common people. He liked to do the same things they did—sing and dance and drink a little palm toddy and make love—and he would much rather make them happy than have priests worship him in gloomy temples, or do favors for rich people and kings. As for people offering him sacrifices of chickens and goats that they needed to eat, let alone beautiful boys and girls, he would shake the heavens with his fury at the thought.

"I will ask Krishna to be my god," I told Manu, my heart glowing. I was past nine now and felt equal to the great decision.

"It comes to me he will not refuse you, even though you are of the sahib-log," Manu answered.

"Since the people make him offerings of fruit and flowers, I will also, if you will tell me where to find his altar."

"Eat the fruit and wear the flowers. That will please Krishna just as much or more."

"If I love him enough, do you think he may fall in love with me?"

"I think he will come in the person of a beautiful young sahib."

"How soon, do you suppose?"

"Perhaps not for six rains."

"You told me that in two or three rains I would be ripe enough—"

"Yea, but you are of the sahib-log. It is the bidding of their god that young flowers be not plucked, and be left on the vine until full-bloomed. Although the new moon of love is beautiful, their god demands that they await the full moon. It be my own opinion that wisdom lies halfway between the feast of the Hindus and the famine of the sahib-log—but I am an old gardener of little wit."

"I told you I am of the Hind-log and the sahib-log, so I, too, will embrace Krishna."

"He will embrace you, have no fear!" Manu chuckled.

A few days later there was a trouble in my heart, and again I spoke to him about the gods.

"I love Krishna," I told him, "but I tremble with fear of Kali."

The glint in Manu's eyes died away and they were dull as stones.

"With good cause, little one."

"I can smell the burning ghats even now."

Manu picked a spray of jasmine that the wild bees loved.

"Smell this, Lola Memsahib, and forget."

"Maybe I should not have taken a name so like Lohar, the name of strength. The boast may anger Kali."

I looked for reassurance in Manu's face, but found none. "It is not well to boast before the Great Ones, but it may be—since you are white—that the Dark Mother will pay no heed."

"Perhaps if I make offering to her shrine—the one close by the well—it would avert her anger."

"It would be a cunning stroke, chota memsahib."

"I would not give her Shikra." This was my little beagle hound, whose name meant hunter. "But I might put there my dolly."

"The *haqir* Hindus put there—for all her shrines are one—a maiden and a youth more beautiful than your dolly, and their bodies were not stuffed with sawdust." Manu spoke quietly, in a casual tone, and his eyes did not meet mine.

"I forgot, Manu, that my word had gone forth from me not to make offering to Kali. But I remember it now, and remember what you told me when I would keep the puppy, Shikra's sister, that I had promised Willie Sahib. That if I broke—the word—that had gone forth—you—would be shamed." I broke out crying.

"Have mercy on your servant, Lola Memsahib!"

"I bid you forget that you saw the drops or heard the sound."

"Little one, have you heard talk of the black sickness striking in the native city?"

"The doctor sahib told Papa so, but they did not know I listened."

"Did you then remember how in Calcutta it took a score of Tommi and four from your father's mess? Aye, you did—and again the sickness is everywhere up and down the river. But your mother has the protection of Yahowah, and your father—"

"Papa quarreled with a Christian guru when he was a youth and has no protection. Yet he, too, would not suffer me to give my doll to Kali, the slayer of the young and the beautiful, as well as the old. I—I will not call back my word that has gone forth."

But I did not know that today Papa had gone into the native city to see to the burning of some dead from whom the people had fled. On the third day thereafter, Papa sent word that he would not be home for dinner, and for Mamma and me not to be alarmed if he did not return at all that night, because he might be called upon to take the guard. At breakfast the next morning Manu came running, his face ashen, to bid Mamma and me come at once to the soldiers' hospital. Mamma began to wail, and when her silly maid went shrieking into the compound, I helped her dress.

"Why aren't you crying, too, you heartless little wretch?" Mamma screamed at me, when I begged her to be still and make haste.

"If I was crying, I couldn't see to find your bonnet," I answered, not in the least aware of what a strange answer this was.

But it seemed strange to be able to talk and walk with that awful aching emptiness in my chest. When we got to the hospital, the doctor sahib hurried into the hall to meet us.

"Lieutenant Riley was stricken yesterday morning," he told Mamma in a queer-sounding mutter. "I thought it might be seasonal malaria and acquiesced to his desire not to alarm you. Now his heart is failing, and I must warn you he's very low."

Mamma started to wail again, but quieted when the doctor sahib patted her shoulder.

"Can I go to him, Doctor?" she asked. "I won't, for my little girl's sake, if you say not."

"You'd best go no closer than the doorway."

Papa looked at us and instantly knew us, but we would hardly have known him. His eyes were sunken in his head, his features looked pinched, and his skin was dark blue. His lips moved, and when I could not hear what he said, I broke from Mamma's grasp and ran to his bedside.

"Stand back a bit," he ordered me in a hoarse whisper. "And to touch me, you'll not, alive or dead."

I could only nod.

"Hark to me, Larrikin, and heed me. Tell Mamma 'tis sorry I am I didn't do for her all I'd promised."

"Don't die, Papa."

"Tell her if Captain Ferguson wants to marry her—and I know they love each other—she's not to wait in mourning for me, and I give 'em both my blessing."

"Please don't die, Papa!"

"I can't help myself, Larrikin. Now shut yon door."

I did so, and when I turned back his eyes that had been stone-dead glimmered a little.

"I heard how ye told the tarradiddle about me being bastard to a lord."

"Oh, I didn't mean—"

" 'Twas a white lie if ever one was told, and I said not nay or yea. Ye knew I'd risen from the ranks and didn't want me shamed. But shamed I never was, and don't you be."

"I swear by Krishna, I'll always be proud."

" 'Twas the Iron Duke himself who 'warded me my sword, when I'd brought him a dispatch through heavy fire. It counted more there—on the field of Waterloo—then winning one on the delivery bed of a fine lady." His voice grew stronger and a trace of color welled through his blue skin. "And my Larrikin must win more than that, if I'm to rest in peace."

In terror of the desperate strain he was under in trying to talk, I tried to interrupt him. A little motion of his hand bade me be silent. Then I thought I should run and get the doctor, but an expression in his eyes made me stand and wait.

"Why shouldn't I talk to my Larrikin, while I still ha' breath?" he asked. "If 'twill shorten my stay by a wink or two, so much the mercy. A fine lady you'll never be, but travel far and climb high ye surely will, if ye don't falter and ye don't give up. And no matter what befalls, ne'er forget ye are the daughter of Tom Riley, who taught himself to read and write, and stand up for such as him against the foe."

A startled expression came into his face. When I moved a step nearer, he shook his head.

"Stay where ye are, Larrikin," he told me in a breathless whisper. "Bless me, if I don't think I'm going this minute."

"No, no—"

"No use to say no to the Old Man. He passed me by at Waterloo, but he won't again. The bullets flew like hail. . . . The cannons thundered and the flags waved . . . and the trumpets sounded shrill. Do no' ye hear 'em? Do no' ye hear 'em! *Hark to 'em, over the hill!*"

Papa lifted his head from the pillow and tried to raise to his elbow. Then he fell back as quickly as did the flower-decked offerings at Kali's shrine.

I called the doctor then, and he held a mirror in front of Papa's lips. Thrice he looked at it, wiping off a faint mist, before he showed Mamma and me the unclouded glass. Still I did not cry. My eyes felt swollen, but so did my neck, and my blood ran fast and hot, and the cold emptiness in my chest seemed filled with live steam. Mamma fainted in the doctor's arms and was revived by smelling salts, but I was never in my life more wide awake.

I remained so, every nerve taut, when, after long hours of people coming and going and talking in low tones, I was sent to bed. There I lay listening to some more of Mamma's crying spells, but they ceased, and before long the murmur in the parlor died away. The front door opened and shut no more, but the side door, into the garden, squeaked softly. The stillness was as deep as in the jungles of Chota Nagpur when I got out of bed and tiptoed to a window facing the garden.

I saw the moon first, full-faced at the very top of the violet-colored sky sprinkled with lonely stars. I had forgotten that this was the night of the full moon, known to me as the most wonderful and the most dangerous night in the month. Good and evil spirits flew far and wide, their power at greatest height. Dead people who could rest well on other nights rose up and walked, visiting the scenes they loved or hated. I could not bear to think of Papa rising from his new bed, so wasted and so pale, but if he did, I knew where he would come.

And this was the most wonderful and dangerous hour of the night of nights, for when the moon began to sail down she would begin to wane. I dreaded to peer into the shadow patches, lest I should find Papa lurking there, his hollow eyes fixed on a stone bench under the peepul tree. Mamma was sitting on it beside a tall man whom I thought was Captain Ferguson. His arm was about her and her misty-looking head on his shoulder.

I put on my clothes, got my riding whip, and went out the servants' door into the compound. Shikra, sleeping by my bed, had wakened and followed me, but I knew he would not make a sound, and when I whispered to him to *"pana* Manu," he led me behind an outbuilding. There we found him sitting in the heavy shadow of the wall, careful not to attract needless attention from who might be near, and taking what comfort he could from his opium pipe.

"Wah!" he breathed, at sight of me.

"Will you come with me, Manu?"

"In the name of the gods, where? If to the sahib's burial ground I—I cannot come."

"Nay, only to the shrine of Kali, close by the old wall behind the shafakhana." The total distance was not more than a quarter of a mile.

"Can you not wait until daylight? It is as much as our souls are worth to come nigh the Great Ones at this hour."

"Nay, I cannot wait. Until I go, Papa cannot rest and his dead eyes will weep, and I—I, too, will die."

"Is it to give Shikra unto Kali? If the sahib has returned from where—where he lies and bade you do so, I myself will wield the knife—"

"Nay, it is not meet that she should have him."

"Your eyes are big and wild. I think it is the diwani. But I will come with you."

I walked hand in hand with Manu, Shikra trotting behind us, until the moonlight showed us the form and face of Kali under a stone cowl. She was pit-black with four arms, each with a red-palmed hand; her eyes were red, and her tongue and face and breasts were stained with blood; her teeth were pointed fangs, and around her neck was a string of skulls and about her waist a girdle of twisted snakes.

I cried out and, jerking away from Manu, I ran and struck her hard as I could with my riding whip. In such fury that I lost all terror of her sinking her fangs in my throat, I dealt her blow after blow. But now the tears that so long had ached to flow came gushing, and the awful tension in my breast suddenly passed off. My arm was too weak to raise the whip again. The next moment I was sobbing on Manu's breast.

Shikra had barked savagely at the image while I was lashing it; now he whimpered at Manu's feet. When I had quieted a little, I heard Manu invoking very Brahm to defend us from Kali's fury.

"Are you still alive?" he marveled, when I stopped crying. "If I had not seen it with my own eyes, I would not believe."

"It is not Kali, only a piece of stone."

"Yea, but Kali's *kama*—" Suddenly he bayed with laughter, loud and harsh and betokening escape from terror and return to the everyday world. "Look you at Shikra—"

The little beagle was standing under the cowl, his leg nearest to the image calmly lifted. I, too, laughed in an old remembrance of joy.

"Now do you the same as Shikra, to finish well the work of this wondrous night!" Manu cried. . . . "Truly, little one, Krishna, too, must be fit to die with laughing, and I think he stands between you and her revenge. Truly, too, the sahib is gone, but I think he will rest well tonight. Now let us go home to bed."

FOUR

MAMMA and newly promoted Major Ferguson were married quietly three months after Papa's death. The only people in the least shocked were the natives, whose notions of the proper disposal of widows ranged all the way from bestowing them upon the husband's male next of kin, to throwing them alive on his funeral pyre. In this case the killing was done in the name of the goddess Sati, who appeared to be later wife of Siva the Destroyer, but who actually was Durga who in turn was Kali, whom I hated with all my heart.

None of the ladies of the station hinted that Mamma had remarried in undue haste. They knew not the day that their own spouses would be carried off, in which case they wished to strike while the iron was hot. I had not the least objection to the match, since I had been taught young the utter gulf between the quick and the dead, and that life was to be lived. My only regret was being five or six years too young to marry him myself. He was a blond Scot, extremely handsome, and the richest sahib on the station; none of which counted with me so much as his grandeur on the drill field when he had cracked his company about him like a whip.

But there might be another reason for my coveting him. It lay way down deep on the dark bottom of my mind, as broken idols lie on the bottom of the Ganges.

I was to be his daughter, my new stepfather told me, as though I were born to him. Since I was going on ten, ripening fast under the Indian sun, it was a big order to feel daughterly to a man of twenty-five, two years younger than Mamma's purported age, and at least four years under her real age. When he kissed me, I liked to watch her smile stiffen and her eyes change expression. But it was dawning on me that in every serious dispute, Mamma prevailed over him, and I did not know to what lengths she might go.

This same anxiety cast a shadow over the most proud occasion of my young life. It happened that the Governor General of all India, Earl Amherst of Arakan, visited Dinapore on a farewell tour. He was to review the troops, then be entertained at a garden party given by the Colonel, to which all the sahib-log big enough to walk were invited. Nor was Mamma able to prevent my going. Under my stepfather's beaming eye, I had picked out from a Parsi's shop the prettiest and most expensive dress I had ever owned—a deep-blue velvet with white lace trimmings in the newest French style.

I had seen a few knights—they were fairly common in India—but this was my first view of a nobleman. Tall, gray, with a fine humped nose, and wearing a red and gold uniform with blazing decorations, he looked every inch an earl. The station people were waiting to be presented to him when he and the Colonel appeared. Big majors looked nervous and their bejeweled wives flustered as their turn neared. Then I thought about my new dress, silk hose, red slippers, and little cap, from under which my dark hair flowed as pretty and fluffy as the brush of a black fox.

When Mamma's turn came to meet the earl, her airs did not appear to impress him. I was so glad that I needn't brace myself any more, and was able to curtsy gravely to the nobleman and wait smiling, my eyes on his, for him to speak to me. This I had practiced in front of the mirror the night before.

"Who is this young lady?" he asked the Colonel, who was still speaking to Mamma.

"Mistress Ferguson's daughter, Lucia, one of the prettiest on the reservation. Lucia—his lordship!"

He gazed at me with glowing and, I thought, startled eyes.

"Pretty, my eye!" he burst out. " 'Pon my honor, Colonel Rogers, the chit's beautiful."

"Thank you, Lord Amherst."

"Do you know it, miss?" Without waiting for my reply, he turned and spoke gravely to the Colonel, unaware of the people listening and watching. "Sometimes they don't know—the real ones, I mean. This is a real one, one of a handful I've seen in India, and perhaps the most unique. Real beauty is as rare as real genius. It's undefinable and"—he glanced, without knowing it, I thought, at Mamma—"and unexplainable. It always thrills me to see one."

"No, sir, I didn't know it," I said when he paused, "but I'll always believe it, now you've said so."

"By God, this is a real adventure!" he burst out. "Yes, believe it and believe in it. What is your name again?"

"I was christened Lucia, sir, but I named myself Lola."

"It always goes with imagination," he told the Colonel. "I sometimes think that it *is* imagination, incarnate." He turned to me again. "I'm an old man, Lola, but I hope I live to see you five—seven years from now. This is my salute to the gift of the gods."

Bending from the waist, he took my hand and kissed it. Immediately he turned to speak to my stepfather; and, trying not to cry, I walked on.

I was both exalted and terrified. A scheme had been hatching in Mamma's mind ever since her marriage. I had had no trouble guessing what it was and was now certain she would put it into operation. Her chance came at dinner when my stepfather, glowing with pride, teased me a little about naming myself Lola. Well aware of Mamma's sharp eyes, I told as plausible a lie as I could invent.

"I thought that since Mamma has Spanish blood in her veins, I'd like a Spanish-sounding name."

"I'm afraid I don't care for it," Mamma remarked, smiling at me. "It sounds like a half-caste's name. There are so many Portugese half-caste girls out here—I don't want strangers mistaking you for one of them."

"I wouldn't mind. Some of them are mighty pretty." But that remark was a mistake.

"Your new papa and I would mind—very much. And being as dark as you are—and speaking Hindustani better than English— well, people who don't know about you might very easily be doubtful of your origins. Darling, you're picking up quite a few native ways, too."

"Lord Amherst didn't find any fault with her," Major Ferguson said.

"He said that he'd like to see her five or six years from now. I'm looking forward to that, too—but I want her to be an English lady, not a Colonial, and I want her to have something more than good looks. What schooling she's getting is haphazard, to say the least. Andrew, if I had any money of my own—and please understand there's not the slightest obligation upon you—I'd spend every penny of it to have her raised in England."

"I want to stay with you, Mamma—and with my new papa," I cried.

Except for this, there was nothing I could say to help my cause. My stepfather had been raised in a strict Calvinist home in Scotland and would be shocked and angry if I took issue with Mamma on anything. Mamma had brought up the subject in my presence only to please my stepfather's sense of fair play, and after supper she gave him some signs and signals I had seen before, then led him off to bed. As if I didn't know what she was up to!

After giving them time to undress, I tiptoed to the back veranda and put my ear to a little aperture in the wall, through which ran a rope to operate their punka. "It's a gloomy old house with grim old servants, where I didn't dare laugh out loud," I heard him say.

"Andrew, don't you see that's exactly what she needs? I warn you, that if she doesn't go—and at once—she's going to *go wrong!*"

"I'd miss her so. But let's talk about it afterward."

"No, I want you to promise me now that we'll do what's right for her. I know it's not your obligation—but I'd love you so much! When I think of her as she is now—in such *danger*—it's like a dash of cold water—"

"You're right, of course. Well, I'll pack her off to Kelso. Now show me how sweet—"

I tiptoed away without one board creaking under my feet. My face was drawn as though I were weeping, but not one tear dimmed the footpath through the quarter to Manu's hut. "Ai!" he called, when I tapped on his door, and soon we were squatting in the shadows of the oleander shrubs, a posture that we both found more comfortable than sitting on the grass. There I told him what had happened.

"These be bad tidings, Lola Memsahib, but I have expected them long ere now," he told me.

"If you will go with me, I will run away."

"It would be poor service to you, as you will see, when your head is cool. And you do not know that woe may be turned into weal? How can you harden your muscles save through labor, or sharpen your wits, save through adversity? And can you find pearls in the brook? Nay, you must seek them in the black waters of the sea."

"I see now that I am all alone."

"It be true that you must walk alone, but only thus may you win your prize. It is always thus, with those who win great prizes. Nay, I am not a mulla, only an old gardener. When I seek to read your riddle, my head swims."

"It is fool's talk, and you love me not."

"I love you more than my first-born, a son who is tall and valiant. Because I am only your servant, I can love you without hating you the while, which few of your own kind can ever do. Memsahib, the nobleman spoke truth. The sahib-log who saw you every day would not believe their eyes, but the great sahib saw you with eyes fresh and unafraid. The memsahib fought the truth bitterly and long, and at last she has sent you into exile, to excape from it."

"If it be true, she will confess it before many rains, and on her knees."

"Thus speaks my Lola Memsahib! I, who am as low as the noble-man is high, also look upon you with clear eyes. But will it content you at last to dazzle a few sahibs and memsahibs in this alien land of Hind? Those who love you, you must reward, and those that hate you, you must cast down, and those that wound you, must suffer the torments of Jananna. Will you be satisfied with beauty, and not the power it may wield? Whence did the beauty come? Did the gods who hate you, for your defiant spirit, give it you? Nay, I swear that you built it into your own face and body."

"It is again the diwani."

"Nay, the moon is old and sick, and my eyes are all too clear. This much more I will tell you, by my soul's troth. You have seen but ten rains, but already the die is cast—and there be many visions before my eyes. I glow with pride, chota memsahib, and tremble with fear."

"Will you make pooja for me every night when I am gone?"

"Aye, I will weary the gods with my pooja-making."

"If I send you a ticket for the great ship, will you come to me?"

"Across the black waters, memsahib? I have little caste already, and that little I would lose. Yet if you need me enough to send for me, by your god Krishna and by very Brahm, I will come."

BOOK II

The Novice

$\mathcal{K}$ELSO on the Tweed had a pretty setting, and a ruin of a cathedral one-third as old, and one-tenth as weird, as some of the ruins in India. Sir Walter Scott was old and sick at nearby Abbotsford, but his tales were hard for me to read and his characters seemed pale compared to the hero Rāma, and the Dwarf, and other half-gods of whom Manu had told me. The sun at summer midday was pale and feeble compared with the Indian sun at winter rising; the fogs off the river darkened my eyes, and the autumn winds bit me to the bone.

My step-grandfather, Noah Ferguson, did his duty by me with grim conscientiousness. He said it was no less because we were not blood kin; I was his son's stepdaughter, and he would see that I walked the straight and narrow path into Christian womanhood. The prayers went on and on in the cold dawns and in the candlelit chill before I went to bed, and the floor was hard to my knees. At mealtimes they were only long enough for the porridge and meat to cool.

Grandsire—so I was told to call Mr. Ferguson—was never deliberately cruel or even harsh: his sternness toward me stemmed from the same sort of piety that I had seen that dreadful night in Chota Nagpur. Indeed his favorite Bible story was of Abraham tying up his little son for sacrifice to Jehovah, only to find a ram caught in the thorns to offer in his stead. He was greatly worried about me, and blamed my "frivolousness" and fiddle-faddle on a bad upbringing among the heathen. Grannam, however, lean and sharp-faced as an ax, was more inclined to believe I was naturally vicious. She wanted to believe it, I thought, so that she could take out on me her smothered fury at her son Andrew's marriage to a flighty widow. While she was burning up my prettiest and gayest dresses and bonnets and little shoes—they were more fit for a Jezebel, she said, than a modest God-fearing lass, which she would make out of me with God's guidance—her face looked as wicked in its way as Kali's.

The dresses the seamstress made for me would uglify an angel. Again I wore my hair brushed back and fastened in severe braids. I was much too old for my years, she was always saying, and as though the repetition was a kind of pooja, I had the feeling not of growing up but of getting younger. My stepfather had written her that my name was Lucia. Grannam said it was too foreign-sounding to suit her and called me Lucy. That was a small thing compared to my losing heart to call myself Lola. In dreams I was ever searching for a girl of that name—a girl whom a great earl had called beautiful—but could never find her. When I wakened and went to look in the mirror, she was not there.

Often I dreamed that I was in India, under a blazing sun, and had forgotten how to speak Hindustani. In those dreams I searched in vain for Manu amid the green and gold, and cuddly, sniffing Shikra lay with his throat cut at Kali's shrine.

At the close of my second year at Kelso, Grannam told me to wash and put on an unrumpled dress because I was to meet great-folk. My weak surge of hope that they would be of Earl Amherst's ilk died away when I saw her glinting eyes.

" 'Tis Lady Kirk of Belfast, wife to a baronet, and her daughter Annie," Grannam told me. "Though good Calvinists, they have lands near Limerick where you were born, and she took a gracious interest in you when I told her so and has given me leave to present you to her ladyship."

Lady Kirk proved to be a large, heavy-featured, iron-gray woman who impressed me more than I wanted her or even myself to know. Her daughter Annie, old enough to marry, looked almost as thin and as cold as an icicle.

"If Lucy's manners are not quite those of our good Scotch lassies, you'll please consider the circumstances of her bringing up," Grannam said with ill-concealed annoyance. " 'Twas in India, you mind, where white people forget God's ordinance, and manners and morals are lax." Both women had expected me to curtsy to them but I had merely bowed my head.

"I'd think they'd be all the more God-fearing," Lady Kirk answered, "considering how the people there die like flies."

"Lucy, with Lady Kirk's permission, you may sit."

My heart had choked at what the lady had said, but now it beat fast and strong.

"My papa died out there," I said as I sat down, "but not like a fly."

"I'm sorry to hear the first part and I don't know what you mean by the second."

"He died brave like he'd always lived."

"I would rather hear that he died in fear of the Lord, as becomes us all."

My face felt hot and was no doubt red, for when Grannam glanced at me, she thought best to change the subject.

"Lucy, you never expected to be sitting down with a lady of title, did you?"

"I never thought about it, Grannam, to tell the truth. But I was flattered to have an earl kiss my hand."

"An earl?" the woman's daughter broke in, in an amused tone. "Who was he, pray tell?"

"Earl Amherst of Arakan, Governor General of India."

"I'm glad you were sensible to the courtesy paid you by such a courtly nobleman," Lady Kirk remarked. "I hear that a good many Anglo-Indians, as they are called, look above their stations."

"Having all those servants goes to their heads," Grannam said quickly. "Lady Kirk, you told me you remembered Lucy's father. She'll be grateful for you to speak of it."

"I told you I recalled her grandfather, Larry Riley. He was a tenant farmer on one of Sir Andrew's estates—and an honest, God-fearing man, who, learning to respect his betters, gained self-respect. Only just now do I remember his son—perhaps there is something in Lucy's face that recalls him. Lucy, wasn't his name Thomas?"

"Yes, ma'am."

"Why, I remember him well. There was a streak of wildness in him, and his father feared he would come to a bad end—especially after he rose from the ranks to a lieutenancy. Old Larry Riley knew the danger that lies in humbly born boys being placed in positions that are better reserved for gentlemen. 'Be gorra, 'tis hopin' I am he won't get no foolish notions,' Larry told Sir Andrew. I remember the occasion as though it were yesterday."

All three women fixed their gleaming eyes on my face. But I remembered Papa's eyes, sunken, dulled by death, then suddenly glimmering. *Stand up for such as him against the foe.*

"Well, Papa did get a lot of notions," I said, trying to keep my voice from shaking. "You see, the Duke of Wellington awarded him his lieutenancy on the field of Waterloo, and Papa said—and I agree with him—that was much more honor than winning one in bed."

"In bed—" Lady Kirk gasped.

"Yes, ma'am. He meant being born to a colonel's wife or the like. Papa went up instead of down. He told me to keep on going up, and I will. I wouldn't be content with being a baronet's wife. That's just one step above a knight's wife, and they're thick as fleas in India. I'm going to be a countess, but not by marrying an earl. I'm going to be created one, by a king."

A long silence followed this, and I was cold in my chest as a snake.

"Fancy that!" the girl burst out at last.

"Mistress Ferguson, this young person is no blood kin of yours, is she?" Lady Kirk asked after one big heave of her bosom. "Have I your leave to speak rather plainly to her?"

"You needn't mince words, Lady Kirk."

"Lucy, I can understand you taking pride in your father's exploit. It does you credit. But don't you know when you talk like that, you only make yourself a laughingstock? What are your gifts and qualifications that you should ever be raised to nobility? Mark you, I'm not angry with you in the least. Can you imagine anything said by a girl of your age and position ruffling me in the slightest? But I do—with all my heart—feel sorry for you."

"Those are my sentiments exactly, Lady Kirk," Grannam said. "Lucy, now you've spoken so freely, you may go to your room."

I went there with dry eyes, and after I had lain very still in bed for a few minutes, I got up and gazed into the mirror. Lola was not there. It was again as when I had searched for her in dreams. Even Lucia, whom Mamma had hated, was not there. There was only a wan-looking peasant's daughter who did not know her place. She was all alone there, as Manu had foretold, but instead of a heroine seeking great prizes, she was a laughingstock.

Then I went to a hiding place and got out three tokens that Manu had given me, whereby to be remembered by the Great Ones. One was a salagram stone and another a dried sprig of the tulasi plant, both sacred to Vishnu, of whom joy-loving Krishna was the avatar. But lest I offend Siva, an equally powerful god, the third was his image, inset in a small lingam of sandstone. I put them on my dresser and knelt before them, but there was no rustling sound as sometimes I had heard or imagined hearing, and no lightening of my heart.

"I *will* be a countess, whether ye help me or not," I told them in Hindustani. "And that is my word that has gone forth from me, and if I break it, may Shaitan take my soul."

I still believed in Krishna the Joyous. As the months dragged on, slow but sure as a buffalo cart on the road to Patna, I clung to that belief with desperate fervency. Often I made pooja to him in the dairy—out of sight of everyone, shaping a little mound of cow dung with my hands, then pouring on a little milk, but I never heard his pipe; and when I had turned thirteen, my worship of him turned to strike at me as though in treachery.

A dour housemaid found the tokens and took them to Grandsire. When he called me to him, he had dropped them in the coal scuttle, and his face was like Abraham's as he prepared his son Isaac for the sacrifice. Grannam was standing by him, with her nose curled and her thin mouth twisted.

"I'll ask you, Lucy, what you mean, by keeping abominations in a godly house," Grandsire said.

33

"They're not abominations. They're sacred objects to the Hindus, and I kept them for—well, what you might call good luck."

"Wicked fetishes, that bit of chuckie and the sprig o' green, or you wouldn't have had 'em wrapped in finest silk. I ken not what they signify, and don't care to ken. But what of yon obscenity?"

He pointed a shaking finger at the lingam. When I started to pick it up, his shout terrified me.

"Don't touch the foul thing!" And when I had recoiled, "Do you not know that when Mag had touched it, kenning not what it was, she nigh scrubbed off the skin of her hands, ere she deemed 'em clean?"

"Nay, master, they're not clean yet, and won't be till I've prayed," Mag, standing behind Grannam, said in hollow tones.

"Why, 'tis a wonder the Lord dina blast down the house wi' his thunders, as he poured fire and brimstone on Sodom and Gomorrah."

For a few seconds I was utterly bewildered. Lingams are seen everywhere in India, some of them twelve feet tall. In one of the temples in Dinapore there was one set upright in a circular, perforated stone: after Manu had shown it to me, and explained its symbolic meaning, I had never given it another thought. Although I had known that the small sandstone lingam Manu had given me was the male symbol of re-creation, I had never dreamed it could be considered obscene. Now that I needed and wanted to be angry, all I could feel was despair.

"I've handled it a hundred times without getting dirty," I said, out of a cramped throat. "There's nothing dirty about it. It's a symbol of Siva—"

"Pick up yon scuttle and dump it in the fire!" Grandsire demanded in a fierce voice.

I stood still and held my breath and suddenly my throat eased.

"No, sir."

"You'd best not disobey me, Lucy."

"My name's not Lucy. It's Lola. And I won't throw my gods in the fire."

"Her gods!" Mag cried. "Would ye but hark!"

"I think a good old-fashioned whipping will do the minx good, and I'll gi' it to her," Grannam said.

"If you whip me, Grannam, I'll kill you."

She drew up and I knew by her eyes she was frightened.

Grandsire snatched up the coal scuttle and, swinging it with all his strength, hurled its contents against the inner wall of the fireplace. The stone fell among the ashes; the tulasi sprig was instantly consumed, and the lingam broke in two pieces.

"That settles it," he said. "As for you, Lucy, or whatever you call yourself, there's a home in Yorkshire for the indigent bairns of officers who died in service, and we'll leave it to the matrons there to make a Christian woman of you. You'll set forth Sunday morn."

SIX

I WENT to my room and began packing my belongings. Although not sure yet where I was bound—certainly not to a home for paupers—my heart was decidedly lighter. Among my treasures was a string of amethysts given to me by a headman in the hills of Chota Nagpur, superior to one I had seen in a shop window in Edinburg priced at fifty guineas. And in fashionable Bath dwelt General Sir Edmund Judson, knighted for his service in India, whose granddaughter Kitty had played with me during his brief stay at Dinapore and sent me an invitation to visit her, in case I came near Bristol. Kitty and I had sworn everlasting friendship in the way of little girls, and her grandfather was both rich and generous. . . . Before I had strapped shut my first bag my mind was made up.

Grandsire offered me some money to pay my fare by river boat to Berwick, and by coastwise ship to Hull, as well as some extra for incidentals. I accepted it wistfully and gratefully, at which his wrath cooled; and by a little play-acting on the way to the boat—I was in high spirits now and enjoyed the game—I won not only his parting blessing but an extra pound which I prized a great deal more. Also I had learned a lesson that would stand me in good stead.

By pinching pennies I made the money last all the way to London. The weather grew brighter every day. Here a fellow passenger who took a fatherly interest in me helped me sell my amethysts— they fetched nearly forty pounds—and recommended me to a genteel inn. Ten pounds of the sum went for new dresses, hose, and shoes, all of these a little less extreme in style and color than my native taste would lean toward, but picked to point up my dark hair and skin, blue eyes, and small, slender, but well-developed figure. Until now I had failed to make good use of a natural aptitude for cunning. I had even felt dimly ashamed of it, as being not quite pukka, forgetting that the Dwarf, one of Krishna's manifestations, had employed it to win a universe. From now on I meant to stay down from my high horse when the gate was too high, and wriggle through the bars.

Kitty Judson gave me a hearty welcome to her grandfather's fine house in Bath, and I tried to make sure it would not soon wear out. It did not take me long to learn how to ingratiate myself with her, the old general, and the servants. Kitty was a pretty blond girl, eclipsed by her frumpy clothes and clumsy toilet. I redressed her hair and directed her purchase of a new wardrobe, effecting an improvement startling and delighting both her and the household. In no time the pair of us, like a dark red and a yellow rose, took the eye of the old roués in Queen Square.

Kitty took her grandsire for granted. Careful not to stand in her light, I made much of him, listening open-mouthed to his stories, filling and lighting his pipes, stroking his forehead to ease his headaches, and rubbing his feet when they were lame, and keeping track of his spectacles, jackets, and slippers. At first I was sparing of shows of affection lest he think me forward, only to discover that his capacity for being petted was practically infinite. The effectiveness of that simple practice amazed me. I wondered if it applied to old men only and some day meant to find out. The cold and gloom at Kelso began to seem like a dream in the night. When in reply to my report, Grannam wrote me a letter of self-righteous malediction, it did not hurt a fraction as much as Mamma's rare prissy notes. My heart felt healed and I glowed with youth and health.

When at the end of the first month I had mentioned departure, Kitty pressed me to stay at least one month more. At the end of that period I confessed to the General that I must start search for some means of support, but he declared he'd be damned if the daughter of a hero and a young stepdaughter of that fine officer, Major Ferguson, was going to become a drudge; by God, he'd support and school me as Kitty's companion until her marriage. Although I had schemed it so, I could not keep from crying. It was a strange fact that when I was hurt or saddened, my eyes ached in vain for the benison of tears, as though my childhood gods had forbidden them. Of late they flowed easily over kindnesses done me and at pitiful scenes in life and in plays and books. Even beautiful music and poetry brought mist to my eyes.

Kitty and I studied under a good tutor, and once I had to dissuade Kitty from eloping with him. We took dancing lessons from an elegant Frenchman and French from a German lady; then spent three glorious months sightseeing on the Continent, during which I became quite fluent in this most delightful of all European tongues. From fifteen on, we made brief, well-chaperoned appearances at balls and levees.

Kitty was still too young to be introduced to Mrs. Grundy, yet too much under her thumb to have beaux. Although we met quite a few young bucks of fashion, it was always in the presence of our elders. We were kissed only by gray-haired cronies of the General, or in games with bashful striplings of our own age.

Bath was a Mecca, as the papers put it, for English society. As General Judson's protégée—as he frequently introduced me—I could in time follow Kitty as far as its fringe and probably catch a well-off husband moving in that fringe. As I drew near sixteen, I was obtaining a more sensible—mature was the better word—attitude toward life. With enough money, I could dress beautifully, entertain, flirt, be flattered, and become a big frog in a pleasant, if not large, pool.

The General's friends and blades of Bath often spoke of me as "a beauty," but never with the voice of Earl Amherst that unforgettable day, and their eyes held none of the same wonder. I thought that my being a dowerless "companion" to Kitty might curb their enthusiasm, but remained oppressed by a notion that I had not fulfilled the promise of my childhood. . . . My dream of Lola's becoming a countess in her own name had been a noble dream—but I had lost Lola in the misty mirror of the past. No more would I dip my hands in cow dung to make pooja to a hero-god.

In June, 1834, Earl Amherst came to Bath from his seat in Kent to treat a rheumatic leg.

We had had a royal duke only the month before—he had taken quiet lodgings—the chance of my meeting him again was not one in a hundred. . . . The upshot was almost enough to restore my faith in kismet. A quirk of circumstance prevented Kitty and me from going to see Macready in *Sardanapalus;* flighty girls that we were, at the last minute we decided to accompany the General to a stuffy supper with one of his cronies. As the footman announced us, I stopped, my heart fainting, in the door.

Although the earl was just leaving, he paused politely to meet the new arrivals. I was able to take the stance considered fashionable; when I was introduced as "Miss Riley," I gave him my best smile and bow. He had wonderfully clear eyes and for an instant they appeared to be troubled by an illusive remembrance. It dimmed out—he spoke a gracious word or two—then he passed on.

"What's the matter with you, Lucia?" Kitty demanded. "You look as though you've seen a ghost!"

"I don't believe in ghosts any more," I told her. Then I went to the dressing room, put a little paint on my cheekbones, and came to a great decision. The General was old and failing, his estates were entailed to heirs of his blood; at eighteen Kitty was almost certain to marry her second cousin, Ronald Atchison, long her grandfather's pick and beginning to be her own. I resolved to make hay while the sun shone. Starting tonight, I was going husband hunting, and would take the first well-to-do, socially presentable, virile, and decent bachelor under forty that came my way.

At midnight in my own room I carefully appraised my assets. Being able to speak Hindustani—only in dreams had I forgotten it—was not one of them, but I could do well with French, and was completely fluent in the fashionable English of the day. If the quarry liked society, I had been prize pupil of our dancing master; if he were of literary taste, I was widely read; if he were a burly sportsman I could play dainty femininity until it came to riding, then probably beat him. If my face were my most apparent fortune, what undisclosed charms could I somehow manage to advertise? Undressed before a wall mirror, I made a close survey.

To start with, my hair was so dark brown that it gave the impression of being raven black. My brow was wide and well molded, my eyebrows were narrow and had a slight upward flare at the temples, perhaps because of the lift of my bold cheekbones. My eyes were an authentic violet with dense lashes, long and perceptibly lifted at the outer corners. My nose was a trifle too long, but not conspicuously so and, as noses go, did well enough. My mouth was too large to fit the fashion of small cherry mouths, but had a childish mobility and warmth; my chin was strong; and my teeth sharp-looking, but of brilliant luster.

My throat would be as easy to chop through as Anne Boleyn's, and had a touching hollow. My shoulders were straight for a good breath, then fell away in what seemed to me lovely curves to long, tapering arms. My breasts, although not large, thrust boldly with the tensure of a hill girl's in India, and I was sure that if Lord Amherst could see them, he would pronounce them beautiful. They were my single most lovely feature, I thought, worth a tidy sum in the marriage market, and from now on I would choose dresses to do them justice.

Below them my body sloped to a narrow waist, trim and strong, the skin as tight over the smooth muscles as though made of elastic. My belly had always pleased me and would have pleased King Solomon, I fancied—but that was a part of the Bible Grandsire never read aloud; the grim being he worshipped was too stern and long-faced to have fashioned a beautiful woman. I admired the long low swell of my hips as must Lohar the mighty bulge of his muscles as he lifted his sledge, and with as honest cause. My slim legs were not at all like those of Venus de Milo, but would almost fit Botticelli's Venus, which I was bumpkin enough to consider the more beautiful of the two.

Indeed, with different coloring, more height and a rounder form, I could have been his model for that lovely picture. Perhaps in an earlier incarnation I had been a pretty Florentine street girl, whom the artist had brought home one night and painted in the morning, by the magic of his imagination creating the miracle of beauty. A like miracle had hovered over me, only to expire.

Between eleven and fourteen I had been increasingly aware of virginity. Then I had been shy of my own thoughts in regard to it—swiftly fleeing from them. At the door of sixteen I was far more consciously virginal than ever. It was a medium of innumerable perceptions: I was made wistful by sensuous music and poetry, the kisses of striplings, manly forms, and now my own image in the mirror. Often when my emotions were stirred by some experience which had no logical connection with love, I felt the recurrence of its yearnings.

If I were a dark-skinned daughter of Hind I would have eaten the fruit long since. In those societies enforcing purdah (female seclusion) I would have been married; among the hill tribes I would either be a wife or still testing out various lovers in the Men's House. The Indian sun might have made me susceptible, but I thought that the more vital girls of my mental and physical age all over the world shared all this with me, except perhaps its frank confession to themselves. My own honesty was an Oriental indoctrination brought about through play with native children and especially by my closeness to Manu.

If it set me a little apart from English girls, yet I was proud of it. True pride, as opposed to false, is ever nothing more or less than an inward recognition of a strength; I was sure that confronting my own nature, which was Mother Nature manifest in me, made me stronger. Standing before the mirror, I put this strength to test.

I must marry well, I thought. Now that I had forsaken my dream of great adventure—forced to forsake it by some loss I did not understand—there was no other means of obtaining a place in society that would fulfill my reasonable desires and satisfy my pride. But a new condition had now risen—I must make that marriage soon! Otherwise I would be in great danger.

"Because," I told myself, gazing into my mirrored eyes, my lips shaping the words, "what I really, truly want to do with my maidenhead is lose it."

SEVEN

*A*T least once in my life, Fate saved me from what surely would have been a disastrous mistake.

It moved in the person of a white-haired, white-bearded Spanish savant, staying in Bath because the hot springs benefited his gout. I was moved by his esthetic face when I saw him at a garden party, and thrilled when he beckoned me to his seat. He was a pale, blue-eyed Asturian holding a chair in French Literature at the University of Madrid, and when he got around to telling me his name, I found out it was Don Garcia Jacinto Ramon de Montero y Vicensa, but I could call him Señor Professor. Although enchanted with my appearance, he looked a little bored with my mother's claim to a noble Spanish ancestor.

He was the most fascinating conversationalist I had ever imagined, and at our first parting, after two hours in each other's company, I had fallen in love with him.

I was never to discover any other term for my feelings toward him. I came to idolize him, to feel empty when out of sound of his voice and sight of his face, to thrill with excitement when I sat at his feet. I could not endure the thought of his having any other inamorata, or I some other lover. I wanted to be Beatrice to his Virgil.

I gave him great delight, so he had suggested an arrangement that would legitimatize my spending from two to four hours every day in his apartment. It was that he become, nominally, my tutor in French and Spanish literature, for which I would make a token payment of a shilling a month. The broad-minded General was perfectly agreeable and rejoiced at my good fortune. In those hours I did very little but exclaim and nod my head with vigor. He said I was a blank page for him to write on, and truly he wrote beautifully. His dissertations in those subjects came to embrace the literature of all lands, history, and all the arts and sciences. Because I hung on his words, his instruction was etched in my brain, and groping for the meaning of the more difficult ones, my own language became immensely enriched. Every spare moment away from him I had my nose in some book of his recommending. Invariably we spent his shilling fee, plus a pound of his own, on a rude dinner of *arroz con pollo,* washed down with a bottle of divine amontillado.

The relationship lasted almost two years. My mind could not possibly have expanded as much in twice that long at the Sorbonne. It ended when Señor Professor returned to Madrid to resume his chair. His gout was practically cured, for which he accredited me more than the baths. At our farewell dinner he gave me a gold locket set with seed pearls containing a miniature portrait of himself by Andrew Pilmer, and a poem in my honor entitled "Persephone au Bain." When I lamented that I had no gift for him, he said I could give him something which would make him richer and leave me no poorer. This I gave him on his lips, and his eyes filled with tears.

I went mooning about, often weeping, for a week after his departure, then woke one morning with a healed heart and refreshened spirit. This was my eighteenth birthday and I wanted a new bonnet . . . I wanted a new dress to go with it . . . and a party to wear it to . . . and a young and beautiful and rich young man to be there . . . and a fountain in the garden whence he would escort me . . . and a surprise taking the form of his clasping me in a passionate embrace. I wanted old Earl Amherst to look at me now. I wanted to fly. I wanted a great adventure. . . .

A few days later, I participated in a street accident. At least it appeared no more than that to my conscious mind; although the air came sharp to my nostrils as in long-ago days I made pooja to Krishna and thought that he was near.

On the sidewalk of a street near the Abbey I met another stroller whom I took at first for a typical buck of fashion—wearing a top hat, large neck scarf, cutaway buff coat displaying two gaudy vests, and long, tight pantaloons of violet stockinet fastened garter-like to his shoes—a style of dress beginning to be disparaged in plain William's court, but strutted boldly in Bath. He stopped, turned sideways, and swept off his hat, meanwhile taking me in from head to foot with a rather more insolent gaze than a pretty girl was accustomed to expect from lordly young roués. I acknowledged the address by the merest inclination of my head, yet I felt vaguely disturbed. The reason seemed to be that I was a good deal more impressed by him than he was by me.

I read admiration in his large, magnetic gray eyes, but no intent toward me. His face did not ask the usual question—whether I was a lady out of easy grasp, or a doxy in ladylike guise—both common hereabouts. Perhaps he had been spoiled by women making much of him, I thought. His clothes indicated riches, his insolence betokened high station, and his looks were striking. He had glossy blond hair, fairly gold, brushed back from a high forehead, and his face was aquiline in the true meaning of that term—like an eagle's. Although he was not handsome in the usual meaning of this term, the strangeness and strength of his face gave an effect of beauty.

He had hardly passed when I heard him speak in the most haughty, withering voice I had ever heard.

"You clumsy oaf!"

I looked back on a scene that I could not dismiss as trivial. Because of factors I did not yet grasp, it had for me the aspect of minor tragedy. A tall man in his middle twenties, soberly and respectably but cheaply dressed, and carrying a big portmanteau, had started to cross the street a few seconds before; I had barely noticed him. He had been unfortunate enough to drop the portmanteau in a mud puddle close to the sidewalk, and mud and water had splashed on the beau's clothes.

The young man seemed utterly crushed.

"Pardon, m'sieur," he said in French. Then in foreign-sounding English. "I contritely beg your pardon—"

At that instant he glanced at me and his gray face turned brick-red.

"Don't beg the *barnshoot's* pardon," I told him in French. "The mud you threw on him's too good for him. Hit him in the face."

Completely to my surprise, the young man struck. It came as an equal surprise—and a painful one—to the dandy, who was staring at me fixedly as though he could not believe his eyes. Although the blow looked awkward, there was a great deal of power in it. Catching the dandy on the side of the jaw, it knocked him flat.

He got up at once, dusting his hands, his eyes shining, and with what I looked at twice before I recognized as a faint smile on his beautifully carved lips. Suddenly I was terribly afraid for the gangling dark-eyed man standing in an awkward position beside his broken portmanteau.

"I won't hurt your friend," the buck told me quietly. Then turning to him, he spoke in elegant French. "We will let this go. I spoke too harshly of your gaucherie, and anyway we must not behave like swashbucklers in front of ladies."

I beckoned to a brawny workman across the street and gave him sixpence. "That's for carrying the gentleman's box to his lodgings."

"Madame, I can look out for my own—" the Frenchman began.

"Tell him where to take it and quit making scenes."

He mentioned the name of a lodginghouse on a mean street. "I insist, madame, that I can fight my own battles without help from English ladies of fashion," he told me, his dark eyes glowing. "Will you kindly give me your name?"

"It is Miss—Lucia Riley." To my amazement, I had started to say Lola.

"I am Rene Saint-Denis, at your command."

I gazed after him as he stalked stiff-backed away, my thoughts in chaos. The other spoke in his perfectly controlled, powerful male voice.

"May I also introduce myself, Miss Riley?" he asked. "After all, I received rough treatment at your hands. Jacques Bonhomme

44

wouldn't have lifted a finger if you hadn't set him on me." Jacques Bonhomme was equivalent to Tom, Dick, and Harry.

"You may, sir."

"Jeffery, Baron Lundy of Blackmoor."

I had heard of Lord Lundy before! Immensely rich, his barony one of the oldest in England, he was enough of an enigma to become the theme of interminable gossip. As a gentleman rider, he had won the Coxley Steeplechase three years ago. Taking up amateur boxing, he had soon won the right to challenge the belt-winner at the famous Pugilistic Club, only to refuse because the champion "is neither gentleman nor riffraff, and I do not like red herring." According to the last report, he was climbing mountains in Switzerland. But no rumor had ever reached Bath of his conquests of women.

"Your humble servant," I answered, bowing, and started to walk on.

"I'll cut your path through the gawkers."

He stepped in front of me and advanced with ready stick on the cluster of porters and peddlers whom the brief encounter had attracted.

"Stop it," I called.

He turned with an amused expression. The men had already cleared the sidewalk, some of them scowling, and a red-haired Welshman muttering curses. Then he fell in beside me.

"Did you think I was going to strike them?" he asked.

"I certainly did."

"I wonder if I would, in case they stood their ground? It's never been necessary. This eagle-beak of mine frightens 'em. If I did— I might be brought into court. By English law they have as much right to the sidewalk as we have."

"Then why can't you be decently polite to them?"

"I've no rancor against them, but somebody has to keep 'em off balance. That's a pugilistic term, and a very apt one. You know what happened in France fifty years ago. It can happen in England overnight. If I were one of them—instead of happily born in the opposite camp—I'd make it happen, and chop off toffs' heads right and left. Of course, my side offers better sport. We're only a handful to their swarms."

"You're a very ready sportsman, Lord Lundy, or so I've heard."

"I find most so-called sport very boresome. But I'm far from bored this moment. Will you kindly explain what you meant by calling me a barnshoot?"

"I didn't know I did. It's a Hindu epithet." Actually it was the most comprehensive of all bazaar invective with an obscene connotation. I had thought I had forgotten it years before.

"My word! This is the most refreshing experience I've had in years. Is it necessary for you to look so belligerent? I didn't settle with the Frenchman for knocking me down, although I could have beaten him to pulp with one hand."

"I'm not sure of that, and perhaps you intend to settle with him later."

"He's not in the least to blame. You pulled the trigger and he went off by accident. I did speak too harshly to him—but surely I haven't met an aristocratic republican!"

I shook my head.

"Could it be that you're a parvenu? No, or you'd have treated those people like dirt."

"I'm the daughter of a lieutenant who rose from the ranks." This was the first time I had mentioned the fact since I had told Señor Professor nearly two years before.

"Well, you can be the daughter of a chimney sweep for all I care. You're one of the few truly beautiful young women in England."

He paused, I thought to watch the effect of this. Instead he was busy with his own thoughts.

"Oddly enough, I didn't notice it at first," he went on in a puzzled tone. "It seemed to come out on you when you were cursing me in an unknown tongue. Your face was transfigured. It still is. I wonder if there is some kind of beauty that comes and goes like inspiration to the artist. Could it be that I was its particular inspiration today? . . . I'm referring, of course, to the violent antipathy I wakened in you. If so, I shall have to keep you enraged with me."

"I don't think that would be difficult."

"Good for you! But tell me—is there any reason I may not pursue your acquaintance? I'm sure you're not married. Are you betrothed?"

I shook my head.

"And I came to Bath expecting a dull time! How soon may I call to pay proper addresses to your elders?"

"Next week, if you like."

"Next week! Why not today?"

His voice was vibrant and his eagle's face betrayed no subterfuge. He had a way of turning his head on his neck as he talked, most strangely eagle-like. I was fascinated by him and proud to be walking with him, but my deeper feelings toward him were confused. Perhaps because I kept remembering the flushed, sensitive face of Rene Saint-Denis—his name, too, was firmly fixed in my mind—I seemed to sense danger. I was not frightened of it, but there was a dim, troubling presentiment deep in my mind that I should be.

Certainly he was immensely distinguished and perhaps an aristocrat of a type rarely seen in England, whose climate and soil were not, according to Señor Professor, favorable to the development of a truly *haute noblesse*. The Anglo-Saxon would not stand enough trampling down. Feudalism had never obtained as strong a hold in England as on the Continent. I thought that Lord Lundy would be more at home as a Spanish grandee—I could imagine him a great margrave in Bohemia or a boyar with ten thousand serfs in Poland. That he was more than equal to all the feats ascribed to him I need never doubt.

I was excited at having encountered such a personage, and exultant at his excitement over me. I had the feeling that Manu's prophecies had suddenly begun to come true. A moment ago I had thought, "What use can I make of his importance in getting ahead?" That train of thoughts had stopped short as at the edge of a precipice. There was a folk tale in India of a conceited donkey who essayed to match his guile against a tiger's. It did not come to my mind, but its lesson had evidently sunk home.

"Why not today?" he repeated.

"I'm occupied today and for several days."

The answer surprised me as much as it did him. I could hardly believe my own ears. Apparently my instinct was to go very slow. All I would do was lose him—

"As you know, Macready is playing at the Bath Theater. Perhaps I could make a party—"

I drew a deep breath. To appear at the Bath Theater with Jeffery, Baron Lundy of Blackmoor, would be a brilliant triumph. But I had better not go back on what I had just said—

"Some other time, Lord Lundy."

"Please, if you want attentions from me, don't be elusive. My time is very short before I must go to Southhampton. Do I have to explain I'm not one of the typical satyrs of our enlightened age? Need I tell you that I am very sensitive to beauty and hold it in great reverence?"

We were walking along a shady street on a warm, sunny, summery day. Cultured Romans had walked here when Bath was called Aquae Sulis, and tall, fair-haired, blue-eyed Celts worshipped Druids, but I saw no toga-draped ghosts, only flitting sparrows, staggering butterflies, flowers, small white clouds, and people coming and going on their common affairs. I wondered what Lord Lundy worshipped. I could picture him in a pew of an ancient parish church at Blackmoor looking like a tethered eagle. I had never seen Blackmoor in Devonshire, but knew it was the wildest, loneliest region in England.

"It's a very high compliment," I said. "It's my misfortune that I'm engaged."

"In that case—" He stopped, again turned sideways, and swept off his hat. I bowed my head and walked on.

Sparrows made short flights; butterflies seemed always about to fall, pearly clouds moved slowly in the limpid blue; people came and went. All that was the same, but my pride had come tumbling down and I was ashamed of my gaucherie. I had acted like a milkmaid, bent on showing the master how highly I regarded my virginity until, persuaded of the fact, he had made off. I, a self-made lieutenant's daughter, neither fine lady nor riffraff, only good

red herring! I could find only one in the least credible explanation
—that in my heart I was still championing Rene Saint-Denis.

The air had miraculously changed from wine to water. I no
longer walked as bold and free or felt so keenly alive.

I was eager to talk over the experience with Kitty but she was
riding with Ronald Atchison, and they did not return until four,
when dinner was called. Since the General was entertaining today
a Mr. and Mrs. Oswald from Bristol, I did not mention Lord Lundy.

We were finishing the meat course when a footman entered and
whispered to the butler, whereupon the flustered look of the former
spread to the latter. When the butler bent to speak in the General's
ear, the old man rose nimbly with a quite dazzled expression. He
hurried out, without remembering to excuse himself from his
guests, and in a few minutes returned with a visitor.

Mr. Oswald and Ronald sprang to their feet at sight of the new
arrival, and we ladies rose more gracefully but almost as promptly.

"Ladies and gentlemen," the General pronounced, his voice ringing with pride, "Baron Lundy of Blackmoor has paid us the great
honor of calling."

All of us bowed like owls.

"You honor me, General Judson, by receiving me on the strength
of such a remote connection," Lord Lundy said.

"The baron met an old messmate of mine in Switzerland," the
General explained, "and consented to deliver in person his friendly
remembrances. Needless to say, I'm deeply grateful."

The old man began to present us to the noble visitor. When my
turn came to exchange bows with him, he appeared pleasantly
surprised.

"Why, General, this is the beautiful young lady who gave me
some directions on the street today," he said, with sparkling eyes.

"What an odd coincidence! Lucia, you didn't tell us—"

"I am delighted to meet her again under such pleasant auspices,"
Lord Lundy went on quickly.

The footman was instructed to provide a chair and another
cover for dessert. When we were seated, the baron began to hold

forth on the General's military history. He appeared well versed in all his principal campaigns and battles, and never failed to infer that the victories were his alone. That he had acquired the necessary information from some retired officer since our mid-morning meet, there was not the slightest doubt.

Kitty, Ronald, and the Oswalds hung on his words, nodding vigorously when the cue came, laughing excitedly when he chose to be amusing, and Mr. Oswald was so spellbound as actually to ape his gestures. This was in spite of the fact that he only occasionally glanced at them and was patently addressing his witty lies to me. . . . It had dawned on me slowly that they *were* lies—somehow quite different from flattery designed to please an old man. But the General himself did not recognize them as that, he knew only their untruth. His kind old face had at first beamed, then begun to flush with embarrassment. Often he tried to disclaim the honors that he knew he did not deserve, only to be told that his modesty became him, but the facts spoke for themselves. Still he could not possibly doubt the great lord's good faith and intentions. His deep, male voice had a mesmeric power and was so thrilling in my ears that I could not, somehow, generate any anger at what I felt was the strange and utterly pointless sport he was making of his host.

Did he think I was enjoying it? The senseless question gave me an eerie feeling.

After dessert the ladies retired, leaving the four men to drink port. Happily, Mrs. Oswald was so dithered by her sudden elevation to the company of a nobleman that she had to run errands to the dressing room, whereby she gave Kitty and me time for confidences.

Plainly Kitty had seen nothing strange or in the least shocking in Lord Lundy's fulsome praise of the General. Perhaps I had had, as Papa used to say, a chip on my shoulder. I resolved to become more realistic. . . .

"He has eyes for no one but you," she began. "Lucia, do you suppose that after seeing you on the street—"

"Don't be romantic, Kitty."

"Anyway he's gone on you. Of all the wonderful—"

"Kitty, can you imagine Lord Lundy marrying a girl in my position?"

Her eyes changed. "I don't see why not—"

"The millennium isn't yet. But I might be able to become his mistress."

"Lucia!"

"Don't try to look shocked, because you're not. I don't mean a light o'love—I mean a position corresponding to the morganatic wife of a king. What would I lose by it? When the affair's over—it would be a mistake to try to string it out—I ought to have, if I'm fairly clever, at least five thousand and maybe ten thousand pounds in jewels and money. Mark you, he'd be getting a virgin who's called a beauty—accomplished—able to preside at his table and entertain his sporting friends. I believe I could get a contract out of him, before I took the irremediable step."

"That's the most calculated—"

"Have I any social position to lose? Instead I'd gain some—on the outskirts of the *haut monde* where life is Bohemian and very pleasant and where I could shine. Would my price in the marriage market be reduced? It might be if I had a perfectly honest love affair with a commoner that happened not to result in marriage. At least I'd have to keep it very quiet. But as the former favorite of a great lord, I think I'd be at premium."

"Lucia, are you serious?"

"I ought to be. It may be my great opportunity. Well, I've looked at the cards and I can't play them, though I don't know why."

"You *did* make an impression on him today. That's the reason he came—"

"Yes, but please don't tell the General."

The gentlemen joined us in the drawing room. Lord Lundy had become rather quiet, making only polite responses, yet he dominated the scene, and not merely by token of his name and place. He was dominating everyone here, I thought, except me. I had the curious illusion of a dual role in a drama just beginning to unfold—both his objective and his antagonist. I did not pay much attention to what he was saying. I thought about Manu—Kali—two flowered-decked immolants under crimson fountains—Mamma—Earl Amherst—Lohar—Krishna the Joyous. . . . A dream was weaving in my brain. . . .

"I would like to make what I hope you'll think is a good suggestion," Lord Lundy was saying as he rose to leave. "Suppose I get seats for the play tonight—"

At that fateful instant—and long ago I believed in fate!—a footman entered and bent low beside my chair.

"There's a young man in the hall who wants to see you, miss," the servant whispered. "I didn't take him for a gentleman, but he said it's very important—"

I rose and bowed and with a hasty "Excuse me" sped out of the room. In the dimness of the hall a soberly dressed figure stood in an awkward position. He moved into better light and I saw his face. He was Rene Saint-Denis, who today had knocked Lord Lundy down.

"I am sorry to disturb you, mademoiselle," he said in French, "but my errand was important in my sight, no matter how trivial it may appear to you."

"What is it, Monsieur Saint-Denis?" I asked, my pulses throbbing.

"I wish to return the sixpence which you spent today in my behalf. I was not in funds at the time. I could not afford to hire a messenger to bring it and I wished to make sure that you received it."

He did not now stand awkwardly, and he spoke with a good deal of dignity. I looked into his round, somewhat boyish face that contained so much so hard to find, and then into his growing dark eyes. If ever I spoke with my heart in my mouth, it was then.

"Why, I have another to put with it, to make a shilling. Do you know a place where that would buy two glasses of French wine?"

"Mademoiselle, I know where it would buy a bottle of the good red wine of the country. It is well frequented by my poorer countrymen."

"Is it a place I need wear a bonnet?"

"They are not often seen there."

"Monsieur, will you do me the honor of escorting me there—at once?"

"It would give me great pleasure," he answered, bowing stiffly.

I took his arm and hurried him out the door across the long shadows of late afternoon. Deep under my happiness glimmered a memory which for the moment I could not quite recapture. . . . But the happiness was sharply felt. It had a pronounced quality of wonder—I knew of no other in the world save this vital yet wistful Frenchman whom I had so briefly met could have brought it to me. Only to him could I have fled from Jeffery. . . .

If that made no sense, it was on a par with the pale memory that now came clear. It was of Manu, lifting me in his arms to carry me away from the Great Pooja of Chota Nagpur.

EIGHT

RENE'S awkwardness was not the fault of his big gaunt frame. It was caused by self-consciousness stemming from a peculiarly sensitive nature. Since the stolidity of the peasant was not in him, I thought he must belong to the bourgeoisie, and his accent and manners were obviously provincial. As soon as he began to talk fluently, his movements and carriage became graceful, in the way, I thought, not of a thoroughbred racehorse but of a rugged stallion. He carried his head somewhat bent and cocked on one side. He began to give me the impression of a great deal, perhaps an amazing amount, of physical strength. I thrilled over it, thinking how he might need it if he should cross certain paths of Jeffery Lundy.

After making various stilted comments on the weather and the glories of the Royal Crescent, he launched forth on the history of the region, speaking so rapidly and employing such erudite French that I had some difficulty understanding him. He said that Salisbury Hill bore signs of habitations hundreds of years older than the Roman ruins, and its name commemorated a Celtic goddess, Sul. It was these ruins he had come to see, and he would be departing soon for Cornwall, to compare them with very early

Celtic monuments on the moors, and these in turn with some in Brittany. No, he was not an anthropologist. He was a hack writer, he said, for various French journals. But he had a smattering of anthropology, and was using a hard-earned holiday to write a monograph on one small phase of Celtic migration, which he hoped might win him some sort of prize from the Académie des Sciences.

Very few of our Little Englanders knew that the Café de Provence existed. It opened on an alleyway and had a dingy exterior: within it was a small, bright French island. A hush fell as we entered, and I caught a rather sheepish look of pride on Rene's face. An English crowd would have taken stealthy notice of us, if any at all; these French people gave us voluble welcome if not a kind of applause by their buzz of comment and pleased smiles. A small orchestra began to play the popular "Dream of Me Tonight," and when we were seated at a wall table, what looked like an old boulevardier, his elegance of manner setting at naught the poverty apparent in his attire, preened his gray mustache and small beard and, by right of his years and ribands, came up to do us honor.

Rene addressed him as mon Capitaine, and told me that he was that famed Captain DeFosse of the First Grenadiers of the Old Guard which stood with the remnants of two battalions at Waterloo, refusing to surrender long after the field had been lost. He kissed my hand and, in a voice rich with emotion, told me that I reminded him of Du Barry when his boyish eyes had last beheld her more than fifty years before. She was then twice my present age, he reckoned, but her beauty was like that of the urn of Monsieur Keats and she was of "Sweet voice, sweet lips, soft hand."

"It was well I did not see her being borne in the tumbrel to the guillotine," he told me. "I would have tried to join her there, her last escort." And I could not feel that this was a romantic boast.

On impulse I said a strange thing. "Perhaps I will follow her there."

"Mademoiselle!"

"You see I know Kali, the goddess of the Little Window, through which Du Barry looked out at her. I met her in India when I was very little, and we are old enemies."

Both men stared at me and had difficulty arousing themselves when two other Frenchmen, Rene's friends, came up to be introduced.

Presently our guests departed, leaving Rene and me to enjoy our wine in solitude. But it was not the cheap red wine of the country. The maître d'hôtel had substituted a bottle of heavenly Clos de Vougeot.

"It is not what the lady ordered," Rene protested, his face clouded.

"No, but what the lady will accept at the same price," I told him, "and anyway it's none of your business."

"The difference of three shillings, fourpence is a trifling but sincere tribute from the Café de Provence to the most beautiful lady who has ever honored us with her custom," the maître said with aplomb.

When he had gone, Rene ran his hand nervously through his carefully brushed dark hair, at which he suddenly became different and better-looking. He had a fine straight nose and truly a noble forehead, and his disheveled locks accented the aspect of sensitivity in his face. I seemed to sense in him a great deal of unapplied and perhaps imperfectly realized power.

"I would like to review, if I may, the incident of our meeting," he said.

"Very well."

"I felt much at fault for splashing mud on Lord Lundy's clothes."

"So you found out who he was."

"The news of his arrival was already abroad, and I soon discovered he was the one. I should not have attempted to cross the street at that slippery place. Anyway, I'm very easily flustered, and too ready to accept blame, perhaps because of a keen awareness of my own faults. Also, I am slow in standing up for myself—perhaps for those same reasons. Truly, the nobleman had no business speaking to me in that tone or calling me an 'oaf,' but except for you I would have continued my way in shame, my resentment slowly growing but impotent."

"I'm delighted I was there to do a little prompting."

"Will you tell me why you did so?"

"I have a vile temper."

"Weren't you angry with him already?"

"I had never lain eyes on him before."

"That did not mean you weren't angry with him. I was watching both of you as I came across the street, and your expression, eager as you approached him, became annoyed as you passed on. I thought you were expecting some address that you didn't receive."

I remembered my failing to impress him at first sight.

"Perhaps I was."

"You're a very beautiful young woman. I suppose you are used to having the fact acknowledged. Now I will make a confession. Showing the way to the man carrying my portmanteau, I made excuses to look back, and took a course that kept you in sight for a matter of two blocks. I couldn't help but observe that you and Lord Lundy very quickly came to terms."

"Why not?"

"Why not indeed? You have no title yourself, but you are far nearer to him in social position than to me. As a journalist, I'm aware of his wealth and place, as well as his quite extraordinary exploits in the field of sports. By and large, he is one of your order. An alliance between you would be far from unthinkable. Yet I was foolish enough to feel jealous. It was jealousy—I suspected it at the time and am sure of it now—that made me in such haste to return the sixpence."

"Well, I'm glad of that. Why were you jealous of him?"

"Not because I'm the son of a provincial tax collector, self-educated, so poor I cannot buy decent-appearing clothes, and so gauche that I couldn't select them if I had the means. I accept all that, and have determined to make my mark in spite of it. I have no energy to waste on jealousy of the rich and highborn. However, to be jealous of him for those reasons would have been no more silly than for the real reason. That was, you are available to him and not to me."

"I feel greatly complimented."

"I am sure you don't. You feel complimented only in a passing and mild degree. Actually I don't see why you should at all. You are constantly being complimented by people you regard as far more important. I grant that your eyes indicate some pleasure in my tribute, and can account for it only by the strange innocence—modesty is a better word—the sensitivity of self-doubt hits it best—that so often goes with a great gift of the gods. You like to be told even by servants that the gift is real. Well, since I owe you a considerable debt—you saved me from a severe wound to my self-respect—I'll seek to pay you in that way. To quote from Monsieur Keats, as did Captain DeFosse —a new planet swam into my ken."

His eyes slowly filled with tears, and I could not believe my own.

"I looked at you with a wild surmise," he went on. "It was that you are the atavar of some pagan goddess. Sometimes I see beauty where more cultured men cannot—I long for it—lust for it—my real jealousy of the rich is because they can buy and live with it. I'm not sure that everyone sees yours—it gives the effect of coming and going with your thoughts and moods; for a moment today I was subject to the ridiculous illusion of being its discoverer. But I soon recovered a small portion of my usual common sense. I saw the pride with which you walked with him, and his fascinated attentions. So now I come to another question, although I already feel sure of the answer. Why did you condescend to come here with me?"

"I didn't condescend to come. I came because I wanted to."

"I'll tell you the reason. As you confessed, you are quick to anger. You became furiously angry with Lord Lundy over something that has happened since your meeting today—a slight of some kind, I suppose—and you were foolish enough to think that you could spite him by spending an evening with a commoner who had knocked him down. Having a lively imagination, you no doubt often conceive and even give way to such absurd whims."

"Then why did you accept my invitation?"

"I would get to see you for an hour or two—sit with you at a table—feast my eyes with beauty, and dream poetic dreams. I have paid as much as two francs—quite a large sum to me—to go into galleries or to hear beautiful music. I'm a realist in my own way."

If Lord Lundy's face had a strange semblance of beauty, for a moment the open countenance of this French journalist had the real thing.

"Well, you're wrong in a great many of your premises," I told him. "In the first place, my social position is practically the same as yours. I'm the daughter of a lieutenant who rose from the ranks and the paid companion of the daughter of the house where I live. Lord Lundy didn't slight me; in fact, he invited me to go to the theater. I tell you again, I came with you because I wanted to."

His face began to light up, and I could not stand his rejoicing or my own.

"But I wanted to," I went on, "for selfish reasons. I'll have a hard time explaining them, but I'll try. The conflict between you and Lord Lundy excited me very much. It did not seem to be over splashed mud—it seemed to be over me. You'll think I've drunk too much wine, but actually my mind feels very clear. I was on your side instead of his because of something Papa told me on his deathbed, but that doesn't explain why the issue became so vital. I thought it was my fight and I felt intensely alive. I felt strong—my name was again Lola, the pooja name—that's Indian magic—of my childhood. I was myself and no shadow of anyone else."

I paused, not merely to collect my thoughts, but to try to see by a tenuous light shining through them as from a vast distance beyond. Rene gazed at me with a look of strain, as though he ached to help me.

"Maybe there's no mystery at all," I told him. "When I was a little girl, I wanted to be a heroine. In my heart I still do. I wanted to have thrilling adventures—to seek great prizes and not turn back from danger. I suppose I wanted to kill dragons. I recaptured that feeling for a moment and it was vastly exciting. A moment later a reaction set in, but it's been with me, more or less, all day. I wanted to sustain it a while longer—to feel—" I hesitated.

"Beautiful?" he asked, his eyes glittering under their dense black brows.

"Brave, I suppose."

"There is a curious link between the two. I don't know what it is

—it's something I can sense but not rationalize—but I know that every brave man has an aspect of beauty, and no cowardly woman was ever beautiful. I'll ask you this. People need weapons with which to kill dragons. What was to be your weapon?"

"Beauty."

"You were going to forge it yourself?" His voice was low and tense.

"Yes."

"Don't you feel that you succeeded?"

"It's no good. It's always breaking."

I had not talked so intimately and freely with anyone since parting from Manu. I had had nothing like this to say to anyone else— I had daydreamed it perhaps, but never meditated it. With Señor Professor I had only listened and taken in. Thinking of Manu now, I floated back to him. Memories of him re-created a scene of hot sky and warmed earth and trees with giant leaves, and wonders very close and exciting. . . . Then platters rattled beyond me—a girl's voice said, *"très elegante"*—and I was back sitting at a wine-stained shabby cloth in a cheap café with a penniless French writer.

"There's a flaw in the steel," I said. "I may remind Captain DeFosse of Du Barry, but I'm afraid of the guillotine—not the kind that chops off people's heads but shreds their hearts and cuts down their pride. I'm not going to try to marry Lord Lundy. I'm going to use him, if I can, in attracting other men. Among them I should be able to find one who'll think I'm pretty and charming and who can buy me pretty clothes and safety. I'll dance and be gay and be flattered. I'll be doing a whole lot better than the daughter of a self-made lieutenant should expect."

"Well, in that case—" The light had gone out of his eyes.

"It is the case, so please take me home."

I summoned the garçon and paid the bill of one shilling.

"I am sorry," I told him, "that tonight I cannot include a gratuity."

I thought he might scowl. Instead he gave me a wonderful smile.

"I'm already much in Mademoiselle's debt," he replied, bowing.

I bowed to him in return. Rene and I went out and walked in silence to the entrance of the alley. The long clear summer twilight still held in the wide street beyond, but the narrow way was dark with many superimposed shadows. Here I stopped.

"I'll go home in a public cab," I told him.

He nodded. "Considering your position and ambitions, I think that's best. I trust you can invent some plausible reason for leaving with me today."

"As it happens, my returning unattended by you has nothing to do with either my position or ambitions."

"I'm sorry I have no funds with which to pay your fare. By paying one debt, I've incurred a larger one. But the greatest of all I can never repay. I won't try to tell you what it is." He bowed, and I thought he might say, "Au revoir." Instead he said, "Adieu."

"There is one thing you can do for me before I go, which I would regard highly, provided you would yourself take pleasure in it."

"What is it, Lola?"

"Thanks for calling me that, although it isn't deserved. I'd like to have you kiss me."

"I would have kissed your hand, but, according to French custom, only those of the *noblesse* can properly kiss a lady's hand."

"I don't want you to kiss my hand. I want you to kiss my mouth."

"It would give me very great pleasure, but it might be seen by passers-by, and even in this dimness your face is luminous and one easy to remember. Also, if it is anyway a consolation prize—"

"Don't be so proud, Rene," I broke in, between laughter and tears. "If you're going to kiss me—"

He bent toward me and lightly touched his lips to mine. I started to turn away, then faced him again.

"Is that the best you could do?"

"*Mon Dieu!* I'm not a clod. Be it on your own head—"

He threw his arms about me, held me close, and crushed my lips with his. Instantly I responded with furious hunger, the reality of a passion for life and love and ecstasy, of which until now I had known only the dream. But I became frightened by its force, and with all my body awake and yearning fled from what I most craved.

"Adieu," I called back, as I hurried into the twilit street. I had succeeded in saying that, by a wrench of my will, instead of "au revoir." But in that small, mean victory I sensed great defeat.

NINE

THE kindly old General was perplexed and distressed over my sudden exit from the company of Lord Lundy. I explained that, until summoned to the hall, I had been so fascinated by his conversation as to completely forget my engagement with an old schoolfellow—surely Rene and I had had the same dear teacher—and hoped he did not take it amiss.

"He was very gracious, of course—remarking on the impulsiveness of youth—but he said no more about going to the theater," the General answered. "It's my opinion that his main, probably his sole interest in it was to enjoy your company there. He was much taken with you, Lucia. I must say you've never had a higher compliment. You were the apple of his eye at dinner—"

The General paused, looking at me intently.

"By the way, Lucia, you do look 'strordinarily well," he went on.

"Thank you, sir."

"You've grown up a mighty pretty girl, and tonight you have a glow—" He took off his spectacles and wiped them. "Lucia, I want you to write a note of apology to young Lundy. It is really your duty, when you dashed off without taking leave."

I took pleasurable excitement in the brief composition.

My Lord,

During your visit with General Judson, I was called to the door on a financial matter, the ramifications of which prevented my return in time to pay you my intense respects. Trusting that you will take them for granted,

I remain,
your obedient servant,
Lucia Riley

The messenger brought back a note, written in an oddly delicate hand on gorgeous stationery under an embossed baronial coronet, which read:

My dear Lucia,

On my third attempt to climb Mount Blanc, I became bored with the contrary weather. When I want a picture for my gallery at Blackmoor Keep, I never make more than three offers. In other words, I try to season a certain tenacity with the salt of common sense.

Will you, your companion Miss Judson, and her cousin Ronald Atchison give me the pleasure of your company to the theater tonight to see Macready in King Lear? *Unless I hear to the contrary, I shall call for you in my coach.*

your devoted,
Jeffery

The General had me go to Mlle Simon for a gown of the latest French style. I chose a blue velvet rememorant of the dress Papa had bought me for my first introduction to nobility, with short leg-of-mutton sleeves just off the shoulder, a closely fitted, low bodice, and a full skirt with a draped front. I wore my hair parted in the middle and drawn back over the ears in quaint-looking buns. For jewelry, Kitty lent me a long chain of encrusted gold with bracelets to match. My breasts had never been so beautifully outlined, and I stretched my neck to try to kiss the lustrous dip of my shoulder. I wished that Rene, too, could kiss it. Then the thought of Jeffery's lips pressed there glimmered strangely in my imagination and quickly fled.

We rode in an all but royal coach to the theater, Jeffery's deep glances taking me in and his long, hard hand enfolding mine. As we entered the box at the theater, a rustling sound rose in the galleries, and then a multitude of whisperings oddly like the sibilant hum of fast-flying water fowl. Pointedly, Jeffery bowed over me as I took my seat.

I forgot him and myself and the throng when white-bearded King Lear cried in an aged but yet imperious voice:

Attend the Lords of France and Burgundy, Gloucester.

I knew the play well, and was soon myself the tragic figure of Cordelia, unable to mouth the declaration her father demanded, ashamed of his senile vanity being paraded before the court, well aware of the evil brooding about me, half pitying Burgundy's blindness to my worth and beauty, but glorying when great France, the scales falling from his eyes, declared before all the world:

> *Not all the dukes of waterish Burgundy*
> *Shall buy this unpriz'd precious maid of me.*

I thought I could never forgive the king for his stupid sternness, but as the dreadful story progressed, I was soon pitying him—wanting to throttle with my own hands his serpent daughters, and hating Cornwall and Edmund with all my heart. Jeffery appeared as lost in the play as I.

"It's a magnificent play, but Shakespeare hedged his bets," he told me after the first act. "As a villain, the Duke of Cornwall could have given a much better account of himself. He could have quietly put the king out of the way the day after he acquired his domains. The week after, he could have cooked Albany's goose, taking the whole kingdom, and had both vixens murdered, not because they lacked attractiveness, but because they were potentially dangerous to him. By the way, the duke is supposedly an ancestor of mine. The legend is, a Lundy married his daughter—although she doesn't appear in the play."

"Surely the Lundy family doesn't go back to pre-Christian times."

"There is some evidence that it does. The three-headed eagle of our armorial bearings was found in an old mine shaft that was used later as a barrow for Celtic dead. We've had a better chance to survive than most families, because of the tin mines on our manor. In fact it's almost worthless except for them—miles of barren moor— the money comes out of the ground. We had no trouble with stout yeomen, as did the farmed manors. We didn't have to supply soldiers for the interminable wars—there was a time when our liege lord believed that the tin was dug by gnomes. The poor devils looked like gnomes, I dare say—white ones instead of brown. In those days they were born, lived, and died deep in the mines, and their food was dropped down the shafts. They say—probably a myth—that in time they were all born blind, but continued to dig the ore just as well by their quickened sense of touch."

"I think that's the most horrible thing I ever heard."

"It isn't very pretty. But the moles were quite happy, according to family legend. It appears that some extra-clever Lundy—they've always been notably clever or practically half-wits—invented a religion for them that turned their labors into religious devotions. He gave them a subterranean god and pursuaded them that the mine was his temple. Their duty was to enlarge it—especially to get out the tin ore which was some sort of abomination—like the Groves to the Hebrews. They were allowed to make human sacrifice to him on great occasions—invariably the sick and worn-out—and I'm afraid, I can't be sure, eat them afterward. The name of the god came down to us as the Erlking. He was quite a brute, I believe— Satan was a tyro compared to him—but if his worshippers worked fourteen hours a day they got along with him all right. Oddly enough, the tin-miners on our lands still believe in him. They call him Old Berkeley—obviously from Erlking. They make obeisances to him when the vicar isn't looking. We haven't discouraged it— it makes them better workers."

"Do they still live and die in the mines?"

"My word, no. You'd think they owned the place."

My mind asked a question that would sound silly in words. Yet I heard myself ask it. . . .

"Do you believe in Old Berkeley?"

He laughed pleasantly. "The miners think I'm his prophet. At least a high prince of his realm. Why should I care? It makes them better workers."

The question had not sounded silly, after all. And he had not answered. . . .

Near the close of the third act occurs the most terrifying scene in all Shakespeare, strangely lighted by the most heroic passage. I could not watch the blinding of old Gloucester by cruel Cornwall, and my gaze fell on Jeffery's face. What I saw there did not, oddly enough, divert me from the drama; instead it was made more real than before. He became in my imagination not a spectator of a play but his own remote ancestor of whom he had spoken, born two thousand years before his time, and a young member of the duke's court. His name was Acquilla, I thought, his lineage was already ancient, and he was a swordsman of great renown. For the moment he was amused by his liege lord's violence and Regan's fiendishness, but he himself would not stick his finger in the old man's eyes. He wanted and would get the dukes estates, but of the king's three daughters, he preferred Cordelia . . .

> Hold your hand, my lord.
> I have served you ever since I was a child,
> But better service have I never done you
> Than now to bid you hold.

A lackey spoke those lines, one of the very few instances in Shakespeare where a humbly born person was shown otherwise than a clod, a fool, or a knave. "A peasant stand up thus!" Regan said. And as she ran him through, the indrawn eyes of an eagle-faced baron briefly glinted.

The curtain fell, hands clapped, and the growing light found me sitting beside an urbane theatergoer, tall, graceful, all but beautiful of countenance, and in almost foppish dress, in the act of stifling a yawn.

"I think you'd be interested in meeting Macready," he said, gracefully rising.

An usher took us backstage. Well born and widely cultured, still the great actor forgot he was just now the most impressive of all stage kings, and flushed with pride over the baron's visit. Jeffery did not shake hands, only gave him a grave bow and a word of praise. It caused me to remember that, except for my own, I had not seen him touch another's hand.

When we returned to the box, Jeffery and Ronald and I entered first, while Kitty paused a moment in the passage to speak to a dowager of her acquaintance. As Kitty joined us, Jeffery shut the door hastily, apparently without noticing her hand still on the frame. She was not quite fast enough in jerking it away, and although she uttered only a deep gasp, the swift pallor of her face betrayed excruciating pain. The very tip of her middle finger had been pinched and instantly turned blue.

"How unfortunate!" Jeffery cried. "In my haste to shut out the busybodies, I was careless—"

"It's no matter," Kitty said.

"Shan't I send for some smelling salts?"

"It doesn't hurt so much now. I'm all right."

"You'll forgive me, I know."

Lord Jeffery took his seat beside me and spoke in an undertone perfectly clear to me but inaudible to our companions.

"You know, Lucia, sometimes I think there's a demon who has become my familiar spirit. He worships me, apparently, and when I'm the least out of sorts, the most curious accidents happen to my companions."

My heart began to thud. "Are you out of sorts tonight?"

"A little—and with you."

"For what reason?" I was able to control my voice well.

"You treated me rather shabbily, Lucia. You went off last night when you knew I'd come to see you—on the excuse of a 'financial matter.' My French valet saw you at the Café de Provence with a man whom I readily identified as the one I'd let walk away—instead of being carted off—after knocking me down. Wasn't that insult added to injury? Jolly well like it, I tell you!"

"If you think that, you shouldn't have invited me tonight."

"There were two reasons that I should. One was to try to find out, if possible, why you avoided me. It may be I'm not attractive to you personally—often the case with people I wish to cultivate, to my great regret. My other reason is the hope we might get off to a better start. I certainly didn't want to forsake quickly a prospect of such pleasure to me. I'm deeply taken with you, Lucia. You are wonderfully beautiful."

66

I must let it go at that, I thought. I must make a polite answer and stay out of trouble. The attendants were turning down the lamps and the curtain was rising on the scene of blind Gloucester being led across a lonely heath. It was not my business. Many people had encountered queer things that had the cast of darkness, but by minding their own business, they escaped unscathed.

But my heart would not stop bounding.

"The demon that follows you about—worshipping you—isn't as forgiving as you are," I said under my breath. "You only get out of sorts—but he causes queer accidents to happen."

Jeffery had keen ears. "Oh, come, don't carry on with my little whimsey."

"I wonder how he got Kitty mixed up with me."

"If you want to continue pretending he exists—for the sport of it— he might realize I wouldn't stand for any reproof to you, but, still wishing to make his point, he used a proxy."

"Well, I won't tell Kitty."

"Why, I'm beginning to think the little fellow did us both a good turn. You couldn't help admiring his spirit. I'm only joking about him—but I do wish you would come to know me better. I would like to open your eyes to a whole new world."

"I wouldn't tell Kitty because she wouldn't believe me. She'd think I'm mad."

"It's best not to tell anybody—anything."

"You're not mad by any chance, Jeffery?"

"I think you would find me the most sane man you ever met."

"Your stick is in my way."

It was leaning on the edge of the box, and as I moved as though to lay it on the floor I could tell that like many bullys' canes it had a leaded knob. Out of sight of everyone, I whipped it hard as I could in the confined space and struck him a vicious blow just above the ankle. He bent over, his body rigid with pain, and for the moment helpless. His white face became beaded with sweat.

"How unfortunate," I whispered. "I was careless—"

He did not answer or glance at me. Badly frightened and gazing straight ahead, I became aware when he leaned slowly back in his chair as though watching the play. It went on with nightmare-like pace and doom, and perhaps because its terror and violence seemed my familiars, reaching out to my own fate, I was soon living it more deeply than before. . . .

Blind Gloucester leaped from what he thought was the Dover Cliff, only to sprawl headlong on the level plain. Mad Lear, his fool gone to bed at noon, made his great outcry against hypocrisy and injustice. The act ended with Lear, "a very foolish fond old man . . . not in my perfect mind," begging forgiveness of Cordelia. . . .

The thought came to me as the curtain fell that I had never seen Macready rise to such heights. Perhaps that was partly because a great lord, on whose words many a flatterer hung—no doubt the idol of the London bucks he must strive so hard to please—had given him a word of praise.

"Magnificent, but mad," Jeffery pronounced, urbane as ever. "Let it be a lesson to us all."

"You're right about that," Ronald earnestly agreed.

"Suppose you and Kitty go to the refreshment parlor and get me a glass of Napoleon brandy. I have a lame shin from an injury I received while mountain-climbing, and its troubling me tonight. I don't want to trust an attendant—often they substitute an inferior brand. Lucia will keep me company."

Waving away the note Jeffery held out, the two departed.

"What a vixen you are, Lucia," he said quietly, when they had gone. "And yet how easily taken in."

"Who's taken me in lately?"

"I have. You actually believed I caught Kitty's finger in the door on purpose."

"I still believe you did."

"Be sensible, my dear. Leaving out everything else, it must be plain to you I'm trying my best to ingratiate myself with you. I'm certainly assiduous in my attentions. Would I start by teaching 'lessons' to your friend?"

"I'm not sure. I don't think I'd better judge you by ordinary standards of behavior. You might suppose I would be greatly attracted to a lord as lordly, say, as the Duke of Cornwall in the play. Not to a bad man—or a madman—but a truly wicked man. I think that real wickedness does exert a tremendous fascination to a great many women. Perhaps it would to me, exciting me a great deal, but I think I'd fight it to the last ditch."

"I'm sure you would," he said with a brilliant smile. "I wish I had a lot of it, instead of only an average amount. You'd be beautiful, fighting me."

"Do you think you would win?"

"We're talking dreadful nonsense. I confess I'm a bit of a poseur—for my own amusement. Don't you think the little demon was an amusing invention? I suppose you know I made up the story about the blind miners—inventing it as I went along, inspired by the expression on your face. Well, I paid the fiddler with that vicious whack you gave me on the shin."

"I suppose real wickedness must be very rare. In India I got the idea that evil is an actual force in the world—not just a lack of good—but nobody believes that in England. I realize now that you caught Kitty's finger by accident. I wish I hadn't hit you."

"Well, let's leave it this way. I'm enchanted with you, but for the present I'm dropping out of the race. As it happens I'm going to Southampton tomorrow, to meet a confrere, and both of us will probably proceed from there to London. When I return—if I do in good time—I may seek another engagement with you. If you decide to accept, we'll make a fresh start."

"That's very gracious behavior, Lord Lundy."

"Jeffery, please. Let's keep that."

He began to talk about the play. Ronald and Kitty returned with the brandy. The curtain rose on the last act, but I could only watch it, not live it, and horror piled on horror finally dulled my wits. When Macready took his salute, he looked straight into our box.

Jeffery talked winningly on the homeward road, and when we stopped in the carriage way he begged to be excused from getting out, on account of his old injury. Ronald had sprung down and given his hand to Kitty, when Jeffery gently drew me back into the seat beside him.

"Lucia will join you in half a minute," he said gravely to Ronald. "I wish to impart a confidence—"

Ronald and Kitty walked off a few steps and politely gazed in the other direction.

"In farewell—and to let bygones be bygones—may I have a kiss?" he asked with great dignity.

I had set out tonight with the intention of letting him kiss me, if he liked, and I wanted to forget what had happened in the mean-time. "If it is your pleasure," I answered.

Still holding my hand, he bowed his tall head. His mouth was soft and of silken smoothness, then suddenly it was burning and I felt the prodigious power of his life's force expressed in passion. As I recoiled, his hand closed hardly perceptibly, yet mine was as helpless as though caught in a steel band. His body swayed a little, and mine was pinned, one arm confined at my side, against the wall of the coach; his free hand lay gently on my throat. I did not turn from his kisses or resist them in any way. He fed from my mouth slowly and with an effect of gentleness and courtesy, although his brow was drawn as with pain.

I tried to think of Rene. I wanted to imagine I was in his arms, but there was a world of difference. The sensation was exquisite, creeping through my body and turning into rapture, but this was invoking its like I had beheld long ago—some experience of child-hood that I could not quite recall—a rapture I had seen, not felt. Not responding, yet I was yielding. Instead of becoming more alive, as when Rene had kissed me with rough ardor, I was floating off into a delicious trance. Then his hand crept from my throat along the slope of my shoulder and moved downward. A sense of de-liverance swept through me, and with a violent movement I broke free from his embrace.

"I'll say one thing more," he told me, "then you may go. What you feared in me—and hated because you feared it—is quite real. But you didn't hate it just now—you found that out—and if I re-turn, you would find out much more. I know you better than you know yourself. It's a case of Greek meets Greek. Wait for me, Lola."

In a dim corner of my mind I wondered how he had learned the name I liked to call mine. Probably his valet had heard Rene use it, at the Café de Provence.

TEN

WHEN Kitty and I were alone, she asked me to tell her "everything that happened." I was able to put on a bright face, and in a lively tone tell her nothing. Meanwhile my thoughts were intertangling as in the delirium of fever. I felt dizzy and bitter cold, and lonely beyond any loneliness I had ever known.

The hall to my bedroom seemed endless, and once I had to stop to rest against the wall. I undressed in a daze, and immediately, it seemed, was in the throes of nightmare. Again I was in India—I could speak only Hindustani but all the people spoke English and drowned out everything I said with shouts of laughter—when I tried to catch Shikra, he bit me on the finger; when after a weary search I found Manu, he had grown long golden hair, and he would not let me comb it because I was "pert" and a show-off.

I'm going to be a countess! Someone was screaming that—a frumpily dressed little girl—as she was being carried by a dancing, laughing throng to the shrine of Kali, and I laughed and danced with the rest till I saw that she was someone I knew . . . someone whose name was Lola. . . . *She needs a good old-fashioned whipping.* It was Mamma saying that, and the whip was a cane with a leaded head, and when I resisted, Lady Kirk cried in a man's deep voice, *"A peasant stand up thus?"* There was safety for me if I could find Papa, but I searched and ran, ran and searched, in vain.

I wakened at dawn clear-headed enough, and, putting on my riding habit, walked toward the Cotswold Hills. I wished I could meet Rene going forth to look at and wonder over Celtic ruins, but I did not, and instead undertook the task I had set out to do. The General's term for it was "pull myself together."

On the way home from the theater, Lord Lundy had spoken again of his early departure to Southampton, and there was no reason to disbelieve it. He might not return soon, and, if he did, I meant to avoid him even if I must invent an excuse for a journey far from his ways. Whatever his passion was, I must escape from it. The solution to that mystery I did not know—there was no use trying to find it by any process of rational thought—if I ever discovered it, it would be by some kind of intuition. Even then it might not be reasonable, but I would know it was true.

The best and safest course for me was one I had already charted —early marriage of the kind Kitty would make. Such a marriage should be in easy reach—I knew several young men in her circles whom I could charm into proposing to me—and with good chances for success. I went home resolved not to let any emotion or passion or lingering childhood dream deflect me from this path. The sword of beauty that I had somehow forged had too many flaws to wield in more heroic battle.

This did not in the least allay the eagerness with which I sorted the letters of the morning post, or reduce my disappointment at not finding the one I sought. It was to be from Rene. I had pictured him writing me yesterday, at least to commemorate our minor adventure of the night before. . . . It had been more than that to me. . . . I had hoped he would suggest one more sally together before his departure for Cornwall.

The disappointment hung over me throughout my day's routine. Even when I did not think of it, there was a bleak spot in my heart. It lifted at every peal of the doorbell, then sank again. When the evening shadows began to creep, I faced the issue squarely.

I wanted to see his big, vital face, to hear his exuberant poorly modulated voice, and when the time turned magical, to feel his kisses in my mouth. I needed the surge of life that they drove throughout my body, because last night I had been wounded in some deep way. My mind denied this—it was no longer trustful of my deeper perceptions as it had been in India—but my nightmares had been Reason's ineffectual struggle against shadows hanging over me still.

It was no trouble to hear reports of Jeffery's comings and goings. The town buzzed with him. He had indeed gone to Southampton to meet Lord Stanley, and rumor had it that both would proceed to Apsley House to confer with the Duke of Wellington and Lord Robert Peel—my first inkling of his hand in the political pot. But no one had breath to waste on an impoverished French journalist, and there was no letter from him in the following morning's post.

Shortly after noon I dressed simply and took a cab to the Café de Provence. The purchase of a bottle of Clos de Vougeot as a present for General Judson could excuse the visit as well as casual inquiries about Rene. But when I entered the shabby resort, I rejected the subterfuge. The impulse was not fine pride but superstitious fear of the scorn of a childhood god. There was ever an intimation deep within my being that the gods I had once loved or hated were parties to the affair of Rene, Jeffery, and me.

The resort was almost deserted, and the only face I recognized was that of our garçon. It had lighted that night, and now it lighted again.

"I've heard nothing from Monsieur Saint-Denis," I said, "and hope you can help me get in touch with him."

"He would be greatly pleased if he knew of your inquiry," he replied, with that wonderful French courtesy unequaled in any land I knew. "It was no remissness on his part that you have not heard from him—a humble man, he feared to trespass on your good nature."

This seen to, and he and I in pleasant rapport, he went on to tell me of Rene's departure for Penzance the preceding day. He would remain there several days, studying *les ruines des celtiques primitives*.

He had left no forwarding address, but a Frenchman in Cornwall would be much observed and easy to track down.

"Here is a half crown, and I wish it were more."

The garçon held it upright, by the edge, his lips pursed as he considered.

"I accept it with a thousand thanks," he told me, "and will buy with it a beautiful kerchief to remember you by."

When I told the General that I was feeling seedy and wished to go off by myself for a fortnight to some quiet place in the county, he looked at me anxiously, thinking perhaps that Jeffery's careless flirtation with me had bruised my heart.

"I think it's a splendid idea," he told me. "But don't pick some dull hamlet where there's nothing to do. Go to one of the less fashionable vacation grounds, where you'll meet some young people."

When I told him I had enough money for the trip, he insisted on giving me a five-pound note. One pound was enough to pay my stage fare to Bristol, and on the morrow, my passage by coastwise packet to Penzance. Arriving about noon of the following day, I put up at the Sign of the Skull and Box and at once bribed one of the hostlers to get track of Rene. I would pay him in reverse ratio to the time he took in the search, I told him. He looked once into my face, believed me, went away, and returned in fifteen minutes.

"That frog, 'en coom yesterday, and 'en gone Burleigh way the day," he instructed me.

I too was "gone Burleigh way the day" in a farmer's cart. At a village on the road, I found where Rene had turned off on a grass-grown lane, and on the following day tracked him to a farmhouse at the edge of the moors. Taking lodgings there, I hired a younker named Jarge to guide me half a mile into the wastes to a shepherd's cot which "the furriner took for eightpence while 'en cudgel 'en brain o'er Merlin's stones."

"Are there many of the witch-stones nearby?" I asked.

"Too many for my content," the youth muttered, with obvious discomfort.

It was my first visit to the moors, so I could not understand a haunting sense of familiarity with them. They presented the aspect of an unpeopled world. The view was enormously far, and since there was so much green, unaccountably forlorn. There were almost no trees, and great masses of granite jutted up in shapes weird and melancholy without being recognizable. We kept to a sheep path between peat bogs until we gained a high heath from which we could spy the shepherd's cot, but save for this and the farmhouse there was no human habitation or mark as far as vision cast. The air was warm and soft.

Where the old gods still reign . . . The thought formed in my mind, and I knew now that it was the association between these melancholy moors and the hot, vernal plains of India.

We came up to a wide stretch of wet-looking sand between granite tors. The path ended at the nearer side and straggled on beyond; no footprint of any kind was visible between. Poles had been erected in the middle of the bed to form an aisle.

" 'Ee step along smart behind me," Jarge directed.

The bank quaked like jelly underfoot but yielded only an inch or two to my weight. Jarge led me through the aisle of poles and onto the grass beyond. When I looked back I had the creepy feeling of having suffered an hallucination. Our farther footprints had quite disappeared and the nearer ones were already melting away.

"Her safe enough if 'ee walk between 'em poles," Jarge explained. "The sand washed up over a peat bog. But jus' back of 'em poles her'll swally up a horse."

The door of the stone cot was unlocked. We looked in, and saw a great deal of Rene without finding his breathing presence. A slab of flint resting on a stone pillar served for his dining and reading table; on it were a lantern, several books, an inkwell and pen, and closely written sheets of manuscript. I could picture him working late the night before, and his aloneness in the wide, silent waste touched my heart. The clothes I had seen him wear were carefully hung, a few cooking utensils cleaned and put away, and some packages of groceries neatly disposed. His bed was two blankets folded on a straw-filled tick on a roped frame.

"I trow 'en away glyming yon fairy circle," the younker ventured, with a vague gesture toward the granite boss beyond.

"I'll wait here for him, but if I'm not back by sundown come for me."

"I'll coom a liddle afore 'en, miss. The shades run fast at shut o' day, and I'd not want 'em to catch me on the moor."

He made off, and I sat in the doorway waiting for Rene. When the sun was two handsbreadth over the western hills, I saw what seemed a tiny upright stick moving snail-slow on the vast down. It disappeared for a while, then emerged as a slightly taller stick, moving a little faster, on top the granite tor. It made a jerky way down; and there, still small, but recognizable by the swing of his long arms and the sweep of his stride, was Rene. I rose and started toward him. I wanted to give him time to wonder who his visitor was, guess, and adjust himself to the fact before we came on each other. I thought he might need to steady himself, as I did. Perhaps he might take a brighter view of the whole situation.

He quickened his pace a little, then stopped, cupped his hands like a trumpet, and called something I could not make out. When I started on, he gestured in my direction, and presently shouted again. The sound came thin but clear, "Stay where you are."

Uneven was his gait from then on, with frequent change of stride, and markedly awkward. When he loomed up wearing rough clothes and mud-bedaubed gaiters, his round face glistened with sweat, and his attempts at urbanity would not have deceived a child.

"I didn't expect to meet you in this out-of-the-way spot, Miss Riley," he remarked in careful English. I thought he had rehearsed it—rather pleased with it—on the way here, only to have it sound ridiculous in his ears.

"That's a mild way to put it," I replied.

He flushed, but that was an improvement on his pallor. "I warned you not to advance farther on account of the danger of quicksand," he went on hastily. "You crossed the worst place, but I've seen other banks that I don't trust."

"Thank you, Rene. Have you had a good day?"

He jumped at the chance to talk about it. "It's been very profitable," he began, falling in beside me as we walked toward the cottage. "I found several celts—that means their worked stones, naturally, not the people themselves—and a small circle of the Breton type that I believe—I'm almost sure—has never been documented."

"What a pleasant surprise!"

"Indeed it was!" His gaze slid sideways toward me, then appeared to bolt like a frightened rabbit. But I had caught a glimpse of his eyes, shining with mingled excitement and anxiety, and I thanked all my heathen gods that I had come.

"Then on top of that to be surprised out of your wits by a visitor—" I said.

"I'm acting quite witless, I know." He stopped and, with an effort of will, steadied himself. "Miss Riley, will you please explain the mystery? I'm afraid I can't behave rationally until you do."

"I didn't want our friendship to terminate this soon. I was lonely in Bath and wanted your company. There is no mystery beyond that."

"That itself seems a prodigious mystery to me."

We were approaching the stone hut and our voices enhanced the silence and solitude of its setting. The ice was by no means broken as I sat down on a stone bench near the door. Rene removed his heavy packsack and set it inside. Then at the spring he filled a washbasin of green-and-white stone and disappeared behind the cottage. When he emerged, his hands and face had the scrubbed look of an urchin's bound for school. Plainly he had something to say.

"Perhaps you were especially eager to leave Bath at this time." His attempt to speak casually was a dismal failure.

"Perhaps so."

"An explanation leaps to my mind, and—since it would seem to concern me—I dare say I'm justified in voicing it."

"Don't be so painfully polite, Rene."

"Excuse me. Remember I have no social graces. I do not know how to handle difficult situations. I happened to learn on the day of my departure that Lord Lundy had gone to Southampton. I can readily imagine that he left on account of some sort of rift in your relationship. Still I cannot see how that would cause you to turn—I mean—pardon me—to wish to resume—" He was stammering painfully.

"If I wanted to spite Jeffery, you don't see why I should come all the way to Cornwall to do it?"

"It seems to me you would have devoted your attentions to someone he could regard as a rival."

"Perhaps it would annoy him worse for me to devote my attentions to a man of humble station—especially one who had knocked him down."

"By the good God! Is that the explanation? I'm well aware that your affair with Lord Lundy had progressed greatly since you did me the honor—"

"How did you know that?"

"I, too, saw Monsieur Macready in *King Lear*. You will wonder where I obtained the money, since I had none to pay your cabfare from the Café de Provence. As it happened, the maître d'hôtel insisted on lending me enough for the cheapest seat, knowing my passion for Shakespeare and especially for the old, mad king. Until then I'd been tempted to write you a note of farewell, despite your saying 'adieu' to me in the alleyway—"

"You said 'adieu' first—"

"What else could I say, mademoiselle, when it stood to reason we would never meet again?"

"But we did, didn't we?"

"Wonder beyond wonders."

"I don't think it's so wonderful, considering my forwardness. Well, your explanation is wrong—at least as far as spiting Jeffery goes. I went with you that night because I wanted to. I wanted to see you again before we parted forever. Is there any mystery about that?"

His lips parted to ask another question, but his eyes asked it instead, and slowly filled with wonder.

"I wanted to see you again—Lola. I longed to see you. I did see you in the mists that rose off the moors in the cool dawns. I could see you clearly as the priestess in the Circle of Stones I discovered today. But to have you come here, warm and alive—to say farewell—" He fell silent.

"I dislike doing all the prompting, but will you go on?"

"It has the aspect of the preternatural."

"Have you any wine?"

"We Frenchmen always have wine. Mine is the cheap, good red wine of the country."

"Will you pour me a glass and drink one with me?"

"With great pleasure."

He brought out a jug in a wicker frame and two chipped tea

cups. We drank slowly, and although Rene seemed more at ease than before, he was not inspired to kiss me.

"If I knew how to cook, I'd prepare your supper, but I don't," I told him.

"I'm a fair cook. If you will share—"

"Jarge is coming for me just before sundown."

He glanced at the sun. "The time is very short. Forgive me, Lola, but since you are really here—on these moors—I'll have to ask you a question I suppose I would ask a winged seraph if she as incredibly dropped down for a visit. Will I see you tomorrow?"

"Unless one of us dies—or you go blind—before then. I certainly wouldn't travel this far for one glass of wine."

"That would stand to reason, but—what can I say? The fact remains that the time between now and sundown is short."

"The time between now and going to the burning ghats is short."

"May I ask another question—a much more personal one?"

I thought I must weep at what I saw in his face, but instead I smiled as to a child.

"Yes."

"Wonders come to pass now and then. Perhaps there would be many more—for us all—if we would look for them and not try to minimize them. I know only how I yearned to see you again, which anyone could understand. But you will understand how I could not possibly imagine its reciprocation. I am an obscure, humbly born, penniless French journalist. I believe in myself—I am aware of certain potential powers—but these wouldn't seem the sort to appeal to a young lady moving in fashionable circles in Bath. However, I realize that it is possible for two people of completely different worlds to find something in each other which each direly needs."

"Hurry up, please, Rene," I said, glancing toward the farmhouse.

"Did you feel that despite your intention to make a brilliant marriage very shortly, that a holiday, as it might be called—having no serious consequences—"

"Yes, I did. I wanted to eat my cake and have it. And here comes Jarge."

"Will you step out of his sight—"

I moved in front of the cottage. "He can't see us now."

"Can it be that you too—"

"Pomme de choux!"

"Forgive me, Lola. I have gone hungry so long—"

He put his arms about me and laid his lips gently on mine. I felt a childlike happiness that somehow added up to safety. A wound was instantly healed.

His lips moved at last and said, "I love you, Lola."

"Are you sure? Please don't be mistaken."

"I'll love you forever."

"If only just tomorrow—"

"If I never see you again, I'll love you always."

"Then give me a kiss of love."

He did so, his body pressed tight against mine. A nightjar swooped down, catching the air in his wings with a bass-viol strum; it seemed a sign of some kind.

A prayer I had made long ago was being this moment answered. I had made a mound of cow dung and poured on milk in obeisant pooja that I might be given a great gift of the gods. That gift was on me now, luminous, magical. I could give it endlessly to Rene as from an inexhaustible fountain. I could see its radiance in his face.

"Oh, do you think there will be no tomorrow?" he burst out, his eyes darkening.

"I don't know. But Jarge is coming now."

I could hear him whistling, not to warn us but to keep himself company, for the sun was down and shades running fast as he had foretold. I wished I had not told him to come. I had only begun to share my gift with Rene. . . . His mouth had leaped to mine in this urgency but forsook it when Jarge stopped a little way behind the cottage and called.

"M'lady!"

I had only to touch my lips in Rene's sight. Jarge was reluctant to come any nearer to the cottage. . . . Perhaps an old shepherd had died here, and the wide-eyed country folk coming to search for him in a silence as deep as this had found a fairy mark on his forehead. . . . But Rene knew I had sent for him. If it could occur to him I had changed my mind, he could not believe it. Rene thought I was concerned for my reputation. . . .

"We're here, lad," he called in great haste.

The lad came around the corner. "I coom as I promise 'ee," he told me, cheered by the sight of us. He turned to Rene with a solemn look. "Gaffer, 'en sent 'ee tiding."

"The old man at the farm sent you a message," I interpreted, when Rene looked puzzled.

" 'En bid me tell 'ee gulls ha' come off the sea to roost in haven, and the kine won't gi' down their milk."

"What does that mean?" he asked.

"Don' 'ee know plain sign? Why, a gale making off Land's End, and if 'en blow up marsh water over the sheep path, 'ee mayn't cross the moor tomorrow. 'En say ha' it as 'ee a mind to, but if 'ee and pretty lady ha' stood up in church, 'ee can coom back wi' us and sleep in her bed. If 'ee twain had put up 'ee banns, 'ee can do as 'ee both see fit. But Gaffer say 'en won't stand for no larking, least-ways open sin."

I wanted to say "We have put up our banns," but my lips were turning cold and pale. Then Rene spoke quickly. With ill-boded sharpening of ear he had understood the dialect well enough.

"The young lady and I are merely friends. If the storm begins to gather, I'll make my way by lantern light and sleep in the hay-loft." He looked at me as though I would be greatly relieved.

"The storm will break," I told him, "and you won't be able to come, and I'll not be able to go. The paths will all be drowned. When you get out, it will be time to go back to France."

"It might be better for both of us if it happened so," he answered. "There is great danger on the moors."

"Danger from whom?"

"From old gods who have power over us because we believe in them."

"They be plenty pharasee on the moor," Jarge said darkly.

Rene glanced at me. "Fairies," I explained.

"Best not to call 'em by right name, lest 'em coom. And if we don' make haste, we'll like enough see 'em's lights, a-flitting all about yeller and green. They be thick as fireflies on eve o' storm."

"Will you come early tomorrow morning, weather permitting?" Rene asked me, his voice trembling.

"Yes, and if it looks as though the weather won't permit, will you come in tonight?"

"I'll come to the hayloft."

Jarge and I set out for the farmhouse, and the shape of Rene slowly dimmed. Dimming too were my regrets at parting with him tonight . . . It was far the best . . . I had acted wisely . . . It was a good thing I had been able to control my shameless heart. . . .

As Rene had said, there was danger for both of us on the moors.

ELEVEN

NO breath of wind stirred all night, and although the sun glowered inimically on first topping the eastern downs, it climbed out of a tattered wisp of cloud into a sky of purest azure. Jarge came in from the dairy barn with two wooden pails brimful of milk, looking defiant in defense of Gaffer's fame as a weather prophet. Honoring it still, I had Jarge's mother fill a basket with eggs, bread, butter, cuts of bacon, a head of cabbage, and a jar of honey, for Jarge to carry to the cottage in case Rene should become storm-bound there. But I was fully resolved not to get in the same fix with him. Although I had lain awake more than an hour after midnight, my head full of wild thoughts and my body of wilder achings, I had wakened serene and sane.

"Mrs. Dawson, have you any mead?" I asked the farm wife on sudden inspiration.

"Maybe a little put by in the cool of cellar," she replied.

"May I buy a flask of it?"

"I'd not say 'ee nay, but I might say 'ee best beware. 'Er taste so good, 'er tempts 'ee to drink more than 'ee reckons, and 'er wondrous warming."

"I'll be very careful."

" 'Tis said 'er a good drink for brides, especial 'em that be shamefaced and shy. Put enough of 'er down old Gaffer, and I'd not trust 'en at prayer meeting. Now if 'ee and yon furriner have plighted 'ee troth—"

"No, we're just good friends."

"I'll sell 'ee a quartern, but won't bear no blame for what fall."

"On second thought, I'll not take any."

Then I asked her to put up a lunch for Rene and me in a separate basket. I pinned my riding skirt in tucks up to my knees and put on stout boots as though going otter-hunting. When the baskets were ready, Jarge slung the big one on his arm and we retraced our steps of last evening. When Rene spied us, he waved first wildly, then with proper restraint. Soon I saw his hair neatly combed, his face cleanly shaved. A good Frenchman, he had used a sweet-smelling soap.

"It's a wonderful day, after all," he told me.

"Jarge, you can come for me the same time," I said.

"Her depend on storm," he answered in hollow tones.

"There's no sign of a storm."

"Her do look sunny, I grant 'ee, and sometime Gaffer miss by nigh a fortnight, but 'en ne'er miss clean."

"I'm sure he's the best in all Cornwall." At that, the boy tossed his head proudly.

"You needn't come for her, Monsieur Jarge," Rene told him with grave courtesy. "I will fetch the young lady to the farmhouse at nightfall, and come back here to sleep."

"If gale hold off, 'ee can, and that easy. But if 'en blowin' and rainin', 'ee had better not stay till nightfall. 'Ee can follow yon brook straight here long past duskdown, but from here to Gaffer's house the path be wondrous mazed, wi' quicksand waitin' nigh."

I could not give the lad tuppence without casting a reflection on Rene, but I complimented him on his sagacity and handsome blue eyes. Gratified, he made off. Carrying our lunch and a flask of wine in his packsack, Rene led the way into the moors, walking slowly and pointing out interesting features of the landscape. This became even more strange—forlorn rather than gloomy, lonely rather than desolate. It did not appear deserted because I could not believe that human kind had ever come here. Rene told me I was wrong about that—flint-workers of unknown origins had lived and died on these wastes, herded their flocks, fought wolves, and worshipped forgotten goddesses a thousand years before they were driven into the forests by fair-haired invaders with bronze points on their arrows and spears. The Tiber wolf had not yet given suck to Romulus and Remus. The bold Phoenician had not spread a sail beyond the Gates of Hercules. Achilles, wondering sometimes about a pale spot just above his heel, had not been dreamed.

The huge masses of granite that Rene called tors were bereft of life, save for mosses growing in their seams, and had an ominous aspect; but small patches of scrub-oak forest clung in their lea, and grass grew rank in the fens. Curlews flushed from the brinks of dark pools and went wailing off; a hawk caught and killed a hare in our plain sight; what I thought at a distance was Fenris the Wolf evolved into a shaggy marsh donkey on some patient, solitary quest. None of these denizens of the moor brightened its mood or relieved its lonesomeness.

"Lola, you are—I was going to say unearthly beautiful—but that doesn't fit," the tall, gaunt man beside me burst out in the silence.

"You mean I'm earthy as that donkey," I answered.

"How do we know his secrets? He talked to Balaam, you remember—there's more to him than we think. Earthy's a good word, but human is better. It's not an ethereal beauty—delicate though it is, it's superbly human. It grew out of the ground under a warm sun. It's as though Mother Nature wanted to show what she could do without help from the angels."

He turned the subject quickly to his own upbringing in bleak poverty near Lyons, and told me his tireless, indomitable struggle for an education. His main studies were economic and he was a serious—though meanly paid—writer of political articles. These bought his bread, all he could ask in the way of material reward, because otherwise he could not fight for the things in which he believed. The money was in the other camp, he said—in the forces of Metternich, who had set his heel on human freedom seventeen years ago.

"With Lord Lundy?" I asked.

"I didn't suppose he would instruct you in his political aims."

"He never mentioned them."

"He has some, I assure you. He may very well realize them. Of course, I represent the antithesis of all he stands for. He doesn't know that—but some day he will know it." He stopped, flushing. "I've forgotten what little manners I possess. I ask you to forgive me."

I was at the point of telling Rene Papa's parting admonition, but I did not, and our talk turned back to the mysteries of the moor.

In high spirits he led me to yesterday's discovery—a circle of large stones enclosing about an acre. It was complete except for what appeared a short, necklike entrance, and here a rudely carved pillar stood upright in a perforated saucer-shaped stone. Instantly I was back in India and then in Kelso watching Grandsire Ferguson throw my evil fetishes into the fire.

"A good many of the circles and particularly the avenues of stones mark burial grounds," he told me. "This one was a shrine of a goddess of fertility."

"The circle represents her womb, doesn't it?"

"How did you know?"

"I recognize the lingam set in the yoni to indicate life-giving. I've seen the same in India."

His face lighted and he began to speak with great vivacity.

"The Indian civilization is very old. But it is rather surprising that the lingam appears in the fertility worship of a people as primitive as these circle-makers. Probably this very circle had only the female symbol to start with. The people didn't know then there was any male principle in re-creation of life. The lapse of nine months between mating and birth was too long for them to discover any relationship—women thought they were made pregnant by fog or the sun or spirits or magical ceremonies. There are tribes today who still haven't discovered the male factor. Naturally, religion centered in women, the magical givers of life; they were the priestesses and the gods were female. When the people finally got the idea of seed planted in the womb, they began to accent the lingam instead of the yoni in religious and magical ceremonies. Then this pillar was set up in the perforated stone. Priestesses gave way to priests. Of course, women lost their exalted position in the tribe."

"I wager the women knew all the time about those nine months. But they were too clever to let dim-witted men know they had anything to do with babies."

Rene laughed happily, and I thought of Krishna. I was imagining myself a priestess of a shepherd tribe, performing ceremonies at this very spot. I had known perfectly well—the Old Mother had told me—that my lovers were not merely joy-givers but necessary co-operators to my fertility. "And I'll bet the mysteries into which the girls were initiated by the priestesses were mainly instructions how to keep the secret from their mates," I went on.

"That's an idea I've never heard put forward by an anthropologist. It's quite reasonable that there could be a period of civilization—its length depending on the strength of the priestesshood and the relative isolation of the tribe—in which the women knew and the men didn't."

"What a magnificent secret," I said, wishing I had been there to help keep it.

"Perhaps the most exciting in all history."

We walked into the circle and sat down on a grassy mound. The stones set here so long ago to make women and ewes bear well and the grass grew green; the wild wastes of down and fen on every side; the black pools and the great grim tors breaking the long curves of the landscape, worked upon my imagination. Coming here with Rene became in some strange way connected with my going to Kali's shrine with Manu more than eight years ago. There I had gone in fear and hate of death; here I had come in hope and trust of life. Once more I was aware of their endless tug of war. And I was no stander-by, but a passionate partisan—a hard fighter on life's side.

Today I was wildly alive. I loved the breath in my lungs and the sparkling streams in my veins; and every movement of my body and surge of feeling and of thought were not only in vivid contrast but somehow in defiance of death.

With an intent expression, Rene was getting out our lunch from his packsack. He had often gone hungry, I thought; anyway the vital, sane French were properly devoted to their palates and stomachs. I sniffed the good food with delight.

"Don't you think the fertility goddess might consider this a sacrilege?" I asked.

"Not for you, it isn't. You're kind of a fertility goddess yourself, I think. I suppose she'll forgive a stray Frenchman."

We ate the bread and honey and cheese, and tippled from Rene's bottle. As my appetite slacked off, I felt a growing excitement in being so close to him and at the same time so far from all other human kind.

"I love life," I said, at some not quite clear prompting. "I want to make life—and fight death."

"What I said just now—about your being a fertility goddess— came from a real flash of insight," he told me earnestly. "I've been thinking about it ever since. Living people often reached godhead in olden times. A skeptic would say to me, 'You mean the tribespeople imagined, or were fooled into believing, that one or more of their number had become gods or goddesses.' But I don't mean that. What is godhead? Does anybody know? Some people are either born with, or acquire, powers so supernormal that a clear thinker cannot detect a distinction from supernatural. In the days of the matriarchies, the unusual women became priestesses. The great beauties—and don't forget that beauty in women is profoundly sexual, the outward aspect of desirability as wife or mother —could become goddesses. The power was there, if they knew how to use it. Elemental power that the people took to be supernatural; and where does natural leave off and supernatural begin?"

"It was dangerous to use that power," I said. "They had to be brave."

"Beauty and bravery go hand in hand. The moment a people's god ceases to be a super-hero in man's image to become a kind of abstraction, the people sicken. What we want to see is his personal power, awake and ablaze. The people of the Renaissance saw it and they became awake and ablaze. But since the glorious youth of the race, most people in most ages have come to demean themselves. More and more they regard themselves as an army of ants. They deny the wonder, let alone the miracle of human life."

He looked at me in startled happiness, then his thoughts rushed on.

"Lola, if you had lived a long time ago—or even today in some corners of Europe—you would be picked as a corn maiden. Your intense femininity, expressed in beauty and passion, would have made you the people's choice. You would have gone through a ritualistic marriage with a corn spirit so that the crops would be bumper. From that to being a corn goddess is a short—a perfectly credible—step. The people wouldn't be fooled. They'd see in you an incarnation of the life-giving force of nature, and whether you call it divinity or beauty is mere verbiage."

"I used to imagine that I was the incarnation of Râdhâ, the cow-herdess, Krishna's beloved."

"Perhaps you are. Her last incarnation before the last god dies and the machines are set up in the temples. You fill me with wonder and joy."

"Do you still love me—today?"

"Always." He leaned and kissed me, and I felt the same as when Manu and I made magic in the twilight.

"Do you love me, Lola?" he asked.

"I don't know. But I love life, and I've never felt it so strong. It makes me feel strong."

I put my arms around his neck and my lips against his. I felt a fullness of beauty come upon me to give to him. . . . I could not have it save to give it. . . . In giving it I possessed it. . . . The more I gave, the more I had. . . .

"You shouldn't have to do all the wooing," he told me with a smile. To my opened eyes it was a beautiful smile.

"I don't mind, if you respond enough."

"I think it's all right. You know how I want your love and yet can't believe you'd want mine. I suppose—when these stones were set here—women were expected to do the wooing. They were the child-bearers—the guardians of the great secrets—it was their right and business to choose the seed."

"It still is." I was greatly wrought up, my imagination was on the wing, and I felt as though I were speaking for all women, and for their goddess brooding over her lost and forsaken shrine. "Women let themselves be chosen instead of choosing. Those who still woo do it in stealth and fear, even in shame, because they've been taught to bow down to men. But I never will."

His eyes searched mine in profound inquiry.

"Lola, will you stand by that?"

"I hope so. I don't know."

"You need never yield, you have so much to give."

His big hands began to fumble at my jacket. His awkward touch and then his gentle caresses brought me to a pitch of life I had never known. Every shading of color in the landscape was lovely and hopeful as each band of a rainbow. I knew the meaning of the Circle of Stones, and curlews flying restlessly overhead were forms of exquisite grace.

Bliss was flowing through me in ever rising waves when the light dimmed. I held my lover close so he would not see the small cloud that had broken from the low-lying bank and drifted across the sun. But at once he lowered me into the hollow of his arm and lay down beside me.

"There is danger on the moors."

"There's always danger."

"The danger is somewhat like that of being on a mountain peak. You have to get down. There's a storm coming—the air's still and heavy—although it's still a long way off, in a few hours we've got to come in off the moor. What will we do then?"

"I'll cross that bridge when I come to it."

"What will we have to keep? Lola, you know I love you. I tried to take for granted that you loved me. Now I find I can no longer do so. Do you, Lola?"

"Would I have followed you here if I didn't love you?"

"I'm not sure. I can't use ordinary standards to judge by. Well,

I'll ask another question that may help you to answer the first. If we have each other—here—now—will you marry me?"

I knew I must speak truth which was at hand, available, in the ancient circle.

"No."

"I was quite sure of that."

Rene kissed me with deep love, then rose. Biting my tongue lest I say some bitter thing that would prejudice the future, I led the way out of the Circle of Stones. A moment passed before I could take any bearings whereby to set a course. All that I knew was that we must not turn back.

There was sadness in his face and, I thought, shame. Touched by both, still I did not speak, but for a different reason now. By keeping the aching silence, I could make him speak.

He did so, at last.

"Lola, will you answer a strange question?"

"If I can."

"Would you have let me take you today?"

"No, but I would have given myself to you. That's a different thing."

"How could you, if you don't love me?"

"You said I have great beauty. You can see it, and so I wanted to share it with you. That's what it's for—that would make it more real. I wanted you to give me rapture and the strength to go on alone."

I had not known the words would come that free.

"You can't expect me, a man, to understand that."

"I don't understand it either. It's just true."

"How could I give you strength?"

"I wouldn't have had to make a marriage of convenience. I might be able to become a great adventuress. Now I have a question to ask you. You're a young, virile man, and, as you said, a realist in your own way. Why did you rebuff me?"

"Because you didn't love me and wouldn't marry me. It knocked down all my pride. I'd show you my independence—that silly gesture people make when they're hurt and afraid."

"Usually it's a gallant gesture."

"Anyway, I knew I couldn't have you—to keep. I'd always long for you in vain. Can you imagine yourself as helpmeet to a struggling journalist? I'd want to give you a beautiful setting—so you could shine before the world as you were born to. There's no hope for us, and we'd better go back."

I listened for a moment to the uneasy cries of the curlews.

"No, I want to climb that tor." I pointed to one farther on the moors.

As we walked slowly on, I told him about my childhood in India. Fascinated, he did not at first notice the ebb and flow of the light as clouds streamed across the sun. They were moving much more rapidly than before, although there was yet no breath of wind on the moors. We were halfway up when the rack massed and lowered.

"We must start back at once," he said.

"Oh, it's a long time till dark."

"I've got to get you clear to the farmhouse in good light. The most dangerous part of the way is from the cottage on. If it clouds over and blows rain, darkness will shut in at sundown."

"Blow, wind! Come, rack!" I whispered, looking away.

He had me take his arm and started walking at a brisk pace. Soon the sky was jam-packed with clouds and the curlews wheeled no more; warm puffs of air rustling in the grass closed ranks in a gentle breeze. It quickened very slowly, but the sun's fall was slower still.

"We're going to make it all right," Rene told me, with what he thought was a reassuring smile.

I was ashamed to plead fatigue and ask him to walk slower. I was not tired in the least and had always taken pride in my physical stamina. But presently I began to limp almost imperceptibly, as though trying to conceal it.

"You're lame!" he cried in alarm.

"It's a stone bruise, I think. I stepped on a sharp flint this morning. Rene—I'll have to go a little slower."

The anxiety in his face touched but did not trouble me. He thought I was lame; but I knew he was. He wanted to help me to safety from the storm, but I wanted to help him to a greater safety. I did not want him to love me in vain; that great force of such potential strength to us both must be actuated. It was like that of the gathering storm, I felt, which must burst to fulfill its being.

When we came to the brook that flowed between the tors to the cottage half a mile below, there was still enough daylight to guide a lover determined on my safety to the farmhouse an equal distance farther. But just then that light became tinted as from a slow-moving purple beam cast from a lighthouse in the sky. The dark-gray clouds turned purplish black. Not ominous to me was the darkling scene; my heart swelled with gratitude to my nature gods. High lightning blazed a jagged path to the horizon; and the Wolf growled deep in his throat. Then a distant sibilant sound rushed and swelled into a wild consonancy of wind and rain.

Rene started to take off his jacket for my use, but it was almost instantly drenched, and I could not help but laugh at his woebegone expression.

"Let's run!" I yelled, tugging at his arm.

"Your foot!" he shouted.

"I'll stand the hurt to get out of the rain!"

He must have thought me a Spartan as we sped down the slope, so swift and light my pace. He must have wondered at the happiness in my face and movements, for we almost flew before the wind that roared with laughter. I was in love with the warm rain in gushing flood. It warmed instead of chilled me; it bathed me as in preparation for a procreant rite; it was a passionate lover to whom I yielded in joy.

We saw the cottage take shape in the dusk. We entered and shut out the storm. But thereby was shut out a force friendly to me, with which my own forces were in tune. I had always got along well with Nature. All my adventures with Manu had occurred outdoors, and I had drawn in the strength of the Indian earth through my bare feet. I had never felt as strong or as brave within walls, perhaps because my darkest hours had been spent there. There I had learned that Mamma did not love me—there Papa had died—within bleak walls in Kelso I had lost Lola.

The great whoops of the wind had become a sullen mutter beyond the thick stone walls, and the rain on the flint roof made stifled splashings. When Rene had ignited the wick with a Vienna match from his store, it gave forth a feeble, yellowish light. The dank air of the stone chamber reminded me of that in the candlelight when Grandsire Ferguson had prayed for the saving of my soul. It felt more chill than the rain.

"I'll get a fire going at once," Rene said, with an anxious glance at me. "You'll be lucky not to catch your death of cold."

When he had poured oil on a block of peat and ignited it, my drenched clothes felt clammy and dismal. I should take off my jacket, riding skirt, and boots and stand close to the fire in my shift, I thought, but hovering beside him on the hearth I felt great strain. My very eyes seemed dulled and I could not recapture the lost wonder or believe what I had so plainly seen in the wild of the storm.

"I'd like a glass of wine," I told him. "I'm cold inside."

"My dear—I'm so sorry and ashamed. I bought the least I thought would make out—I had so little money—and we drank the last at lunch."

"That's all right," I told him quickly, torn by the sadness in his face. "I don't need it. I'm getting warm now."

We had drunk our wine in the magic circle under the midday sun, and the cups were empty. He had been wise to resist the spell; I had been an outlaw in the throes of summer madness. When the rain stopped blustering, Rene and I would take his hurricane lantern and make our way to the farmhouse. Great Pan was dead.

My stomach faint, I went to the basket the farm wife had prepared intending to get out the cold bread and warm it by the fire. When I removed the cloth, I saw a small, earthen jug I could not account for. With trembling hands I removed the cork. . . . It couldn't be because I had told her not to send . . . we hadn't plighted our troths . . . she had warned me of its beguilements. . . .

Then I cried out with joy, because I had kissed the round, sweet mouth of the jug, and it was—indeed it was—mead!

"What is it?" Rene cried in amazement.

"Mead! Mead!" I exulted. "Mead from thyme honey! Mead, the drink of the gods!"

TWELVE

RENE'S face lighted at my joy, but his knowledge of the gods was scientific rather than from folklore or first hand, and of course he could hardly begin to understand it.

" 'Er taste so good," I told him, bringing the jug and two cups to the fire, "but 'er tempts 'ee to drink more than 'ee reckons, and 'er wondrous warming." I gave him what could never be written, an almost perfect imitation of the farm wife's dialect.

He took boyish pleasure in the show.

" 'Tis said 'er a good drink for brides, especial 'em that be shamefaced and shy. Put enough of 'er down old Gaffer, and I'd not trust 'en at prayer meeting. But if 'ee and me ha' plighted our troth—"

"By the good God, I can plight mine to ever remembrance of the wonder of this day." He was a Frenchman and not afraid of eloquence.

"Before we drink—why don't you take off your miserable wet clothes and put on those?" I pointed to his carefully hung street clothes.

"I would've, but you had no extras—"

"You can lend me your shirt, can't you?"

"Better than that! By Jove, I have it. It is old and patched—"

He rummaged in his bag and produced a *robe de chambre* of worn-smooth huckaback. I began peeling off my clammy garments and letting down my hair in the full glow of the fire; he disappeared in the shadows behind me. Spreading his blanket on the cold stone floor, we were soon seated there, snug as the proverbial bug in rug, with the flask and cups between us. Such a firelit, cozy scene might attract evil spirits—I had learned that long ago. Perhaps one of them would prevail on the Gaffer, his farmer son, and Jarge to light lanterns and torches and come searching for us. No, they would first climb to the hayloft to look for a light, and see through the blown rain the red peat flames bursting from our chimney. If the Gaffer still thought I needed protection, Goodwife would set him straight.

" 'Ee mind 'ee own business, Gaffer," I could hear her telling him, respectfully but firmly. " 'Em young folk ha' plenty vittle and peat, and can look out for 'emsel." But she would know better than tell him of the jugkin of mead she had slipped into our basket.

I poured some of the golden nectar into the cups.

"Why," he exclaimed when he tasted it, "this is hydromel. It's still made in Brittany, and was a ceremonial drink of the Romans."

"Do you know any of the ceremonies?"

"No, but I might invent one. Wet your lips with it."

I did so, and he leaned and kissed them.

"I know a ceremony performed by the bee-keepers in western England a long time ago," I told him. "It's called the bee-bride's words, and a marriage wasn't considered blessed until they were said over cups of mead. They appealed to me, and I learned them."

"Please repeat them."

"The groom sang first to the bride:

Sweet as honey, loving as mead,
You shall be my queen indeed."

"Enchanteur!"

"Then the bride sang to him:

Flowers unplucked will wither soon,
Eat my honey with a spoon."

"There's the pagan spirit for you! No wonder it appealed to you."

"I suppose I recited it for you in defense of my own behavior today."

"It needs no defense, Lola. You were only being yourself—the beautiful woman that you are. It happened that you've never been indoctrinated in the taboos. There's an evil principle in nature, but you know only the good—however wisely it may be banned by society." He paused, his eyes widening. "Listen to the storm."

The wind was howling in the chimney like Jove's wolves and the windblown rain flailed the flint roof.

"And we're so warm—" I said.

"I'm too hot. The drink and the fire combined."

I did not speak with words or had any need to. Event set into motion long ago quickened its pace; charms worked stronger; what was as true to nature as the wind blowing the rain, and the brooks rising became a potent magic. I was gloriously happy as it revealed my companion of today, my lover of tonight. He gave the effect of being roughly carved. His was a woodman's body, I thought, tireless as an ax in the long, gaunt arms. The massive head and round, sensitive face gave it great human dignity and meaning.

"You remind me of a picture I saw in Florence," he said. "It's the most beautiful in the world, I think. Lie on your right side, Lola."

I did so and he rolled his coat as a prop for my head. He posed me carefully, finally draping my hair over the right shoulder.

"It's more beautiful than the original," he told me quietly. "The old man would say so himself."

"The old man—?"

"The picture is by Tiziano Vecellio—Titian—I believe she was his mistress and a duchess—anyway he loved her, as you can tell by the expression on her face. It's known as 'Lady on a Couch.'"

Rene lay beside me, and began to pay me other tributes in amazed joy. I surrendered to an ecstasy not dreamy but entirely vivid. I heard the wind in the chimney and could almost catch the rhythms of an elemental ode. I saw the firelight's change and play, causing shifting highlights on Rene's flesh and my own. Every nerve-end waited for his gliding hand, leaped at its touch, and thrilled long in its wake.

It roved in light circles at ever slower pace while my whole body waited in almost unbearable suspense. This broke in waves of sensation so acute that it did not seem even momentarily relieved, then began to rebuild. The waves increased in intensity until they eclipsed all other consciousness, forming a continuous current. All my being became concentrated in one agony of rapture. Then I thought that I cried out, but presently there was no sound but the wind and the crackle of the fire. I became aware of tenderness and warmth in Rene's arms.

After a time he reached for and got my cup of mead and held it to my lips. I drank a little from it and he drained it.

"Will you marry me, Lola?"

"I'll tell you tomorrow."

"You must tell me tonight. I love you."

"I love you, Rene. That's all I know."

We could still draw back . . . There came a moment of deep silence between one gust of wind and another, and the flames hummed low without crackling and appeared to sink a little. It must have been that brief lull that made the next gust sound forth so loud. Rain flung against the wall like a wave of the sea, and the blaze leaped. I could imagine a shout of *"Lola! Lola!"* in the chimney.

My hand moved to his side, paused, then moved again, the wise priestess hand, more potent than all the winds and seas, more kindling than the lightning. Then my arms flung wide.

THIRTEEN

*T*HROUGH my dreams I was aware of my body's glowing and my heart's happiness. I wakened in the intimation of breaking dawn, although the clapboard over the window showed no crack, and the round glass set in the door—long ago salvaged from a wreck —had the merest haze of gray. I rose stealthily, opened the door, and looked out. The wind was down, the rain had ceased and a ghostly presage of light lay over the moors. I returned and kept vigil over my lover until the dawn came through our doorway and I could see his face.

He was sleeping very deeply and many little pleasantries of love were required to waken him. The stillness after the storm, the light growing in the doorway, and the freshness of the air, became symbolic of the morning of the world. Until that morning Eve had not known her beauty, but she had dreamed of it in the night; and by giving it to her mate she discovered its power and purpose. Men who loved woman truly held it yet.

We rose and put on our dry clothes and looked to our belly-needs. Then we went out and sat on the stone bench overlooking the moors. Rene got out his clay pipe and a packet of cheap tobacco, and, although his hand shook when he filled it, smoking calmed his breathing. He looked at me and gave me a grave smile.

"You said you'd answer my question in the morning."

"I will." Then I hesitated to speak on, not in doubt of the answer, but in awe of its momentousness.

"Will you marry me, Lola?"

"No, Rene."

His face told me that it was the answer that he expected. He received it as a true Mussulman receives strokes of kismet, whether good or evil, too proud of soul to show, or hardly to feel, joy or sorrow.

"I wonder if I should ask why. I doubt if I have the right—and if I do—I don't know whether I would benefit or suffer from knowing."

"I think you should ask me, Rene."

"Then tell me, please."

"That's not going to be easy. If I said, 'I love you too much to marry you,' I wouldn't mean I'd be a handicap to you in the way you spoke of yesterday. I would mean that to give you more than this would handicap me."

"Do you mean for some sort of career?"

"If I married you, Rene, loving you as I do, I wouldn't be free. Everything I did would affect you for good or ill; knowing that would restrain me. Grandsire Ferguson would say I wanted freedom to walk a primrose path. But I think I want it in order to have adventures—to put it another way, to be an adventuress. I've always known what that meant. One who seeks great prizes, and won't turn back from danger."

"So far I've helped you along?"

"Yes."

"For that, you've rewarded me with your love. But I can't have it always."

"Yes you can, all your life. I've given it to you for a keepsake."

"But if you go on with me," he said, after a pause, "I won't help you along. I'll handicap you. Is that true?"

"If I let you. I might be tempted to, because you're my first love and I think my great love."

"Do you think you'll ever marry?"

"My mind has changed about that, too. I was going to marry for safety and become a chota memsahib—compared, that is, with my girlhood dreams. I feel I don't need to do it, now this has happened. If it serves my purpose to marry, I will, but it wouldn't be fair to marry someone I love as much as I love you, or who loves me as much as you do. Manu said something that applies to that. He understood me better than anyone—or else he dreamed wonderful dreams about me." I paused and Manu and I were again squatting among the oleanders, saying farewell.

"It comes back to me now," I went on. "He said he could love me without hating me the while. I think you could, too. But I won't marry anyone who can do that—it would be a dreadful sin. If I marry, it will be someone who can hate me as well as love me, and in that way take no harm or do none to me. A man whom I can use and reward for that use and to whom I needn't be bound."

This was the clearest I had ever seen. I had spoken of what I saw, letting it come to me. I did not wholly understand it, but I felt its truth.

"You say you're going to do so and so," he said after a long silence. "You'd better ask help from your gods."

The warm sparkling sweep of my blood seemed briefly checked.

I no longer had the sprig of tulasi and the salagram stone that Manu had given me. But my emblem of Siva had been restored to me incarnate.

"I listen to what you say," he went on, "and believe it because you say it, but the fact remains I'm going to lose you. Tomorrow I'll be setting out for Brittany. I'll have some cheap clothes on and a few more expensive in my valise, and my bag of rocks and pages of manuscript, and my job to go on with in Paris. The crowds will engulf me. I'll think of their affairs instead of the doings of gods and goddesses, heroes and heroines—I'll be lost in them—I'll remember the moors and the magic made there as though from an earlier incarnation. I won't have you to look at, Lola, or to kiss. I may forget your face and body, to keep them from haunting me. I'll never again climb to the peaks."

"Oh, I'll come back and we'll go there together—"

"No, don't come, unless we're both free, and you will stay. If I'm married to a woman of my own kind, I might be unfaithful to her, but not with you, Lola. I mean—if I had you again, my marriage to her would be nullified. I'd be the husband of a ghost."

"What does that mean, Rene?" I asked, my pulses throbbing.

"What can it mean, except that you and I are married? Last night before the fire we became one flesh—it was validated in the dawn. I can stand to lose you once, but I've got to think of it as by death. You've either got to go on with me, or to be dead to me. If you won't come with me, set me free."

"Rene, I set you free. I too am free. But tomorrow will be here before we know it—"

I swayed toward him, but unconsciously I swept my gaze over the moors, to make sure that Kali—or some other harbinger of ill— was not watching us. There was no one standing tall on the distant tors, the moors beyond were unvisited and naked to the sun. Finally I glanced back toward the farmhouse. Jarge should be coming soon. . . .

He was coming now, I thought, with Gaffer. . . . No, the taller figure was of the right height to be that rangy old man, but walked too young. It had to be the farmer, although I did not remember that much difference in stature between him and Jarge. . . . It must be a ceremonial visit requiring them both, to find out how we had fared during the storm, perhaps for the elder to explain why he had not "coöm" last night. . . . Perhaps a letter, too important-looking to be delivered by the younker alone, had arrived for Rene.

Both disappeared in the low ground beyond the sand bed. In a moment I saw Jarge returning while the tall man came on alone. His stride was young and lithe.

I looked quickly in the other direction, laying my arm across Rene's shoulder.

"It was all my fault, wasn't it?" I asked, in a thoughtful tone.

"I don't know what you—"

"I invited you to go to the Café de Provence, then followed you here. Well, I want you to promise me something. If anybody says anything to me about it in your hearing, will you control yourself? No matter how angry you are, will you keep still—not raise a hand—until I ask for your help?"

"I'm always too slow to anger—"

"Then it's agreed that until I call on you, I'm to fight my own battles. That's your solemn promise."

"If you want it so." I dropped my arm and he looked sharply into my face. "What in the good God's name—"

"We're going to have a visitor. It's Jeffery, Lord Lundy."

FOURTEEN

RENE turned white but his head shot up, and I was proud and glad that he was my first lover. He glanced toward the approaching foe, then turned his head to smile at me. When Jeffery was about fifty paces off, he looked at him again, then rose leisurely. His posture did not appear awkward as he waited and although his eyes were shining with excitement, he held his own well. I remained seated.

I noticed first that Jeffery was dressed in hard tweeds and wore a short-brimmed, low-crowned hunting hat. His boots and breeches were bedaubed with mud well above the knee, and from the rumpled state of his clothes I was sure that he had traveled fast and not taken them off last night. His eagle countenance had never been more impressive, not handsome and yet barely falling short of beautiful, and at first there was nothing in it that I could read. He had meant it so but was not able to maintain it for very long. He made a slight but somehow stately acknowledgment to Rene's bow, then turned his gaze on me. In spite of himself, it was deeply searching in intense anxiety. Then the skin appeared to tighten over his facial bones and his eyes darkened.

"I see that I'm too late," he said, with a bitter smile. The words were for me; the smile was for something or someone that dwelt within his being.

There was nothing I could say and the silence grew long.

"It was the fault of the storm, you understand," he went on, as though in self-justification. "The message of your having arrived in Penzance reached me in Southampton by the same ship the following morning. One of my employees had taken ship with you. I already knew that Monsieur Saint-Denis was in Cornwall, but I had never dreamed that you were enough involved with him to follow him. I felt it in my bones I shouldn't leave Bath at this time—" Jeffery stopped in an agony of self-fury, then again smiled.

"Pardon me, Jeffery." I turned to Rene. "I think Jeffery wants a private conversation with me. Would you mind waiting in the cottage? I'll call you, if I need you."

"I think that would be best."

"Aren't you betrothed to Lola?" Jeffery demanded.

"I haven't the honor of your acquaintance, Lord Lundy," Rene answered with quiet dignity. "It is for Lola, not me, to answer your inquiries."

Lord Lundy bowed gravely. Rene responded with awkward movements but with an inward grace. Then he walked away and disappeared in the cottage.

"To resume the recital of an enterprise that failed, I took ship within the hour and arrived in Plymouth late that night," Jeffery went on, as though unaware of the interruption. "I started at once by stage over the old post road to Callington, striking the turnpike at Bodmin. My scout had learned while the ship docked at Penzance that Monsieur had set out for these moors; and after riding one horse to death and exhausting another, I was within ten miles of the farmhouse when the storm broke last night. There was no way to go on. There were only sheep paths that were immediately lost in darkness and rain. I spent the night with a shepherd, setting out at dawn. But the brooks were up, my guide could not keep to the flooded paths, and this greatly belated arrival is the result."

"I'm very sorry you went to so much trouble." My voice trembled but was quite clear.

"Lola, didn't you expect me?"

"No. It didn't cross my mind."

"I hoped to the last that you knew I would come—that you wouldn't be here otherwise—and would wait for me before you took some irremediable step."

"I came here to be with Rene, not to play any game."

"Oh, I knew you were greatly attracted to him, but I thought mainly in connection with me. We both came into your life the same moment—he was my natural antagonist. Even if I had no part in your plans, how could you underestimate me in that way? How could you fail to know that I'd follow you?"

"You'd gone to Southampton on your great affairs. You told me in your coach that you were no longer involved—"

"You believed me? *This* is my greatest affair. Could you imagine a man who spent nearly a year of his life in steady practice in order to win a steeplechase—another year to win a boxing championship that I didn't even claim—still another to become a mountain-climber—could you imagine that man letting any business prevent him from following you here? You—the greatest prize that ever came my way?"

I could not bear seeing him so torn. He was still so like an eagle, which screams in pride while he soars seeking prey but when wounded makes no sound.

"Won't you sit down, Jeffery?"

"Thank you." He sat erect, his long beautiful hands in his lap, gazing out over the moors.

"This is a very strange thing," I said. "There's a pattern running through it—from the moment I met you and Rene until now. If you want to talk—maybe you can help me see what it means."

"No, because you are its central mystery. You can understand it only through self-revelation. I suppose the pattern is always strange when the central figure is a truly beautiful woman. She is so involved with the greatest of all mysteries, procreation. All who can realize her beauty are profoundly affected by it. It draws the lightning."

The strain in his face eased as he talked.

"Lola, it's too late now for any more games. I'm going to employ truth as far as I can see it. I want you to hear me out. Then you can decide whether there can be anything more between you and me."

I nodded and waited.

"I had no ordinary approach to life in the first place. The house of Lundy is one of the oldest in England, as you know, but has always been more or less isolated from the court and from public affairs. Our wealth came out of the ground—ships came for it bringing the best from all the world. In our hall is a bronze bowl worked with gold, bearing a Phoenician inscription of the time of King Hiram. Rugged men, the younger sons either became soldiers or drifted to the colonies; the barons stayed close to Blackmoor, reigning over their immense bleak domain, spending almost every day shooting and hunting. I was raised on the moor and in my dreams I was an eagle seeking hares and other prey. I came to look like an eagle."

"You do, Jeffery."

"Blackmoor Keep is one of the oldest seats in England. It's had additions like most of the old houses but the central tower is almost certainly pre-Roman. It's very large and gloomy—countless antlers and boar heads and shields and weapons on its walls don't lend it any cheer. I was an only child and had no playmates. I was passionately in love with my mother, a very beautiful woman from an old

Welsh house—fey if ever woman was. My father was a weak man, and I detested him. I despised weakness in any form. I didn't hate him, but I wanted him to die so I could have Mamma to myself and come into the barony."

"How old were you then?"

"I'd always wanted him to die. I realized his weakness as I came into my strength. At nineteen, my philosophy of life—you might say my religion—was a deeply imbedded active force. At one pole stood Old Berkeley—his name derived from the Saxon Erlking. I told you I invented him and his blind worshippers in the mine, but I didn't."

"I knew you didn't."

"The legend is well established. Not only our miners but a good many in Cornwall propitiate Old Berkeley—rams are sacrificed to him to this day. I conceived him not only superstitiously but intellectually. I saw him not as Satan, who is merely in revolt against Jehovah, but a much older god, one of the vassals of the true creator of the universe, representative of the principle of evil. In my theology, evil was the positive principle in creation, good the negative. As a child, I began to realize that doing good not only fails to profit but is actually weakening. Good-doers start out with the idea of loss instead of gain. Jehovah promises rewards in heaven—but he is not bonded. His promissory note is not a mortgage that can be foreclosed."

"Who was the real creator in your inverted religion?" I asked, trying to reach Jeffery through his words. "In India, it's Brahma. Did Jehovah and Satan correspond to Vishnu and Siva?"

"I'll go into that, perhaps, at a later time. I discussed it once with a great prince in eastern Europe—again with a Slavic philosopher whose teachings will rock the world—once with an archbishop. It's an interesting hypothesis, decidedly more reasonable than the theologies that millions of our fellows swallow without a gulp."

"What happened to your father? Perhaps I shouldn't ask, but you said you wanted him to die, so you could have the barony and your mother to yourself. You said he was a weak man who didn't deserve great prizes."

"Aren't you seeking great prizes?"

"Yes."

"Then I'll tell you. I didn't kill him—I only let him lose his life trying to keep up with me. You see, he fancied himself a sportsman. The silly fool was always mouthing 'stiff upper lip'—'never say die'—'play the game.' So I took him mountain-climbing—almost my first fling at it. I picked a comparatively easy peak in the French Alps and suggested we take no guides. He was too sporting to protest or to insist on our roping up until the going got hard. Suddenly it got very hard, and he became exhausted and lost his footing."

In fancy I could see the murdered man spinning down, rebounding from the rocks, and could hear his screams shrill as an eagle's. But with my own eyes I was looking into Jeffery's face and wondering what had changed it since I had seen it last. I was unable to find the flaw that had kept it from being beautiful. The back of my neck prickled and tingles were creeping around my waist and down to the calves of my legs. These were not cold or unpleasant. . . .

"I find, Lola, that a leopard can't change his spots—even when he is in love," he said after a long pause.

"I'm amazed that a leopard can fall in love."

"He can—with a leopardess. He's not tempted to fall in love with any other creature—there is no other as beautiful. I'm ashamed that I ever tried to appear to you other than I am."

"It was only a feeble try and it didn't succeed."

"I succeed with others when I choose. The truth is I didn't want to deceive you. I wanted you to know me as I am—I wanted you to *join* me. I couldn't believe—I can hardly believe it now—that a woman as elemental as you are could reject me for such other lovers as come your way."

"Don't you think, Jeffery, you might be—mad?"

"If so, it's a very profitable madness. Twelve years ago—when I was nineteen—I became Baron Lundy of Blackmoor, recognized by the nobility of all Europe as one of the truly significant titles— far more illustrious than those of the new duchies. Its revenue is fifty thousand pounds per year. I am lord over a few hundred shepherds and farm folk, and absolute monarch of a thousand or more miners and their families. That is not so in name. According to English law they are freemen, who may work or idle, come and go, as they please. Actually I have the power of life and death over them, and they know it. Instead of hating me, as soft, stupid people would suppose, they idolize me. I told you something different before— now I'm telling you the truth. They stoned to death one of their number who broke one of my rules."

My cheeks burned and my eyes felt weak as though the pupils were too large. I could not stop breathing deeply and rapidly. These things I could not hide from him, and I could not hide from myself other signs and tokens throughout my body. But my brain remained perfectly clear.

"I dare say that Old Berkeley teaches them a lesson now and then," I said.

"It's not necessary. They're completely devoted to me. As I said, Old Berkeley is the personification of a force—one that I know how to use in a limited way. The great Slavic genius I spoke of told me that in a very few generations it will rule the world, although, perhaps, under some other name. All the people on earth will be willing slaves to a few men who can employ it in a truly great way— idealizing those men—deifying them. The times are not right for it yet—the opposing institutions are too strong—the Slav thinks that it can't prevail until Europe lies prostrate again after great wars. Anyway, I have neither the genius nor really the desire for such a role in history. I'm too devoted to hunting and to the arts. I am childishly ardent in all my pursuits."

"I wouldn't say you were childish in the way you came into the barony," I said.

"My predecessor was only forty-one at the time. If he were alive now, he might live twenty years more."

"Your predecessor was your father."

"Lola, I don't think you can question my sanity on that score. For a few minutes' pleasure in the bedroom, he brought into being a rival. He proved no match for him."

"It's a terrible sanity."

"Why are we taught that patricide is the crime of all crimes? Because the graybeard lawmakers stand in such terror of it. They know it is the most natural of all crimes. Every historian—every philosopher worthy of the name—knows that. The weak must get out of the way of the strong."

He paused, then asked bluntly, "Lola, don't you want the strongest lover you can get?"

"It's natural for women to want strong lovers to make them strong children. But there are many kinds of strength—"

"Let's not employ euphemisms. I'm talking about elemental strength—the kind I have—and you have. Let's join them."

"Do you mean—permanently?"

"For always. I want you for my wife."

My thoughts became entangled with chaotic emotions. "I find that amazing," I said.

"Do you?"

I steadied myself. "No. I find I'm not amazed at all."

"Will you marry me, Lola?"

"I wouldn't be amazed to hear myself saying yes. Instead I'm going to ask you a question. It's a very important one. What will happen if I don't?"

"You'll marry Saint-Denis and that will conclude our relations."

"What if I don't marry him, either?"

"Don't suggest such a thing, Lola. He had the head start—you championed him against me on the street that day—by your marrying him, I can write off your loss as unpreventable, on the assumption that you fell in love with him that night—an *idée fixe*. I wouldn't want to believe that you refused me because of a passing sexual infatuation for a person whom no one would presume to introduce to me."

A peasant stand up thus? I had once thought of him as Acquilla, out of pagan England. Instead we were sitting on the same bench; he was a man of lightning that I had drawn. I felt the intense heat of his life's flame. It was flowing through me as though taking the place of my own. It seemed to me that I was being possessed by him.

"If you marry him, you'll disappear with him," Jeffery went on in quiet tones. "You'll not be the rare sort of being that you are now, and I'll be rid of this torment."

"If I married you, wouldn't I stop being what I am now?"

"You would become something much more."

"How long have I to decide?"

"I'm leaving in a few minutes. If you'll come with me, very well. If you can't make up your mind that soon, write to me at Blackmoor in a few days. But if there's any doubt in your mind, don't go back into your lover's arms until it is removed. From this moment he is to have you—or I am."

He rose with the swift, easy motion of an eagle taking wing, but was arrested on the balls of his feet as though by a tether. I looked up into his eyes I had once thought were steel gray. They were not, however—that grayness was intensely animate. I would go and look at an eagle in a cage.

"Will you come, Lola?" he asked.

"Not now, Jeffery."

He raised his hat and walked away in long strides. At every one, I felt more listless and cold. The cloud shadows on the moor stealthily ingressed the regions of sunlight. Jeffery stopped and looked back. I rose, my arms stiff and trembling at my sides, and walked with a quickening pace toward the cottage. As I neared the door, Jeffery strode on.

Rene was sitting on the edge of the bed, one hand on his lap, the other under his chin, his head bowed in deep thought. He sprang to his feet.

"Lola!"

"Shut the door."

"What's frightened you?"

"I'm frightened only of myself."

"He wanted you to go away with him—"

"Yes, just to his hall to be his baroness. The rest is imagination. But I want to get rid of it, Rene."

"Let's start at once for Boleigh. There's a magistrate there, and a Methodist church."

"I can't marry you, Rene, but I'll love you always. Now do what I want."

"What is it?" He caught my hands. "Calm yourself and tell me."

"Shut and lock the door. Don't wait. Hurry."

My hands were already flying.

FIFTEEN

AN hour after Jeffery's departure, I climbed a tor to try to find out if he had left the farmhouse. I did not see any sign of him there, and presently discovered him and another horseman much nearer than I had expected on the winding moor road going toward Bodmin. I returned to the cottage and asked Rene to cut short his stay here and leave at once for Falmouth. We would travel and live together, and I would stay there with him until his departure for France.

He agreed without asking questions. He packed his few belongings and mine; the pots and kettles and bedding could be retrieved by Jarge. Rene carrying his heavy packsack and his big valise, I unburdened except for a light bag, we left the cottage with hardly a backward glance. He knew that I was too badly frightened to take tender leave of the beloved spot, although he did not ask why.

My impulse was to make haste on the path to the farmhouse. To curb it a little—and thus not make sorry show in his and my own sight—I asked him to take the lead. He walked briskly enough to indicate only reasonable haste to be on our way, but I knew that he, too, wished to be gone from the moors in case Jeffery should, on an afterthought, return there.

As we came on to the sandbed, my thoughts of our footprints soon fading out brought sorrow to my heart. We had raised no monument to our strange adventures. We had marked no path for our returning. We had wrought no change in the scene, to commemorate the great change wrought in us. The rains would wash out our marks and the wind would howl with no thought of our passage. The Circle of Stones that had worked magic all but forgotten these thousand years would forget again and lie impotent and forsaken. The ghosts of old shepherds might still haunt the cottage, but the hearth would be cold, and the beauty and rapture we had made there would illumine it no more.

The peat bog under the thin layer of sand quaked beneath our feet. I was thinking about it idly when, without any foreshadowing of thought or event, a wave of icy terror broke over me, stifling my heart. Rene was just entering the aisle of poles. With a scream, I dropped my bag and sprang toward him. In that same instant I saw his head and back lose their level, as though he had become a dwarf. He cried out in warning to me, but I had been warned by my soul and my hands were leaping toward him even now. When they clutched his coat collar, I tugged backward with preternatural strength.

A monster had seized his legs. By an agony of effort I broke its hold; there was a sound like the smacking of a giant's lips; and I shot backward, dragging Rene behind me five yards across the bank. Falling hard on the quaking ground we had just traversed, we could not believe we were safe, and half crawled, half ran to the green moorland. There we stood panting, with clutched hands, gazing at the deadfall we had so narrowly missed. My small bag lay on its side where I had dropped it. Of Rene's heavy valise there was no trace. Our most distant footprints were already melting away.

"Qu'est-ce que?" Rene gasped, his eyes round and filled with darkness.

I did not answer. Horror was on me, cold and deadening, and I was trying to cast it off so I could realize my own identity in time and place. I was not wakening from a nightmare, only coming out of shock caused by an actual experience of nightmare aspect. Thin though the summery air was, I heard Gaffer's shout as he drove his cattle out of sight behind the hill.

"Let's go to the farmhouse," I said at last. "We can climb the tor—"

"No." And then when I turned to him, Rene spoke quietly and firmly. "No, I'm going to find out what this means."

He threw off his packsack and turned back across the bank toward the aisle of poles. I followed him closely, intent on the inquiry as he was, no longer troubled by the tremor of the peat bog under the wet sand. As he neared my bag, he tested the ground at every step, working his way to the nearest pole. By employing a good deal of strength he pulled this out, to find it supported by a big circular cork taken from a sein or a buoy at a point barely covered by the sand. Probing with this, he advanced a foot or two farther.

Suddenly the sand offered no resistance. He thrust the nine-foot pole down and out of sight save for a few inches of its top.

"No bottom," he told me.

Then he set about a long, grueling task. It was to probe the gulf of quicksand and reset the stakes on either side of the isthmus of safe ground that traversed it. It meant that both rows had to be moved about three feet. As he grunted and sweated, horror went out of his eyes, and I could read nothing but resoluteness in his face.

"This means we could never prove—" I began. Then I stopped, in distrust of my voice.

"We couldn't anyhow. And while we were climbing the tor or getting the farmer to come here to investigate, Jarge or someone might try to cross. I wouldn't want even a marsh hare to fall into this hellhole."

He gave a violent thrust to the last stake. "Not," he added, grinning at me, "that a rabbit would have sense enough to go through the aisle."

The grin did wonders for me. When he led the way between the poles onto the trembling ground beyond, my knees were again steady, my blood warm, and my pulse fast but strong. When we gained the footpath he stopped beside a granite up-cropping.

"Let's talk it over now," he said.

"Yes, I want to."

"It's a good seat for one, and you can sit on my lap." When I was comfortable, he lighted his pipe, then took my hand. "The sooner we face it the better," he went on. "It's going to look different when we're among those farmer folk; and the farther we get from the moors—the more we mix with other people—the less we're going to believe it. We'll start thinking that the quagmire bed shifted under the sand—after Lord Lundy crossed. We'll wonder if the storm didn't blow down some of the stakes, and, in trying to restore them, he put them in the wrong position. This soon—you and I together—we know better."

I nodded and pressed his hand.

"It seems too monstrous to lay at the door of any sane man," he said, after a thoughtful pause. "But perhaps you don't know how some people on the Cornish coast used to make their living. They moved the lights and the buoys so that ships would strike the rocks and break up. They had nothing against the crews—they just wanted the cargo to drift in to the beach where they could get it. These were relatively simple people—with only a little of the knowledge of evil possessed by a king of the moors."

"Why do you call him that?"

"It came to my lips and I think it fits fairly well. He told you of his family's long reign over the greatest of the southern moors. They were of Celtic origin, I think—Lundy is a Celtic name—and as for ancient lineage, the Hanovers or even the Stuarts may be upstarts in comparison. As a child with a powerful imagination, he could have learned evil from the wasteland as readily as good. Both themes are found in nature."

"You don't have to prove to me that Jeffery would be capable of it."

"I almost refuse to believe it—and I'll tell you why. I hate to tell you—it's a dreadful thing. An imperious man like he is, a ruthless hunter who has killed hundreds of stags and many thousand brace of wildfowl, an emulator of the cruel lofty kings of the Middle Ages, might not hesitate to remove a rival from his path. But how did he know that I—not you—would walk in front?"

I waited a moment and then answered. "He didn't know."

"But he loves you! You said he proposed to you today—"

"But I didn't accept. That made the little demon that waits on him very angry."

"I don't know what you mean."

"I'm just repeating one of Jeffery's lies. He's quite a picturesque liar, like so many criminals. He's not a priest of evil—he's not king of the moors. He's just a highborn, brilliant Burke or Hare."

"I can't imagine anything more terrifying than a highborn, brilliant Burke or Hare. I suppose you know that before the end of their careers, lowborn stupid Burke found self-justification for his murders, believing he had every right to butcher poor people who came his way or who stood in the way of his low desires. The brilliant doctor who bought the cadavers had no objection as long as his scientific studies were not interfered with. I mentioned a moment ago the murderous kings of the Middle Ages—some of the Borgias and the Medicis and your good King Harry and dozens more. All were highborn, almost all of them highly cultured."

"The Borgias and the Medici lived so long ago—"

"While Burke and Hare lived just yesterday—and Baron Lundy of Blackmoor lives today. Thousands of their ilk are alive on earth every day of every century. Lola, there's a great difference between doing evil and loving evil. What is evil? Just a lack of good? Madness? A disease? No, by God, it isn't! It's a definite actuating force in the world. It's the stuff of religion the same that good is. Brilliant, cultured kings and prelates have always killed ruthlessly in the name of religion, but with benefits accruing to themselves. Isn't that demonry out of the seventh hell?"

"Yes." I was startled at the thought. "But Jeffery didn't try to kill you—or me—over religion."

"Lola, are you sure? With the usual benefits accruing to himself?"

"You mean he considers himself a high priest of a new faith?"

"A very old faith with scores of different names. He was bold and intelligent enough—in his pursuit of you—to call it by its right name."

"Then his imagination ran away with him, as mine did in India. For a while we both imagined I was a priestess of a fertility goddess—"

I stopped, because of the expression on Rene's face.

"It's plain, now," he said in great pain, "that we have gone from the moors."

"Rene—"

"I'm defeated just the same, as far as having you beside me, your real presence, always. But I would rather be defeated by your noble inspiration than by what people call the hard facts, the expediencies, of reality. It's so hard to believe in wonders—so much more sensible to deny them. Pan is dead. There's no mystery in the world —only cause and effect. King Hamlet's ghost did not walk the parapets, driven there by murder—that was only Shakespeare's craft as a playwright. There's no poetry in life except what madmen wrench out of their frenzied brains."

"Please, don't say that."

"Lola, I accepted the mystery of Jeffery the same as I accepted yours. That pattern you spoke of—I could almost but not quite grasp its transcendental meaning. I sensed that he or somebody like him would be drawn to you by some elemental attraction. I was caught up in its storm. Don't let me fall!"

"Good God, I was only hunting for protection for both of us. Don't you see that if Jeffery is only a brilliant, vicious criminal, so vain that he'll kill to get what he wants or to console himself for a defeat, then we'll know better how to deal with him? He'll get over a passion in time—he'll drop one feud for another. He gave up mountain-climbing when he couldn't climb Mount Blanc—he made an excuse to give up the championship belt in boxing. Even if he's insane, he'll get another obsession. But if he's a zealot in demonolatry and visions me in some great role in the drama, his shadow will be over us all our lives."

I was searching Rene's face as I spoke. It was deeply thoughtful and oddly lighted.

"He undoubtedly visions you in some great role in the drama of his life. He knows—not just believes—that you are one of the most beautiful and rare women of our generation. He met you under circumstances that appeared fateful. Beyond that, we can only conjecture his motives and future actions. But I know how it is with me. I'll always be poor in worldly goods—I'm a man of the people and my pen will wield power only if I remain one. Yet since I met you, I've felt a participant in a great adventure. I've had a great experience, the like of which will never come to me again. I felt— I know you won't laugh at me—a hero. I became one, in my inmost being—I sailed with the rest to Ilium in quest of Helen—I knew Achilles."

I broke out crying and tried to stop his lips with mine. But he kissed me and spoke on.

"That was the way you made me feel. You inspired my imagination to flights utterly beyond me before—and what is imagination but a glimpse of what might come to pass, seen from what *has* come to pass? I'll keep faith with that experience all my life. I'll never doubt it, no matter what you say. I'll derive strength from it all my days."

I was weeping as I had never wept before, feeling no need to fight back or hide the tears, or to clamp bands about my heart.

"You can have many as wonderful, Lola, if you don't deny the wonder of this one," Rene told me, his face lit by vision. "Only by faith in the wonder of life can you become that great adventuress that as a little girl you avowed yourself. The gods give only to those who believe in them and—when the need comes—defy them."

SIXTEEN

AT that moment I saw Gaffer, tall and lean, trudging behind four plodding cattle. He came around the side of the tor, and at sight of us stopped, leaning forward from his hips to gaze.

"There 'ee be!" he called, in a pleased tone.

I dried my eyes and beckoned to him. I wanted to look into his face and hear his voice and be healed. He came walking briskly.

"How are you feeling, Gaffer?" I asked.

"Hale, thank 'ee. And I want to tell 'ee 'twas no lame bones that 'strain me from succoring 'ee at the cottage in the storm, along wi'

Dora's man and Jarge. We had dressed to go afore the gale broke, and fixed a fire pot and lantherns, then Jarge clumb to the hayloft and see 'ee on the moors making in safe. Arter while 'en see the blaze of 'ee chimney through the rain, for eyes like a kestrel, 'en ha'."

"We were all right, Gaffer."

"I was still troubled in my mind. 'Ee was safe from the storm but I didn't know what was between 'ee. But my daughter Dora say how 'ee 'fess to her 'ee two was sweethearts soon to wed, and if 'ee saw fit to sleep together, 'twas no business but 'ee own, and me and her man and Jarge was not to catch the ague a-succoring 'ee when they was no need."

"Good for Dora!"

"Ter'ble strong-minded, 'er is. Jarge reckoned to set out the morn when 'ee'd waked and got about, but we spied 'ee chimney-smoke, and 'fore long we was all a-dither over 'en ludship's cooming."

"No wonder," I said smiling. "He's quite a great lord."

"We knew 'at at first look at 'en. It coom to me 'en was Lud Lundy o' Blackmoor, the greatest in west England to our thinking, and 'en truly was. 'En'd not let Jarge take 'en all the way. 'En had 'portant business wi' 'ee, 'en say, and when Jarge had shown 'en the way to 'em poles, 'en sent Jarge back."

"Did Jarge say that any of the poles had been blown down by the wind?"

"That 'en didn't, but I reckon 'en didn't notice."

"We thought Lord Lundy might have straightened them up. The next time you go through them, test the ground carefully. We thought there was a soft spot—"

"If 'ee walk into a soft spot there, 'ee ne'er walk no place else again. But I'll bid Jarge 'ware. And Jarge ne'er coom to see how 'ee fare for peat and belly-timber, 'cause when 'en ludship coom back, 'en say 'en nay."

Gaffer had spoken in an easy, quiet tone, yet his pause gave the silence an effect of depth. A donkey brayed stridently far away on the moors. I felt an artery pulsing in my throat. Rene's eyes darted to mine.

"Did he give any reason?" I asked in a casual tone.

" 'En say 'ee two had 'portant business to talk o'er, and Jarge or no-body was to coom to 'ee or spy on 'ee or nigh to 'ee side at all."

"What do you mean, Gaffer, by our side?"

"On the cottage side of 'em sands."

"Drop the subject," Rene said in French.

I did so, trying to drop it out of my mind. Rene explained to Gaffer that we were cutting short our visit to the moors, and wanted cartage for ourselves and our baggage to the nearest village on the way to Falmouth. That would be no trouble to provide, the old man answered. The moor ponies, of which he had a fine pair, could fetch us to a good inn on the Falmouth road before dusk.

Rene and I paid our contracted debts, and out of his sight I gave Dora a sovereign. She and I looked into each other's eyes and made no unnecessary comment. Jarge drove the cart and entertained us well with a history of the landmarks and the legends of the moors. The innkeeper was delighted to hear that we were honeymooning in these parts, and furnished us with a hearty supper and then not his biggest but best bed. This we put to good use in the way of our kind, loving and being loved to our heart's content, for we were living for the immediate glimmering moment, without thought of the future and with only joyous recallings of the past.

The boniface of a cheap, comfortable inn in Falmouth was like-wise delighted, cut the price of his best room when he looked at our baggage, and saw to it that we took in all the sights. So we visited the great Tudor castle of Pendennis, were shown the difference between Smithick and Pennycomequick, and climbed the lighttower at Saint Anthony Head, like any summer visitors. Our host himself supervised our hearty meals; and after explaining that the famous Falmouth oysters were out of season, he fixed us a mussel chowder, according to a recipe passed down by the old wives since King Egbert's time and which the royal cardinal had blessed for its wondrous powers.

Despite the smart to his pride, Rene had consented to my paying the fare for a three-day stay. His ship for Brest was to sail at mid-night, and the final glimmer of the long, summer day was still hold-ing when we sought a last aloneness with each other. The tide of his outgoing was already making. The kestrels circled, shrieking; there was an aliveness in the air; but I did not understand until I looked out the window. The full moon was sailing up the wan sky. This was again her night of nights; at midnight she would reach her very zenith, then in one climacteric second begin to wane.

The gray light grew silvery as the big stars came out, and I stood bathed in it in the darkened room. Rene gazed at me as though to paint my portrait, warm and breathing, for him to keep. Then I gave him many more mementoes of tonight, and he told me of their loveliness, and of how he would treasure them when he lay chill and alone. The running tide was the mighty tide of the effulgent moon. It would roar against the rocks and overflow the creeks and flood the beach pools. The moon's face would be everywhere in the dark, far-flung waters. Everywhere the tides of life sprang with it, the earth nursed its young, and the grass grew wildly in the night that it might bear seed. The tides of my being were likewise deep and swift, and the inkling came to me that I, too, might teem.

Weeping at last in some poignancy of triumph, I went to sleep and dreamed of Manu and Shikra and me on our terrible mission to Kali's shrine. . . . I had whipped her bloody breast. The little dog and I attested our defiance and brought her to contempt before the Great Ones, in the full light of the moon. Now she could not lay her red hands on Manu, because he had seen and would tell the shades of her shame, and they would mock her with ghostly mirth. She could not sink her fangs in my throat, because Krishna had bellowed with laughter and given me his protection. . . . But perhaps she could reach me now. I had a lover and might soon have his child.

The dream faded, and in only a moment Rene was waking me, saying it was time that he boarded the ship. Would I go with him to the dock? Would it be better for both of us if we parted now?

I got up and dressed in the chill candlelight, dreaming no more. . . . Seeing Rene's shabby bags, a half-drunk driver made no move to help him load them into the mud-spattered cab; at the dank dock a porter demanded his tuppence in advance for carrying them into the custom house. I could not bear to look at Rene's flushed face.

"I'll carry the lighter bag, and you carry the other," I told him. To the porter I made a remark in an undertone that Rene did not hear. "I didn't want you to touch them in the first place. You smell like a rotten lobster." It was small comfort to see him goggle, but the best I could do.

An officious customs officer made Rene empty his poor belongings on the table in sight of everyone. I wondered if some such incident had happened to Shakespeare, when he, too, was an unfamed scribbler, which had later caused him to speak of "the insolence of office."

Rene had bought the cheapest passage, affording him a bunk in the steerage, so we said our farewells sitting on a forsaken box beside the gangplank. We laughed over our adventures, when we were not shiny-eyed with solemn happiness, and neither of us mentioned Jeffery. For a parting gift he gave me a spearhead of beautifully worked blue flint he had found near the Circle of Stones: it had been thrown in battle or in defense of the flocks when London was a tide marsh. I gave him a flask of thyme-honey mead that our host had procured for me from a Stithian beekeeper.

"Lola, will we meet again?" he asked.

I shook my head in doubt.

"Maybe I'll see you on the stage. I think you may touch there, in the course of your adventures. If I do, I'll watch you through happy tears. I know that you did right in parting with me. As your lover— for these few days—I've grown taller. As your husband, I would have been dwarfed."

"Don't say that."

"Why not say it, when it's true? 'You are too dear for my possessing'—you shine too bright. And always I would know that I'd clipped your wings. As it is, maybe I've given them more power and sweep. You've given me a pride I can never lose. Will you always look to it, Lola?"

"I don't know what you mean."

He began to speak with the eloquence of deep emotion.

"Will you never let me fall? You can keep faith with me by keeping faith with yourself. Fly high and far. Don't ever bow your head. It may be that you can make a great name. I want you to win homage from crowds and kings. But I'd rather you lose the fight than to turn from it. Remember that all you are—all you have—you made yourself. So keep your sword bright. Win great prizes. Have glorious adventures!"

The humming sound that the wind made in the vessel's rigging was like that I had heard when Manu and I made pooja to the Great Ones, long ago.

BOOK III

The Worldly

*I*T seemed that my sun had gone down as when I had left India, but instead a light that I had held slowly burned down. I could not see by it any more and began to doubt what it had shown me before. It was nothing like the sun, my bleak heart told me. It was an artificial light.

Perhaps I was only suffering a reaction from my exaltation on the moors, mainly caused by parting with Rene. That would account for the darkening of my spirit and my dimmed eyes when I looked in the mirror. The parting had been made more complete in the early morning hours following his sailing: the moon and I had reached our fullness and begun to wane.

But it would be young again, I would find Lola again. I was able to throw myself into the preparations for Kitty's wedding, its date set forward by the General's developing illness. Busy early and late, I could avoid solitude, and especially lying awake in bed, tossed between faith and fear. That did not change the fact of the General's slow resigning of his life and Kitty's soon departure out of mine.

Where were Rene and Jeffery? I was entirely reasonable about not having heard from my lover—it was too soon, the boats were too slow, he was delayed in Brittany—and I had been foolish to expect a letter today, although tomorrow it could not fail. . . . But when just short of a fortnight the missive arrived, and when I was alone with it, the door locked, in my room, its carefully drawn lines left me dizzy and cold. . . . He had returned to Paris. The Republicans were crushed—the new prime minister was a lackey of Louis Philippe—Rene's attacks had attracted attention but would probably fetch him to prison. It went to show that our decision was the right one. He was at present faced with another of great moment in his life. He wanted me to be happy always. He would love me always. Adieu. . . .

I had dreaded hearing from Jeffery but pricked up my ears to hear of him. There was no letter from him in any post, and the gossipers who mentioned him assumed that he was in London. He had told me he expected to return to Blackmoor in something like a week—when two more weeks vanished without trace, I began to feel a kind of disgust with myself every time he crossed my mind. I could not explain it and so get rid of it. It was as though I had committed some appalling gaucherie. I imagined myself telling Kitty what had happened, only to shudder with humiliation at her expression. I knew now that if Rene had died in the quicksand, I could never have accused Jeffery publicly—the same expression would be on the judge's face.

I assured myself that I was not envious of Kitty's flutterings. Her way was not my way—I would be starting soon up a steep path to some great fulfillment. On that day, I would do penance for the present hollow in my heart and the cracked ring of my voice. Certainly she could not ask for a more zealous co-worker for her great affair. We discussed every detail of the ceremony and reception; I taxed my brain for ideas to make them a brilliant success, and I toiled till my eyes and fingers ached over the invitation list.

"But I don't see Lord Lundy's name!" Kitty exclaimed, when she read over the sheets.

I stared as if incredulously at the listing of peers and peeresses, then laughed.

"He was too much on my mind, I dare say. But Kitty, I'm afraid we're both going to have a disappointment. He told me at the theater that he was going to attend Parliament—"

"You haven't heard from him since?"

I shook my head. "He wasn't very impressed."

"He seemed so. Well—catch somebody like Ronald. Not that there is *anybody quite* like him. I'm *so* happy."

When we made a final survey of her trousseau, Kitty opened an exciting-looking package just arrived from Paris. Blushing, she showed me its contents—a *chemise de nuit* in the most risqué style, not beribboned as much as the English nightgowns, but lower-cut and of translucent silk instead of linen.

"Don't you think it's *shocking?*" Kitty asked, when I had exclaimed to her heart's content.

"It doesn't shock me. If it shocks Ronald, take it off."

"Lucia, you say such startling things. But I'm much more worldly than I was even a month ago."

"Is Ronald impetuous?"

"That's no word for it. I wish I could tell you all that's happened—but I can't. No, I can't tell even you—Ronald wouldn't want me to—although he loves you as I do. But I'm so glad we held back—a little. We both have our bridal night to look forward to—I mean, for what it's meant to be. And if I had even fallen by the wayside, thinking I was in love when I wasn't and swept off my feet, I'd want to kill myself."

Then a question came dimly and reluctantly into her eyes, and she changed the subject quickly.

Among the "regrets" was one from Jeffery, posted in London. I picked it up—the fine precise handwriting swam before my eyes—and put it down. To console Kitty, there were an imposing number of acceptances on stationery stamped with coronets. Peers and peeresses from all over England were glad of an excuse to visit Bath—more than thirty in all, she exulted—besides a fine array of baronets and knights. The great Duke of Wellington wrote a note to General Judson, regretting that the "damned rascals snapping at Peel's heels" kept him from a pleasure he would sorely miss. If he had accepted, I intended to ask him if he remembered a Tom Riley whom he had promoted on the field of Waterloo.

I was Kitty's maid of honor, and there was no oil in my lamp. I was curiously unprepared for the spite of the bridesmaids, baffled by it, and unable to combat it. It stemmed partly from an ill-favored but highborn girl who had expected the foremost place in Kitty's train. She was the niece of a peer and had done Kitty social favors. I had suggested that she be maid of honor, and was perfectly agreeable to taking a more minor part, but General Judson had insisted on our keeping a girlish pact made years before. That Kitty's paid companion, of unknown and no doubt dubious antecedents, should shine second to the bride at Bath's most fashionable wedding of the season was not so much a cause for spite as an excuse to vent it. My receiving Lord Lundy's single attention to any young female in Bath had helped incite it, and made me a prominent target for them all to shoot at, instead of sniping at one another. I had been much talked of, it seemed, since that memorable night.

Before and after rehearsal, and at the wedding-day breakfast, they played a fine game. . . . We were a pretty bevy, they admitted, but Kitty outshone us all. Her beauty was not spectacular—no real beauty ever is—instead it reflected her good breeding. . . . She had a kind heart, too, and was very democratic, as the saying goes. . . . So many of the nobility would attend—it was a pity Lord Lundy could not leave London. He was supposed to be studying political issues for the coming Sitting, but his instructress in these solemn matters was the tall, stately daughter of a marquis, the present toast of London, and their nightly study rooms the most fashionable resorts. What a sobersides the scamp was turning into!

I appeared obtuse and very gay. Actually the gloved thrusts from girls as pretty and young as these, who I felt should be confederates instead of foes, cut deeper than they knew. It smacked of treachery in our own camp. I was unpracticed at parrying them—there had been only one woman with whom I had been forced to compete, and I had not laid eyes on her since leaving India. My instinct was to make a solid front with them against our ancient enemy—those who would have us at their beck and call, who presumed to pick and choose us at their whim, who so often made light of the gifts we gave them, and who dared to believe that the seed was mightier than the ground wherein it grew. I was a fool. . . .

At the ceremony I alone among Kitty's attendants stickied my face with tears. But the girls looked down their noses during the reception, when the very best of the gallants gave me their deepest bows; and an old countess kissed me because I reminded her of Maria Smythe, later Mrs. Fitzherbert and the belle of London.

"I saw her when I was a little girl," the old woman told me with tear-dimmed eyes. "She was much too good for him—you know whom I mean." She meant George IV, of whom Maria became the morganatic wife. "Perhaps she was beautiful—perhaps only radiant —perhaps both mean the same," the countess went on; and as the other bridesmaids listened and the people waited, I thought of the Earl Amherst at a reception in Dinapore, and forgot, for the moment, my second meeting with him. "I'll pray for you, my darling," she said, when I kissed her hand. "Beauty has a hard row to hoe in this half-blind world."

The row became hard to hoe less than an hour later, when the toasts had been drunk and the ball not yet begun.

One of the bridesmaids who had not taken part in the sniping told me that a late arrival named Mrs. Terrance, wife of the younger son of a Welsh viscount, had noticed me and asked that I be presented to her. In fact she was under the impression that she had met me somewhere before. Glowing with my recent triumph, I skipped with the girl across the floor of the ballroom, and took no alarm at finding three other bridesmaids chatting with the new-comer, a fat, expensively but dowdily dressed young woman whose back was to me.

But when my sponsor said, "Mrs. Terrance?" I knew that I was at bay. I could tell by the sudden silence and the glints in the girls' eyes. The woman turned, and it was quite true we had met before. No longer thin and cold-looking, she was still Lady Kirk's daughter Annie, and the chill of my prison in Kelso was on my heart.

Her face wore a long-cherished malice. "A peasant had stood up thus" to her and her mother, and although the offense was six years passed, and the offender a desolate girl of twelve, they had not for-gotten. At least she had remembered my name, when one of the bridesmaids had mentioned me as the maid of honor, or had asked who I was because of an unpleasant association with my face; and vain of her vixen tongue, she had seized on the opportunity to put me again in my place. The other bridesmaids must have been called up to see the fun. I was stunned that they would sink to it, but I dared not let myself be saddened lest my own steel be dulled.

"I was right, Dorothy!" the woman burst out. "And now I remember her well. Your calling her Lucia threw me off." Then, smiling into my eyes, "Weren't you introduced to me as Lucy?"

"I'm flattered that you remember, Mrs. Terrance."

"And didn't Dorothy speak of you as *Miss* Lucia Riley?"

"Why, yes," Dorothy said. "She's still one of us spinsters."

"I have some memory of a title in connection with you. I do believe it was that of countess. Will you straighten me out on that, Miss Riley?"

"With pleasure. I told you and Lady Kirk that I hoped to be made a countess in my own name."

"But you didn't say you *hoped* to be made one. You said you *would* be made one. You'd not be content to be the wife of a knight —such titles were thick as fleas where you came from—or even a baronet. I was so impressed that a young girl could be so confident."

"I was only twelve or so." I was quite sure that the soft answers would stimulate her flow of venom until, like a cobra towering before a mongoose, she would lose her cunning and lash out too far.

"Mother was so old-fashioned," the woman remarked to the audience. "She thought it was not admirable self-confidence but— since Lucy herself was so frank—plain impudence." She turned again to me. "Then Mother spoke of knowing your father."

"I beg your pardon, ma'am. She spoke of knowing him before then."

"I believe you're right." It was coming now, I thought. "She recalled him at first sight of you. Of course, that made your assurance more startling to a gentlewoman of the old school. But you know, my dear, that your grandfather, Larry Riley, would have been equally surprised. A fine type of Irish peasant, who left readin' and writin' to his betters, he was highly respected by the gentry. I'm afraid he would have spanked you."

She had thought all this up before. I had to think hard on the spur of the moment.

"You remember so well." I was ready now.

"I trust you are well along toward your goal?" Her mouth took the wormlike twist I had seen on the face of her mother.

"It's another hard row to hoe. You might help me along, if you choose."

"How could I? The mere wife of an 'Honorable'?"

"I would like to make a reputation as a great *modiste*. When the ladies of fashion flock to me, I will, of course, find opportunities for further advancement. If I could start out by working a miracle—say, on you, Mrs. Terrance—choosing colors for you that harmonize instead of fight—jewels in good taste instead of gawdy—making you look as though you had lost two stone in weight—and my crowning achievement, putting collars on you that will appear to lighten your heavy jowls—"

Throughout all this she was swelling up and turning livid. I thought quite possibly that she would slap me—and my arm was poised at my side to retaliate with all my strength. Instead she turned to Dorothy with all the presence of mind she could muster.

"She has a ready tongue of the kind heard at Cheapside, but I really don't care to continue her acquaintance. My father always said you can't make a silk purse out of a sow's ear—"

"I didn't promise I could do anything about your ears." Very Krishna must have inspired me to that stroke.

"Pew!" she spat out vulgarly—and turned her back on me. It seemed to me that the bridesmaids were standing in the same position, their arms at their sides, their shoulders slightly raised, their heads slanted forward, watching me from under their brows. I had seen people take it before, when they wished to make themselves as inconspicuous as possible—maybe the instinct behind it was to drop their chins on their throats to protect them from being cut. I laughed jubilantly and made off.

My triumph was by no means over. When a moment later I encountered Forest, one of the General's footmen who was setting out punch glasses, he gave me a startled look, and then his small, quiet, secretive smile that I had long ago learned to cherish.

"Miss Lucia, ye must be feeling fine," he remarked.

"Why do you think so, Forest?"

"A while ago I seen ye, and ye looked in poor fettle. Now I could light me pipe from the spark o' your eye."

"Thank you, old friend."

"Mark what I tell ye, Miss Lucia. I've seen 'em come and go—
the proud and the humble, the comely and the plain. But I've ne'er
seen a young lady who can hold candle to ye when your chin is up,
and that dark flush on your face. Ye'll pardon my plain speaking."

"I'll bless you for it. Anyway—I told you—about Papa—"

"That's why I'm so proud of ye. Ye've shown us what can grow
in common ground. Mark, I don't make free wi' ye. Do ye think I'd
give them high-fliers the satisfaction when I want ye to top 'em all?
I bow to her ugly ladyship 'cause I have to, but I bow lower to ye
because I don't."

I slipped my hand into his and squeezed it. Then the groomsman
who was to escort me in the Grande Marche, a great beau, who until
now had shown no enthusiam for his office, came up preening his
feathers. When the march was over—I had been most demure
throughout, meeting and passing with small, wistful smiles—at least
eight burly young men made for me as though I were the ball in
a cricket match. They minded their manners with difficulty. They
looked flurried and smelled sweaty.

My program was immediately full, with candidates for every extra.
My heart was filling up with joy like rice-field ditches with the rains.
My name was Lola and I would slay many more dragons and I was
going to be a countess and long ago I had been a priestess of the
Magic Ring. I was the beloved of Krishna and when Old Berkeley
had seized my lover to snatch him down into a black abyss, I had
grappled with him and broke his hold and beaten him back. When
the time came round, I would return from whence I had gone,
whether to Troy where Helen was, or to the underworld with
Persephone, or to Avalon with Morgan le Fay, and make a bed with
my mortal mate . . . and live happily . . . ever . . . after. . . .

But it was a false dawn.

I had danced once and begun to dance again when I saw General
Judson, leaning heavily on Forest's arm, tottering toward the door.
I sped after them and helped lift him on his bed. Forest asked me
whether he should summon Kitty. I told him not to alarm her yet;
and he must go back to the ballroom, where he was urgently needed.

When I was removing the General's shoes, he spoke in a feeble voice.

"You go back, too, darling. I'm all right now. Greeting all those people was too much for me—"

"I'd rather be with you." This was quite true. I was frightened by the tautness of his skin over his facial bones. I had seen that look before.

"Go and enjoy yourself, Lucia. Dance with the young men. I've never seen you so beautiful—"

"Don't talk any more until I've made you comfortable."

I undressed him without any trouble, put his nightshirt on him, and fixed him a drink of whiskey. Then I rubbed his feet until they were warm. By now he had forgotten he had asked me to go, and when I sat down beside him to rub his forehead, his worn old hand clasped mine. He dozed a few minutes, then wakened with a start.

"Are you still here?" he murmured.

"Yes."

"I dreamed you'd gone—"

"Why not sleep a little more?"

"No, I want to tell you about the dream. . . . It was so strange. . . . You were smiling at me and you wore a green dress and the sunlight was warm and beautiful. Then you began to fade away. I strained my eyes and could see only your outline . . . and the shadows fell . . . and I felt very cold. . . ."

I, too, was turning cold with terror.

"Give me another drink, Lucia."

I held the glass to his lips. He took a deep sip and in a moment spoke again. His voice was no louder and trembled just as much, but there was more strength in it—the strength of his will somehow made palpable. I thought of him as fallen mortally wounded in battle, but still giving commands.

"I know what the dream means," he said.

"I was rubbing your forehead—and stopped—"

"Don't treat me like a child."

"Forgive me, General."

He lay a moment in silence, gathering strength. Dim and far away

I heard the strains of "Dream of Me Tonight" pouring from the harps, flutes, and violins. Sometimes it loudened as a door was opened—and I thought of the old beadsman flattered to tears in his ashes on St. Agnes Eve. Eyes looked love to eyes—and I thought of Belgium's capital gathering her beauty and her chivalry on the Eve of Waterloo. I had read of both before I knew Señor Professor, and because he had loved them and I had loved him, they had become inextinguishable lights in my brain. I saw by them now. They gave meaning to life and to death. By them, I could read the old man's face.

"The dream was a foreshadowing of my passing," he told me solemnly. "It will come very soon. You were the symbol of life. Ah, yes—you've always been so in my soul—why haven't I recognized it before? You are youth and beauty—the springtime and the sunlight and the warm earth. You have blessed me all these last drear years and made them bright. And what can I do, Lucia?—there is nothing I can do—to repay you."

I would have wept, save for the pain and sorrow in his face. I had to keep strong to fight it.

"You took me in and loved me," I told him, covering his chill face with kisses. "What can I do to repay you? I love you."

"Hark to me, Lucia. Open my desk and lift the little panel between the inkwell and the pen holder. Get out the envelope—quickly."

I did so and started to hand it to him.

"Hide it under your clothes," he went on. "It's a hundred pounds in notes, left from my last withdrawal. It's all I can leave you, Lucia. Everything I have is entailed to Kitty and my son at Gibraltar."

I stuck the envelope in my stocking and sat by him again. I was watching his lips with frightened but sharp eyes. I must not miss one word. . . .

"The world is so harsh—and so blind. Perhaps you could go far, Lucia—but I don't know the road—and whatever it is, it's so easy to fall and fail. I think you had better marry soon as you can. Take someone like Ronald, whose station is not too far above or below your own—that way lies safety—and common happiness. Won't it content you, Lucia?"

"Did you want safety? Would you have become a general—"

"I'm a man. This is a man's world. One thing more. I'm telling you what comes into my heart, though I have no proof. I don't want you to marry Lundy. Not because of his high station, but because—I think—I feel—he's the most evil man I ever knew."

"I won't ever marry him." That was my word that had gone forth from me the same as in long ago, I thought—and I found myself thinking in Hindustani.

Some of the strain went out of his face, but the peace was in confederacy with death.

"General?"

"Yes, my darling Lucia." It was the faintest of whispers and there was no light in his eyes.

"Tell me again what you told me when I first came—about the last charge of the Old Guard at Waterloo."

"What did you say?" The question had half wakened him from his deepening sleep.

What had I said? Had I no more sense than try to excite a man who by saving his strength had only a few days—perhaps a few hours—to live?

I could have explained it to Manu. Manu would have understood without an explanation. The dying man was aged and had cheated sharp-fanged Kali's lust for the young and beautiful and brave, and all she would get would be a bag of lame bones; still I could not resign him to her yet. It was not enough that a little breath should linger in his body while she turned contemptuously away, certain of her worn-out prize, letting it fall like a dead leaf into her lap. I would make her itch for it even now. When Kitty and the others came, they could shelter the dim spark from the wind as long as it lasted, but I wanted it to burst into flame if for only one fierce leap. I wanted him to die fighting the red-handed goddess. I hated her. . . .

Then I felt a surge of shame and guilt, for someone knocked on the door. It was Forest, and he asked quietly, "How's the master?"

"What do you think?"

"Miss Kitty missed him, and when I told her that he was tired out and gone to bed, she sent me to tell him she would come up in a few minutes. But perhaps I should summon her at once—"

"He's resting. She needn't hurry. When she sees her chance to slip away—"

"Very good."

Forest went out. I sat limp and half alive. Then the old man stirred and said softly but distinctly,

"Waterloo."

My pulse leaped and I felt my eyes rounding as they fixed on his face. But I did not speak. I who had spoken so boldly to one I hated was afraid to speak to one I loved.

"Yes, I fought there," he went on, color stealing into his gray face. "I was in the Duke's center, a captain under Halkett, when Napoleon sent forward the Guard." His voice was gaining strength. "God, how they charged—"

His hand moved in mine in the start of strong gesture. Instead of freeing it, I held it close. He fell silent, a dazed expression on his face. Then after a deep, sharp gasp, his lips moved again.

"I thought—pardon me—that someone—asked me to tell—"

I wanted to cry, "I did!" I wanted him to see once more the brave flags amid the dust clouds above the dauntless line; the sunlight on the steel, the faces of his comrades, and the nearing implacable foe contemptuous of death. I wanted his heart to glow again with the glory of human valor and human being; and the smell of powder smoke and blood to be sharp in his nostrils. I would return to him the thunder of the guns and the trumpets sounding shrill. *Do no' ye hear 'em? Do no' ye hear 'em! Hark to 'em, over the hill!*

Instead I only pressed his hand in silence.

In a moment his breathing became quiet. The dangerous flush on his face faded out. He was sleeping peacefully when, after the few minutes I had kept her away, Kitty came in.

Other people began to come and go. One was a doctor, many were old friends—one who came and departed on the following evening, promising to return the next morning, was a clergyman. Mostly they leaned and looked at General Judson, and spoke in low voices to other visitors to his bedside. When he roused a little from his slumbers and muttered to them, they made soothing replies. His worshipful the Mayor of Bath called on the third day of his repose; he was followed by an earl and a viscount; that night a bishop prayed over him, and in the morning the servants left their labors in house and garden and stables for a last sight of him.

Most of them crept to his bedside, looked at him in silence with streaming eyes, and turned away. But his Welsh groom made bold to speak to him.

"Do ye know me, master? I'm Davie, who rode behind ye many a league."

Some of the callers looked embarrassed, one or two pained. But when the doctor opened his mouth to speak—"Best not to disturb him, Davie" would be the burden of his words—I whispered sharply, "Let him alone." My prayer went shooting rocket-like aloft, it was so fervent.

I saw the old man's purple lips move and take unmistakable shape. Davie turned to us, wrapped in impenetrable dignity.

"Ye see the master knew me."

But except for this brief last stand, the old soldier fell that night like a withered leaf into Kali's lap.

EIGHTEEN

THEY—meaning some people I had never seen before—put what remained of General Judson in a box, and put the box under the floor of the church. Kitty and Ronald moved out of his house, and a man I had seen once or twice a year prepared to move in with his wife and family. To me he was exceedingly polite and thanked me warmly for the help and happiness I had given his father and his niece. It would be thirty days yet before he could wind up his affairs in Gibraltar, and in the meantime would I please consider myself his guest? In the interim I could be looking for other lodgings.

Although this had nothing directly to do with that, I wished I had not defended myself so well against Mrs. Terrance.

I began to look for other lodgings, but of far more urgency was my going to see Madame Celeste Renalt, who lived in a big comfortable cottage near St. Swithin's. She was a tall, fair Belgian of about fifty who had once promised the world a great ballet dancer. Breaking her leg in a fall, she had come to Bath, hoping that the mineral waters would help its mending. It had never regained its grace, and she had since supplemented her small income by teaching the ballet when she could, other stage dancing when she wished, and ballroom dancing when she must. Except in the latter case, she would accept no students without native talent, or keep any that did not progress—much to the ire of some of the gentry's daughters.

At sight of me she had trouble controlling her expression. She could not prevent a glint of excitement in her eyes. Well, she asked, *que diable,* did I want?

"I want to make my living and a career dancing on the stage," I answered.

"Have you studied the ballet since you lost your milk teeth?"

"I've never studied it at all."

"It's too late to begin. But there are other dances that are not so difficult—that do not demand the flesh knit with the bone in a certain fashion—dances that succumb to great native grace without years of wooing. I wish to the good God you have it. Your countenance and from what I may judge of your form—but off with your clothes, so I won't waste my breath."

Presently I stood before her naked, as my father used to say, as a jackdaw.

"Turn slowly," she ordered.

I did so.

"It is—in my opinion—divine. Stay where you are a moment."

She disappeared and presently returned with an elderly Frenchman with a bored expression and drooping mustaches. The first became instantly animated, and the second quivered a little.

"Name of a name!" he burst out.

"Raise your eyes, old goat, and look at the shoulders!" Madame cried. "The set of the neck and the head. The slope from the armpit.

The breast not in suspension like a hillside but apart and alone—
la mamelle de nymphe d'amour."

The old Frenchman did not reply, but walked around me nodding
his head and clacking his tongue.

"Celeste, may I call Monsieur Lavelle?" he asked.

"You certainly may not."

"I would feel more secure in my opinion, if it is supported by his.
Nevertheless, I will voice it, but please understand it is made in haste
and subject to reconsideration. I think mademoiselle is one of the
fifty—I may venture the score—most beautiful women in Europe."

He tossed his gray head defiantly and went out.

Madame had me flex my thighs and arms, and appeared satisfied
with the tensure of my muscles. When at her direction I had put on
my shift and outer skirt, she called through the door for Henri. This
young handsomely bearded Frenchman proved to be Monsieur
Lavelle, but at first he would not glance at me and appeared a little
aggrieved.

"Yes, Madame?"

"Don't be a lout, and play what you think she may interpret well.
Mademoiselle, forget we are here and let your soul and body move
to the music."

Monsieur Lavelle sat at the pianoforte and began to play an
amorous waltz. I fancied myself dancing with Rene. I changed
partners when Monsieur Lavelle began "The Dance of the Perjured
Nuns," a composition that had raised the hair of all Europe only a
few years before. It was from the opera *Robert the Devil,* and represented the wicked glee of some women sworn to celibacy rising from
their graves to celebrate the breach of their vows while on earth. The
melody breathed evil incarnate, and I danced it with a tall man of
eagle countenance.

"You interpreted that quite well," Madame told me.

The next piece was "Arkany," a Hungarian dance, with the
rhythm of a running horse; and I wished for a Gypsy to dance it
with. When I regained my breath, he had me try the bolero, and
although I did not know one step, I was able to interpret it with
gusto and a kind of fury.

"Magnifique!" Monsieur Lavelle cried, after the last crashing chord.

"I believe, my dear, it's your forte," Madame said. "Do you love Spain?"

"I once was in love with a Spaniard," I replied.

"You look Spanish, and Lucia is a Spanish name."

"Monsieur, do you know an Indian temple dance?"

"No, but perhaps—"

Monsieur Lavelle played some weird-sounding strains that were his idea of a nautch dance, but when I tried to interpret them, I got red in the face and ashamed.

"I will accept you tentatively as a student in Spanish dancing," Madame declared. "Two hours per day, five days a week, fifteen pounds per month. After two months I will be able to tell you whether I can continue with the instruction." She went to a desk, opened a book, and dipped a pen. "You said your first name is Lucia—"

"My real name is Lola," I answered.

"Why, that is much better. It's fit for a stage name—it's at once musical and strong. Let us choose a last name to go with it—Spanish, of course—I want you to think of yourself as a Spaniard."

"Lola Lopez?" I suggested.

"I think you should avoid alliteration."

"The Spaniard I spoke of was named Montero. I don't think he'd mind if I took it."

"Ah, your first lover!"

"No, my beloved."

"Better yet. Lola Montero you shall be! I christen you so! Today we have made history—perhaps. You are beautiful enough, God knows—perhaps too beautiful. I do not know what I mean—it is a presentiment—I must meditate on it. *Diable*, there is the knock of the Jones child. She's ugly as sin and I hate the ground she walks on, but she will yet be a great ballerina. Go quickly, Lola, little one, lovely one! I shall be busy—"

She hurried me out of the house. I felt neither elated nor depressed, only bewildered. I wished Manu were here. I could not believe in my new name until he certified it. Whom did I have left but Manu? Kitty had become one flesh with Ronald, Rene was lost in the crowds of Paris, General Judson was a pale shade in Kali's kingdom. It might be that I still had Jeffery, that the bond between us was not yet broken and could never break as long as we both lived. I had a presentiment that there would be a letter from him, waiting for me in the house that was no longer home. . . .

A letter was there for me, but it was from Rene:

Beautiful Lady,

Do you remember how the orchestra played "Dream of Me To-night" when we entered the Café de Provence? I hear it everywhere now. It is sung on the streets for two sous. Just before dawn, next Thursday, let us dream of each other. Dream of the peat fire, and the blanket on the floor, and the little jug of mead and two cracked cups. Then we will confide the consequences to each other.

Perhaps you have already taken another lover. What a fool I am! If you are a goddess or if you are a mortal, it is your right and your need. Have I not taken to live with me a woman of Corsica, black-eyed, black-haired, with a form that suggests yours, a peasant who is thus also in tune with the earth and the moon? But I sought to vision her as your proxy. It is not fair to her. I shall try to love her for herself alone.

Did you know I am becoming a toff? Don't laugh at me, but about ten of us, journalists and lowborn artists and a mad poet have formed a riding club. We rent horses from a stable near the Boulogne Forest —fearful Rosinantes no doubt, but we could stay on no other sort— and race with one another, chase imaginary foxes, and shout "Tally-ho" like lords. But will you believe me, a riding master there told me my hand and seat were those of one who had ridden all his life!

No, do not dream of me, and I will not dream of you. What good are dreams? Of what good is this letter, a little spilling over of my hopes, the main tide of which is dammed up by my fears? I am a very lion one moment, a kicked cur the next. Praise the good God that your good heart did not betray you into marrying me.

Adieu! With my heart's love, adieu!

I went to my room and lay down on my bed and was very still.

On the morrow's appointed hour I went to Madame's in a kind of frenzy. She did not tell me so, but I knew she had never had a more zealous student, for I strove with all my might and main. She too was all business today, and so were Monsieur Lavelle and the old Frenchman who came in now and then, passed judgement on some exercise I was practicing, and shuffled out. Madame addressed me as Miss Montero, spoke sharply when I did poorly, evenly when I did well, and never complimented my appearance or progress.

She had had me buy a pair of castanets—the little shells of pomegranate wood cost nearly a pound—of the width of my hand. She asked me if I could distinguish their difference in tone, and when I picked one as being deeper than the other—the male, she said, as opposed to the female, and always worn on the right hand—she appeared relieved. For a solid hour I practiced the golpe—a note struck with the middle and fourth finger in time with a piano note endlessly repeated, changing hands when one began to ache. The secret I had to learn lay in the back-spring of the hand and I could not perceive the least difference in the tone from first to last. Madame's tone, however, became less sharp.

Fifty minutes of the second hour went to general exercises—bowing, bending, twisting, kicking, and the like—and only ten minutes to some simple steps of the *sevillanas*. I thought that these were to stiffen my sagging morale.

Yet in twenty lessons, with hours of practice at home, I was able to satisfy even the old Frenchman with my golpe, double golpe, choque, and muted choque; I won rhythmic nods from Madame with my carretilla; and I was making progress in el choqueto, el picoteo, and el redoble. My arms began to rhyme with my legs in the *sevillanas*.

Also I had begun to realize the existence of an invisible foe. Often when I had thrown myself into this joyous dance, Monsieur Lavelle strumming his guitar with great passion, my body filled and running over with its rhythms, I was attacked by self-consciousness invoking a sense of shame or even guilt. On the first few occasions

Madame stopped the dance and shrieked at me. Was I a woman or a cow? Had she not taught me streams of movement instead of jerks? I shrieked back at her to keep from weeping. The fourth time she gave me a hard slap in the face, which I instantly returned.

"Get out!" she yelled. "Leave my house and never show your face here again! You heifer on two legs! You fisticuffer!"

I had turned, my face drawn and my eyelids burning, when the old Frenchman spoke quietly.

"Wait, Miss Montero." Then to Madame, "Celeste, did you observe that she struck you with the back of her hand?"

"What of it, you old fool?"

"Thereby she kept from breaking her castanet, which to my mind is a sign of an artist. Moreover, you struck first, and I honor her for the retaliation. Also, she is not a heifer on two legs, but a lovely dancer. I do not know what is wrong, but it cannot be made right by abusing her. I will ask *you* a question. Are you a dancing teacher or a fishwife?"

I could not believe my ears to hear such language from the shabby, meek-looking little man. Madame stood straight and still for a moment, then bowed her head.

"I beg your pardon, Miss Montero," she said with the dignity of sincerity. "And yours also, Chevalier Camille."

He turned to me again. "Lola, what comes over you, to cause you to stiffen in that way?"

"I get ashamed and want to run and hide."

"Of what are you ashamed, my dear? Can you tell me?"

I could not tell him if I tried. By not trying—by opening my heart to him—the words spoke themselves.

"I'm ashamed of being a show-off."

"Ah! Did someone used to call you one? Someone jealous of you?"

"Yes. Of course. My mother did. Every time I skipped and danced in front of people."

"Is your mother alive?"

"Yes."

"Do you love her?"

"I did love her until I learned to hate her. I thought I'd got over it."

"People never quite get over what they feel in childhood. The next time you have the feeling, say to yourself, sing to yourself in rhythm with the castanets, 'Hah, hah, hah! Mamma's jealous of me! Hah, hah, hah!' I'm sure it will help."

But I found it only a palliative, not a cure. I was never again attacked in his presence, but often when I was alone with Madame and Monsieur Lavelle I spoiled a whole figure before the defiant outburst set me free. Once I shamed Madame in the presence of two star pupils.

About the end of the first month of lessons I said goodbye to Forest and a few other servants whom the General's son had decided to retain, and moved bag and baggage to a boarding house. It was a respectable place and the people staying there—two young couples without funds to set up housekeeping, some elderly women who were not gentry but whose favorite word was "genteel," and bachelors starting out in business—were rather complacent over the address. All had felt a little lift in their self-esteem when a girl only recently maid of honor in a fashionable wedding, and before then—the old ladies kept track of such doings—the escort of a real lord, came to share their abode. No doubt some of them had heard me spoken of as "a beauty" and, remembering that it was only skin-deep, they were willing, with various reservations, to acknowledge it.

The attitude changed subtly within a very few days. I lived in the same kind of rooms, ate the same food, bathed in the same tub, and went to the same privy, all of which, by the principle of sympathetic magic, ought to have made me another pea in their pod. While my taking dancing lessons and practicing endlessly in my room was at first an invigorating breeze from the Great World, they soon shut the window. In the first place, you didn't hear of the *best* young women going on the stage. Moreover, being a dignified actress such as Sarah Siddons, and kicking up one's heels in a dance were two different things.

I had known long ago what it was to lose face. I was losing it rapidly these days in this little humdrum, insipid world from where, twenty or so hours of the twenty-four, I had no place to go. It was an odd fact, although not any more happy because of its oddness, that of the young men who had paid court to me when I was Kitty's companion, I saw no hair or hide. Her friends who used to include me in their invitations either forgot me or ignored me completely. It was seen that I had no callers; the old ladies who kept track of the post perceived that almost all of my letters bore the same female handwriting. So it was time—high time—I stopped putting on airs.

Truly I put on not one. I went out of my way to be not only courteous but companionable to my fellow boarders, which seemed to have a completely opposite effect than I intended. I declined to "walk out" with the young men, only because I did not want to be kissed by them and their conversation was crushingly dull.

My luck was hardly any better with the servants. Save for my long stay at Kelso, I had always made out well with the whole staff from butler to boots—thick as thieves, in fact—but here the pursed-lipped, long-faced housemaids were painfully stand-offish toward me. Not so a freckled bus boy new from the country! Truly his bashful adorings were my only real happiness in the house, which otherwise reminded me of my bleak prison in Kelso and might have the same effect. It was becoming harder for me to dismiss disparagements as beneath my notice. In the cheap dim mirror in my room I could hardly recognize Lola.

Mamma's seasonal epistle was the usual masterpiece of detraction. Kitty's twice-weekly letters failed to raise my spirits and instead often darkened them by arousing jealousy and shame. Long and brightly written, they were just what I could expect from a blissful bride. It was such fun to be the mistress of one's own house. She described in detail the "improvements" she was having made, every new dress, and the parties she went to and gave. She had never dreamed that married life could be so wonderful. She would tell me a great deal more if it weren't too sacred. . . . Instead of trying to call back the moors with their enchanted places, I sought to bar them from my mind.

I lived for my two hours, five days a week, with Madame, Monsieur Lavelle, and the old Chevalier. Only then did I deeply breathe. The hole in the coat, the fly in the ointment, was one I steadfastly ignored. It was that my progress was not wholly satisfactory to Madame. Occasionally I danced so well that her eyes burned in her head. Too often—usually when I was in the easiest passages—she looked drawn and ill. She did not shriek at me any more, and again spoke glowingly of my appearance.

On the way to my lesson near the end of my second month, our courier, my ardent admirer, stopped me on the street.

"I've got a letter for you, miss," he told me in great joy. "It came from Lunnon, and may be from the King 'isself for all I know."

He fished it out and I saw a baronial coronet embossed on the envelope.

"I haven't time for it now, Fred," I told him. "Please put it on the rack for me."

He looked puzzled a moment, then nodded. I thought he must know a good deal about human nature. . . .

After lessons I ran an errand in town, so that all the boarders would have a chance to see and talk over the letter. It was strange behavior for one who had been offered Lord Lundy's hand; but there is no flower, not even beauty, so quick to wither in a drought as pride. When I came in, two of the old ladies were sitting on the hall seat where I had never known them to be perched; and one of the young men emerged from the parlor to speak to them at the moment of my entrance. I did not glance at the rack and headed toward the stairs.

"How are you this evening, Miss Riley?" Mrs. Watson asked.

"Very well, and I hope you are."

"Why, bless me, you didn't stop for your letter! I'm quite sure I noticed one—"

I walked to the rack, took the letter, glanced at it, and looked back at Mrs. Watson.

"How are your geraniums doing?"

"Oh, very well—"

"Isn't supper ready? I'm famished!"

"Not for fifteen minutes yet. You've plenty of time—"

I spoke pleasantly to the others, then walked leisurely upstairs. . . . This was I, Lola, who was going to be created a countess. This was the glory I could not share with Rene.

I had taken great pains not to guess what was in the letter. It had been an unnecessary precaution—I could not have possibly guessed. It read:

My dear Miss Riley,

Under the doctor's care and progressing nicely, I have discovered that I owe you an apology—provided I am addressing the right party. Having a passion for the arts, about two years ago I was so taken with De Quincey that I, too, decided to try eating opium. Failing to conjure up such beautiful visions as he did, I switched to Indian hemp. The effect was amazing. I was capable of great flights of imagination but unfortunately forgot them as soon as the effect of the drug passed off. On eating a fresh batch, I picked them up where I had dropped them. Thus there was a certain continuity— let us say wisdom in madness—in my aberrations.

My servants have told me that in one of my worst attacks, I devoted certain attentions to a Miss Lucia Riley, of Bath. I instituted inquiries and have discovered that a young lady of that name lives at the address written. For any untoward behavior during the spell, I beg your humble pardon. Should I ever encounter you again, I hope you will identify yourself, so I may again voice my regrets. Indeed I would be grateful if you would recount to me such of my words and actions as you may remember. The good doctor wishes to record them for the benefit of his fellow toxicologists.

I am enclosing a draft on Lloyd's Bank for fifty pounds. Perhaps it will help compensate you for any inconvenience or irritation I might have caused you. And with the most cordial wishes for your health and prosperity,

> *I remain,*
> *your ob'd't servant,*
> *Lundy*

A candle was burning under my hot-water pot, and for a few frantic seconds I was in danger of giving both the letter and the draft to the flame. I stood still, with a feeling like coldness in my chest, and suddenly I was neither frightened nor ashamed. I put the draft in my purse and hid away the letter. The money would pay for lodging and lessons for two months. I did not know what use I could ever make of a confessed drug addiction by a peer of the realm, but as a cobra in death battle with a mongoose, I thought that Jeffery, too, had struck too far.

The next day, I danced so well that Madame called in the Chevalier to watch. Especially I outdid myself in the fandango—one of the most fiery of Spanish dances, the end of each measure dramatized by a pause in which the dancers freeze in the attitude of the instant. When I finished, glowing, the old man solemnly kissed my hand.

"Hommage à la divinité!" he exclaimed.

I continued to shine for the next few days. Madame went back to shrieking and cursing at me for the least fault, and never re-marked on my appearance; and she, Chevalier Camille, Monsieur Lavelle, and I were all wonderfully happy. Then, after sauntering dreamily and sweatily home after a marvelous lesson in the popular bolero, I found another letter on the rack. I looked at it several seconds before I recognized the handwriting.

It was from my mother, the second I had received in two months and it had been forwarded from the General's house. It announced that my stepfather had died suddenly in Bombay, and, having set sail at once, she had arrived safely in London. She wanted me to meet her there at the first possible moment. She had engaged lodgings for me at the Blue Shield, a respectable inn, and enclosed I would find stage fare. She had a trifling task for me to perform, which would profit me greatly. Also, she had a curiosity to see me, for although I had become estranged from her by nearly nine years' absence, blood was thicker than water.

NINETEEN

$\mathcal{B}$LOOD was mighty thick. Mine felt as though it could hardly flow. It was understandable, I thought, that a little girl who had once idolized her mother, only to be rebuffed, unloved, and finally exiled, would come to hate her. But I had hoped that the hatred had long ago changed to disdain. Now I could almost hate myself for my fluttering heart.

Two of my most fortunate capacities were for food and sleep. Very rarely had I been so disturbed that I could not make a good meal; almost never had grief or anxiety cost me a good night's sleep, although often I had lain awake too joyful to close my eyes. On the night following the arrival of the letter, I heard every toll of the town clock and felt every breath I breathed. During some of these I was dreaming, but knew it all the time. It was as though I were trying to dive into the sea of sleep but could only struggle on the surface. I wished Manu would bring me a cup of coconut milk, spiced and mixed with arrack. I wanted Manu more than anybody in the world.

When I went to my lesson, Madame looked at me in bitter exasperation.

"What in the devil is the matter now?" she demanded.

"I don't know. I got a letter—"

"You got a letter. Oh, the good God! What have I done, to be so accursed? Why can't I lock my doors to everyone who can dance, and take only sows and heifers? I would make more money, and retain my sanity and perhaps a little sweetness of disposition. They would not have spells. They would not turn into dancing bears when they get a letter! Only yesterday the Jones child, may she burn in hell, hopped about like a sick ostrich. Why? Because her *papa* had scolded her for throwing her dinner on the floor. Not spanked her, mark you—only scolded her— when he should have boiled her in oil. Oh, very well. Tell me about this precious letter. Tell me all, and on your own time."

"It was from Mamma. I haven't seen her in nearly nine years. She's in London and wants me to visit her."

She turned and yelled at Monsieur Lavelle, "Take yourself off. There will be no lesson today." Then to me, "I couldn't face it—I would lose my lunch."

She paused, looked at me keenly, and her manner instantly changed.

"Forgive me, little beautiful. I am an old fishwife, as Chevalier Camille says. What has frightened you so?"

"My mother."

"My God, I would like to strangle her with my own hands! She casts you off when you are ten—you can starve or sicken or go into a workhouse or into a whorehouse for all she cares—and now that the wound is almost healed, she commands you to visit her! Must you go?"

"Yes—because I'm so frightened of her."

"Of course. What a fool I am! She hurt you so when you were little that you still cringe from her like a whipped dog. Yes, you must go. You must defy her until her power over you is broken. What dreadful power mothers wield over their daughters, and fathers over their sons! Oh, if you could pay her in her own coin—"

Madame paused, her eyes narrowing.

"Put a flea in her ear!" she muttered, as though swearing. "Turn her mother's pains and benefits to laughter and contempt—"

I laughed hysterically at the two cheek-by-jowl quotations. Then I heard myself starting to ask a question. . . .

"Suppose I do break her power over me. Suppose I get so I'm no longer ashamed of 'showing off before company'—"

I was stopped by Madame's eyes. Although her expression appeared almost the same, these had subtly changed. The question I was starting to ask became frightening.

Madame had braced herself. "Go ahead, Lola."

"You know what it is. Can I ever be a great dancer?"

She led the way to a stiff little sofa where we both sat down. The action gave her time to collect her thoughts.

"Let us for the moment put aside the word 'great,' " she said quietly. "If you had asked me, only a week ago, whether you could become a popular dancer—a successful dancer—I would have had to answer that I did not think so. Your lights were too often turned off. You doubted yourself too many times. You lack the rhinoceros hide so useful to that kind of career, whereby to deliver, night after night, a high level of performance. At times you danced well, at other times you were unbelievably awkward. I was preparing to discontinue giving you lessons. A few days ago something happened—I cannot guess what—that worked an amazing change. You danced not well, but superbly. The old man was wildly excited. But I was sure it would not last long."

She took my hand and held it between both of hers.

"You asked me if you could ever be a great dancer," she went on. "I'm quite sure you cannot. You have not the genius for it. I have a strange feeling, which I cannot rationalize, that you are too completely feminine—perhaps all great artists are, in spirit, hermaphrodites. You can express the woman's soul but not the universal soul. But by the same token, you have great beauty. Byron had it, but his poetry was not great like tormented-looking Keats's; Helen could start a war, but old blind Homer wrote of it to the world's wonder. Lola, I think possibly you can capitalize on your beauty on the stage. If you use dancing to call attention to it—not even attempting either creation or superb interpretation—you have a reasonable chance to win riches and fame. Delicate though it is, it remains a carnal, not a spiritual beauty—it is a weapon for winning victories, not a heaven-sent grace—it is pagan and earthly. I believe in it enough to continue to give you lessons, if you so desire. They will be lessons not in interpreting music or human emotion, but in flagrant salesmanship of your charms. The women must be made to feel that they are you—you are, somehow, their personification—and the men to crave your embrace. I have never before undertaken to teach the dance *d'amour,* but Chevalier Camille has great respect for it, and is willing that I try. And since I cannot promise you any success—many people love beauty, but a great many hate it—I ask your permission to step down from my office as your dancing teacher and give you my best advice."

"I'd be very grateful," I said, bowing my head.

"It is to set your cap for a virile young man who can buy you pretty clothes and lights in which you may shine. Marry him, love him, and submit to him. It's been the law ever since Lilith, and she was cut out of the Bible. That's the way we get along best, the world being what it is. Somehow we've lost so much of our power—"

"We lost our priestesshood," I said.

"Whatever it is, we can't get it back. I sense it stronger in you than any woman I've ever known, but the odds against you are still too great. At most you could win only a skirmish or two—and at what dire cost!"

Her eyes had become round and empty as she prophesied, and I knew that we had made pooja together as we sat talking, and she had spoken truth. I left her soon, saying that I would decide later whether to study under her any longer; and when I opened the door of the boarding house I found myself dreading to look at the letter rack. In a few seconds I would look, I thought, and find it empty. My mother might write again, hoping to catch me with some instructions before I took stage for London, but it was not very likely. . . . I had heard from Jeffery only a few days before. . . . I had not answered Rene's last letter. . . . This morning no news would be good news.

I did look, and there was a square white envelope at my place on the rack. It would be from Kitty, I thought. Instead it was from Rene.

I took it to my room and laid it down while I washed my hands and face. Opening it carefully, I saw there were only a few lines, quick to read, quick to put behind me. They were:

My lovely Lola,

When this reaches you, I will have married Mlle Guitera, the Corsican girl I mentioned in my last letter. She is of my own social plane, she, too, is a journalist, and we have found a good measure of happiness in each other.

By this act I am locking the door that could never open anyway but which, if it remained unlocked, would admit dreams I cannot afford.

I will always love you.

Rene

I went to lock the door of my room, only to discover that I had done so on first entering. Then I was troubled what to do with the letter—I did not want to keep it, or to put it in the dust bin. Finally I put it with Jeffery's and my mother's letters: they were three birds of a feather, I thought. Now if Madame would send a note hurrying after me, saying that the lessons had been interrupted by my forthcoming journey, and the future was uncertain, and I might find opportunities in London with which she did not want to interfere and which if missed might not come again, so she had decided to terminate our arrangement at once—why, I would have four!

I began to pack my bags with patient neatness and care. Into them went all my prettiest clothes, and a good part of the plainer ones. With them I packed some small treasures, and then distributed my money as safely as possible. My lodging had been paid for the next fortnight, so I need say nothing as yet about retaining it. Later I observed the amenities with the boarders, and gave the post courier two shillings for the forwarding of any letters, and an extra for himself. To the bus boy, behind a door, I gave a kiss.

My mother was staying at a luxurious hotel on Pall Mall. When I had put up at the Blue Shield, a pleasant and inexpensive inn a half-hour's cab ride distant, I dressed carefully and rather plainly, and waited upon her in the parlor there. She sent word I was to be shown up to her room. A flunkey bowed me into an antechamber, then a door to the past opened and she came through.

"Lucia?" she said musically, without any show of emotion, and with a bright smile.

"Ma'am?"

I stood gravely, which I had long ago learned gave an effect of strength, and, by that giving, restored strength.

"How *pretty* you are! We must kiss!"

She kissed me on the cheek and never knew whether or not I responded.

"Now let me look at you," she went on. "Why, I'd know you anywhere! Not quite so tall as I pictured you, but quite as pretty as you promised to be, all those years ago."

I was doubtful of my prettiness. I knew I was not beautiful, this moment—I was missing it farther every weak beat of my heart. When my face paled and my eyes lost their luster, my skin had a sallow look. On the contrary, my mother was extremely pretty. I had hoped that she would have aged a great deal—she was in her early forties—but I could see very little change in her hair, her skin, her figure, or teeth, or even her neck and her hands. She dressed richly and well. She had a decided manner, obtained by success in Anglo-India society.

"Do sit down," she proposed.

I took a chair, and she chose the biggest and most comfortable. She was not concerned with what I said or did next, but I was anxious over her least expression. The scene was different from when I was last with her, but our relationship appeared to be taking up where it had left off. I felt penned up with her. I had no real defense against her. I felt no safer than before, not even any taller.

"In your last letter—the few lines I got from you about six times a year—you said you were still being tutored by a Spanish professor of high rank."

I had received a lesser number of lines from her about four times a year. I did not say so, though—I did not want her to know I had noticed. I was hiding what she did not need to hide.

"Yes, ma'am."

"What are you doing now?"

"Taking dancing lessons."

"Preparing for the stage?"

"I hope so."

"Since coming to London, I heard that General Judson had died, and Kitty married and moved away."

I had not wanted her to know that. I felt as though my face were dirty and I wanted to wipe it.

"That's true."

"I heard, too, that you'd moved to a cheap boarding house, but my informant didn't know the address, so I used the old one."

I nodded.

"Lucia, there's never been much love lost between you and me. Perhaps I'm an unnatural mother—but you might have been an unnatural child. The point isn't worth discussing. But you need money to go on with your lessons, and I'll pay you a hundred pounds for something I want you to do. You won't relish the job, but you can stand it. It won't take you fifteen minutes."

"How may I earn a hundred pounds?" I asked.

"Sit down at my desk. You'll find pen and ink and plain stationery of the kind you use."

I took the seat and dipped the pen.

"You're writing me a letter. Date it last Sunday—that's the twelfth—and write your Bath address in the upper corner. Begin it 'Dear Mamma,' and write a paragraph or two about your progress in your dancing lessons. I think you'd better put in a line or two about Kitty."

I wrote without glancing up for about two minutes.

"I've done that," I told her.

"Now write this word for word." She began to read from a sheet of scratch paper. " 'I was interested to hear about the Lieutenant Colonel. . . . I am glad you are having such nice times with him, and I know that if my stepfather knew it, he would be glad. . . . He was such a gentleman. . . . He knows that you need companionship now more than ever before in your life. . . .' "

"This is very sweet," I remarked.

"That's my business, Lucia. Your business is earning a hundred pounds. Continue, please, with a new paragraph. 'You didn't say whether the Colonel is a gentleman. . . . Of course, I assume he is. But you made a mistake once before, you remember. . . . I don't think Papa was to blame for deceiving you when he was so in love with you, and he certainly did his best to make it up to you, but

I've found out the danger of social mismatches, and you are a very trustful person. Papa, too, could talk well, you know; he was so ambitious and had studied so hard.' "

My mother paused; I raised my pen and I looked up. "The idea being that Papa married you under false pretenses?"

"You will see as I go on. Your father has been dead nearly ten years and will take no harm from this letter."

"No, I don't suppose he will. And it will explain to the Colonel how a young woman claiming descent from Spanish noblemen might have married a lieutenant risen from the ranks."

"You were always very clever, Lucia. Now's not the time for it, I assure you. To go on with a new paragraph, 'By the way, Mamma, the old professor from Madrid—I told you he was of ancient lineage —knew your family and was much impressed—' "

I was writing when there came a knock on the door.

"It's that silly maid with a package," my mother said irritably. Then calling in a disgusted tone, "Come in!"

It was not a maid with a package. It was a tall, well-dressed, aristocratic-looking man in his late forties. I did not notice much more than that, for the moment: I was occupied with my mother. She had stiffened and her eyes had rounded, but she was recovering swiftly and with wonderful presence of mind. Still I had not the slightest doubt that our visitor was the Colonel.

My mother shook her head at him, with a playfully wrinkled brow.

"Anthony, you rascal, you know you have no business coming up unannounced!" she said.

"I know it, but—"

"You'll have to take yourself off. The young lady and I have business."

"Nonsense. Now I'm here, I'll stay. Moreover, I want to meet this young lady. If secretaries like her can be found—"

"I'm only an acting secretary, Colonel," I said. "I'm Lucia Riley, Mrs. Ferguson's daughter by her first marriage."

"What?"

I rose and bowed.

"I'm Lieutenant Colonel Reeve," he replied with a deep bow. Then he turned to my mother. "Dash it, Lenora, you didn't tell me that Lucia was in London—"

"She arrived only this morning," my mother answered. "It was to be a surprise—"

"Won't you take a chair, Colonel?" I said. "I know Mamma wants to finish this letter. Mother, what if I read back to you what you've already dictated?"

My mother turned white, and her paint looked as though it could be scraped off with a pallet knife. Colonel Reeve looked from her face to mine.

"That isn't necessary," my mother answered, her voice almost steady. "The next figure, Lucia, is—five hundred pounds."

I shrieked with laughter.

TWENTY

THE next I knew, Mother had rushed toward me and was trying to snatch the letter from my hands. When I thrust her away, she clawed at my face. I slapped her as hard as I could, almost knocking her down.

"What in the devil does this mean?" Colonel Reeve was shouting.

"That girl—my own daughter—trying to blackmail me—" My mother burst out sobbing.

"I want the straight of this," he demanded in a cold voice. "If either of you claim to be ladies—"

"I'll give you the straight of it, if you can make her shut up," I answered.

My mother stopped crying instantly. "Tony, Lucia has always been bad. She's got too much of her father in her. Now she's trying to go on the stage. She wants money—and I was so ashamed—so frightened—that you just heard me offer her some. I don't know what she's written on that paper—"

She had walked nearer to him, to make her plea, forgetting the sheet of scratch paper she had dropped when she attacked me. I crept forward and picked it up.

Again she flung herself at me, trying to tear the page. I evaded her until the Colonel could seize her arm.

"Enough of this!" he commanded, in his military voice. "Control yourself, Mrs. Ferguson!"

"You believe her and not me," my mother wailed. "How could you? Anthony, I confess I'm in this creature's power. I beg you to forgive my behavior, but you don't know how long and terribly I've been provoked. It's true I was going to deceive you. I wanted to give you certain information—every word of it true—but I wanted it to come through my daughter instead of direct. I was having her write a letter, as though from Bath, that I intended to show you. It answers a question in your mind, one that you were too great a gentleman to put to me. If Lucia says that it contains a lie, it's just further evidence of her viciousness. Now, Lucia,"—she turned to me, with a wonderfully simulated triumph—"you may let him read both my writing and yours."

I handed him both papers. He sat down by the window, put a monocle in his eye, and read with rigid attention.

"The pertinent passages are approximately the same," he pronounced in formal accents, as though sitting on a court-martial. "However, Miss Riley wrote 'My mother wants me to say' or 'Mrs. Ferguson directs that I write' here and there in parenthesis."

"She was planning to blackmail me even then," my mother cried.

"If you please, Mrs. Ferguson, I do not wish any comments until I ask for them. Miss Riley, you knew your mother would look over the letter and see your insertions. Of course, she would not be able to use it. If that was your purpose—and I can conceive of no other —why didn't you refuse to write it in the first place?"

"I didn't know what she wanted me to write until she read it to me," I answered.

"How much had she offered to pay you for writing the letter?"

"A hundred pounds."

"Let us hear no more about blackmail. If that had been your game, you would have complied with her directions until you could get

your hand on the page in her handwriting. As it was, you were
going to lose a hundred pounds."

I nodded my head.

"Will you tell me why you were so adverse to testifying that your
father concealed his humble birth when he proposed to your mother?"

"Because she hates me," my mother broke in.

"I will address you later, Mrs. Ferguson."

"Because it wasn't true," I said.

"How could she know? She wasn't born!"

"Mrs. Ferguson, I asked you to wait your turn, but since you've
spoken that far, I will reply. You were having her write that she
did know. It's as short as it is long. Miss Riley, why are you so
certain that your father wooed her honorably?"

"Because he was an honorable man. I've heard her say dozens of
times, 'I shouldn't have married you. I knew you'd never amount
to anything, the son of a tenant farmer.'"

"I haven't the least doubt that you're telling the truth. If the
letter had been written as she directed and shown to me, I would
still have wondered how a humbly born youth could deceive the
descendant of Spanish nobility, no matter how well he had educated himself. I met Lieutenant Riley and have a quite distinct
memory of his rustic speech. In plain words, I don't think I'd
have been taken in by the letter, but I might have been, had I met
you personally, and you had repeated the charge. Mrs. Ferguson,
it is a very grave charge. Even if it were true, you have no business
making it against a dead hero who cannot defend himself."

My mother had turned white. "Tony—"

"Pray wait till I am through. I shall speak briefly but very plainly.
I have every reason to believe it's a false charge. Moreover, you
tried to bribe his own daughter to make it for you. You spoke of
her wanting to go on the stage—I have no doubt you tried to take
advantage of her need of money. Your purpose in the despicable
business was to support your claim that you are of good birth—
such good birth that you would not have intentionally married a
humbly born man—indeed of good enough birth to fit you to be

my wife. You are a low and odious woman. I'm ashamed I was ever taken in by you."

My mother walked toward him, her eyes blazing and her fingers parted and curled. "You get out of here—"

"You'd best not put hands on me, Mrs. Ferguson. I'll be leaving in a moment, and I intend to take your daughter with me. Lucia, I'm proud of you! You've proven the lady while your mother has shown the contrary. I salute you, and desire to pay you some attentions—those of a gentleman of the old school. Will you do me the honor of being my guest for dinner?"

"Get out of here! Both of you. Take her to dinner or take her to bed, for all I care, you worn-out old waxwork. All I wanted from you was your uncle's title. I'd have had to put up with your priggishness for another ten years—"

I was listening with a good deal of enjoyment to my mother's carrying on, but could not give it my full attention on account of Colonel Reeve's putting himself in a new role. A moment ago he had been a stern and extremely impressive judge; now he was paying earnest court to me. If his words were still formal, his voice had become warm and his face was flushed with excitement. I was seeing it really for the first time. It had been half concealed by his judicial wig.

When the door had slammed behind us, and I was being escorted to the Colonel's carriage, an idea startling and momentous began to shape in my brain. It was that my resounding triumph over my mother, which even now I could hardly believe and was thrilling me to the core, might lead on to great things. Calm though he had appeared in his judicial office, every inch a pukka sahib, his best nature had been deeply stirred. His exultation was warmly human and there was something quite knightly in his manner and expression. Under this were the figure and face of a sincere, likable, and capable man.

He was, indeed, I thought, a gentleman of the old school. If he were an actor, he would always be assigned that part, and instantly recognized by the audience. He had the fine, plain bony countenance that English gentry bred, at once delicate and completely male; his premeditated actions appeared stiff, but his natural movements had the grace of the expert horseman he undoubtedly was; his public-school reserve cloaked lively emotions and probably a good deal of sentiment. I did not think he was a "broken-down waxworks." My mother's rage had laid bare the cankerous resentment of the real parvenu against gentility, almost never seen in humbly born people who have made their mark through worth. There was a good deal of gray in his brown hair and mustache, but his blue eyes were young, his voice firm, and his well-tanned skin had youthful tone and glow.

Feeling adventurous, he suggested that we dine at a famous Hungarian restaurant in Soho. Luck was with me on the way there, in our getting acquainted. The military campaigns in India had been General Judson's most devoted study and chief subject of conversation—it had been part of my job to discuss them with him—and Colonel Reeve was amazed to discover that I was well grounded on the battle of Mehidpur where he had been baptized by fire, and quite thrilled at my detailed knowledge of the hard-fought war with the Burmese, in which he had won his coat. I had soon discovered that he was second-in-command of the 2nd Wiltshire Rifles, one of the old-line regiments stationed in India; and was a thoroughgoing professional soldier. As such, he did not know India nearly as well as I did. He was well versed in the facts and figures and interpreted them through the eyes of the typical burra sahib: what he considered its truths were frequently the cherished illusions of his class. I had walked in the Indian dust; to me she was Mother India; I had eaten and slept in her arms and perceived her through my pores.

Colonel Reeve would not dream of bragging, but he was putting his best foot forward, and I soon gave him a chance to mention his titled uncle. I had already thought him too consciously pukka—his manners too precise—to belong to the nobility, who were almost always childishly frank and free; and since the only inherited title held by commoners was that of baronet, I felt sure such was the plum my mother had craved. He told me that Sir Spencer Reeve of Wiltshire was a childless widower of seventy. Colonel Reeve was technically heir presumptive—unless all signs failed, heir apparent.

"I've heard of that baronetcy," I fibbed. "Isn't it a very old one?"

"It goes back to James II," he answered modestly.

"Much older than, say—the baronetcy of Sir Andrew Kirk?"

"At least fifty years older."

To become the wife of Colonel Sir Anthony Reeve was a far cry from being created a countess, but, in that event, I would at least precede Lady Kirk through the door!

I had instantly noticed that his beautiful clothes and the stunning pearl on his neck scarf had not been bought out of his screw from the king. The hired carriage was an elegant one, and our table at the Bathori, shown us by a knowing seneschal, one of the most choice. The Colonel's first order was for a magnum of Ambonnay champagne and a bottle of Tokay blanc from the Balaton, the first to be set aside and chilled, and the other to be served with our goulash. And all this was an even farther cry from my boarding house in Bath.

All went marvelously well. He was inspired to tell me of his work and play in India. The station of Poona was a delightful one; the shooting was excellent; he was still head goaler of the regiment in a Manipuri game called *pulau,* played on horseback, but some of the youngsters were pushing him hard. The heavenly wine went not to our heads but to our hearts. The Gypsy orchestra cast sorrowful spells upon us with its weird wailings, then inflamed us with rhapsodies. I knew now that we were both thinking of the same thing.

When the candles burned blue-green and the brimming glasses of champagne flung quivering amber lights on the white cloth, he leaned toward me, his eyes shining, and spoke in deeply earnest tones.

"Lucia, you may wonder why a man of my age—I'm forty-eight—has never married."

"Yes, I do wonder."

"It was always something I was going to do a little later on. At the moment there was either a promotion to make for, or the rumor of war, or no young lady to my taste available. I was never a lady's man. I didn't enjoy dancing or flirting, and perhaps I had set my standards too high to be readily met by such ladies as I encountered. Yet all the time I felt I should marry. There's no real doubt in my mind that the baronetcy will pass to me in a few years, and if I have no heir, it will descend to a remote branch of our family. I want to say, though, that I'm glad tonight—more glad than I can express—that I never did."

"I'm glad too, Anthony," I answered when he paused.

His face lightened. "Your saying that emboldens me to continue. When fate—and I believe that's what it was—brought about this present brief holiday in England, I decided to look for a gentlewoman of thirty or so, or, which seemed the wiser choice, a widow nearer my own age, yet able to bear me an heir. She could not expect much in the way of romance. I'm a bit of a duffer, and too long a bachelor to be an ardent wooer. But I could give her such love as derives from common interests and companionship and—you will pardon my plain speaking—from the marital bond."

"That's a great deal to give." My heart had begun to leap.

"I had always expected to marry a lady of position," he went on. "You know what I mean—an acknowledged member of the English gentry. But today I have met a young woman—a mere girl, she might be called—who has all the qualities I hoped for in my wife, despite the fact that she's the daughter of a self-made officer who entered into—I must again be frank—a most unfortunate marriage. She is loyal to her own. She has high intelligence and culture. Her manners are lovely and most winning. She has courage and a high temper, but a native sweetness apparent in all actions. In addition to this, she has great beauty. Such beauty as I never, in my fondest dreams, hoped to win."

"I'm afraid you give her too much praise."

"No, I do not; and considering the difference in our ages— thirty years—I would not presume to pay court to such a girl, save for feeling that I could give her things that she has always lacked, and wants and needs. I refer particularly to an impregnable position in society. Also I can offer her a comfortable home—indeed a luxurious home, as long as I remain in India where money goes far. I have a thousand pounds a year of my own, and will come into as much more with the baronetcy."

"I've had no home since General Judson's death," I told him, seeing his face through tears.

"Lucia, I couldn't have gained my present rank if I had any serious vices. There is no other woman in my life. These are the essential facts I want you to consider. I am not of the age or the disposition to embark on a romantic courtship; and what I propose is, in a sense, a marriage of convenience. I appeal to your intelligence rather than to your emotions. Therefore, now that I have made up my mind that I desire it, I see no reason to delay."

"Anthony, are you asking me to marry you?" I asked, steadying my voice.

"Yes, Lucia. But you needn't answer until you've thought it over. You can wait until the week before I sail."

"To Hind?"

"I have never heard it called that by an English girl. Yes, to India."

"Would there be room in our household for Manu, a Bihari who took care of me when I was a little girl?"

"Of course."

"What if it doesn't work out well, Anthony? Suppose we don't become fond enough of each other? I'm of humble birth, as you know, and you are a great gentleman. We may not find enough in common."

"In that case, you can return to England and we will obtain legal separation. But you understand—that would prevent you from marrying again until my death."

"That's fair enough. I don't need to wait. I accept your proposal."

TWENTY-ONE

FOR the last hour at the Bathori and during our homeward ride in the carriage, Anthony's exultation took a different shape, or at least had a different aspect. It was less solemn and while it was more intimate, I had the feeling it was less inspirational. I thought it mainly a shedding of his public-school reserve as his skin and body and mind became flushed with wine.

He began to reveal to me not his most deep but his most practiced prides and ideals. Thereby I had a chance, this soon, to find out what he expected in a wife. I did not know when again he would be so voluble; and perfectly clear-headed now, I marked him well! I had known what I was doing when I accepted his proposal made on noble impulse, and must meet his terms. He could not make compromises, but I could. He would not pretend to be in the least different from what he was, but I could accent or conceal traits that he liked or disliked. Well I knew that my hope of success as the wife of Lieutenant Colonel Reeve lay precisely there.

The phrase on which he put the most accent in voice and facial expression and lift of his shoulders and head was "gentleman of the old school." It was his watchword, his shibboleth, and his fetish. Gentlemen of the old school were confined to Old England—their like was not found on the Continent—and the bedrock of English greatness. The more he spoke of the solid worth, standards, lack of fiddle-faddle, and traditions of this old-fashioned gentleman, the surer I was that he did not exist in reality—that he was a sentimental concept flattering and comforting to its holders, a defense against overshadowing by the nobility and a protection of their privileges against the lower orders. I had never heard the expression "a nobleman of the old school," or "a plebian of the old school." The class in England properly called gentry, well off, well born, were between the upper and the nether millstones.

Anthony told me, with glowing eyes, of old-school gentlemen who had preceded him. He recited incidents of their relations with tenants and servants, all reflecting a kindly patronage on one side and recognition of quality on the other; I found out how they put upstarts in their place; how sporting they were whether winning or losing; how they felt about their horses and dogs. Now I was to be taken into this plain, unvarnished order of merit. Its country was to be my country, its god, my god.

I was increasingly amazed over Anthony's admitting me there. I had few of the marks in appearance or manner; and the thing that had turned the trick—my righteous but unroarious fight with my own mother—was the epitome of unladylike behavior. Undoubtedly he had fallen in love with me at that moment. His rather dormant imagination had been wildly aroused; I had an inkling that he had spoken more nobly than ever before; and in spurning his highest dogma to propose to me, he had become, for the moment, a different man. But I must not for a moment assume he would continue to spurn the deep-taught canons of his class. I was lucky enough that he would give me, if I were a good wife to him, kindness and security and, as he perfectly put it, marital love. Being a good wife to him meant being, as far as I could fetch it, his idea of a lady of the old school.

That would be my goal; and when we parted for the night, I had no illusions about its being beer and skittles. It was difficult enough to be challenging, and its prizes were greater than any I could believe were in my grasp. I could go back to Hind. If he still lived, I could have Manu.

Anthony and I were married quietly by his schoolfellow, an Anglican clergyman, and we had a gay wedding supper at the house of a former messmate attended by various officers home on leave and their pretty wives. Time began to move in a way new to me—a wide, smooth, unhurried stream, with no sharp contrasts of light and shadow. I knew neither high exultations nor sharp poignancies, thrilling victories nor stunning defeats. One day merged mildly with the next, and all days were very much alike. Formerly, my nights' sleep had seemed passages, often weird, sometimes perilous, between one island and the next of a long chain; I had wakened with a sense of undertaking a new adventure. Now I drifted pleasantly, secure in my husband's tranquil love, through failing or growing light.

Because of the long journey through ever warming waters under an increasingly ardent sun, touching at ports of ever more familiar smells and sounds and sights, India did not burst on me like a tropic dawn. I supposed that in a little while I would be hers again, and she mine; but there persisted a feeling of alienhood—I had left here an Indian, but had returned a pukka memsahib. I could get rid of that, I thought, when Manu came. Out of sight of my husband and the other sahib-log, he and I would walk barefoot in the dust.

Anthony and I had hardly settled in the big, handsomely furnished bungalow, Number Two house on the Regimental Row, when he wrote to the commandant at Dinapore, requesting that inquiries be made for his wife's servant whom some of the older khadims around the post would doubtless remember. My husband's manner in this matter indicated that he was indulging a girlish whim, but I did not blame him in the least for that—he could not possibly realize my need, and I must not let him do so. Instead, I was deeply grateful for his tolerance and discomfited over the trouble I was making him and his correspondent. Tolerance was the right word, really, I caught myself thinking. At the same time I sent a letter in Hindustani to a teahouse Manu used to frequent, the address he had given me at our parting.

While waiting for the replies to the letters, I indulged no other whims. They were too expensive in respect to my husband, too dangerous to the success of our wedding. The lesson was well taught not more than a month after our arrival at the station, when I found myself attracted to big, open-hearted, open-eyed Jenny Dorsey. Jenny was the wife of a sergeant. There was more to her than any Poona woman I had met except Colonel Radford's wife, a middle-aged woman of true grace, and the highly educated, homely wife of Dr. Haines. I had met Jenny going to the commissary and was charmed with her bright face and big laugh. When we had talked a moment, I had invited her to tea.

She looked at me with something like compassion. "Mrs. Reeve, you're new to the army, aren't you?"

"Yes."

"I can't very well come to your house for tea, but you can come to mine—if you will."

We had a lively two hours, comparing notes on India, and when I began to recount them that evening to Anthony, I saw that he was embarrassed to the point of pain.

"What have I done wrong?" I asked. But I already knew, and needed only to know the degree of the offense.

"I should have warned you, dear, against any familiarity with the enlisted men's wives."

It took pains to speak evenly and calmly.

"I realized that Jenny and I couldn't mix in public—"

"You called her by her first name?" he interrupted.

"Yes."

"You didn't stop to think that was a tacit invitation for her to call you by your first name?"

"As a matter of fact—I asked her to."

"What if Sergeant Dorsey—not on the field, mark you, but at a regimental cricket match—called me by my first name?"

"Anthony, I admit that after I told her I was coming—she didn't invite me, you understand—I invited myself—I thought I'd better make a short call—"

"Not call, my dear. A lady calls only on another lady—it is part of the social ritual. Mrs. Dorsey is a good woman as far as I know. But you know what I mean by a lady."

Yes, I knew. Papa had told me on his deathbed I could never be one—at least a fine one—but he was wrong. By being the daughter of a self-made officer, I got one foot in the door; and Lieutenant Colonel Reeve had dragged me the rest of the way. Now it was my duty to lock the door behind me.

"I take back the word 'call,' " I said, my chest aching. "I started to say I was only going to stay a little while, when I admired some flowers on the table, and she told me that Mrs. Radford had brought them to her—"

"She wouldn't miss telling you that!"

"I asked her about them. She didn't lug it in. Mrs. Radford drops in there every few days. On the table was a book Mrs. Haines had lent her. Well, of course, I thought—"

"It's not quite the same with Mrs. Radford and Mrs. Haines, Lucia, my dear. Mrs. Radford is the daughter of a viscount. The aristocracy can take chances—ignore convention, I should say—in a way that would invite criticism to members of the gentry. It's my own private opinion that she carries it a bit too far. She doesn't want to be referred to as 'Honorable,' and once when she was made a judge of a dancing contest at an enlisted man's hop, she danced afterward with the male prize-winner. Mrs. Haines is the wife of the regimental doctor. A medical officer doesn't have the same standing in a British regiment as one who commands troops."

I wanted to ask, "Not even the same standing as an officer risen from the ranks?" I did not. I must be a good wife to Anthony. He had given his name to the daughter of such a one. He was gentle and kind with me.

"I won't go to see Jenny—Mrs. Dorsey—any more."

"Thank you, my darling."

It was not fair, I thought, to blame anyone for his religion. Once instilled in him, he cannot help but act upon it when it comes in conflict with any other. A few would die for it, a great many would kill for it. I had discovered Anthony's religion before I married him—it was just a little more strict than I had realized. It had its God—the most pukka of all Pukka Sahibs who, after discarding the goats, put all the sheep in orderly pens. Its code of morals and ethics was admirable as long as their extension did not conflict with its basic tenets. If being a gentleman interfered with him being a gentle man, I knew which would win.

It came to me suddenly that although my mother had badly bungled her attempt to prove her ladyship to Anthony, she had known what side her bread was buttered on.

So I became the Lieutenant Colonel's lady, according to the Mede- and Persian-like laws laid down by Anglo-Indian society. I received and paid only proper calls; with the good ladies I kept to the approved subjects of conversation; brightening up when we gave or went to parties, I never "showed off in front of company," being only legitimately flirtatious and sweetly gay. Tony did not object if my jokes barely bordered on the risqué, which was enough to fascinate the more staid ladies and enthrall the young bachelors. At the first military ball we attended I became at once the most popular matron on the station, much to my husband's pride, and held the position without rancor from the Colonel's lovely wife, who was

fast becoming my best friend. I dressed prettily and rather childishly, as Anthony desired; rode every day with the ladies or occasionally with the bachelors, but never the same one twice in a row. My
mother had done so well in India as the wife of Colonel Ferguson
as to gloss over the fact that my father had risen from the ranks. At
least no one dared to throw it up at me.

I made a prayer to my childhood gods—took it back—made it
again to a Mrs. Grundy kind of god who seemed to have such
matters in charge. It was that I might never be such a fool as to
trade my pleasant mess of pottage for a vague, perhaps visionary
birthright.

My name was Lucia Reeve. When I thought of Lola Montero,
I felt inchoate emotions overcast by anxiety. I was troubled and a
little ashamed because I did not get close to our servants; but perhaps I could not have done so, had I tried. When I looked in the
glass, I did not find beauty imaged there, instead the vividly pretty
young memsahib that my husband loved. My lines had fallen in
such pleasant places. I was so lucky to have been so rash!

Our letters to Dinapore had gone by post pony overland to
Benares, then downriver. The reply from the commandant there
arrived in a little over four months and was pleasant and humorous
as the occasion called for. Inquiries had been sent on foot. But the
memsahib must be patient—after all, India was a somewhat thickly
populated country. Servants did not always stay put. A good deal
could happen to ten years.

I heard from my letter more than a month later. The reply came
from the proprietor of the teahouse, written by a professional scribe
in ink of several different colors, containing many allusions to my
eminence and glory, but one of the most moving I had ever received. Manu was well remembered and had made it his custom to
call monthly there for mail, until his fate had taken him to Patna,
two years before. Since then he had called personally twice, and
sent couriers twice to inquire in his stead. The writer would send
word by journeyers to Patna to seek him out and bid him return to
receive memsahib's favor. If he still breathed, she could expect an
answer within one, at the most two rains.

My tears had begun to flow before I had read three lines; before the end I was weeping in a childlike transport of mingled joy and pain. Anthony heard me and hurried in.

"Darling, what in the world—"

"Manu's alive! At least he was until just lately. He kept his promise to me all these years—"

I stopped, because of the expression on his face. It was kind, but a little embarrassed, too. He wanted to understand, but, of course, he could not, and that always annoyed him.

"Darling, I don't think it calls for any such outburst of emotion. Perhaps you're not well—"

To steady myself, I recited the main contents of the letter.

"I still don't see it's anything to cry about," he said, smiling down at me. "In the first place, you don't know whether the writer is telling the truth—he'd naturally play along, you know, for any advantage that might accrue to him—and if he is, Manu's keeping his promise to you was partly good business. No doubt he's fond of you, but, of course, he was always looking for a main chance—"

"Will you write to the Commissioner at Patna to try to locate him?" I broke in, when I could hear no more.

"I can't do that, my love. I don't know him personally—he'd think it was very odd—you're letting yourself be carried away by a childhood sentiment. If you want my opinion—any further search for him would be beneath the dignity of both of us."

I nodded and was grateful for his kiss. Yet from that moment my relations with him began to change. I knew it was a dangerous change, stemming from what I could very easily argue was weakness, but which my heart knew was strength. I felt immensely strengthened by the almost assurance that Manu was alive and would come to me. I did not feel such a deep need of the security Anthony gave me. That meant I might risk it some day, and thereby lose it. To be a good wife to him would be a harder task from this moment on. Lola, her wings clipped, was sprouting stout plumes again. The danger at once frightened and thrilled me.

I knew of only two events that would restore my safety. One was to become convinced of Manu's death. The other was to have a baby. The first was opposed by a superstititious feeling of great persistence and force. The chances of the second were diminishing rapidly with the passing seasons, as my husband became ever less hopeful, and, as if in consequence of that, less passionate. He had a deeply ingrained feeling that passion was something "to be satisfied," but never lovely in itself. An increasing amount of his energies went to riding and shooting. I found that I did not mind very much—I had my own dreams. In these my partner was usually Rene—sometimes someone I was unable to recognize—occasionally to my amazement it was Jeffery. When this occurred, the bliss was intense, but I wakened with a sense of having narrowly escaped a rushing darkness, eerie, evil, and obliterative as death.

In the house was a music box made by some tireless German craftsman that played eight pieces at one winding of the spring. These were mostly French and Italian airs, melodious and charming. I had it put in my room, and when there was no danger of interruption, I stripped to my shift, tied on my castanets, and danced to them to my heart's content.

Near the close of my second year at Poona there came another letter, addressed to me in an ornate script by a hired scribe. I slipped it out of sight until I could take it to my room, and while carrying on some sort of a conversation with Anthony, I was thinking how few people I knew to whom I could confide the fever in my brain and the tremor in my hands. Manu himself—Rene—my dancing masters—some humble people I had known and, strangely enough, the most exalted, Lundy of Blackmoor. I need wear no veil before Jeffery. That might be more true of complete antagonists than of ordinary lovers, I thought. When the sinner confesses his most hidden sin to God, he becomes a saint. When he confides his last goodness to the devil, he becomes his brother.

Behind a locked door, I opened the letter in wild hope and terror. It had been dictated by Manu and his spirit came into the room. He had pledged his labor for six months, to provide for certain loved ones; and would start forth for Poona when he had raised the bond. If I were rich now, and it was my desire that he come quickly, I must send him fifty rupees, enough to redeem him from what remained of the debt when the sum would reach him and speed his journey. If my purse were thin, he would stop along the road betimes to earn his onward passage. For it was not meet that the servant of Lola Memsahib beg in sight of the gods.

Since Anthony had only a smattering of Hindustani, I read the letter aloud to him, making such changes as I thought best. I should have known he would be unpleasantly surprised. He had long ago concluded that Manu was lost or dead.

"He probably has children and a wife or two," Anthony said. "Don't you think you'd better send him a ten-rupee note for the sake of old times and tell him to stay put?"

"I think his children are all grown up," I answered, my throat tight. "He's over fifty."

"When you fell under his influence, you were a mere baby. You gave him the affection you couldn't give your mother—"

"He gave me the love she wouldn't give me. I've loved him for it ever since."

"I wish you wouldn't speak of *loving* a native. Although I know what you mean, it doesn't sound right. He's not an old English nanny or even a butler that the young master or mistress may feel a warm affection for all their lives."

"No, he's not. I never had an English nanny. I never saw an English butler till I moved to the General's house. He's an old low-caste Indian—"

"And you, my dear, are the Lieutenant Colonel's memsahib. You may very soon be Lady Reeve. What you feel for Manu is a hold-over from childhood that you had better let die."

"It never will die."

"Please temper your language, Lucia. What you say isn't true—"

"It is true."

"If so, I'll ask you not to let him come."

"You promised me when you proposed to me that he could have a place in our household."

"I know I did. At that time I didn't realize the hold he has on you. I don't like it, Lucia. I ask you to relieve me of my promise."

"If you don't let him come, I'm going back to England and take him with me."

"Lucia! How can you say such a thing? I don't like to remind you —" He paused.

"Of all you've done for me?"

"I suppose I was thinking that. I could hardly help it, could I?"

"No, you couldn't help it. But he's done just as much for me as you have."

"Great heavens!"

"I'll be grateful all my days for what you've given me. I'm trying every day to repay you. Manu didn't make me second lady of a regiment—he didn't rescue me from poverty—but he did save me from death."

"Do you mean he saved your life in some accident—"

"He saved me from death. He went with me to fight death. I can't explain it any more."

"Lucia, this is the first time we've ever stood apart on any issue. This is the first barrier that has ever risen between us. But I'll meet you halfway. Let's put this precious love of his to test. Don't send any money—don't write him. Then if he makes the journey all the way from Patna, I'll feel that his devotion to you is real, and he isn't trying to take advantage of your childhood affection for him. In that case, I'll put him in our service for as long as he proves worthy of it."

I turned away and looked out the window. On the brown drill field small geometrical forms in scarlet ever changed to new forms. These were the sepoy troops, natives being drilled to fight other natives. Farther on were the lines where they were quartered; on our side of the field were the Tommies' barracks and a row of cottages where the married soldiers lived. For an officer's wife to drink tea with the wife of a sergeant would be detrimental to discipline. It was detrimental to the discipline of society for a memsahib to love an old servant more than her husband—indeed it was an offense akin to sacrilege. But I did—and once I had been Lola, who had not let man-made discipline—man-decreed sacrilege—check the great beat of her woman's heart.

"I'm not going to test his love," I said, hardly knowing what I was saying amid my soaring thoughts. "When I have to test some-one's love, I don't want it."

"Lucia, you've been parted from this man for eleven years. You've come back to India as the wife—"

Yes, I had come back to Hind! I had returned to Lola's birth place. Somewhere the brawny Lohar hammered the great iron. By Manu's acknowledging her, she had found strength to lash the breast of Kali. She had bowed her head to the red-handed goddess at General Judson's bedside, and he had not heard again the trumpets of Waterloo, but she wished to God she hadn't or never would again.

Kali, I hate you! I was born and shaped to fight you all my life and became formidably armed. This now is a tiny skirmish with you on a small, obscure field, but I do not know why, and if I tried to find a practical reason for its truth, I would doubt that truth.

"I'm going to send him the money out of some I'd saved when we were married." I had been about to say some money that General Judson had given me, but that would not be true. I was going to spend that as he would like, according to my love. To Manu I would send ten pounds of a fifty-pound note, not as its giver would wish—indeed as he would greatly fear—according to my hate.

"Very well," my husband answered. "Understand it is very much against my advice and wishes. I hope it will work out well. If it doesn't—I'm frightened of the consequences."

TWENTY-TWO

I SUPPOSE Anthony wondered how I was going to transmit fifty rupees clear across India with the least assurance of their safe arrival. Manu himself had told me how it was done, when he had wished to send five rupees to an uncle in Madras in a family crisis of fifteen years ago. It was a simple matter of depositing fifty-five rupees with a Marwari money-lender in Poona. On the receipt of the draft, Manu could collect the sum from another Marwari in Patna. In the letter I enclosed a pass to the reservation, and a charm which I had bought for three annas from a holy man. It consisted of the names of beneficent spirits written on a scrap of paper. By washing off the ink and swallowing the water, Manu could face the journey without fear.

It was then mid-January. In the next two months my husband never mentioned the affair and was gentle and often affectionate toward me, partly perhaps as balm to his conscience for the wish, father to the thought, that Manu would devote the money to his own uses and probably write for more. As the drought deepened under the blaze of the April sun, I pictured him traveling southwestward on the great highway from Allahabad to Jubbulpore—southward to Nagpur—turning sharply west through Berar—almost to Aurangabad, of the tomb of the Queen of Aurangzeb. His bare feet made an endless chain of prints in the dust. At night his stick fire flamed and flickered out as he slept safely under a peepul tree beside the road.

Late in May, torn and tattered clouds began to stream across the sky. Sometimes at sundown they thickened into banks, and a wind with coolness in it, almost a dampness, rustled the dry reeds. A day or two later uncertain thunder rumbled in the distance and a few big, warm drops of rain squashed in the dust. On the last night of the month, the wind soughed all night, and lightnings played all over the starless sky. The clouds did not break at dawn, but darkened and lowered. There came a moment of deep suspense—all the high gods stopped their businesses—the fowls in the yards stretched their necks—the dogs sniffed the air—only the cart buffaloes cared naught, sullenly plodding before the goad that was god. Then with great choral music, as when a sea storm had broken on the moors, down flung the rains.

Manu was late for our appointment. I sat nearly an hour at the window before I made out a dim form, a pack on his shoulder, wearily walking up the alleyway behind the officers' row. But his step hastened as he saw the gate of our compound. The *chokidar* would be squatting in his hut out of the wet, and I could not suffer my beloved to knock and call. Shrieking, "Manu! Manu!" I rushed out into the vertical flood. It was warm and loving—it was washing away my sins—the thunders were roaring "Lola!"—and when Manu dropped on his knees, his arms extended toward me, I seized his hands and knelt before him. We raised our tear-wet faces to the rain. Its roar in the trees deepened and became the mighty laughter of Krishna . . . Krishna the Joyous . . . Krishna our own. . . .

My hand clutching his, we ran to a little room opening off the larder which I had forbidden the other servants to enter. There I had fixed him a cot, a chest containing clothes and bedding, a washstand, and a lamp and little pan for preparing opium pellets. I left him to put on dry clothes; when I returned, he was squatted on the mat, having a pipe to drive off weariness and fever. Now that he had removed his turban, I saw that his long hair was streaked with gray; perhaps his brown skin was stretched a little tighter over the bones in his face. Otherwise he seemed unchanged since we had squatted together in the oleanders saying farewell.

Time sprang back like my hand after striking a golpe on my castanet, and I gave him back his words.

"Are you still alive? If I had not seen it with my own eyes, I could not believe."

"How could I die, when I had gone with you and saw Kali whipped and shamed?" he answered.

"Will you live forever, even as a god?"

"Not as a god, but as one who fears no god, for as long as you will not make offering unto her. The money you paid for the charm sent me in the letter was thrown away."

"Once I yielded to her and I have made offerings to other gods, Kubera, the god of wealth, and perhaps Ganesa, the god of wisdom."

"That I see. It is no harm, when the way was so lonely and steep. But it comes to me that you offended them both, when you bade me come."

"Perhaps I do not need them, when I have you."

"By your leave, I will lay bare my heart. Lola Memsahib, we have been parted for eleven rains. You are wife to a pukka sahib and mistress of a rich house. Is it not a long way from the child who kissed her servant's hands when the memsahib had ordered her banishment across the dark waters? I am newly come, the cup of my returning new raised to my lips; and if you will give the word, I will straightway go. I will dwell as I have dwelt since then, with my heart gone from me, but yet taking joy in my children and their babes and in food and sleep and a pipe after labor, and in little things. But if I look upon you at sundown and at sunrise, if I lie one night at your call, then if you send me away from you, my spirit will depart from me also, and I will be like unto the living dead."

"Why should I send you away, beloved?"

"Have you great riches of your own?"

"Nay."

"Have you a high place across the black waters?"

I shook my head.

"You have not forgotten the day when the boats floundered in the river. On the day following you went with me to see Lohar straighten the bent keel. On that day I saw you with clear eyes, and visions came unto me of the years to come, and in time I told you those visions, and they set your heart on fire. But now the fire burns low. You are happy in the place you have won. When I asked at the gate at what house dwelt Memsahib Lola, young wife of the Lieutenant Colonel Sahib—the writing of his name was deep in my bundle, out of the rain—the sepoy mocked me for a fool, saying none of the memsahib-log was named Lola, and if I were seeking the wife of Ree-va Sahib, who was young, and joy to the eyes of all the poor and lowly, and who spoke Hindustani as though born in the bazaar, her name on the lips of her husband and friends was Lucia."

"Then you remembered calling me Luch-cha (rogue) in sport."

"Aye, but on the night we went to the great pooja in Chota Nagpur, I beheld you as Lola, the daughter of Lohar. It was she with whom I went to the shrine of Kali on that terrible night of the full moon. Do you not know I will ever be a reminder of what is lost? Because you love me, you cannot shut your ears to your true name. It may be you will no longer make offering unto Kubera and Ganesa, and will again make pooja unto Krishna the Joyous, the god of common folk. That is not well—at least it is not wise for—one of the sahib-log."

I knew all that. I might have known that Manu would know it, at first glance at me. I stood naked in the mirror of his eyes.

"Nay, it is not wise."

"I will tell you what I see, as though we had made mounds of cow dung, and poured on milk," he went on. "You cannot have me and this, too." His gesture indicated the big house and all it stood for, and his eyes glowed in the dark room with prophetic fire. "The magic we have made together was weakened by our parting, but it will regain its potence if we unite. For know, Lola Memsahib, that I love you beyond all heaven and earth, and for that you will reward me, even as I foretold."

"What will be your reward, Manu?"

"That you will be true to thy name."

I had only to say it was *behudgi* (fool's talk). No, I need not say even that—I had only to quiet my heart a little, close and doubt it a little; and then he would look into my eyes, pick up his pack, and go out the door. Instead I heard my voice thrilling and strange.

"I will not let you go."

"Even if I bless you first?"

"Nay, I cannot. If I did, would it not be offering unto Kali?"

"Aye, but I know not why."

"Then would you go to the burning ghat?"

"Yea, very soon."

"You shall not go from me. I love you."

Manu knocked out his pipe and cleaned it well. The glow in his eyes had died. Then he groped in his pouch.

"Here be ten rupees left of the sum you sent me. You had better save it for the hour of need."

To delay that hour I resolved to devote the main of my energies to preserving what I still called my marriage.

I could call it that, but really it did not amount to that any more. Anthony and I shared the same house, very rarely the same bed; and very few of the same interests. He was proud of me as I appeared to his competitors and associates, but ashamed of—at least resentful toward—what he thought was my real self. He thought I did not love him as much as he loved me. I was sure that I loved him a good deal more than that—love being a word of many meanings. I perceived his stature in his own faith and field—I still thrilled over his high-mindedness in Mamma's parlor and his noble proposal—and felt compassion, itself an aspect of love, for his constant cramping of his own best nature. His love for me was mainly part of his religion—I was his lawful wife, and it was his duty to love me and he always did his duty. I was sure now that I could never surrender to him enough to allow him to feel the possessive love that the word meant to him; but I knew how to fascinate him and raise his self-esteem. I could raise, I thought, the level of his happiness.

Manu became my groom, the office that would permit us to be together the most in my husband's absence, and the least in his presence. Manu was not a good rider, but I got him a plug he could stay on, and on country lanes the beast's head beside the tail of mine permitted us easy conversation. I almost never mentioned him to Anthony and I thought he was becoming reconciled to what he considered an act of insubordination on my part, hardly short of mutiny. I entertained him by the hour. I shone when he wanted me to shine, and when he did not, went into eclipse. I was Lola only in Manu's eyes, in which sometimes I saw her reflected. Sometimes the image dimmed even there.

For the first setback after Manu's return I was not in the least to blame. Sir Spencer Reeve had remarried the year before—a marriage for companionship, he wrote, to a lady of mature years—and envisioning a quiet, elderly couple drinking tea before the fire, Anthony had not been worried about the succession of the baronetcy. But the end of the rains brought a triumphant letter dripping with joy and gladness for Anthony to share, announcing that Lady Reeve had presented the old Benedict with a son and heir! Some of his friends had been doubtful that a marriage between a gentleman of seventy-two and a lady of forty-two could be a success, but they had been proven false prophets!

"I'll bet it's a little bastard," I remarked, instinctively trying to ease the tension in Tony's face.

"Lucia, I don't appreciate that kind of humor at my uncle's and my aunt's expense."

I had forgotten a like difference between my husband's age and my own. It was the darkest anger I had ever seen possess him, and there was nothing I could say to turn it away. I nodded and quickly left the room. Perhaps I would have done better to have struck back; a blaze of rage might have welded again our breaking bond.

The next event of large and clear-cut bearing on the issue was a street incident oddly reminiscent of that in which I met Rene and Jeffery. On the way home from a ride with Manu, I had stopped in the town, and, leaving both horses in Manu's care, went into a shop. Emerging, I stopped to look at some brasswork in the shadow of the doorway and in sound of Manu's voice. He was talking to a fine-looking sepoy from one of the native regiments quartered across the drill field from ours.

"My memsahib is the wife of Lieutenant Colonel Sahib," Manu was saying in the informal vernacular.

"She is the most beautiful memsahib I have seen," his companion replied. Then asking the question uppermost in the native mind about any marriage: "Has she borne him sons?"

"To her deep sorrow, no."

At that moment a tall man in mufti, pausing to light his pipe, pricked up his ears. I recognized him as Captain Henry, a late arrival at the station in command of a company of Rajputs, and already known as a martinet. But I was not warned in time.

"Why is it that memsahibs are so often barren, or else have only a miserly two or three?" the sepoy asked, unaware of the sahib standing behind him. "Think you they are cold to their lord's plowing, or do their furrows lack richness?"

Captain Henry took two lithe strides, seized the sepoy by the shoulder, whirled him around, and smote him hard in the face.

"That will teach you to keep your dirty tongue off memsahibs," he said in a brutal voice.

The Captain knew Hindustani, but he did not know Rajputs,

however he might presume to command them. They were one of the most proud and courageous clans in India. I had already suspected that the sepoy was one of them, and I knew it when he struck back as swiftly as one of his desert wolves.

Captain Henry reeled back from the blow, then took a threatening posture. However, he soon thought better of teaching any more lessons here and now to this lithe son of the thirst; perhaps he remembered his dignity as an officer.

"Report to the guard, sipahi," he commanded in cold, clipped tones. "You are under arrest." At once he walked on.

Throughout the incident, my instinct had been to remain unseen. I was a lieutenant colonel's wife who must not figure in street fights. But it had never occurred to me that since he had struck first, Captain Henry would order the man's arrest.

"I saw what happened and I will speak for you to the sardar," I told the sepoy. After writing down his name and his number, I sped home as fast as I could and reported the entire incident to Anthony.

"I'm sorry you happened to be present," he said.

I was incredulous. "My God, I'm glad I was! You can't tell what that beastly man will do. He may try to get him sent to prison—"

"He'll be lucky to get off with ten years."

"What?"

"It's a capital offense for an enlisted man to strike an officer. The fact that the officer was in mufti would ordinarily mitigate it, but in this case I presume the sepoy struck his own captain. You thought he was a Rajput, and Captain Henry has the only company of Rajputs on the reservation."

"Anthony, you heard me say that the brute struck him first—"

"When he heard the sepoy using obscene language about white women? Pray don't apply such terms as 'beastly' and 'brute' to your defender—for he was defending you as well as all other memsahibs. You particularly, in fact, since the conversation began with you. It was held with your precious Manu. I'll personally congratulate Captain Henry for striking him—it was very mild punishment to say the least. A just judge at the court-martial can't increase the sentence for what the fellow was saying to another native, but he certainly doesn't need to reduce it because his remarks were properly rebuked. The judge will consider only the sepoy's blow—"

My husband spoke on, but I did not listen. I only stood there, my heart torn at what I saw in his face. It was not his own nature that had cast the dark pall of anger there, that had hardened his eyes and drawn his mouth into an expression of cruelty. It was a mask of evil put on in invocation of evil gods—the gods he must invoke when the good gods would not let him speak in their name. . . .

"May I say one thing more?" I asked, when the cold, rasping noise finally ceased.

"Of course, Lucia."

"The sepoy had no notion of being obscene. The natives' sense of imagery causes them to compare the male sex organ to a plow, and the female to a furrow."

"How did you know that interesting fact?"

"I listened to a great deal of native talk when I was a child."

"It gave you some strange ideas, to say the least."

"I'm going to see that the truth comes out at the court-martial. If I have to, I'll go before it and testify to what I've just told you, and that I took not the slightest offense at it. I don't think the judge advocate would dare refuse me."

"You would use those very words?"

"What's wrong with them?"

"A lady does not speak so in public. Lucia, I've done the best I can. I forbid you to appear at the court-martial."

I nodded and at once went into the courtyard and ordered my horse resaddled. On this ride, I did not take Manu with me—it was only to the shafakhana to see Dr. Haines. He received me in his cluttered office, and at the first glance into his wise, kindly face much of my pain was healed. Again I recited the street incident from first to last, and he wrote it down word for word.

"The fools!" he cried, when I was through. "They'll keep on this way until there's a great rebellion that will bathe India in blood. Well, I'll go before the court. I'll insist on being heard as an expert on native idiom—by God, I've written on it for the Indian Survey!

No fear I won't be heard! I'll show that Henry's blow for chivalry was nothing but a piece of damned stupidity. That ought to temper the sentence."

"What will happen to you?"

"I won't be very popular with the pukka sahibs, but I don't think I'll lose my standing with the burra sahibs—such as Henry Lawrence. I wouldn't mind being transferred for the good of the Service—especially if I could get in a regiment on the Afghan border. I'd like to know those desert men better."

He paused, his eyes full of thoughts, then leaned toward me.

"Look, Lucia. I wish we could get the court-martial delayed. If it's held now, we can't save that fellow's skin altogether. But in a very few days—and this is a military secret that a doctor has no business knowing—the sepoy regiment is going to be sent to the Northwest Frontier. Hell's going to pop there soon—thanks to some more fools. This fellow would, of course, be left behind, under arrest. With Captain Henry out of the picture, I could do a lot more for him."

When I had risen to go, he looked at me searchingly.

"You know, Lucia, I'd like to write a monograph inspired by you. I'd like to give it a fancy title—'Beauty and the Beast'—the Beast being the shape of humanity. Do you remember that in the fairy tale he was really a prince who had been enchanted by an evil witch, and Beauty restored him to his rightful form? Humanity, too, has been bewitched—often it appears in such ugly guise—it does such inhuman things. Science can't undo the spell—lawmakers can't—religion is too frequently turned to the Beast's uses. One great Beauty revealed nearly two thousand years ago did more than any other one thing to save us, but it's been blackened by hypocrites. Our only real hope lies in the Beauty of Woman. If only she could realize her power!"

I left him with revived hopes. But he was not able to postpone the court-martial, and the stern judges conceded only that since the prisoner had not intended any insult to white women, his offense of returning Captain Henry's blow was moderated. He was neither shot nor sent to penal servitude. Instead he was paraded before the regiment, his insignia cut off, and drummed out of the army.

But the following morning, when the sepoy regiment received orders to march to the Northwest Frontier, Captain Henry's company of Rajputs refused to fall in line.

TWENTY-THREE

STERN measures! That was the term for what must be taken, loose on the lips of the women. They've got to be made an example of. Young wives of the junior officers, new off the boat, mouthed the sentence till it turned into a kind of shibboleth, to identify the mouther as a pukka memsahib. But something more than pukkahood had set the lips of the officers in grim lines. Unless sternly dealt with, they said, the mutiny might spread first to the other companies of the regiment, then throughout the Bombay and Bengal armies. The four chapatties (unleavened bread) would be passed to the four winds—each receiver making four more, the old Indian way of spreading an alarm.

The mutinous troops were given one brief moment to reconsider, then were arrested and ironed. Now, while the other sepoy companies seethed with excitement, the guard stood over them with ready rifles. There was no time to send for instructions from the High Command; at General Headquarters the brigadier and his staff sat in solemn council to decree the punishment.

"They won't have any trouble deciding," a major's wife told me. "You see this has happened before—twice that my husband told me about—and they only have to follow precedent. In each case the fire was put out before it could spread."

I knew of those two cases. About eighty years ago, thirty mutinous sepoys were lashed to the mouths of cannons and blown to pieces. Less than twenty years ago, the 2nd Bengal Infantry had refused to march to the Burmese War, and again the big guns—although at a somewhat larger range—had taught all India a lesson.

The thought of appealing to Anthony brushed my mind and vanished. I was willing to hear from him that he could do nothing in a matter serious as this—actually a crisis endangering the empire. What I could not bear to hear him say was that stern measures were not only necessary but right—that God intended for England to rule India and the Indian people would be the first to suffer if our hold were weakened. True, it was damned unpleasant business. I had better put it out of my mind as something that couldn't be helped. Why didn't I get a good book, and go to my room. . . .

There was no use of going to Major Haines. A regimental doctor did not have the standing of an officer commanding troops. . . . For a moment my hopes leaped at the thought of our Colonel's wife, Mrs. Radford. She was the daughter of a viscount, and the greatest in India sat at her table. Then I remembered what she had told me when I had confided to her the growing rift between Anthony and me.

"I've stopped trying to do big things out here. I do only little things. I can get a doctor for one native woman about to die in childbirth, but not for a thousand. I can bring a little gift to a corporal's wife dying of heartbreak, but I can't make a dent in the dogma of the military caste. I haven't the stuff of heroism. I'm a woman Nicodemus, who with a troubled mind and heart goes on her way."

So in the end I went to Manu. To whom else on earth could I turn? The way of it was to put on a riding habit and order my horse. Manu rode well behind me until we went out the main gate of the reservation, then drew his horse's head beside the tail of mine.

"Which way, Manu?" I asked.

"Do you wish to ride far, memsahib?"

"I do not know."

"The memsahib must ride very far to escape the sound of the guns."

"Will there be guns, Manu?"

"Assuredly there will be guns, perhaps the great guns, perhaps those fired from the shoulder. In either case, the memsahib must ride far to escape their sound."

"What is to be gained by staying near enough to hear them?"

"Nothing that I know of, memsahib."

"When do you think they will be fired?"

"Before sundown."

"The sun is even now halfway down the sky."

"It will fall quickly, memsahib."

"Why do you not call me Memsahib Lola?"

"I cannot—when we are both so weakened and afraid."

"Yea, there is something to be gained, though I cannot count its worth. It is pain—and anger."

"Truly."

"Would you rather have pain and anger than weakness and fear?"

"Yea, memsahib."

"If we would have them in great store, it is not enough to hear the sound of the guns. We must also see their fires of death, and our brethren die."

"That be true."

"Do you know a place where we may go?"

"The crest of Pak Pahari looks down on the sepoys' drilling ground. You know the road."

"Aye, so I do."

We rode that way in silence until we were winding up the hillside.

"Manu, why did the company of Rajputs disobey the sardar's command?" I asked.

"If you asked them, they would tell you that their tribe had made truce with the Sons of Allah of Bahawalpur, kinsmen of the Pathan."

"Is it true?"

"It could well be true that their particular clan, dwelling on the border, and tired of fighting over the water or the grass, have declared truce."

"Is that the reason they refused to fight the Pathan?"

"No, memsahib, unless my mind tricks me."

"Was it in fury for the unjust punishment meted out to one of their clan?"

"Their fury had no vent and darkened their souls. Before then, the hand of Henry Sahib lay heavy upon them, because he knew not how to lead them, only to drive them, and they hate his shadow on the ground. During that darkening, came the order to fight their ancient and most feared enemies. They remembered then the sooth-saying that none who go through Khyber Pass shall ever return. So their hearts failed."

"But they knew they would be shot as mutineers. Any chance was better than none."

"Death at the hands of the Pathan, who howl as they come waving their great knives, is many deaths in one. They sucked in fear of it with their mothers' milk. They have heard how the Pathan women cut apart the enemy dead, so they may not be born again in mortal form. They would face it, if their hearts were high, but these have been brought low. It may be they themselves do not know their terror, but I stood near when they refused the order, and I saw it in their eyes."

"Manu, I will speak not as Lola, but as the memsahib of the Colonel Sahib. These men had taken oath to obey their officers' commands."

"Even so."

"A soldier is nothing if not brave. It is right that those who desert should be shot, for their faithlessness and as an example to the rest who are afraid. It is a misfortune that the Rajputs have such a captain as Henry Sahib, who darkens instead of brightens their hearts; yet it is still the duty of the General Sahib to shoot them."

"Aye, it be his duty, by the light he sees."

"By what light do we see, Manu?"

"I know not. It shone upon us long ago. It is very bright here on the crest of the hill. If you are the memsahib of the Colonel Sahib, it would be best that we descend and wait in the shade."

"It is only the sunlight, Manu."

"Aye, the shine of the hot sun."

The rim of the reservation, along which sentries marched, lay only a furlong below us. The naked brown drill field was nearly a mile wide at this place, but looking across to the guardhouse, we could see that the day's duty was under way. Two regiments of redcoats were forming for a parade. At this distance we could not see whether they were Tommies or native troops; indeed it was hard to tell them as men with white skins or dark skins or guts or brains instead of merely military formations. They formed swiftly changing geometrical designs, then began to move in two columns into the field. Their pace was very slow.

Between them was another formation—a moving frame with thin red borders, containing a white rectangle that moved with it. If one looked closely, one could see that the frame was made of men wearing red coats, its contents men whose coats had been taken off. These men did not keep step with the rest. They gave the effect of moving on rollers instead of feet. That was because they were taking very short, quick steps. I need not ask Manu why that was.

Behind and at one side of the formations were what looked like little dogs pulling tiny carts from which thin things projected behind. In the language of the military, guns were being moved into position. We were not near enough to hear the drivers' shouts or see the animals surging in their harness; the operation appeared smooth, sedate, as inconsequential as the detail of a dream.

The two columns halted in the center of the field, and each became two long, parallel red lines. Between them the white rectangle became a much shorter white line. What had been the sides and back of the thin red frame curiously folded up and then parted in the middle. Both sides, now short red lines, moved to opposite ends of the white line, and then very slowly approached each other. These were not any longer stiff and straight, but wavered sideways and up and down.

"What are the guards doing?" I asked Manu. I was almost certain but I wanted to be sure.

"They are taking off the leg irons, memsahib," Manu answered.

"Won't the prisoners run when the big guns begin to shoot?"

"No, memsahib. I have never known condemned men to run from the guns and so make sport for the watchers. Besides, these be Rajputs. They will stand still and straight and wait for Kali. They have resigned themselves unto her."

"It is merciful compared to tying them to the guns' mouths."

"Even so, I would that the sahibs had used the little guns instead of big ones. Then the Rajputs could go whole to the burning ghats."

"They are half through freeing them already."

"Yea, memsahib."

"Soon the regiments will march away?"

"To a safe distance, memsahib, but where they may yet see what befalls when soldiers disobey commands."

"Will the guns fire until Kali takes all who have so disobeyed?"

"Perhaps not. It may be there will be only one volley, or perhaps two or three. It is said there were three when the Bengali foot soldiers would not march to Burma."

"The work of taking off the irons is almost done."

"Yea, memsahib."

"There is nothing that one memsahib and one old Indian can do to save them."

"There be naught that a wise memsahib and her Indian servant can do."

"If the diwani came upon us, and we tried to stand between them and the sahibs' guns, we would be dragged away in shame. Then in their fury the sahibs would order many volleys till not one of the Rajput stands. Thus would they show that no memsahib and her old Indian servant could change in one jot or tittle the law of the sahibs."

"Truly it would be the diwani, such as came upon Lola and Manu, when she led him forth under the full moon to lash the breast of Kali."

"What Lola struck with her riding whip was only an image of stone. This is the law of the sahibs."

"Even now, the regiments swing into columns and the dust lifts under their marching feet."

"Kali will soon be full fed."

"She is never full fed, memsahib. Ever there be blood upon her breast and her mouth and her hands."

"The Rajput stand very straight and still."

"They wait for Kali, memsahib."

"They are alone on the wide field."

"I would that the diwani would come upon us."

"It cannot. I am a memsahib and you are an old Indian, her

groom." But my throat filled, as when Manu and I had made pooja to Krishna the beloved.

"Do you remember Lohar?" he asked. "Can you hear the ring of his mighty hammer against the iron? But I remember the ring of a child's voice when her word went forth from her never to make offering unto Kali. I would that you and I could stand with the Rajput as Kali comes in the form of shrieking shell, and defy her to the last."

"The sahibs would not let us stand with them. They would know the diwani was upon us and drag us away in shame."

"See, the regiments are again forming their lines."

"So near?"

"They are in no danger. The gunners will fire point-blank and the balls will fly true."

"If we turn away our eyes, only one—or two—or three volleys will be fired, and those who yet stand may live. If we defy the law of the sahibs, all will be slain." Yet I had taken a step nearer my horse.

"Do you not know that the Rajput would gladly die together, if they might die in pride instead of shame? Every one who might be spared would rather die with the rest, if one proof could be given of the compassionate heart of God. Aye, we would be dragged away—"

"But not in shame—"

"Nay, not in shame! Instead in the pride of the groom Davie whom you saw call back the General Sahib from the red breast of Kali. Then the Rajput would mock Kali when she comes even as did Lola, long ago."

I was springing on my horse. "Come quickly, Manu," I cried.

"Aye, Lola, lay on whip and spur," he shouted behind me. "I be not far behind!"

There was no path down the steep hill to the rim of the field. But the horses were instantly maddened and bounded like barasingh, the great stags of the north, over the rocks and through the thickets. Manu was a poor horseman, until now riding only on open roads and level bridle paths, and perhaps he thought my backward glance was in fear of his falling. Instead it was only to see his face. There was no fear left in the world, even of being too late. Manu had hooked his reins over the pommel and was hanging on with both hands. The thorns had snatched off his turban and his long hair streamed behind.

A sentry taking shelter behind a rock shouted at us as we rode into the field. The most direct course to the Rajput was straight toward two of the four guns beyond, and as yet the line concealed us from the gunners, but I need rally no courage to use my whip and spur, and Manu's tame old horse came bounding behind us like a sheik's Arab charging into battle. There was no other sound but the drum of hoofs on the sun-baked ground. The dressed troops had eyes for nothing but the prisoners waiting for death.

We were still three furlongs from them when the cannon mouths blazed, and the earth shook and the air rocked with their rolling thunders. Shrill through the crash rose a long scream that met and passed us and ceased. The line of Rajputs was not quite so long, and there was a gap in its center wide enough for two horsemen to stand abreast. I drew my rein a little to head for it. The white shirt of a mutineer standing next to the gap suddenly turned red as the red tunics of the watching soldiery, then he sank down with his prone, quiet brethren.

At that instant frantic shouts rose here and there along the dressed ranks, and several horsemen dashed into the field.

I drew up and stopped just in front of a little cluster of dead men. Manu took his position full beside me. I looked into the faces of the yet alive, and there was such glory in them that no future punishment dealt to them or to Manu or to me could ever strike full force.

TWENTY-FOUR

*M*ANU and I dismounted and waited silently and with a mysterious calmness for the approaching officers. They rode fast, then slowly; they checked their horses a little behind that of the General; all their faces were similarly set and all except one had a gray cast. One—my husband's—was white.

"What does this mean, Mrs. Reeve?" the General asked quietly.

"What it seems to mean, sir, I suppose."

"Are you aware that by military law we would have been justified in regarding your action as aiding and abetting the mutineers and kept on firing?"

"I didn't think about that."

"I believe I know what you did think. I heard your testimony, as given by Major Haines, in regard to the sepoy who struck his captain. He was a member of this company. You believed that the company mutinied because of an injustice done him, in which you were involved. The real reason they mutinied was that they are cowards. They are afraid to fight the Pathan."

"My groom told me so. I've been afraid lots of times myself, and sometimes turned tail."

"Both of you get on your horses and get out of here as fast as you can."

"So you can fire some more volleys?"

"That is our affair, not yours."

"You'll have to take us by force."

"What are you saying?"

"I'm going to stay, and my servant will stay with me. Whatever we've done, wrong or right, we're going to stick by it as long as we can. We'll both fight as long as we can with our whips and our hands. We'll do that much before you drag us away. All India will know it—England will know it—and it will do some good in the long run."

He was still a long minute, then he turned to Colonel Reeve. "This is a public matter, involving the welfare of the Empire, so I feel it my duty to speak plainly."

"Yes, sir," my husband answered.

"Mrs. Reeve, perhaps it was so all India and England could know it—and know of *you*—that you did this."

"No, sir, it was not."

He turned to Captain Henry. "Can any of those men speak English?"

"No, sir."

"Gentlemen," the General went on, addressing his fellow officers, "Mrs. Reeve has taken advantage of us. It's quite true that if the word spreads that the wife of an English lieutenant colonel rode into the field to shelter a company of mutineers from cannon fire, the consequences would be more disastrous than I can readily imagine. It might set off mutiny in all the sepoy armies. I'm sorry to reveal this disadvantage in her hearing, but it is unavoidable, if the disgrace is going to be kept quiet. Mrs. Reeve, did you tell anyone of your plan?"

"No, sir."

"Before you and your groom left the reservation, did anyone tell you that the mutineers were to be gunned?"

"No, sir. I asked Manu during our ride what would happen. He thought they would be gunned."

"Will you make a written statement that on returning from your ride you took a short cut across the drill field—that a cannon ball passed near you—and not realizing that these men were the target, you rode toward them seeking safety?"

"I will, if you will remit all punishment but dishonorable discharge."

"I had ordered only one more volley. For your information, all four crews had orders to hit once and to miss once, four punishing balls in all. But as much as it goes against the grain, if you agree to my proposal and give your oath to live up to it, I'll be inclined to let the men off with drumming them out of the regiment."

"General?" It was a voice rough with fury.

"Yes, Captain Henry."

"Pardon me, but before you agree to remit the punishment, I ask permission to put a question."

"Very well."

"The mutineers know why she came. How are they to be stopped from telling it all over India unless they're shot or sent to prison?"

Up spoke Dr. Haines, who had got down from his horse to see if any life remained in the fallen Rajputs. He was always speaking out of turn. He seemed unable to learn military procedure.

"I can handle that, General."

"What do you mean, Major Haines?"

"If you care to do what you said—on Mrs. Reeve's agreeing to make the statement you propose and live up to it—I can bind the Rajputs with her."

There was no sound for long-drawn seconds, and the General's face was like flint.

"Under those conditions, I will remit the punishment to three months at hard labor and then drumming them out of the army. Mrs. Reeve, do you give me your word of honor to perform your part?"

"Yes, sir."

"Major Haines, you may try to bind the mutineers; you speak Hindi better than any of us. But take note they have broken one oath made with lifted hands."

The doctor turned to the mutineers and drew their eyes to his. "The General Sahib has asked me to say that the memsahib's coming among you was the fault of her ignorance of the punishment being meted out, and while riding across the field, she was frightened by what she thought was target practice by the gunners. Ye know better, but if ye will take oath before Brahma to tell that tale and never reveal the truth to wife or friend or priest or anyone, the General Sahib will spare ye from the guns, and restrict your punishment to three months hard labor and then being drummed out of the army. Will ye touch your hands to your foreheads, in fealty to that oath?"

They did so, dropping on their knees, their faces lighted all alike as though by an aimed ray of sunlight.

"Major Woolford, you served in Rajputana," the General said to one of his staff. "Do you think that oath's any good?"

"I must say I never heard of a Rajput breaking an oath made on his knees," the officer answered. "The stiff-legged devils don't take that posture often."

"But will the Tommies believe it—and our own people throughout India?" a colonel asked. "I don't want them to know that a lieutenant colonel's wife—"

"I can answer that, as far as most of the important white people are concerned," Dr. Haines said. He had turned white and his voice trembled. "They wouldn't believe the truth, but they'll be glad to believe the substitute. They like substitutes for any truth that hurts their eyes. Some of the Tommies who saw it will be disappointed that a wonder turned into a joke. The sepoys in the lines who've had their hearts lifted up can let 'em fall. I'll not be able to persuade my wife—"

"Major Haines, I don't consider those opinions are either proper or timely, and I'll ask you to apply for transfer to some other regiment," the General broke in. He turned in his saddle to the grim men behind him. "Gentlemen, it is to be understood that I made the compromise because I had no other choice. You will now take your posts, designating the captain of each company to make the explanation I have given." He looked down at me without the least acknowledgement of our fellow humanity. "Mrs. Reeve, please leave the field through the East Gate so you won't encounter any troops. I'll be grateful if you and the groom get out of their sight as quickly as possible."

I nodded my head. Manu bent very low as he held out his hand for my step into the saddle. We rode into the lonely emptiness of the field.

We made our way into our compound and dismounted. I gave my reins to Manu.

"I told you, Lola Memsahib, on the night of our first parting, that you must journey alone."

"I'm not alone."

I went to my room, bathed, and put on a pretty dress of the kind my husband liked. I was waiting for him in the library when he returned. He came in quietly, a forlorn expression on his face, and, loosening the collar of his tunic, dropped into a chair opposite me.

"Would you like tea?" I asked.

"If you please."

I touched the bell cord, and, when the tea was brought, I put in sugar and milk. He drained the cup and put it down.

"Won't you have some, Lucia?" he asked.

"Not now, thank you, Anthony."

"Then we might as well get this over with." He spoke wearily and in a kind tone. "I'm going to stay with the regiment. I spoke to the General about resigning, and he asked me not to do so—anyway I didn't want to. If the Queen knew, I think she, too, would want me to stay. I have been a good officer, and I can serve her in no other way."

"That's a fine thing, Anthony."

"Thank you, my dear. Now as to our separation—for we both realize it's inevitable—"

He paused and I nodded.

"I feel it would be much better if you would return to England," he went on. "Of course, you can take Manu with you, if he wants to go."

Again I nodded.

"What would you do there, Lucia?" he asked.

"You knew I once planned to go on the stage. I'll do that if possible, and, of course, use a stage name. If I have to take other employment, I'll use my maiden name as far as I can. I don't think there's any law against that, is there?"

"I think it would be better to call yourself Mrs. Lucia Reeve, which will imply separation. Unless, of course, you go on the stage. In that case I would prefer you use a stage name."

"Very well."

"Now this is more painful. You are a young woman with your life before you. It is nothing to me that I can't remarry, but it may prove a great sorrow to you. However, you're not afraid of convention, and I don't think you would hesitate to live with the man you love. I'd not want you to hesitate—you are certainly entitled to love and be loved—one great innocent mistake should not deprive you of it. If it becomes known, I will, of course, appeal to the Ecclesiastical Court for a divorce *a mensa et toro*. As you know, that doesn't permit remarriage—no English divorce does—but you and your lover can establish what amounts to a common-law marriage, which under those conditions is regarded with a good deal of tolerance by the greater part of society."

"I won't oppose the suit, and I'll let you know when it's necessary."

"I appreciate that attitude very much. I'll settle on you half of what I have—"

"No, I'll make my own way. I have enough money for Manu and me to get to England and to keep us going several months. I haven't been a good wife to you. I tried and failed. All I want is a gift in token of forgiveness. Any little token you want to give me."

To my amazement he bowed his head in his hands and wept. I went to him and stroked his hair and kissed his cheek. Soon he regained his self-control.

"I want to give you the scarf pin I wore on the day we met," he said.

"If you wish."

"Will you accept a loan of five hundred pounds, to repay when you can in comfort? I couldn't stand for you to be in want."

"I'll accept it gladly."

"Will you forgive me for every harsh word I've ever spoken to you?"

My eyes filled with tears, and I nodded.

"You've never spoken one to me," he went on. "You've never been anything but lovely. You said you hadn't been a good wife to me. Perhaps the reason you couldn't be—I mean, my idea of a good wife—was my own lack of faith. I wanted to trust in you today—"

He stopped, to try to shape his words. I did not want them shaped. I wanted them blurted out.

"Will you speak just as plainly as possible?" I asked. "You just made a very puzzling statement. You said you wanted to trust in me today—"

"I wasn't able to. I didn't have the faith—perhaps I didn't have the vision."

"Trust in me to do—or not to do—what?" I spoke quietly, in a calm tone, so not to interfere with his thoughts.

"I meant trust your motives. I should've—you are my wife—instead I was like the others. You see, we've all been trained the same. Dr. Haines did believe in you—maybe the Tommies did, as he said, until the wonder turned into a joke. Maybe we officers—we pukka sahibs—disbelieved as some sort of self-defense—in defense of what we stand for, blinded by our own dust. I've never known such pride as rushed into my heart when I first saw you riding into the cannon. But there was a drop of poison in it that soon spread—"

"Pardon me, Anthony. You're assuming that I understand something that I don't. You said you didn't trust my motives. Do you mean—it's awfully far-fetched, but I mustn't misunderstand you —that you and the other officers thought I was trying to make trouble—that perhaps because my father was humbly born and I'm so close to Manu that I hated the pukka sahibs and on a wild impulse took sides with the mutineers?"

"God, no! It couldn't cross our minds that you were a traitor."

"I don't know that it would have been treason. This is their country, not ours. If I did it from love and not hate, you needn't have been ashamed. But none of you thought that. What did you think?"

"Oh, I assumed you knew! I wouldn't have mentioned it again—"

My heart felt meager and useless, without strength to beat, but I looked my husband in the face and asked, "What did you think? What was the drop of poison? I'm sure I know now, but will you say it in plain words?"

"We knew you pitied those men, Lucia. But you heard what the General said."

"That what I did was not for them, but to show off?"

"Partly."

"When he asked the question, I don't think he said partly."

"He should have said 'self-dramatization.' That was the doubt I felt. You'd wanted to go on the stage—"

"Perhaps he was right. How do I know? My mother always said I was a show-off."

"For God's sake, don't compare—"

"I won't. Mamma didn't want me to show off because she wanted all the attention herself. The General didn't want me to because it was bad for the Empire, and you didn't for that reason and because it shamed you. But it comes to the same thing, doesn't it?"

"I told you that if I were capable of more faith—"

"You had faith in me the night you asked me to marry you. You didn't think I was showing off when I defended Papa that afternoon —you said I was standing up for my own. I thought—I felt—I was standing up for my own today—my own human kind—but I dare say I wasn't. I was only trying to attract attention. It's a dreadful thing that God lets us fool ourselves in that humiliating way. I fooled both of us before—but this time I only fooled myself."

His eyes slowly rounded. "Am I the base Indian who threw a pearl away richer than all his tribe?"

"That's only poetry."

"Lucia, if you'll stay with me, I'll resign my commission—we have enough to live on—and we'll go to some new country—"

"I can't stay with you any longer. Not even tonight. You can tell the people that I had a touch of sunstroke while riding this morning —that's a better story than the other—I didn't know what I was doing when I rode into the field. Manu and I will start at once and put up at the first dak bungalow—there's a fine moon and we'll get there before midnight. It's a very hot night—I couldn't stand it and insisted on starting at once for the cool hills. You can send my baggage after me—my ayah can pack it—and a Company dooly, with orders to take me to Bombay. I'm sorry for all the trouble I've caused you. I wish you every happiness."

"Will you take the pin—and the loan?"

"Of course. I'm not trying to hurt you. I'm trying to help you."

"I'm going to send a guard with you."

"I don't need it, but it will look better."

"Look! Look! Is that all that's left? Not what I see, but what others may see? Your eyes are dry. Won't you even cry?"

"My mother asked me that, one day. No, I can't cry."

TWENTY-FIVE

*M*ID-AFTERNOON of the first day's journey after the first night's stop, the dooly-bearers stopped chanting of the joys of good food and faithful wives and sang a song about me. One after another made up a verse, then all joined in the refrain.

The memsahib is a small memsahib, as memsahibs go;
She is not much taller and fatter than a Bengali virgin,
That the rajah buys when he is old and feeble.
  Jog along, jog along, down the long road.
  Food and rest are waiting for us, Hai!
This morning she got out of the dooly and rode her horse,
But we were fresh then, and hardly missed her burden.
Tomorrow I hope she will ride in the afternoon.
  Jog along, jog along, down the long road.
  Food and rest are waiting for us, Hai!
What has the memsahib eaten since her breakfast?
It is more fattening than rice swimming in ghee!
She will not be able to get through the little door.
  Jog along, jog along, down the long road.
  Food and rest are waiting for us. Hai!
I will tell you what she has eaten. Bread made of lead!
But a horse is stronger than we are. Perhaps he would fall down
If again she would spring on his back and ride.
  Jog along, jog along, down the long road.
  Food and rest are waiting for us. Hai!

I had them stop and put me down, and did my best to answer their broad grins. It was a poor attempt, for an hour was striking that I had waited for, in deep dread, all day. Both the scene and the time were as favorable as I could hope for. The lengthening shadows promised the first breach of the heat. The buffalos were lurching out of their wallows, soon to file back to the village. The countryside was completely Indian—a village in the distance shaded by tall palms; a farmer coaxing impounded water into his thirsty field; a pilgrim kneeling by a wayside shrine; a cobra sunning in the dust. I mounted my horse, and, when I had ridden well out of earshot of the dooly-bearers and the guard, waited for Manu to come up beside me.

"Yea, memsahib?" he said.

"Did you think I had something to tell you?"

"I have known it all day."

"Do you know what it is?"

"I know it is in my kismet, and what good to go forth to meet it? In its hour, it would surely come."

"Manu, Hind is my native land. I was not born here, true, but I remember no other, and I have made it mine by loving you, its son."

"Yea, truly."

"You have a wife and tall sons and grown daughters and grand-children, all dwelling in Hind. But I have no one but you. My husband has cast me forth. With him, I lose the protection of Kubera and Ganesa, for truly I have played fast and loose with them. Shall I find Krishna again? He gazes upon my dim eyes and into my bleak heart and will have naught of me. Now I set forth for the cold island. Once I thought he forsook his cowherdess playmates to visit its green moors, but then I was beautiful and young—I had seen but eighteen rains. Soon—in a few moons—I will have seen two and twenty rains. All who loved me save you are gone—Rene my lover, and the old General Sahib, and Kitty. The dancing-teacher mem-sahib and the old French knight and the music-player do not want me unless my heart is light. All I have won is gone—my gold and my izzat. So it has come upon me that I cannot take you across the dark waters."

He rode in silence for a moment, not a trace of expression on his face.

"Memsahib, hast thou ever seen the little piece of iron which sailors look at, to find their way on the waters?"

"Truly."

"A lascar had one and showed it to me and asked me which way it pointed. I told him to the south. 'Fool,' he said, 'it points north.' But, memsahib, that depended on which end of the little iron one judged by. Now it comes to me that all you have said—save that part con-cerning my loved ones—points not to my parting with you on the shore, but going on with you across the waters."

"Again, Manu, you are looking at the wrong end. You loved me with tenderness when you first cared for me. But you loved me in pride on the night that the boats caught fire on the river, and I did not run crying to your arms, but flung the burning brand into the water. Are you my servant?"

"Aye."

"Despite our hearts put in each other's keeping?"

"Aye. My heart beats with thine, or leaps or falls."

"My pride is your pride, and my shame your shame?"

"Aye, for I can love you without hating you the while."

"So could Rene, whereby I could not make a marriage with him. Manu, I have been cast down. It is no longer meet that you should serve me, until again I arise. You would be cheated, and I would be shamed."

"Memsahib, I rode with you into the cannon's mouth. Do you not ride again into cannon?"

"Nay, I walk humbly, in great fear. A wheel has turned full circle, and again I am sent into exile. You would have gone with me before, if I had bid you, but I did not, although not knowing why save in my silent heart. Now the truth rises to my mind, where I may see it. Did you not tell me I must walk alone?"

"Aye."

"If you went with me, it would be a great cost. To your loved ones, you would be as one who has drunk the cup of death. On the cold island there are few of your kind, with whom to sit at the rice bowl and to tell old tales, and to smoke and spit and be as brothers. There the sun in summer midday is not as warm as here at winter rising. It is a weak sun, half the time hidden behind clouds. The rains are chill, and the east wind bites to the bone. Yet if I could be your sun, I would bid you go there with me. If I could keep you warm with happiness and pride, I would wear you like a jewel on my hand. I cannot now—I have been brought too low— it may be I must again dwell in shadow as in dark days at Kelso. When the day comes that I can—and that day will come, if we both live—I will send word to my beloved servant to come to me."

"Your servant obeys your command." Manu answered, tears rolling down his face.

"I will leave you enough rupees to pay your way under the deck of the great ship. I will write you every month in care of the Dak-khana in Patna. And from henceforth, until we say farewell beside the ship, we shall take no thought of our parting, and shed no tears, and look not to the past or to the future, but live for the day, the hour, and the moment, and see and hear and smell and touch all that we may, as when we journeyed together into Chota Nagpur. And you shall be happy in my love, and I will be happy in yours."

This last we achieved. We made boon companions of the dooly-bearers, and sang saucy songs to them in reply to their own. We would not put up with my homely Mahratta ayah's weeping and wailing lest she never see Poona again, and frightened her into silence with spine-chilling charms. We forgot about time, traveling when we pleased, stopping where and when we liked for as long as we liked; we went down byways out of the dust and dim paths through the forests; we visited solemn temples and frivolous bazaars. We struck up friendships with Gypsies, holy men on pilgrimages, Marwaris with laden ponies, Mohammedan women dressed like goblins in absolute purdah, all but naked jungle men, plowmen in the fields, and girls coming up from the brooks with water jars on their heads. We looked, heard, smelled, and felt, without the darkening thought that together we would not pass this way again.

At night we put up at dak bungalows when they were handy; otherwise we stayed in native houses, our bedrolls spread on the floor. But I could not control the passage between my falling to sleep and waking again. Therein I was repeatedly warned not to confuse the holiday with the days of reckoning to come. I would be given this merrymaking with no penalty added on, if I had learned my lesson. That lesson was a relatively easy one. It did not demand that I abandon my goal; it only required me to pursue it in a sensible fashion. I was not to yield to my rash impulses. I must be temperate in all things. I must have more regard for appearances. I must not fly in the face of public opinion.

When we arrived in Bombay, I found that I had missed the big Indiaman sailing around the Cape of Good Hope, and the next sailing was the *Lord Clive,* what the English tars called a "morpha-dite boat," meaning one equipped with both sails and paddle wheels. She was one of the Company's first ventures in steam, and was in disfavor with Anglo-Indians on account of her cramped quarters and sluggish pace. Her present voyage was one for comfort-loving travelers to shun. She would carry us only to Suez; from there we must cross overland to Cairo on the Nile, descend the river to Alexandria, then take a Peninsular and Oriental Steamer to London. As a consequence, I was able to get a stateroom to myself and had the pleasant prospect of riding a ship of the desert.

There were no other prospects, just now, that I cared to entertain. The ship was to sail on the tide just before midnight, recalling to me another sailing near that hour, and my parting with Rene. Manu and I had hoped the rains would break before our farewells were said—one of the reasons we had dawdled on the road was to await the good omen—but they had held off, and the sun glowered in red fury as it plunged into the sea. There was no breeze in our faces. The dock was thronged with people who might as well be enemies, since no look or word or gesture indicated they were friends. Manu could not go aboard with me because he wore no badge.

We stood beside a white wall hot to the touch.

"Will you forgive me for breaking faith?" I asked.

"I know not whether you have broken faith or kept it, because I know not who you are, nor who I am."

"Are you not Manu, named for the Vedic hero? Am I not Lola, named for the blacksmith?"

"I cannot tell. I wander in a dream."

"Have I broken faith with Lola?"

"Nay, because she is gone. By that token, you have not broken faith with Manu. Manu found himself in Lola. He, too, became a hero, who rode into the flame to stand with the Rajput. Now that she is gone, he is only an old gardener of little wit."

"Will you remember me as I was, when we rode into the fire, ere the sahib lay me bare as a braggart?" I asked.

"Aye—and as you ran into the rain on the day of my return."

"Will you live on, taking joy in your loved ones, in good food, and rest after labor, and the company of your friends, and a pipe of refreshment?"

"You have quailed before Kali, but have not yet made offering unto her, and until then, neither you or I may die, even though stones be heaped upon us high as a tower."

"I cannot believe it now. What we defied was only an image of stone, painted black and red, with no power to slay. But to the law of the sahibs, that has power not only to slay but to rend the living heart, I will now make great offerings. Yet I would have you believe, when I cannot, that we will again ride together into the flame."

"I will believe it, memsahib."

"Will you call me Lola?"

"Nay, I cannot. My heart fails."

"Yet I speak to my servant Manu. The moons will wax and wane, and the rains will break and die away, and you shall labor in the gardens and take what joys come to your hand. Every month you shall go to the Dak-khana for my letter. I will not send for you until the faith is found again never to lose again, and on that day you shall take leave of your loved ones and give all your possessions to your heirs and say farewell to Hind. For you then will become a bairagi, setting forth on a pilgrimage never to return to your familiar scenes. To all you have known and loved, you shall be as one who has drunk the cup of death."

"Truly, I am your servant."

"You shall cross the dark waters without loss of caste, and in me you shall live again. That is my word that has gone forth from me, and if I break it, may you be shamed."

"There is even now a flush upon your face—"

"It will soon pale, like the flush of the sun in the sky, but it will return. Now put your hand in mine."

"See, it is strong again and trembles not."

"It was my will to kiss your mouth in farewell, but now I bow before the law of the sahibs and make sacrifice. Even now they gaze at us, because you stand beside me instead of behind me, and there be tears in both our eyes. But this hand that was ever raised for me—that I will kiss in token of our bond."

It did not matter that two or three sahibs and memsahibs saw me do it. They thought their eyes had tricked them.

BOOK IV

Krishna the Joyous

*W*HEN the *Lord Clive* had steamed or sailed or both, depending on the weather, out of sight of land, I lost sight of my landmarks behind me and before. I had no sense of forward movement; the sea was all around me when I went to sleep and when I wakened; it changed with every least change of light and wind, but we remained a rocking, rolling island, moored amid its storms, calms, currents, and rolling waves. The clock of my heart kept ticking, but I did not look or listen. In this curious backwater in the stream of my life, I had one pleasant interest.

It was in a sailor to whom I had spoken when he was securing the captain's gig on the small passengers' deck abaft the wheelhouse. I was so glad to be taken with his appearance—fitting my notion of a young Viking. Not very tall, but compactly built, he had genuinely golden hair, a grave, plain countenance sun and wind-tanned, with manly features lighted by eyes of deep marine blue. When he was too shy to volunteer it, I made bold to ask his name. It was Martin Nelson; he was the ship's bosun; and he had come from Hammerfest in the northmost tip of Norway on the Arctic Sea.

When I commented upon his being so far from home, he made me a wonderful answer.

"I've sailed fur'ter t'an t'is from my old home in Norway," he said, using good English with a pleasant accent. "From Drake Strait to Alaska to the Great Australian Bight. But my new home and me—we go toget'er."

As I vegetated on the sterndeck, my most pleasant diversion was watching Martin at work with the other sailors, a good many of them lascars, on the main deck below. Hard as the task might be, it never appeared to demand his full strength—he always could turn and smile at his fellow or make some quiet comment. He climbed the rigging as though he were swimming straight up. In rough weather, when the other passengers fled from the blown foam, I watched him battle the elements with the same poise, never angry, apparently never hurried, but always beforehand with the emergency, more than equal to the occasion. The effect was one of grace. I had never seen a more graceful man, unless it was Jeffery, and his was of another order, another meaning.

Once, indeed, he moved at full power. The same event brought a brief passing breach of his perennial good nature.

A sudden, violent squall sent my deck companions scurrying below. Taking shelter in the lee of the wheelhouse and clinging to a cleat, I watched the furious assault of the wind against this moving, man-made tower, far out and alone in its kingdom. It would topple us over, it thought. It had caught us off guard and would bludgeon and stamp us down. Little it knew our garrison—such men as Martin Nelson, strong and cunning of hand, composed of mind, resolute of will, great of heart.

Mate Green ordered all hands aloft. Precariously perched, they began reefing the shuddering, popping sails. Above all the rest climbed Martin, swinging in a long, sickening arc. Suddenly the canvas he was hugging swelled out black and round against the gray clouds. He hurtled headlong clear of the mast, then plunged down.

If he cried out in the death horror, I did not hear him above the roar of the storm. But he did not crash to the deck or pitch into the sea; an invisible hand appeared to catch him in mid-air. The acceleration of his fall appeared curiously reversed, as though the hand that had seized him gave beneath his weight, but did not let him go. It checked swiftly, was briefly arrested; then I saw his dark shape rise several feet. The instant that I perceived that he had fallen across a taut line stretched between the rigging, I saw him start to slide off.

As he slid feet forward, his arm rose in a powerful sweep to grasp the rope. He caught it, and for a second he clung with one hand, and the tension of his body told me he was giving all he had to save himself from a shattering plunge to the deck. I shrieked as I saw him conquer; both of his hands were now locked on the stay; before I could grasp my breath, he had swung along it to the mast and had slid down the rigging to the deck.

The entire incident, from his fall to his safe landing, could be measured in seconds, and by a queer chance Mate Green, going about some other business, had not seen it. The result was the most heart-warming piece of comic relief that a laughing god had ever let me see.

"Why aren't you in the tops, takin' in sail?" the mate bawled, his voice thin-sounding in the bluster of the storm.

Martin answered instantly in a rumbling roar of indignation, "You son of a bitch, didn't you yust see me blow down?"

After a few seconds of consternation shared by all hands, Martin pulled up his shirt, revealing a red welt across his snow-white chest.

Kali drew back balked and shamed. My eyes filled with tears in pride of her conqueror, and that night, when the squall had been entered in the log and the accident was only a subject of coarse jest in the fo'c'sle, I lingered on the afterdeck long after the other passengers had gone to their cabins. It was a calm night, and the watch coming on at midnight would have little work to do. I hoped to talk to Martin and tell him how glad I was that he was still with me on the earth.

He did not take long to spy me in the dim moonlight; and, bashful though he was, I need not call him.

"Mr. Green, I'd like to look at Cap'n's gig, to see if she's well secured," I heard him tell the mate.

" 'Tis true her lashings might be loosened in the squall," the man replied. "Take a good look at her, while ye're about it."

The gig lay lashed to the rail of the sterndeck. Martin looked at it in the moonlight, and then turned to look at me. I did not require him to call my name, but went and stood beside him.

"I saw the accident today," I said. "I waited up to ask you about it."

"Aye, aye, ma'am."

"Did all your past life pass before your eyes as you were falling?"

"No, ma'am. I had time to t'ink of yust one t'ing. It was whet'er I was going to hit the deck or fall into the sea."

"Wouldn't you have been killed in either case?"

"Aye, but I'd rat'er fall into the sea t'an have my bones broken. She couldn't 've heeled 'round to pick me up, but it would have been a clean deat' in the big water."

"Have you time to sit down a few minutes?"

"Aye—if you'll be so sociable wit' a common sailor."

"Aren't you an uncommon sailor?"

"No, ma'am, but I'm a good sailor. I could hardly help it, loving ships and the sea. I learned to pull wi't my fat'er on an oar as soon as I learned to walk."

I led him on to talk of his parents and his home in Norway and his voyages, and then asked him what harbor he was making for at last.

"I've never t'ought of the harbor. I've only t'ought of the sea. I want to sail it in my own ship."

"Do you think you ever will?"

"It's not easy for a fisherman's son wit' only a little schooling to be an officer, let alone own a fine wessel, but I'll try, I bet you."

"I bet you will too."

"I wrote to Ingar about you, Mrs. Reeve," he ventured presently. "Who is Ingar?"

"She is a girl in Stavanger. I t'ink I will marry her, if she'll have me, when I pass t'ere again."

"What did you tell her about me?"

Martin became abashed. "Maybe if I told you, you would t'ink I was too forward."

"You brought it up. Now you have to tell me."

"I wrote to her how all the sailors were so pleased to have you on the ship. She is not much to look at—the ship, I mean—and she can only go eight knots under full steam in good weat'er, but she is staunch and not a hungry ship, and we have a friendship crew."

"You were writing about me, not the ship, but tell me what does 'friendship crew' mean."

"It means the men sign on year after year, and stay toget'er, and get along fine. T'at is always sign of a good ship."

"Why were the men pleased to have me aboard? They must have generals and their wives sometimes—"

"It was different wit' the generals and their ladies. We could look at 'em, but t'ey did not look at us. I cannot say what I mean—my head is too t'ick. You do not hide yourself from us. You watch us like a child does—you want to come and help us heave on the capstan—you do not like to leave us to fight the gale alone. Do not t'ink we do not see and know. When you hear us laugh at somet'ing, your face tells us you want to laugh, too. When I had hung wit' one hand to t'at line, my arm almost yerked out my shoulder, and t'en caught it wit' my ot'er hand, what do you t'ink I heard?"

"I don't know—"

"T'rough all the noise of the wind and the wave, I heard you holler wit' joy t'at I was saved."

He wiped his forehead in a bewildered way.

"I'll say one t'ing more, t'en I'll go. Maybe I've said too much already. The generals and t'eir ladies are very fine folk, but you are a real princess."

"You're mistaken about that, Martin. I'm the daughter of a lieutenant who rose from the ranks—"

"You could rise from the gutter wit'out changing t'at. You are a princess because you are so beautiful. Somet'ing really beautiful speak to the heart as well as to the eyes. It make the heart leap up. I have had t'at happen when I see a ship out at sea, going somewhere, wit' men like me standing the watch, and ot'ers asleep, or eating or talking in the fo'c'sle. I don't know t'ose men, but I know t'ey are like me. I have seen it sometimes in the sunrise or the sunset, and t'ought of all t'at color, red and gold, and all t'at light, which would amount to not'ing unless people like me could look up and see it. We look at you and we feel t'at beauty is not reserved for rich people, like the beautiful pictures in their fine houses—we know t'at you won't toss your head and turn away when we look and look at you. And tonight you have stayed up late to tell me you are glad I am alive."

"No, I said I'm glad we are both alive."

"T'at is what I try so hard to say. Because you are a princess, you are not afraid to share wit' ot'er people—you are not afraid you won't have enough left—whet'er it is beauty, or kindness, or yust the air we breathe. My head is too t'ick to make it any clearer, and I go now—"

He shot up from his seat beside me, and I was not equal to the occasion.

"You would make a good captain, Martin. You would have a friendship ship. I'm sure you'll realize your ambition."

"Maybe—if I keep on believing it. It is easy to believe tonight. Sometimes it is pretty hard."

He touched his cap and went down to the main deck where he belonged.

I went to bed aglow with pride over winning such a tribute from a man 'fore the mast. It made me feel not only proud but lofty— and there was something about that I either could not or would not explore. I was glad I had told him that my own father rose from the ranks. I was sure, though, such a meeting should not happen again—for his sake, not mine. . . . But my dreams were curiously troubled. I seemed to mistake him for Lord Amherst until I saw that he was wearing a sailor's cap, and when he wanted to change it for the Captain's, I would not let him. The scene changed, and I was going to school again to Señor Professor, but he buckled on a sword and looked like Anthony. "Please don't speak of loving an Indian," he said sternly. "I know what you mean, but it doesn't sound right." Then Martin Nelson returned to the dream, wearing Papa's sword and walking proudly, but I ran and hid. . . .

I wakened rather low of spirits and for the remainder of the journey to Suez was prey to anxiety over the future. The adventure waiting for me there—to cross the desert on camelback to Cairo— was no longer a thrilling prospect; it would bring me that much nearer England and to a battle for which I felt inadequately armed. . . . I could not marry again. I could not dance consistently well

enough to win fame and fortune. The beauty that Madame thought
I might capitalize felt dimmed, despite Martin's tribute to it; except at rare moments, it was only the vivid prettiness I had seen
in the mirror of my room in Anthony's house, from where I had
been cast forth. I had forgot what beauty meant. Martin had
tried to tell me, in his dialectal English, but I had not believed
him or wilfully misunderstood. . . . I had waved and smiled at him
from my seat on the upper deck, but had not again spoken to him
intimately. To arrange it would be difficult; not to do so seemed best.

We anchored off the sun-baked port just before dark. Our trunks
were to be lightered into shore tonight; the passengers and their
handbags would follow in the morning. I was a little troubled about
the brief farewell I would take of Martin amid the flurry of dis-
embarking—it would seem so anticlimactic to that strange hour of
moonlight—but it would have to serve. I would make him a little
gift to remember me by. It would not be adequate to the occasion
but expedient.

Well, I could write him a letter, too—one for him to read when
I had left the ship. There was no harm in that. It would be perfectly
safe . . .

Safe. . . . The word formed on my lips as I stood looking into the
little mirror of my stateroom. My eyes became suddenly round.
My hand reached for the bell cord, but it fell away, and the same
continuing moment found me shutting the door behind me and
hurrying up the companionway. It did not matter tonight if I went
onto the main deck ordinarily closed to the passengers; port officials,
native dragomen, and porters busied there. I saw no one I recognized
but Mate Green.

"Mr. Green, could I speak to Martin Nelson?"

"He was going ashore. I don't know whether he's left—" The mate
stepped nimbly to the fo'c'sle companionway. "Nelson!" he shouted
above the din.

"Aye, aye, sir!"

"Break out. There's someone to see you."

Martin appeared in a moment, wearing clothes that reminded
me of Rene's. As he passed by a bucket of burning tar, I saw that

his blond hair was wetted down and his face had the scrubbed look that I remembered when Rene had emerged from behind the cottage soon after I had met him on the moor.

"Mrs. Reeve wants to speak to you," Mate Green told him, then walked briskly away.

"Yes, ma'am?" Martin was looking at me gravely, trying not to reveal—almost not to feel—any excitement.

"Can you come a moment to the passengers' deck?"

"You bet you."

The deck was deserted and dark except for the faint glimmer of the young moon. She had been old and sick when together we had seen her last.

"It's about time to say goodbye," I told him.

"I didn't t'ink you'd bot'er about it," he replied.

"I'm sorry we didn't meet again. We could've—if I'd had more of what you told me you needed to become a captain. Do you remember?"

"I yust said I needed to believe I could—"

"That's what I mean. It seemed such a long way from the passengers' deck to the fo'c'sle. Yet I went there tonight in just a few steps."

"It is a long way, Mrs. Reeve, by one way of t'inking."

"That's the way I've been thinking, but I stopped. You've made plans to go ashore, but it will only take a minute to give you something to remember me by—if you want it. If you do, I'll have something to remember you by."

"I'd like any little t'ing you want to give me. In port tonight I'll get somet'ing for you—"

"It's this." I put my arms around his neck and kissed him on the mouth.

I did not know what I had expected, when for so many days I had dwelt upon the distance between the passengers' deck and the fo'c'sle. For nearly four years I had been indoctrinated in that great expanse; once when I crossed the gulf with Manu in the mouths of cannon I had been wonderfully rewarded only to come to disprize the reward. Whatever I expected, it was not like this.

"Yesus!" he breathed—and the joy in my heart broke out of my throat in laughter.

"I'd like the same kind of gift from you."

He could not speak, but the strong arms that had balked Kali held me close, and I felt the beauty and bravery of his being in every drop of my blood, and the long hunger of my mouth was being assuaged.

"What were you going to do on shore?" I asked.

"Can I tell you the trut'? I wouldn't want to lie to you now."

"Of course."

"I was goin' to drink wit' the boys, and after while I was going to take an Arab girl to spend the night wit'."

"Would you rather spend the night with me?"

"Aye." He was able to say that only with a great heave of his chest and did not attempt anything more.

"Would you think it was wrong? If you do, I can't invite you."

"I could not t'ink it was wrong when you looked me in the face."

"I'm separated from my husband. I'll never see him again. Still his pride would be deeply wounded if this soon after our parting, I had a lover. He's a pukka sahib, and if he knew my lover was for only one night—and a man 'fore the mast—all his memories of me would be spoiled. Do you think anyone would know?"

"I'll do my best so no one will ever know."

"That's all right. There's always danger. I've one more question. Are you in love with Ingar?"

"Aye. To me she is the prettiest and sweetest girl in Stavanger."

"You were going to take an Arab girl tonight—she might understand that—but this would be different."

"You can be sure it will never come between Ingar and me."

"That's all I need to know."

The rest had been taught me aforetime. If there had been guilt in my heart, I would seek in vain for its cause, and would hope for the power to triumph over it, because my soul would confide its falseness. There was none, and instead, joy.

I had been wounded, but was again whole. I was alive without compromise, and I could give without stint. I did not know what

other women had become under man's dominion, but I knew myself. I was still the bestower of beauty, the custodian of the Mysteries, the priestess in the Circle of Stones.

TWENTY-SEVEN

THE day came that I was hurrying up the shady street toward Madame's house in Bath. Two months had passed since I had
said goodbye to Martin Nelson, certain now that he would some day
sail his own ship; equally elated, I knew of nothing to stop me
from winning fame and fortune on the stage. A housemaid I had
not seen before let me into the small stiff parlor I remembered well.

"'Oom shall I tell Madame is calling?" the maid asked with the
priggishness of her kind. I looked too pretty and too happy for good
to come out of it, she thought. What wonderful fun, I thought! No
doubt convinced that the *salon* was a den of sin, likely any moment
to be flattened with fire and brimstone, yet she would not trade
her job to be housekeeper to a clergyman. The more frequently and
severely she was shocked, the better she liked it. She was able to
see herself as Virtue incarnate, the devil lusting to get at her and
gnashing his teeth in vain.

"You may say it's Mrs. Lucy Reeve," I answered, quite sure that
the name would mean nothing to my old companions.

"Well, she's busy right now with Miss Jones, and anybody less
than 'Er Majesty 'erself would have to wait. But she'll be through
on the hour, and if I can tell 'er your business—"

"I want to take dancing lessons."

"In ballroom dancing? I'd thought you'd have learned that when
you was single. I don't 'old with no kind of dancing myself, but
ballroom dancing is better than some I could name, for young folk
only, the partners keeping at arm's length."

"Have you ever heard of the cancan?"

"That, I 'ave!"

"And the Dance of the Seven Veils?"

"Ow!"

"I want to dance them before Queen Victoria!"

The woman thrilled with horror, her eyes shining and her long, sallow face attractively flushed.

"And you look so young and innocent!" she cried. "I'm only the 'ousemaid, and 'tis not for me to express my opinion of what I see and 'ear. But things have come to a pass, I do say."

Rejoicing in my good deed as I sat in the waiting room, I was delighted with what I could hear from the *salon*. The Jones child must be a big girl now, but as obnoxious as ever, to judge from Madame's shrieking and her full-throated wails. When she finally emerged, I saw a lean creature of fourteen or so, with an extraordinarily homely but completely fascinating face. Butter would not melt in her mouth, just now, but the stone floor melted into air under her feet. Her flesh was knit with her bones in a way I had never seen in human form, yet defying description. Despite my heart's sudden heaviness over my own prospects, it leaped at sight of her. What wonders of growth and change lay in reach of human beings! What myriad forms of beauty with which to feed the hungry!

Occupied with herself, as are so many artists most of the time, she looked at me without seeing me. Then her eyes sharpened and she stopped.

"Who are you?" she demanded.

"Lola Montero."

"You used to take lessons right ahead of me. I never saw you because I never was on time."

"I can imagine."

"I thought you'd gone for good."

"Well, I hadn't."

"You're not going to try to be a ballerina—" Her eyes gleamed with murderous jealousy.

"Perish the thought!"

"You couldn't if you tried. You haven't got the body." She sighed and her eyes softened and became lovely to look at. "Well, I might as well tell you—not that it's any news to you—you're the most beautiful woman in England."

"In all England?"

"Maybe not. The most beautiful I've ever seen. Are you married?"

"Yes—and no."

"Have you a whole lot of lovers?"

"That's a secret."

"You must have at least one, if you're divorced. I never heard of a man committing adultery—what they do must be something else. Madame says I can't have a lover until after my debut, and if I get pregnant, she'll cut my throat. But you ought to see me as Cassandra, spurning Apollo."

"I'd love to."

"You can come in and watch me some day. No, I don't think you'd better. I'd try to be beautiful and forget to dance. That's why I mustn't ever fall in love with any of my lovers. I can only fall in love with Agamemnon, damn his eyes."

With that, she made a beautiful exit. I had no doubt she would be the toast of Europe before many snows.

I heard the swift, exasperated step of Madame. While my skin tightened and crept, she flung open the door of the *salon*, looked at me, and screamed.

"Lola! Papa Camille! Monsieur Lavelle!"

I had thought Madame would be a little tamed and less tall. I had feared that the old Chevalier had caught a croup and calmly died. I was sure Monsieur had found a better opportunity. Instead we were all four weeping in one another's arms.

"But I made a pronouncement," Chevalier Camille cried. "The beauty of Miss Montero is slightly more mature and definitely enhanced. I am sure that Monsieur Lavelle will agree with me it is one of the score most notable in Europe!"

"As for me—it is alone in the world!" Monsieur Lavelle replied, his forefinger brought in a fine sweep under his nose.

When we were seated in the *salon*, I told Madame and the two monsieurs a little of my recent history, then blurted out a question.

"Will you take me back?"

"My dear, if you only knew how we've missed you!" Madame cried. Then she began to talk with her old *élan*. "But, Lola, I warn you that England is changing rapidly. Have you noticed it since your return?"

"I came straight here from London—"

"William was a good enough king. Not knowing what to do next, he usually did the wrong thing—but he meant no harm. Now there is a young woman on the throne, very lovely of person, and who for three years was flirtatious and gay and human as I could ask. But in February she married an intensely good young man named Albert. Would you believe it, every stitch of clothes she wore at the ceremony was of British make?"

"Shocking," I said.

"From her shift to her veil, not a French thread! Already, at her table, the merest shadow of the risqué is *verboten*. We will all have to be so proper! It has already affected the length of our petticoats and will soon be reflected on the stage and in the very boudoir. Lola, has your husband merely kicked you out, or has he divorced you also?"

"I was going to ask him to divorce me—"

"Do not, for the love of God! If he does so on his own account, keep it dark as murder. When you are ready for your debut, let no one know that Lola Montero and Mrs.—whatever the name is—are the same person. A divorced woman will soon spell but one word to the Queen and her court and the setters of the tone—adultery. And do you think it would occur to anyone that the shoe might be on your husband's foot?"

"I just found that out from the Jones."

"In any case, if you become known as one—"

"There are always Brussels—Paris—Berlin—Warsaw—Munich—Vienna," Chevalier Camille broke in. "Stop frightening the little girl."

"I would like to make my debut—if it ever comes to that—in London," I said, when I had a chance.

"Of course," the old man told me kindly. "One's own country! One wants to prove oneself to one's own people. You shall, my dear."

"Monsieur Lavelle, play the fandango," Madame ordered. "We will see what four years of married life have done to her legs."

Both Madame and the old Chevalier thought it best that I should employ Spanish dances on which to improvise a beauty show. They would lend it more respectability if prudery became the fashion, and they were boldly flirtatious to start with. Taking lodgings at a respectable inn, I soon was immersed in lessons and practice, my life revolving about Madame's studio and its affairs.

Papa Camille had conceived the undertaking in a somewhat higher light than had Madame. My dancing must do more than display beauty of form and face and movement—it must not only excite but woo the audience and reflect the mystery as well as the passion of love. He soon discovered that when I danced unsmiling, with a dreamy, almost forlorn expression, the violence of the dance became strangely dramatic and the sensuous gestures and postures at once more modest and exciting. At the end of ten two-hour lessons, he and Madame had agreed this was the right track; with a hundred more—five months of intense study and practice—I should, with good luck, be ready to make my debut on the London stage.

"How are you fixed for money?" Madame asked.

"If I don't buy any clothes—and if I go back to the boarding house —six months from now I'll still have three hundred pounds."

"Your professional wardrobe alone will cost a hundred, and the two hundred you'll have left would be the barest margin of safety in undertaking a career. I don't want you even tempted to make an arrangement with some old roué. Moreover, I shan't have you dressing like a beggar or living with those old tabbies—you'll have a hard enough time keeping up your spirits as it is. Lola, you are a superb ballroom dancer, and I have more applicants for lessons than we can accept. You shall teach the young heifers for four hours daily in the waltz, the polka, the galop, and the minuet. For this you shall have a good lunch—Papa Camille is an inspired chef— and free instruction."

I was too happy to weep, as often I had been too sad; but Madame attended to it, and she, the old Chevalier, and Monsieur Lavelle kissed me solemnly.

"This is my Happy Isle," I told them.

It was quite true. It was my Garden of the Hesperides, where there was never fog or rain or snow; where every day was halcyon, and every soul that came or went was blessed.

I had an inkling that Kali might take angry notice of my joy, but no sword fell on my head or earth gave way beneath my feet that day, the next, or the one following. On the evening of the fourth day, when I was making my toilet for dinner, someone knocked excitedly on the door.

"It's Mr. Tucker," rose a flurried voice. Mr. Tucker was the proprietor of the inn, and usually as rosy and hearty as tradition required. "A gentleman's sent up his card, and he's waiting below."

"I'm not quite dressed. Will you put it under the door?"

"This 'ere's no card I'll ever lay on the floor. But if you crack the door, I'll hand it to you."

He did so, and I stood where I was, with the card in my hand, while the latch clicked and Mr. Tucker's heavy steps died away. The card read *Baron Lundy of Blackmoor*. I was trying to feel surprise. If I could regard Jeffery's return as a surprising event, it would have a different meaning. I need not then admit to its foreknowledge, which would be to confess a bond between us that only death could break.

TWENTY-EIGHT

TRYING to break out of a gray mist of feeling, I went to look in the mirror. Instantly I was reassured; as I rapidly continued my toilet, I was aware of a mounting excitement that did not befuddle me but was like a brisk, cool, breeze blowing across my brain. My eyes felt sharp; I was conscious of danger but exhilarated by it; my movements were quick and positive; there was a dark-red flush on my face. In place of the black dress I was wearing, fit for a governess, I put on a little green frock, almost too demure for evening

wear, with a white Lord Byron collar. In this I put the pearl Anthony had given me for a parting gift.

As I entered the parlor, Jeffery rose and bowed. I had thought
I had half imagined his resemblance to an eagle, but there it was,
more plain than ever. In this light his eyes looked a brilliant black.
The grace of his movements was at odds with the tension in his
face. I gave him a low bow.

"Why, Lucia," he said quietly.

"Won't you sit down, Lord Lundy?"

"Thank you."

He sat in one of the stiff chairs with horsehair seats and backs
that would not show dirt, beside a half-withered potted palm, and
amid other emblems of imitation elegance; his hat, gloves, and stick
lay on a rococo table with a marble top. Yet he lent distinction even
to this scene. Two stout, middle-aged women, who despite different features appeared almost indistinguishable from each other,
bustled in and sat down on the sofa across the room prepared to
strike some elegant poses: instead they quite forgot themselves
and sat perfectly still, their eyes and mouths rounded.

I had seen him, I remembered, four times before—once on the
street where I had met Rene; once in General Judson's house; once
in the theater where we had gazed by Prospero's magic into the
evil court of a pagan duke, the last time on the moors across the
quicksand. The new encounter was in the continuance of a pattern
of which he and I were the dominant threads. This was the fifth
time they had crossed, but they had never dissociated; they were like
two motifs in the pattern of a dance duet; when the dancers appeared to go different ways, always the dancing of one remained in
time and rhythm with the other. If in the intricacies of the pattern
they sometimes appeared lovers, sometimes enemies, their true relationship was to be found only in the finale, when the interweaving
of the two themes brought on the catastrophe. A third thread was
manifest in the web, crossing and recrossing both of the others in a
complex design, but without volition. In the dance, it took the form
of a marionette worked by strings in the partners' hands.

Since I had last seen Jeffery, I had received a letter from him.

At the time I had felt it fitted into the pattern; now I realized it was extraneous. I could hardly believe that Lundy of Blackmoor had written it.

"I received your letter," I told him.

"One of my reasons for coming here was to apologize for it. Not because it was beneath me—for that I must stew in my own juice—but because it was beneath you. The attack was unworthy of such an adversary. I was not in my right mind when I wrote it."

"How did that happen, Jeffery? I thought you were always in your right mind."

"On that day, a bird flew away." He stopped, looking startled and a little amused. "Excuse me—my mind wandered. I should have said that I had just suffered a disillusionment. I had been enchanted with a girl I had met in London—a girl completely different from you—tall, fair, with the high-bred beauty of the Norman. Her house is a very old one, as English houses go. But when I set out to propose marriage, I found that I could not. I was too haunted by you. That night I became befuddled with drink—a thing I had hardly thought possible—and in my pot valor I decided to get rid of you with a lordly letter of dismissal. Every version became more and more inspired—you saw the final masterpiece. Instead of a dismissal, it was a patent attempt to keep you from dismissing me— to goad you into sending back the money with a savage reply full of insults and accusations. In the morning I tried to retrieve the letter, but it was too late. I have since been able to smile over your making no reply at all and spending the money. But it's on the wrong side of my mouth."

I did not smile at all. I was steadying my voice for a question. I should know about what to expect for an answer, but wondered whether I could believe my ears. The women across the room could hear our voices and catch a few words—of course, that would make no difference to Jeffery. Well, I had believed my ears before. . . .

"What accusations, Jeffery?"

"Lucia, you recall my telling you about a little demon that follows me about and champions me fiercely. We found him a convenient metaphor, and I'd like to employ him again. If after my departure from the moor any accidents happened to either you or your lover—such as having a finger or toe caught in a door—I thought you would very likely accuse him."

I believed him without difficulty. "In a way of speaking, my lover did have his toe caught in a door. Not only his toe but both legs."

"You must mean that he walked into quicksand."

"Yes, the poles had been moved."

"You thought the poles might have been blown down by the wind and, in resetting them, I misplaced them. You could hardly think they had been moved deliberately, because the mover could not possibly know whether you or your lover would enter the aisle first."

"Rene mentioned that. It didn't carry much weight with me."

"Why was that, Lucia?"

"I was quite sure that the imp—shall we call him Young Berkeley, as opposed to Old Berkeley?—would expect Rene to enter first. It was a rather frightening place, even when the poles were in the right position. True, you were much more put out with me than with him. What had happened wasn't Rene's fault—he'd got in your way by accident—he was man enough not to get out of your way, but I think you were big enough not to hold any rancor against him. On the other hand, I'd decided to stay with him instead of going with you to Blackmoor Keep. So whoever of us entered the aisle first, you'd be satisfied."

"If Young Berkeley thought that, his malignant jealousy got the better of his judgement. The Frenchman is already lost in the Paris crowds dense as quicksand."

"I'm not, though. I'm still here."

"Yes—thanks to an unknown god." His eyes glowed as he looked at me. "When I saw you last, I was too deeply torn to have any strong grasp of the situation."

"Who might be the unknown god?"

"He's not in my pantheon. All of mine are unequivocally evil—even to their servants. He must have been one of yours."

"You're a deeply religious man, Jeffery—in your unspeakable cult."

"I'm as conscious of the mysteries as you are."

"I wonder if that is what marks you from thousands—perhaps millions of people who would like to follow in your footsteps," my mind was working swiftly and well. "When they are jealous, they want to kill; they would gladly take life for even a small gain. When they are angry, they want to hurt someone. There must be a dreadful lot of evil in almost all of us—the moment that it's sanctioned by authority—say, by a general's command to wipe out a city—how many of the soldiers turn into worse than wolves? Look at the great pogroms. Those people are restrained only by fear of retaliation. Faith like yours would strengthen them to act and even enhance their power to act successfully. The same thing is true of doing good. A good act is dangerous, too—most people flinch from it. But if they have enough faith in good, they gain not only courage but power to do it."

"You've stated a social fact that will be the cornerstone of the great evil societies of the future. In the meantime—in spite of the wide gulf between our philosophies—I want you alive in my world. That is true whether or not I win you. No doubt there are a few other people—women, of course—who could give my life as much meaning, but the chance of meeting one of them is extremely remote. I've tried to think it through, but in vain. It may be we are complements—but what is the whole? As human beings go, perhaps both of us are highly representative of elemental forces in dynamic relation. Can you say we are not linked in this world and, if it exists, the next? I can't."

The two women rose and with uneasy expressions went out. They could not have overheard enough either to trouble or entertain them; I thought they must have been frightened by the stillness in Jeffery's face and body and his grave, quiet tone. At least he did not look and act according to their notions of the nobility. Also he had remained unconscious of their existence, always a frightening thing.

"If you felt that way about me," I said, "what did you think when I married and went to India?"

"I took pains to investigate Colonel Reeve and was sure you would soon return."

"It's been four years."

"I passed them pleasantly and even profitably. I developed myself, and hastened the day foretold by a great Slav. Also, I have a new game to play."

"As profitable as mountain-climbing?"

"Not directly, but wonderfully exciting and educational. I want to tell you about it—but not here. Lucia, will you go with me to dinner?"

"I would like to very much—but I want to stay on neutral ground."

"I can understand your caution. We can go to Antoine's or—quite a different proposition—the Munichgarten. I have my coach—"

"I'm not dressed for Antoine's and if you'll condescend to the Munichgarten, I hope you won't mind going in a public cab. You see, Jeffery, I can't tell when I might provoke—indirectly, of course —Young Berkeley."

Antoine's was an elegant but dubiously French restaurant; the Munichgarten a plain but authentically German one. The customers here were almost altogether blond, blue-eyed, and in good flesh; the waiters were serious-looking mature men most of whom wore steel-rimmed spectacles. You could run your finger under the table without finding a speck of dirt; the smell was of tobacco smoke from long beautifully fashioned pipes, mixed with beer and cabbage. The laughter was louder than at a French restaurant and the jokes broader but less risqué; everyone beamed at everybody; even the English customers, after a few minutes of doing their national duty in the way of acting superior and reserved, broke down and became more jovial and noisier than the natives.

In the purveyance of music, this rathskeller, where it was all but impossible for a gourmet to spend more than five shillings at one sitting, surpassed every restaurant in the kingdom save other Germanic ones. The music was furnished by five adorable-looking men with whom I instantly fell in love, individually and collectively. None was under fifty. All had large mustaches, which, after dipping them in beer, they wiped vigorously with diaper-size handkerchiefs. All wore baggy trousers, although their coats and waistcoats were varied and dashing. To a man they had round bellies like a baby's, not one the discouraged paunch so common on middle-aged

Englishmen. A fat-fisted little man played the piano, his pale eyes glued on the notes; there were one bass violist, one flutist, and two violinists. As soon as they finished a piece, they talked amiably together, utterly oblivious of the audience, for about five minutes; then conferred briefly with the air of conspirators about to set off a bomb. In sudden amicable agreement, they nodded ponderously, rapidly sorted their music, the pianist poised his hands over the keys, the flutist fixed his fingers on the stops, the violinists held their bows like sabers, and the bass violist counted slowly, *"ein— zwei—drei."* At the third count, heavenly melody soared glimmering through the hall.

I, delicate and dark, Spanish-looking, so beautiful tonight that our waiter was beside himself with excitement, was no alien in this blond assembly. I would have liked to talk to Emil about his *Weib* and *Kinder;* I liked Bratwurst with boiled cabbage, beer, pumpernickel bread, and Limburg cheese. The other patrons looked fondly upon me; the fat herrs wished they could kiss me. But after one troubled stare, in which he was careful not to be caught, everyone avoided looking at Jeffery. That he was a great lord, no one could doubt; but no kin to old Count Von Kassel, in Bath to treat his rheumatism, and whom Emil pointed out to me. I wondered if Jeffery's companions were all dead, or had not yet been born. A lieutenant at the Barricades, a small, sallow-skinned Corsican named Bonaparte, might have made bond with him; he had told me about a Russian prince and a great Slavic philosopher in whom he had confided. I wondered what the Duke of Wellington, with whom he had a political connection, thought of him. Old now, the guns of Waterloo echoing but dimly, idealized by the nation and by himself, wanting to sit in the sun and believe that all was right with the world, he probably refrained from thinking about him at all.

What did I think of him? Knowing him better than anyone, unless it were some of his old servants, I conceived him through imagination and revery, not through thought. Why was I with him tonight? The answer seemed to be that I could not help myself—certainly every dictate of sanity would forbid me the company of one who had set a death trap in my path. But that answer was wrong. I was no chickadee charmed by a snake—I had come with him not in weakness but in strength. Ever since I had fallen in love with Rene, I had met Jeffery's challenges: through Rene— and his proxy, a Norwegian sailor—I had found either the courage or the need, or both, in some unknown relation. My intense fear of him was always exhilarating. When it tended to die away in passion for him, I drew into great danger. . . . I became intimate with death. . . .

"What is your new game, Jeffery?" I asked.

"I wonder if I can tell you about it, so you'll understand. My forefathers called it hawking—the common term today is falconry. The sport went into decline in Europe two centuries ago, when fire-arms became cheap and efficient, but it has never become extinct. I can't understand why I didn't take it up years ago. I have a spiritual bond with hawks and eagles."

"Can you fly with them yet?"

He smiled strangely. "Yes—again in spirit. Lucia, it is the most exacting, difficult sport—truly, it can be called an art—of which I know. I began in an offhand way, but soon became so fascinated that I abandoned almost all other pursuits and pastimes. The great market for falcons is Valkenswaard in Holland. There I bought gerfalcons, peregrines, goshawks and the like, and hired an expert hawker—a Dutchman who knew everything extant about training and managing the birds. Fool that I was, I thought I could leave the drudgery to him. I didn't know that a falcon worth its salt has to know its owner's voice, be able to recognize him at a quarter of a mile away, and hate, fear, and love him like a passion-ate woman."

"I wouldn't think the falcon would find any difficulty in your case."

"The largest and best falcons are invariably females. Few women on earth would be worth the trouble. I won't go into the infinite labor of training the devils—taming 'em without breaking their spirit. But at last, if all goes well, all the patience and labor is paid for a thousand times. It's wonderful enough to flush woodcock or snipe or grouse with your dogs, and see a peregrine overtake one of them faster than a greyhound overtakes a rabbit, and kill him in mid-air with one thrust of his talons. But you should see a gerfalcon spiraling up over a flock of wild ducks, then stooping like a down-pointed skyrocket. The duck she's picked out may be flying ninety feet per second, but the falcon calculates the angle of attack to the last inch. Those two streaks rush together and become one as by implacable doom. I wish I could show you a Greenland falcon being flown at herons in passage. They climb desperately and swiftly at sight of the killer, but it mounts in ever narrowing spirals until it's well above them, screaming in triumph, then stoops with incredible speed. Usually it binds its prey, and they fall to the ground together."

Jeffery had sat perfectly still as he talked, his eyes fixed on my face. These appeared large and handsome, intensely animate without being warm; I thought their expression might change with the modulations of his deep, male voice, but it never did. I, too, sat still, my spine tingling, my lips parted as though avid for his kisses. My brain was dizzy with voluptuous imagery. . . . The white heron flew high and swiftly, the sunlight trapped in her wings. Then the falcon came stooping, tearing off her feathers with his claws, driving their cruel barbs into her tender flesh, binding her fast in their downward plunge. Her body cushioned his fall. It was in a far, lonely place, where no fowler could despoil him of his prey. His great hooked beak closed on her throat. She felt an ecstasy of pain. . . .

Come with me, Jeffery. Let us make haste to the moor. You shall bind me to you as we fall. In a shadowy valley between the tors you shall consume me. . . .

But as I felt an ecstasy of pain, the round-bellied bass violist counted *"ein, zwei, drei"* and his four round-bellied comrades joined with him in an old Germanic folk tune, "I do not know why I am so sad."

"I believe it's a wicked sport," I said, the spell suddenly and completely broken.

231

"Not as potentially wicked as, say—mountain-climbing." I thought that his eyes had darkened as though a light behind them had been blown out.

"Do you see anything wicked about it?"

"Do you mean—employing the wings and the beaks and talons of one variety of birds to kill another kind? It's no different than using the noses and the swift legs of dogs to kill other animals."

"Dogs are willing slaves. They hunt for their masters. But falcons hunt for themselves, only to have their prey stolen from them. No, you just made it sound wicked—I don't know how. Perhaps men have no right to pursue birds in their own element, where God promised them safety except from other birds. A fowler stands on the ground and shoots at them, but the shot can't follow them when they dodge. You ride on the falcon's wings. I suppose it reminds me of desert men in India hired to kill other desert men, whom the sahibs themselves can't catch."

"The same thing occurred to me—in a broader way. I told you that hawking was educational. I was wondering how, when Europe again lies prostrate after a great war, a few men could go about ruling the whole world—making the whole world their mine, in which all the others would be blinded and put to work, worshipping them for it. They have only to turn loose the hawks on the herons until they are glad to find safety in the dark."

The thought was too horrid to hold, and I spoke quickly.

"You said one bird flew away."

"It was a huge gerfalcon, caught full-grown in Greenland. I paid a hundred guineas for her at the auction at Valkenswaard—a record price since the days of the great falconers. From the first she was utterly fearless and malign—attacking any living thing she could get at—and on me she vented the fury and hatred of her captivity. She would leap straight for my face, her talons spread, until the leash jerked her down. I tamed her partly by gentleness, partly by cruelty that she full well understood. She became, I believe, the premier falcon on earth. Her vision was incredibly keen. No matter how far away a duck flushed or a heron passed, at ranges no other falconer would believe, she would mark it down, pursue it with implacable ferocity, and, unless it gained shelter, kill it. Her speed was dazzling, and her stoop deadly accurate. Very rarely did she bind—when she had killed, she took a long low swoop over me, screaming in triumph, then sped like an arrow to her fallen prey. You know how a savage dog will take his master's hand between his teeth without scratching the skin? I could let Vivian come to my ungloved fist—"

"Vivian?"

"I named her after my mother, who was Welsh of the ancient house of Rhys."

"A pretty compliment to the bird."

"Both were complimented. Then it happened I invited to Blackmoor a French actress with whom I was deeply taken—I shall call her Madeline. Madeline did not care for hunting, so that I found myself neglecting Vivian—flying her only an hour or two every morning. She drooped and wouldn't feed, so I persuaded Madeline to come with me for a full day on the moors. We were alone with the falcon, and, in the course of that day, both of us became impassioned—partly, it seemed, by the beauty of Vivian's flights. Immediately after this, the falcon went on a rampage of killing. It was in the spring, and herons and rooks passed frequently, and snipe, ducks, and woodcock were everywhere—she would kill, let the bird fall, and dart after another. She followed a flock of pochard ducks, killing three as a wolf kills sheep. Her stoops were marvelous to behold. Her last kill was a gray goose almost out of sight in the sky—she struck it three times before it hit the ground. Then she hovered over me with a furious scream and raked away."

Jeffery lifted his glass of what he said was excellent Mittelaarst and wet his lips. I got the curious impression that he was steadying his voice.

"The last I saw of the bird," he went on, "she was a speck in the distance heading northwest. Whether she ever got back to Greenland, I don't know. I never saw her again."

"I've heard of canaries being jealous—and parrots—"

"I was closer to Vivian than to any dog I ever owned, or any human beings—except two—that I've ever known."

I wet my lips with common beer.

"What happened to Madeline?" I asked, in an idle tone.

"Almost at the very moment that Vivian disappeared, I realized what Madeline was. She was an imaginary you. She resembled you somewhat, both in appearance and personality—through some aberration on my part, she became your proxy. I couldn't bear to touch her again, or even look at her. I gave her fifty pounds and packed her off."

"That was the sum you sent me with the letter, evidently the usual consolation prize. When you first started to speak of it at the inn, you mentioned the loss of the falcon, as though you had confused the two incidents. Yet they must have happened a long time apart—"

"I lost the falcon hardly six months ago."

"There must have been a strong connection—"

"There was. That night I again wrote to you. Although I had found out your husband had been stationed in Poona, I didn't know whether he'd been transferred, so I made inquiries of your mother, at her new residence at Knightsbridge. She told me she was expecting a letter from you shortly that would clarify the matter. If I left my letter with her, she would forward it."

"You did so?"

"Yes."

"You're well acquainted with her?"

"I either know personally—or know about—everyone ever closely connected with you."

"Whatever was in the letter, my mother knows and has made as good use of it as she could."

"It was about falcons. Some of the finest in the world are sold in India, and I inquired as to the possibility of getting a cast of saker falcons from the Punjab. I may have mentioned seeing you and Monsieur Saint-Denis in Cornwall. It seems to me I did—but I'm not quite sure."

"Do you suppose, Jeffery, that you wanted my husband to know I had had a love affair with Rene?"

"Perhaps Young Berkeley wanted him to know."

"Jeffery, I want to ask the orchestra to play something."

"May I do it?"

"I'd rather. I want to speak to them anyway. I danced it with you once—in imagination. I'd like to know if it fitted you."

I rose in the next interval and after thanking the old fellows, I asked them to play "The Dance of the Perjured Nuns" from *Robert the Devil.*

"Vell, ve is all goot Cat'olics from Sout' Germany but Herr Lodberg, who is a good Lut'eran, but religion is one t'ing, and opera is anodder," the bass violist told me. "I don't t'ink His Holiness vould vant dem mixed up. So ve vill play dat vicked dance, because it is very fine moosic."

It was fine music—but it did not pertain in the least to Jeffery, Young Berkeley, or to Old Berkeley. I could have danced it as well with Rene.

"Have you anything more to tell me, Jeffery?" I asked. "If not, you can take me home."

"Will you come to visit me at Blackmoor?"

"It would be a fascinating adventure, but I can't."

"I'll take you down into the mine. It's warm and black as hell."

"I don't want to change gods."

"Do you understand that I won't give you up?"

"If so, I'd like to know what you intend to do."

"I'd tell you, if I knew."

"You said you wouldn't kill me."

"I won't kill you except to save my own life, or to take you with me when I die. To that I give my word."

"Are you going to make me wish I were dead?"

"I can't imagine you making any such wish—ever. But perhaps I can persuade you, finally, to join forces with me—body and soul. Oddly enough, I'm in no great hurry."

"When may I expect to see you again? Or I should say—when will you act again?"

"Perhaps not for a year or two. I've got a new cast of gerfalcons which look very promising. Also, I'm thinking of going to India to hunt tigers. But ultimately I think that you'll see that I'm your mate—in this and in all other worlds. You will yield to my rough wooing."

He rose like a falcon freed from the hood.

TWENTY-NINE

*T*HERE had been days of wind and rain, and sometimes fog that I thought must be an intimation of what death was like, and once in a while a sunny day to promise something better by and by. Hardy birds in plain colors, highly respectable, good-citizen birds that knew life was not a bed of roses, but that developed character, birds that went about their business and did not hold by pampering, remained with us; and so did some ruffian birds that took no moral satisfaction in the cold, rough weather but had not been permitted, for guilts that they well knew, to go south with the flighty songsters. They took another satisfaction though—in being just as low, impudent, and ribald as they knew how.

But my heart quailed when I thought of the colder climes, where the snow lay deep and still, and the brooks were frozen to the pebbles in their beds; where the heads of the pine trees bent with their white load and the tall oaks stood naked in the wind. There the owl could fly at noon, so dark were the days; but even when he dipped his beak in the warm blood of his slain, he had no spirit to sound his triumphant horn. There the wolves were saddened and wailed to the winter moon. Bears borrowed from death's great store of sleep to spare themselves the travail of cold and hunger; and the black-belled elk, bereft of his proud horns, plunged breast-deep in the drifts ere he grubbed his juiceless forage. The lean lynx, wild-eyed with hunger, crept from one frozen ambush to another. The hare cared little if he lived or died, if only he could be warm.

I do not know why I am so sad. But I did know, as the turned year brought winter to bay, then to savage, stubborn retreat. When sap flowed again, when the birds came back, when the cuckoo cried again, I must set sail from my Happy Isle. I was even now assembling my cargo—tricks and turns, pretty prancings, bows and postures and flirtatious acts, packaged in gay, spangled dresses, shawls, and little shoes. Madame was writing to the managers of the theaters in London, recalling old times to old-timers, instructing the newcomers as subtly as possible in the all-but-forgotten fame of Celeste Renalt, ere she sought engagements for a Spanish dancer of great beauty and promise. Monsieur Lavelle pounded keys or tooted or strummed late into night in the polishing of what he bravely called my "repertoire."

When one afternoon I had rehearsed the dances in costume from first to last, in the midst of his fervent praise Chevalier Camille broke into tears.

In this half-year I had not heard from Rene. Jeffery had set sail for India almost immediately after our dinner at the Munichgarten, and I wondered if he were fated to meet Anthony, there being tigers in the Western Ghats behind Poona. Late in March I received a letter from him, posted in Calcutta fifteen hundred miles from our drill field.

Beautiful Lucia,

I have just seen my first tiger wild in the jungle, the most splendid male creature I have ever beheld. He was with his mate, and I think that at last I have found a Roland for my Oliver. I shall follow him into his fastnesses, where I will slay him or, hardly less magnificent, he shall slay me. He is gold and black, the color of heaven and of hell. The moors shall know me no more until our account is settled.

I am in love with his sinuous mate. I have seen only three other living beings I regard as beautiful, two of whom were named Vivian. Do you think she will return my passion? How can she help herself when I have slain her lord who alone, until now, is worthy of her? How did the sphinx come into being except by a lion's slaying of some beautiful woman's lover and taking her for his own? Is not the centaur the fruit of a great passion between a hero and a wild mare on the desert?

What if she sees me in the arms of a dark woman of the hills, small and beautiful of body, whom I mistake for someone else? There will be such killings as her villagers, created for her sustenance and amusement, have never dared dream!

I write this in camp, and shall send it out by a runner. If it does not arrive, it will be because Kali or her lord have lain in wait for him by the footpath—that I shall know tomorrow. If he is slain I shall take it for a sign. I wish you were with me here, in the firelight, breathing this sultry perfumed air, listening to the almost inaudible sounds, beholding the leaping shadows and the sinister pattern of moonlight woven by the rifts in the canopy of boughs. If you were here, the tiger and his mate could go their way in peace! But when you receive this—if you do—you will be preparing for your debut on the London stage. You will soon be showering your beauty like largess on the half-blind mob. How can you be so untrue to me, who wants every jot and tittle of it for my own?

your faithful
Jeffery

My letters, like accidents, were wont to come in threes. Jeffery's arrived on the cycle-moon; as she grew fat and then full, my fears were allayed. The letter that came to Madame of my concern brought wonderful news. Mr. Lumley, manager of the Royal Theater, offered Lola Montero a between-acts performance in the latter part of April—if she pleased his patrons, he would engage her for the remainder of the season. On the second night of the waning moon I had bad dreams—perhaps no worse than had visited me a hundred times before without ill omen. There was no letter in my key box when I set out for the salon; and in the clear, lukewarm spring sunlight, starting sap and kindling seeds, the nonsense passed out of my head.

But the courier was late, and again I met him on the sidewalk. Again he was pleased and a little excited—but the letter he was fishing out could not be from Jeffery—I had heard from him about two weeks before. "All the way from India," he told me, handing it over. I had forgotten that the Indian mail arrived at two-week intervals.

Although I recognized my husband's handwriting, I did not open the missive on the street. I carried it, its lips still locked, to our dressing room. There I opened it slowly and carefully, showing I was highly interested but not in the least frightened. The handwriting was neat—the lines and margins orderly. Whatever it had to tell me was three months over the dam. All right, I'm ready. . . .

My dear Lucia,

To my great regret, I am appealing to the Court for a divorce from you a mensa et toro *on the ground of adultery.*

The corespondent I am naming is one Martin Nelson, the boatswain on the Lord Clive *which carried you to Suez. I had not asked you to be continent and did not expect it after you had broken all ties with India, but I cannot help expressing regret that you did not remain so until you were united with your French journalist, of whom I have happened to learn. Also, I must express pain that you chose as partner for your first adventure a seaman who boasted among his fellows of his conquest of the wife of a servant of the Queen.*

True, the evidence I submit to the Court is only the signed statement of an English gentleman that he saw the said Nelson enter your stateroom, which you could very easily contest, but I hope you will keep the promise that you made me, and permit the divorce to be granted by default.

> *I remain,*
> *your well-wisher,*
> *Anthony Reeve, Colonel,*
> *2nd Wiltshire Rifles*

There was a small coal fire in the grate that would instantly turn the page into soft, black dust. Instead I went to the old Chevalier's room and knocked on the door. "What is it, my little lovely one?" His voice was sweet to me as rain after bitter drought. I handed him the letter.

He sat down, put on his glasses, and, reading a sentence at a time, translated it into French. When he had finished, he beckoned to me.

"Will you sit on my lap, Lola?"

I did so, and he held me across his breast as though I were a child. I looked up into his worn face, and its beauty brought to me what pain could not—a plenteous stream of tears. He did not move or speak until the paroxysm had passed.

"Your papa died young?" he asked.

"Yes."

"My little daughter died young. Such a lovely thing for death to take! But the river of the days flowed on; and again I tasted wine and laughed at a jest and loved, and was loved, and looked without bitterness on other little girls playing in the sunshine. Indeed the sight of them returns her to me, and without tears. I make bond with every one; I would give my life for every one, not from any heroism—of which God knows I have none, being too old and fat— but in hatred of the death that took my own.

"Now this letter. It is written by a good man who is self-defeated. How could he write it to one as lovely as you are? Because he can't believe in your loveliness. Poor fellow, he is blind. He throws up at you that you had a lover before you married him, and is aggrieved that you did not tell him. What in the devil's business was it of his? If nine out of ten men look well at themselves, they will know they have married above them. By and large, we are bastards compared to our women.

"Also this letter-writer is aggrieved because you gave your favors to a sailor. Is it any of his business, when he had kicked you out? He is a servant of the Queen, but does that of itself make him superior to a servant of mankind fighting the gale? The sailor boasted among his fellows? I do not believe it! You would not have accepted the embraces of a scoundrel—your eyes are too clear. It may be that he told some intimate in great happiness and pride, and that man was not to be trusted with such a lovely secret. If at the time, when you looked into his eyes, you felt that you were doing right, never doubt you have done right. If he proved base, you have still done right in your own sight. I have lent money to my friends who came to hate me for it. I pity them, but do I wish that my heart had been harder? What good is a hard heart? I might as well have six feet of hard ground over my head.

"You will be leaving soon, Lola. My days will never be as warm again. But I will look upon the pretty young girls who come to take lessons, each with such potentiality of beauty, and I will still be moved by that miracle in Eden, re-enacted when any scrubwoman gives suck to her babe. Now I will seize upon the old man's privilege to give advice. Stick by the people. Do not turn against them for their blindness, their meanness, their selfishness, and their cruelty. Do not forget they are halfway in the devil's power. All they have to fight him with is that miraculous, unweighable, immeasurable thing, the human spirit—without it they are worse than wolves and tigers—yet they have won countless magnificent victories. The conflict goes on, appalling to contemplate; the tide of the battle ebbs and flows; we can see such little gain since Genghis Khan turned Eastern Europe into a slaughterhouse; and that little we may soon lose. You, Lola, have a magic sword—beauty. It is another name for the human spirit, made visible or palpable or audible in millions of people, and in you made strangely plain to all who have eyes to see."

He paused and I spoke.

"My word went forth from me—that's the translation of a Hindustani idiom—to reward those who love me, cast down those who hate me, and bring to those who wound me the torment of Jaranna."

"What's wrong with that? It will serve them all right. You are a woman, not a saint. If you reward those who love you, those who hate you will be cast down by what they have lost, and those who wound you will be tormented without the lifting of your hand. But stand up for yourself and your own. Evil is abroad in the world—there's much fighting to be done. Now I will tell you what!"

"What?"

"Go and teach your class to waltz most beautifully. Think of the joy they will give their clumsy partners! I am very pleased with my philosophizing, and I will sit awhile in the sun, thinking of all whom I have loved, and who loved me. And at one o'clock you shall sit down to *potage d'oignon, lapin et choux verts, et pâté d'amande!*"

THIRTY

THE third letter of my three was a command to appear in court to answer a suit for divorce.

I did so, and standing before a wigged and robed judge, I admitted committing the charge. But I would not be branded with a white-hot iron; I would not be whipped by a beadle or stoned by the folk. I was only instructed that my husband's suit for divorce *a mensa et toro* was hereby granted, and I was never in his lifetime, under pain of the charge of bigamy, to marry again. The judge himself was sorry that so young a woman must be forbidden the joys of matrimony, but as ye sow, so shall ye reap. Moreover, by my rash and immoral act, I had deprived my husband, as long as he lived, of the same joys.

I went away, and after awhile the shapes and shadows and silences of the courtroom passed out of my fancies and finally from my dreams. In the dim scenes of sleep, the people again were human beings, not robed and wigged monsters who spoke with human voices but who were really ministers of death and doom. Far at sea now from my Happy Isle, I went in hidden fears and tremblings to see Mr. Lumley, manager of the Royal Theater, who seemed pleased enough to see me.

"This is the best theater in England, and my public demands the best in the way of performance," he told me. "When they get it, they are highly appreciative. When they don't get it, most people show disapproval in a genteel manner. However, the London theater has not entirely escaped from the rowdyism of my grandsire's day. I make bold to call it rowdyism, in spite of its being perpetrated by gentlemen of name and frequently of title. Have you heard of the Corinthians?"

"I think so, but don't remember—"

"A number of fashionable bucks call themselves so. Their leader is the Earl of Lambeth. They are likely to take omnibus boxes at every change of bill, or when a new actor or actress is to perform. If they are pleased with a performer, his or her fortune is half made. If not, they express their disapproval so emphatically that he or she is forced to leave the stage."

"What do you do in that case, Mr. Lumley?" I asked.

"I keep a male and female stand-in who can substitute for any performers thus forced to retire—and at no trifling cost," he answered. "Frankly, I don't think it's fair for a dozen or two gallants, regardless of their high station, to appoint themselves arbiters for the entire audience, but I know better than to defy them. We are changing our bill on the night you come on, so I am expecting them to appear in force. However, we have a good play, the first act of which should put them in a pleasant humor. Anyway, Madame Renalt would not have sent you here unless you were an excellent performer, and your personal beauty should carry you a long way."

When I had rehearsed in costume the two dances I had chosen— improvisations on the beautiful sevillanas and the more difficult and dynamic fandango—Mr. Lumley's fears were put at rest. I asked one strange and, as far as my common sense went, foolish question.

"I have the honor of knowing Lord Lundy of Blackmoor, at present in India. Is he one of the Corinthians?"

"I cannot say that he ever was, although he sat with them occasionally. Certainly he never partook in their sports. If he is a friend of yours, I'm sorry he's not in London. His support would be of great value, and his approval a fine feather in your cap."

The bill was printed, in which the management declared its pride in presenting, between acts, "Lola Montero, the famous Spanish dancer, fresh from her latest triumph in Madrid, appearing in England for the first time in her native dances." Backstage for three previous shows, I took lessons in its cant and custom, and learned my way about in the wilderness of painted cloth. When the players found me sincerely interested in their "triumphs," they made me their intimate and gave me tips for my virgin flight.

Truly they were the most charming company I had ever met. None were dancers to be put in the shade by my own soon

243

"triumph." All were "wedded to the theater" and loved their spouse to distraction, regardless of her frequent coldnesses, infidelities, and failure to support them in the style to which they were accustomed. I wanted to be one of them.

The musicians and the stagehands took to me kindly. On the great night, they gave me many a good wish, and the director as well as the stars in the company kissed me. Through a peephole in the curtain I watched the audience assembling—that dread court whose laughter or tears or clapping hands were the players' palm, whose coldness froze the marrow in their bones. One actor, who gave the impression of being boonfellow with the nobility, announced the arrival of various lords and ladies. However, he was behindhand on the up-to-now sensation of the evening. The news whispered up from the orchestra shot an electric thrill through everyone on the stage. Entering a box with his mistress, Countess Meran, and the Duke of Beaufort, was the darling of the courts—the rage of Europe —the master pianist Liszt.

Two omnibus boxes on opposite sides of the theater remained vacant until the curtain bell. Suddenly they filled with the best bucks of London—many of them of noble lineage, all rich, setters of the fashion, patrons of the sports, formidable roués. Foremost among them was the Earl of Lambeth, easily recognized by his small body and big beard. These were the Corinthians, whose verdict hundreds would await before daring to cheer or jeer.

If I pleased them, my fortune would be half made, so Mr. Lumley had said. He would be horrified to know that I was not going to try. Instinct warned me that they were my natural enemies, the foe against whom I must stand up for such as Thomas Riley; and if I truckled to them, I was doomed to defeat. The terror in which some of the players held them made me all the more defiant. In my kindling heart they represented my mother—Lady Kirk—Mrs. Terrance—Captain Henry. The issue that I had always felt so strongly, but could not clarify in thought, had never seemed more clear-cut.

The curtain rose on *Money,* one of Lord Lytton's best plays. The audience was immediately captured, and the Corinthians appeared enthralled. "You won't have no trouble, Miss Montero," a veteran scene-shifter told me as I waited in the wings. "Them lords is in a fair good fettle." Hearty hand-clapping with some shouts of "Bravo!" and whistles from the back benches, rewarded the troupers at the close of the first act. For about five minutes the gentlemen and ladies in the choice seats stretched their legs and took refreshment; then the curtain bell rang again. I thought of Papa—Manu—Rene—Martin Nelson—Madame and Monsieur and the old Chevalier. Feet clumped; a rustling murmur came and went in dying waves, then abruptly ceased. The director of the orchestra poised his baton.

I came on the stage in a dead silence, looking about as though at an unfamiliar scene. I was in Spanish peasant dress; in one hand I had a pouch made out of a red kerchief; on one shoulder I carried a basket of fruit. This I put down with a sigh, and, tempted by a bunch of grapes, began to eat them, spitting out the seeds. The orchestra began to play very softly a gay Spanish air. I cocked my ears, took a few dancing steps, and then untying the kerchief, took out castanets and slipped them on my hands. The music dimmed out; then recommenced with the first chord of the sevillanas.

I did not realize the instant that I began to dance it, but in a moment knew perfectly well that I was dancing better than ever before. . . . I was dreaming of a young and beautiful bull-fighter who had his pick of the highborn señoritas, and scorned to look at a peasant girl. I was forlorn but torn with hopeless passion; in vain I displayed my charms; I promised him such a night of love as he had never dreamed; then I grew angry at his blindness. . . .

Almost from the first measure I had felt the good will of the main part of the spectators. In a few minutes more I had won something more than that—their growing and excited joy beating up to me in what seemed palpable waves; they were yearning to me, and I was in an ecstasy of surrender to them. Yet I remained conscious of the enemy, watching with cold, malign eyes. I was nearing the climax of the dance when he struck.

"Stop the show!" The shout rose from the omnibus box occupied by Lord Lambeth and about ten of his henchmen. Immediately all

of these and the Corinthians sitting opposite took up the cry; and their toadies throughout the theater made it their cue to hiss and cat-call. Then the nobleman himself arose and repeated the command in a stentorian shout. White-faced in the wings, Mr. Lumley signaled frantically to the orchestra. Flushed with fury, the leader lowered his baton. I stood still in the sudden silence, but my arm was at my side flexed as though to return a blow.

"Ladies and gentlemen," Earl Lambeth continued in a far-carrying voice. "This performer is not a Spanish dancer recently from Madrid. She's an Irish girl from Bath named Lucia Riley; and has just been divorced for adultery by her husband, a brave officer and gentleman in India. This audience has been swindled."

For a long-drawn second the audience appeared paralyzed by amazement. Then in the crackling air a woman screamed; and through the hissing and hooting the Corinthians began to shout "Get off the stage!" Not only their lick-spittles but some of the people whom I had captivated now turned on me, some to display moral outrage at an adulteress, others to help trample one who they thought was down. But I was not down. As the shouting spread and loudened, I did what I had planned to do in the event of attack.

I picked up my pouch, sat down on a make-believe stone bench under the imitation palm, and got out a Spanish cheroot, a "property" for my encore. I lighted it with a friction match, and since I had occasionally smoked with Manu, I was able to give every indication of absorbed enjoyment in it. I pretended not to see Mr. Lumley gesturing frantically from the wings. Since the uproar continued to increase, I was sure he would make his appearance in a few seconds more.

Presently he emerged, waving his hand for silence. "Silence, silence!" shouted the Corinthians, triumph sweet in their mouths. The crowd instantly stilled, hungry to hear every word of Mr. Lumley's pronouncement.

"Ladies and gentlemen, I will personally investigate the charge made by his lordship and his friends," he declared. He turned to me and spoke in a tone of self-righteousness. "Miss Montero, as you call yourself, is it true that you are Irish, not Spanish, and the divorced wife of an officer?"

I answered loud and clear with a saying made famous on the English stage.

"Yes, but I didn't think Jemmy Twitcher would peach me."

The original line from *The Beggar's Opera* had been spoken innocently enough at a revival of the old play in London many years before. At that particular time Lord Sandwich, one of the king's ministers, was trying to crush the people's hero, John Wilkes, who was his own former companion in debauchery. In smug rectitude Sandwich had exposed some privately printed pornography of Wilkes's invention that had been sent to him in trust. When the audience of that day heard the line, so applicable to the topic on everyone's tongue, it gave forth a bellow of joy that almost lifted the roof. Lord Sandwich was then and there dubbed "Jemmy Twitcher" and called so to the day he died. It was forever a tribute to real, not counterfeit, English sportsmanship and born of their high sense of justice. Ever since then the line had been remembered as a crushing rebuke to hypocrisy.

At least a hundred people in the present audience got the point and gave forth a joyous roar. This hundred was already held in great respect by people sitting near them, and these picked up the laugh and spread it far and wide. Although few of the new laughers understood the joke, they perceived it was at the expense of the Corinthians, whose heavy hand they had begun to resent, and who now, like a cobra fighting a mongoose, had lashed out too far.

"Lola, you're all right!" came a great shout from the benches.

It caused another laugh, and a fat gentleman in the pit saw his chance to win one for himself.

"Lucia, me love, I'm Irish, too, and the saints bless ye."

"What have you got to say now, Jemmy Twitcher?" an old gentleman piped shrilly from a box. This inquiry was instantly popular; it was repeated with variations all over the theater. "Come on, Jemmy, make us another speech!" "Jemmy, has the cat got your tongue?" Then a big, bull voice, "Let me teach him how to talk, the dirty sneak."

The sallies were greeted with jubilant roars rising above a continuous low ripple of laughter with an effect curiously like high waves crashing on a beach amid incessantly boiling surf. But the thrilling storm slacked off when a soldierly figure in the front box rose and called, "Atten-*shon!*" At least a dozen soldiers or ex-soldiers or would-be soldiers repeated the command with severe glances at the frivolous. These instantly sobered; presently all eyes were fixed on the tall, gray, middle-aged man standing stiffly as on parade.

But the people's faces were solemn without being long. They were ready to hear an authoritative opinion on this matter; however, it had better be in accord with their own opinion! If he betrayed the trust they were putting in him, I thought they would tear him verbally limb from limb.

"Ladies and gentlemen, like my friend in the pit I, too, have Irish blood in my veins!"

This was received with a shout of approval. "Good for you, General!" someone bellowed.

"But even if I hadn't, I'd like to ask why a British audience should object to a British subject dancing Spanish dances as beautifully as we've just seen. That's the kind of thing—failure to honor our own —that causes artists to take foreign names. I think I speak for us all when I bid the Corinthians, or whatever those gentlemen call themselves, to either stop interfering with the show or take themselves off!"

A gale of applause rose, punctuated by lusty shouts of "Throw 'em out!"—"Give 'em the chuck!"—"Rout out the rascals!" But it fluttered down to deep silence when the speaker raised his hand.

"As to Miss Montero's past misfortunes, we don't know the circumstances, and it's not in accord with British justice to hold them against her, let alone to voice them publicly," he went on. "For my part, I wish her every success she can win!"

This was solemnly received except for one irrepressible voice from the gallery.

"For my part, sweetheart, I'll take the old bugger's place."

Mr. Lumley had signaled for a roll of drums, which was given with great dash. When he had caught the audience's attention, he spoke in the elegant but far-carrying voice of an old showman.

"Miss Montero, the verdict in your favor is overwhelming. Do you feel able to go on with the performance?"

"Give us a dance, you darling," a woman cried.

I could only nod my head to her, in grave danger of breaking into tears. The audience seemed to realize this, and fond, happy laughter rose up to me in a warm tide. I peeled off my peasant dress, revealing a richer costume glittering with sequins, put on a mantilla in place of my headcloth, and sounded *el redoble* with my castanets. The orchestra began the first magnetic strains of the fandango.

No matter how badly I might dance, I would have still charmed the throng. Instead, its lover and beloved, I became a lambent flame.

THIRTY-ONE

IT was incredibly wonderful to be kissed and hugged by my fellow performers, beaming musicians, and complete strangers. It was marvelous fun to watch Mr. Lumley's anxiety to get my name on a contract, and see him turn pale when three rival managers, ostensibly coming to congratulate me, warned me in undertones that haste made waste. It was sweeter than honeycomb to hold court in the wings to the great as well as to the humble, and yet never forget that it was the latter from whom I held fief.

More notes than I could read, mainly written on programs, were brought up by the ushers. The number of johnnies who offered to escort me home had been unequaled since the last appearance of Charlotte de Hagn. A countess gave me her flowers; and a quaint old fellow presented me with a shamrock, along with a heart-warming Irish blessing. Then the whole backstage throng was electrified by the sudden, dramatic appearance of a tall, thin, green-eyed, spectrally pale young man, with an unbelievably high forehead and flowing golden hair. "Liszt!" the sibilant whisper rose.

The men gaped as at a visitor from another planet, and the women were in danger of swooning.

I gave him a deep bow. He replied, and taking my hand kissed it with histrionic but indescribable grace.

"You must come soon to Paris, Aphrodite," he told me. "That is the only Olympus for such as you and I."

If the words were theatrical, his voice rang with sincerity. Then he bowed to the stunned spectators and walked dreamily away.

After midnight I was carried off to supper by about eight young Oxonians, holidaying in London, all of us packed into the coach of one of the more affluent. We went to Dolly's Chop House where we ate prodigious steaks, drank gill-ale, and sang "The Bride's Lament," "Widdecombe Fair," and other melancholy ballads, making very large and happy hours of the so-called small ones. When I gave them a Hindu lullaby, an ethnology scholar came forth with what all the young men considered a brilliant suggestion. Since I had lived in India, no doubt I knew that polyandry—being polygamy on the other foot, as he explained to the less learned—was practiced and completely proper in nearby Tibet. What if their whole band should marry me and take me back to Oxford to reign over their diggings? A law-student, seconding the motion, said that since polyandry was not recognized in England, the arrangement would not get me into trouble with the judge.

Declining this handsome offer, I settled for two rounds of goodnight kisses. When I wakened at noon, the pages brought up a full score of bouquets and a brimming platter of letters and calling cards. Many of the notes proposed invitations to after-theater suppers, and a few hinted at future friendships of pleasure and profit to both the writers and myself. Three were from ladies, all of whom wanted to be the first to present me—of course, in my role as a Spanish dancer—to London society. Since Madame had told me what this meant—being either patronized by the Lady Kirks for no fee at all or treated like a lackey for two pounds—I thanked my gods for the ability to decline. One letter, long and rambling and smelling of midnight oil, proved by a cipher concealed in the apocalypse that Lola Montero was the real Whore of Babylon. The rest were bonafide offers of engagements in England or abroad.

Remembering Mr. Lumley's voice and expression when he had questioned me on the stage, I appeared quite stupid in rejecting his advice to accept a "modest" salary, "best in the long run for both of us," and insisted on a handsome one for as long as the iron was hot. "That's the way it goes," he told me with an air of resignation when we had signed the contract. "You would think that artists had diamonds to sell, instead of God-given gifts. Except for us managers, they would be born to blush unseen."

I was no desert rose in the nights and moons to come. I gave thirty performances in various London resorts before taking off for Belgium; then in a great theater in Brussels I danced "Eve of Waterloo" in romantic waltz time, contrived if not composed with the help of the maestro, containing such sound effects as a cart rumbling over a stony street and with a stunning finale of cannon fire. If a long way from art, it thrilled the patriotic burghers, and was my mainstay in Ghent, Antwerp, and Liége. Turning southward with the birds, at Luxemburg I danced before the Grand Duke. Setting no world on fire at Metz, I did wonderfully better at Strasbourg, and raised the roof in Geneva. I loved all these cities in the direct ratio to their love for me.

Steadfastly I kept in mind that art, in its narrower definition, was not my business. I gave the people what they wanted from me— thrills old as the earth, light and warmth and beauty of a sort that any parlormaid or porter could understand. I wooed the galleries and took my chance on the boxes. Half of my success was my sense of sharing with the audience every movement and feeling, no matter how I made believe to be miles away. The throng was never just so many ticket-buyers. Seeing through Martin Nelson's clear eyes, I knew them for people like me, as the crews of the passing ships had been men like him. They liked pretty music, not too deep, as I did; they loved life and they hated death. Beside them I took my stand.

Turin—Milan—Venice—Trieste—and over the mountains lay Vienna! In all of these old and noble cities I made friends with fellow players and sometimes with artists of great note. I never dreaded a journey to a new Troy; the trip itself was an adventure in fresh scenes and companionships. I was too excited to be lonely in most of the many hours that I was alone. I made no arrangements with affluent admirers, regardless of their titles or degrees, and I was not lucky enough to fall in love except briefly and idolatrously with Robert Schumann, whom I met in Leipzig and whose passions were already engaged.

To the greatest and noblest of the continental cities, my feet did not find their way. I had not forbidden them to go there nor knew any good reason they should not; it was as though we were a lugger trying to cross a bar in a heavy wind, tacking in only to fall off.

Indeed my whole attitude toward Rene was unreasonable and tricky. He was no longer an "obscure" journalist—often the leader in *La Républicaine* was by his fiery pen—and if I asked six Frenchmen in succession as to his whereabouts and condition, I would no doubt be told. If his door were still locked, which was highly probable, I could come and go without our setting eyes on each other. If it had somehow come loose, I need not see it; certainly he would not call my attention to the fact. I would have to go myself and test the latch. . . . But I could not bear to think of his coming to the theater, his face merely one of hundreds of dim circles, then going his way in silence. On the other hand, if I discovered him there I would dance for him alone.

I was playing a somewhat different game with regard to Jeffery. In the course of every extensive conversation with an Englishman or a titled European, I mentioned his name once in a casual way. Thus I confessed before my gods my concern with him and showed them I was ready to hear any news of him that they desired. However, I never made any direct and vigorous inquiry, lest they send me some I did not want to hear. I recognized the process as a kind of pooja, stemming from guilt, fear, and erotic excitement. By the same token I confessed to myself an intense preoccupation with him, most of the time eclipsed by other interests, sometimes like something quite lost or forgotten, but to which presently I would turn a little corner of thought or feeling and behold again. There was enough terror in it that I could not breathe quite peacefully until his name was said and its sound died. I wondered if everyone had a hidden lust and walked a tightrope between desire for its fulfillment on one side, fear of punishment on the other, with black guilt gaping below.

In the great cosmopolitan city of Geneva I thought nothing, at first, of meeting a French actress calling herself Mab de Lille. I had met a score of her ilk behind the scenes; and because she was a bright blonde, the fact dawned on me rather slowly that her face and body resembled mine in a remarkable degree. Watching her act, I saw that her facial planes and expressions were enough like mine so that people with good eyes might mistake us for sisters. When I was dancing, she, too, perceived our resemblance, and waited, pleasantly excited, to greet me in the wings.

"You're really beautiful while I'm just pretty," she said wistfully, "still we might be kin."

"What's your real name?"

"Susanne Millard. I was born in Lille."

"Mine's Lucia Riley. Lille's a long way from Limerick. Still—"

"Did your papa travel a good deal? I'd love to be his bastard daughter."

"I'd love to have you be. He fought at Waterloo, but straightway went to Ireland."

"Why, that's perfect! I was born in 1816—your papa could have got to Lille in a day's ride. Is he nice? Mine isn't one little bit."

"He was awfully nice."

Meanwhile a dim gleam of intuition was brightening in my brain. Jeffery had spoken of a French actress whom he chose to call Madeline. He had entertained her at Blackmoor and had taken her hunting with his great falcon Vivian, and they had made love in the grass. Vivian had run amok and "raked" away. He had sent Madeline away because . . .

I wondered if Mab's thoughts, like mine, were wandering far.

"Let's have supper together after the show," I suggested.

She gave me a deep, wondering glance. "Let's not ask anyone else," she said quickly.

After our last bows, we deserted our good companions and sneaked away to a nearby supper parlor. Her face was beautifully flushed, and I was sure that she, too, was waiting only for the right moment to reveal herself.

"There's no chance of my being your half-sister," she confessed, when we had ordered a wienerschnitzel and a bottle of Rhine wine. "I was born a year too late. It would have been so nice—I couldn't resist the white lie."

"It's a wonderful compliment, especially since you made yourself out a year older than you are."

"I have one sister—in a Brussels brothel—and no one else to speak of. Still—there may be something between us. I may be mistaken—anyway it may not be important."

"I think it may be very important. I think you're the girl whom Lord Lundy spoke of as Madeline."

"And you're the one he called Fata Morgana. I thought so at first sight of you, and when I saw you dance I became almost certain."

Her eyes had grown big.

"I'm so glad we found each other!"

"Oh, yes. Yet I can hardly believe it. You see—I knew long before Jeffery did that I was only your stand-in. He took me to Blackmoor in your place. Well, I thought by now you'd be either his wife—" Mab paused.

"Or—?"

"His mistress—"

"Or—"

"I didn't mean—"

"Yes, you thought there was a third possibility. I saw it in your eyes and heard it in your voice. What is it, Mab? I think we must be completely honest."

"I thought if you were still alive, you'd be one or the other."

"Why did you think that?"

"He was madly in love with you. Madly is an overworked word as applied to love, but in this case it seems the right one. Also he's the greatest lord I ever saw. He makes Louis Philippe look like a straw man."

"But if for some reason I didn't surrender to him, you thought I wouldn't be alive. Why did you think that?"

The girl turned slowly white. "Don't you know?"

"Was it just intuition, or did something happen?"

"He didn't kill anything, if that's what you mean. He only started to and—but I don't know whether I can tell it. Not that any part of it is very strange—when I think it over to myself, one happening after another, I can't understand why it affected me as it did. I tried to tell it once to a lover, but became embarrassed—and then ashamed. Look, Lola. There *is* a close tie between us, isn't there?"

"Heavens, yes."

"You seem so much older than I, and yet so much younger. I feel you'd understand everything I've done or felt. That's because you're so beautiful—maybe it's what made you so beautiful. At first I wanted to tell you that story to warn you of some awful danger. Now I feel that you know the danger better than I do."

"Please tell me."

"All right. He met me in Brighton and invited me to Blackmoor. He hardly put his hand on me for the first two or three days, and I didn't know what to think. Then he asked me to spend a day on the moor with him, while he 'exercised' his favorite falcon, named Vivian. He let her chase ducks and it was thrilling to see her overtake and kill them. I'm ordinarily kind-hearted, but I loved to watch them fall, and I could see them way off across the moor. It was as though my eyes were twice as strong as usual, and I twice as much alive. I wanted to kill something, too—see it bleed. I threw my arms around Jeffery and got his lip between my teeth and bit it until he slapped my face. Then we made love—but it wasn't that—I can't describe what I felt. Up in the air above us I heard shrill shrieks, and turning my head a little I could see the falcon hovering over us, screaming as though in jealous fury. I laughed at her and couldn't stop, and at the end I was screaming too—laughing screams."

Mab stopped and looked at me with round, guilt-haunted eyes.

"Did Jeffery tell you that part?" she asked, swallowing.

"No."

"Jeffery stood up then, his eyes shining, and stretched out his arm with his hand shut. 'Fist!' he called to the falcon—meaning that she was to come and light. Instead she darted away and began killing birds. She killed three ducks out of one flock, then circled over us, screamed, and darted away to attack a flock of herons. Jeffery kept shouting 'Fist!' but she kept on killing. I began to feel ashamed not of him, but for him—standing there naked, golden-haired, so tall, his skin snow-white under a golden down all over his trunk and limbs, his own face like a hawk's. Once he did something that I knew was a weakness. 'You fool!' he yelled at the bird, his face terribly drawn, 'she isn't the one!' "

Mab fell silent because the headwaiter had come up and was standing just within earshot. His hair was beautifully brushed and his mustache elegantly waxed; he wanted us to see that he was much too fine for this position, just as he perceived that we were lowering ourselves to eat here; and in the same straits of circumstance, we should make friends. If I had come here alone, I would have been a little flattered by his choosing me for his confidences, quite a little bored by them, and very eager for him to know I was Lola Montero, in very good circumstances indeed, and able to eat where I pleased.

Just now, however, he was a source of acute annoyance. I did not want anyone to come between me and my visions of Jeffery, naked on the moor. No, Mab wasn't the one of whom Vivian need be jealous. She had been only my delegate and I had almost felt the first shock of union with my lover. Now I saw him standing with his arm outstretched, still expecting with all his will power the falcon to obey his command. But he had already descended to appeal to her. The climactic second was at hand wherein he must punish her revolt.

"We're doing very nicely," I told the waiter, with a bright smile. He flicked his napkin and stalked away.

"Do you want to hear the rest?" Mab asked me, her eyes misted with tears.

At that instant, I came to her help. She was no longer my proxy in a lecherous adventure. We were sisters of a sort, and I loved her.

"Yes, if you want to tell me."

"I do. When Jeffery couldn't make the falcon come to him, he turned white. I suppose it was with fury, but I can't swear to that.

Then he got his gun that he had leaned against the rock. I knew what he was going to do. The next time she circled over him he was going to kill her."

"Instead she flew away?"

"She didn't have the power, poor thing. But I prayed hard as I could pray that she wouldn't yield. Have you ever had the feeling that the whole world hangs on one little event?"

"Yes, when a Welsh groom asked an old dying general if he knew him."

"Did he know him?"

"Yes."

"I'm so glad. Lola, the falcon didn't yield. I knew then she was going to be killed, but her soul would be saved. Does that sound silly?"

"It would sound silly only to a fool."

"She climbed very high and attacked a wild goose. But there was nothing wicked in her killing now, as when she'd killed for Jeffery— I guess because it was her nature to kill—the only thing God had taught her—it was only pitiful. As the goose dropped, she kept diving at it, nearer and nearer Jeffery's gun. When she'd caught it again, an eagle appeared from nowhere and pounced down on both of them. For an instant all three seemed to stand still in empty air, then the falcon and the goose fell side by side, stone-dead at our feet."

Mab stretched her hands with a quick movement across the table. I caught them, and they fluttered in mine before they became still.

"Go ahead, Mab."

"Jeffery turned to me and said quietly, 'Eagles frequently try to steal the kill.' But the expression on his face—I don't know what it was. He was watching the eagle as it climbed in great splendid spirals toward the sun. In just a few seconds it disappeared in the glare. He looked shaken and utterly mystified. Then he turned to me and asked in an absent-minded way, 'What color was that eagle?' 'Brown,' I said. 'Yes, I dare say it was dark brown.' And I felt cold to the marrow of my bones."

"Mab, were you *glad* the eagle had killed Vivian?"

"Oh, yes! I couldn't bear for Jeffery to kill her. I wanted her to die a natural death. You see, her screaming and the panic of all the birds could easily have attracted an eagle. It didn't even mean to kill the falcon, I thought. It was just diving at the goose."

"You had the feeling that she'd escaped from Jeffery?"

"Yes—forever."

"What happened then?"

"Jeffery walked quickly to the dead falcon and turned her over with his foot. She had a big hole in her head and her breast was covered with blood. I saw his face as he looked down at her—there was no pity in it and no sorrow, only a terrible dark pride, as though he himself had been wounded and would never let anyone know. He was standing there stark naked—I was naked, too—there wasn't a cloud in the sky and the moor was open as God's hand as far as I could see."

Mab choked and tears began to roll down her cheeks.

"My sister," I said—not knowing what I was saying.

"I'll tell you the rest. You can decide for yourself what it means. I couldn't speak or move, but soon he turned to me and said, 'I think we'd better cut this short. This is the second Vivian I've lost,'—I supposed he meant another falcon—'and I won't be very good company. I'm sorry to disappoint you about going down into the mine.' 'That's all right,' I said. 'You can get dressed now,' he went on, 'and then go back to Brighton.' He hardly spoke to me after that, except to say that my clothes had been torn and mussed, and he wanted to give me fifty pounds. I took the money, and one of his carriage men drove me to the stage road. That's the whole story."

I filled her glass with wine, and she drank it to the last drop.

"I don't know what it means either," I told her.

"I've never heard from him since, but I heard something about him. A French marquis told me that when he came back from India, he had a man and a woman with him whom he said were man and wife to be employed at Blackmoor. The marquis said that the man is only a screen, and the woman is his mistress."

"Indians?" I asked.

"Both are Levantines. He thought the woman was a Thracian. Anyway, he said she was highly educated and one of the most beautiful women he'd ever seen. I can't help but think that's a lucky thing—for you."

THIRTY-TWO

*L*ATE in the wonderful Rhineland springtime preceding my twenty-fourth summer, my bright little path again crossed the blazing highway of Liszt. Only thirty-one years old, he was widely famed in France, Belgium, and England, while in Germany, Austria, Hungary, Poland, and Russia he was idolized in an almost hysterical fashion. There were a thousand stories told about him, every new one sure of an avid hearing. When on a secret visit to Italy, he had walked into a great music publisher's in Milan and announced himself by sitting down at the piano, the proprietor in an inner room, hearing the keyboard in melodic convulsions, exclaimed, "That's either Liszt or the devil!" He was at present separated from Countess Meran; according to reports, he had had two love affairs of late, one with George Sand and the other with the beautiful actress Charlotte de Hagn.

George Sand was fourteen years older than I and dressed like a man. The poet Musset and the great Chopin had been among her previous lovers. . . . The number of notes passed up to me from the audience at the Royal Theater had been unsurpassed only at Charlotte's last appearance there. . . . I wished I could fall in love.

With the *Kapellmeister* of Coblenz, who reminded me of Chevalier Camille, I went to hear a concert by the great virtuoso. Each new arrival of the swelling crowd brought a heartful of excitement to add to the great store accumulated there. The people took their seats with a kind of stealth; there was almost no sound; every face was grave; as the hall filled to overflowing, the suspense became almost frightening. One great whispered gasp, which I thought was a thousand people catching breath, broke from the throng as the rising curtain disclosed a great black piano, lighted so that it appeared to project from the shadows behind. To me it suggested a beast of the apocalypse in suddenly arrested movement, one wing raised, waiting for his master in deadly hatred of his dominance, but powerless to resist.

The master appeared as from the limbo of tormented souls. Even as the still, small voice, not of my conscience but of my common sense, reminded me that this was at least partly showmanship, I got goose flesh from top to toe. His extremely tall, very lean figure was stooped as though under a heavy burden; his countenance suggested Dante's and out of its pallor his eyes glowed spectrally; his blond mane swept his shoulders. One could imagine that his dress reflected the sin of which he was being purged—inordinate vanity. Over his white cravat he wore the Golden Spur; the ribands and jewels of other orders decorated his lavish Hungarian attire; his first act was to remove his white gloves and throw them on the floor. He lifted his head a little to the thunders of applause, and glanced dreamily at his white hands.

In a moment the great black beast had begun to utter sounds of familiar character and meaning, but with such passion that they seemed outside human experience. The effect was at once enrapturing and terrifying. No matter how great a showman, Liszt was now in an agony of emotion all but unbearable to see and hear. I felt, I think, the revelation of truly appalling conflict between his flesh and spirit.

His choice of compositions dramatized its totality and terror. The romantic beauty of Chopin and the idealism of Beethoven were portrayed in contrast with the sensuality of *Don Juan,* the eerie magic of *Erlkönig,* and the cynical deviltry of *Robert.* At least this was what the consonant tempest told me, whatever it might tell the others. But one of its effects upon us was notably general—every mother's son and daughter was transported.

After the concert, my escort's position as *Kapellmeister* and my reputation as a popular dancer gave us entree backstage. There the master was holding court to good burghers and their stout wives though with not very good grace. Nor was this the result of weariness, as he pretended. He was not nearly as weary as I expected and was merely bored with the adulation of these plain people. While a man of noble ideals, guileless and companionate, he was known as a prodigious snob. He played up to the boyars and gave short shrift to the bourgeoisie; and he loved the peasantry, with whom he was kin, only at a distance. I had been intrigued by this curious infirmity in so great a man and thought it might be a symptom of the same inward conflict I had heard thundering from the keys. At close range, I was angered by it, and unwilling to have him take it out on me.

"I'll wait for you in the greenroom," I whispered to my escort, and slipped out of the slow-moving line. Then there were quick, light steps behind me, as sometimes I had heard in nightmares, and a long shadow leaped ahead of me. I turned and looked up at Liszt.

"Why are you going?" he asked me, in a deeply troubled tone.

"I won't go if you don't want me to," I answered without thinking.

"Who are you? Aren't you Lola Montero, whom I saw dance in London?"

"Yes."

"Didn't I come up to speak to you?"

"Yes. You said I must go to Paris, the only Olympus."

"Then why should you go away without speaking to me? Is it my fault that those Dummköpfe keep you waiting—"

"They're not Dummköpfe. They're the people who pay money to come and hear you play. What would you be without them?"

"*Gott im Himmel!* It is true—I am the Dummköpfe! You were so angry you would not speak to Liszt! Ah, but you must! I've so much to tell you, so much to hear! You will go now to the salon of the Countess Von der Hellen? I will fly there to meet you!"

"I am with the *Kapellmeister*—"

"Bring him if you must! If he smells of cheese, the countess shall receive him for your sake! There will be only a few, thank God! Do not fail me, Lola! If you do, you'll never be forgiven by God or man."

The *Kapellmeister* did not smell of cheese and probably took ten baths to Liszt's one. He was an immensely dignified little man, and I went with him proudly to a towered *Schloss* overlooking the river. The fat, motherly, jolly countess made us instantly at home among

a small company of artists, scholars, and *Meinherren*. She herself
had seen me dance in Vienna the year before; she said she had felt
not only beautiful, but slender and mysterious.

When Liszt appeared, he looked wildly about until he saw me,
then threw me an ecstatic kiss. Although he did not come near me
for nearly half an hour, I could tell that I was the main subject
of his conversation with the others. Actually it was more oration
than conversation, accented with vigorous gestures. His hearers stood
leaning forward, their lips parted to speak, but rarely got a chance.
Presently he sent a pretty, buxom blond girl to ask me a question.

"The master told me to ask you where you were born, Miss
Montero?"

"In Ireland."

"I don't know how he'll like that. He says you're the ideal
Magyar type, and has just bet a crown you were born in Transyl-
vania and have Báthori blood in your veins. Don't you think you'd
better have your mother or someone—"

"No. But you can tell him I once ate at the Báthori restaurant in
London."

"What audacity!"

She hurried back, her eyes glittering with excitement, and out of
the corners of mine I watched her report on the bet. For a few
seconds, Liszt looked crestfallen, then he said something that won
a hearty laugh from his hearers. His remark did not have to be
very funny to do that—merely, perhaps, that there was a stray
Magyar in my mother's woodpile. When the *Fräulein* repeated my
remark about the restaurant, the master led the laugh and was
presently thumping his palm with his fist with wonderful esprit.

Elsewhere in the room a conspiracy was on foot, manifest in an
ever spreading murmur, to persuade Liszt to play. Evidently he very
rarely did so at social affairs—the hostess so honored became an
envied woman, and his idolators dared propose it only because of
his high spirits. While the delegation was being formed, the pretty
Fräulein came to me again.

"He took it in wonderful part," she said, speaking rapidly and
gazing straight in front of her with somewhat glazed eyes. "He

said if you didn't have a Magyar parent, you should have a Magyar child. It doesn't seem very funny when I repeat it—it was the droll way he said it, I suppose—anyway all of us roared. I hardly dared tell him your joke about Báthori—you see, the Hungarians fall on their faces at the very name—the family's older than Moses and almost extinct—but I did, and expected him to be furious at your impertinence. Instead—what do you think?"

"I give up."

"He said you were the first *complete* woman he had ever known. All the rest either borrowed from the men or else were weak and sickly and fainted at his concerts. You ought to have heard him talking about *strong* women—he was looking right at me all the time without even seeing me, and I'm strong as a horse—women who are true to their sex, who wouldn't lie down and let men trample on them—I guess it's all right for them to lie down for other purposes—women who make men bow to them in worship of their beauty. Why wasn't I little and dark and mysterious instead of big, blond, and obvious? Well, you can get him if you want him. Marie's sulking in Italy and he's broken off with Charlotte de Hagn. You may not believe me, but it's true. In one night changed from a stage dancer to the mistress of the most—*Gott im Himmel, he's coming now—*"

Liszt bowed to me, then tossed his yellow mane.

"Lola, my friends have asked me to play. I have agreed to do so —one composition only—played to you! Would you like a Bach fugue?"

"I don't understand Bach very well, *Meinherr.*"

"I wish all my hearers would be as honest. What would you like? If I know it, I'll play it!"

"I'd like *Serenade* by Schubert."

I thought he looked faintly embarrassed.

"Well, it's very popular—perhaps a bit vulgar—"

"Please don't play it if you don't like it. It *is* very popular, if that makes it vulgar. Everybody loves it—if that makes it bad."

"*Donner und Blitzen!* Because most people love my playing, do I play badly? Have I forgotten what all this is for? Poor Franz Schu-

bert—silenced at thirty-one—the most universal musician of us all—
the greatest poet that ever wrote in notes."

He had the lights turned very low, then he walked quietly to the
piano and without one histrionic gesture sat down and played.

We did not know why we were so sad. We became one with the
dead singer; the yet living song; this great man who interpreted
it so beautifully, but could not interpret himself; and with one
another. The Rhine flowed under the windows, and it alone would
not die. We could reply only with tears.

Afterward Liszt talked quietly with Countess Von der Hellen;
then she called me into another room.

"Little one, the master is a very timid man," she said.

"I thought he might be."

"He is terrified of being rebuffed, and he asked me to speak to
you. He has rented an old house on an island in the Rhine near
Bonn and is composing a rhapsody there. It won't come clear to him,
and he thinks that you can help him."

"How?"

"By going out there tomorrow evening and staying with him. If
you care for each other, he'll want you to remain with him a
fortnight. He thinks you're one of the most beautiful women in
Europe. I think so, too. Are you free to go and would you like to?"

"I'm free to go—and I'd love to go."

"I was hesitant to ask you. It's an office I've never filled before.
You've made me very proud that I accepted it."

As we came into the salon, Liszt's burning eyes met mine. I
nodded and smiled a smile that I at once realized was the kind I
might give a child. His face became luminous with beauty.

THIRTY-THREE

*T*HE island Liszt had rented in the Rhine was of elongated
diamond shape, its sides smoothed by the waters. It had always
been and was still a fortress, although now the turrets of its small,

ancient castle stood unmanned, the keep had been turned into a studio, and no pitch- and fire-throwers lined its battlements. It presently defended not river pirates, but Liszt's privacy.

Liszt sent a boat for me late in the afternoon. I was received, with ceremony and many signs of honor, by a seneschal, and my expectations of a Bohemian household had to be abandoned. The maid confided that Meinherr would be pleased if I wore my loveliest gown. A lackey at the door announced that Meinherr would receive me in the drawing room at eight. When, arrayed in my best, I descended the curving stairway, I found a footman waiting to announce me to Meinherr. Although greatly impressed with the magnificence, I remembered how Martin Nelson had called me a little princess and did not stub my toe.

Liszt, formally dressed, was seated grandly in the great hall. But the moment I looked at him I knew that all the fanfaronade was only an outcropping of his essential childishness. Just now he was imagining himself a margrave, but as between Jeffery and Rene, he was much more akin to the latter. At that moment my anticipations of the adventure became far more pleasant. I was seeking not only a great experience but a notably happy one.

During the marvelously served and appointed dinner, he felt the necessity of impressing me with his boon fellowship with princes and princesses, grand dukes and duchesses, lords and ladies. I did not know quite why, since his genius was so manifest in the molding of his countenance and—when the conversation turned to more interesting topics—in the play and power of his thoughts. Plainly he was under considerable nervous strain. It was a curious role for me, to be trying to put Franz Liszt at his ease in his own palace, but I was dealing with an extremely sensitive, temperamental man and these first hours with him were crucial.

After dessert we went onto a balcony overhanging the river, and there I led him on to tell me of the Lorelei. Presently he talked about me and soon began to kiss me. These were deep and sometimes violent kisses, and I wondered why they did not excite me more. I soon guessed the reason—their ardor was largely feigned. If Liszt himself did not know it, the fact remained. I did not think it was a case of fatigue or inherent frigidity or lack of our appeal for each other; rather he was self-conscious to an inhibiting degree. I, too, must fight against a crippling embarrassment.

"Wunderschön, wunderschön!" he exclaimed, in deep, ringing tones. The exclamations were forced, I thought, but instead of being estranged and chilled, suddenly my heart opened to him. Until this moment I had been seeking a magnificent adventure—to captivate one of the geniuses of the age and be his inspiration for a great rhapsody. Now I felt compassion for his painful striving toward me. His very greatness intensified his need. For his sake more than mine, for his pride not my own, I wanted it fulfilled.

I was a little disturbed by his insistence on haste, but complied with his wishes when he asked me to go to my room. The only lamps I did not extinguish were one close to the door, its flame reduced to a blue drop, and one shaped something like Aladdin's, save for a missing handle, hung high in the sky. It cast blue-gray squares on the floor under the west-facing windows and caused a faint reflected glimmer on the polished posts of my bed.

Liszt came before my eyes could become accustomed to the almost total darkness, so I knew of his entrance only by the click of the latch and the swift shift of light and shadow from the hall. I heard the bolt slip home but could not yet make out the shape of my visitor. Only as he passed in front of the all-but-expired lamp, by which it seemed an owl could not find his roost, did I become aware of his visual presence. He was wearing a long robe more dark than the darkness.

He sat down by the edge of the bed and began to woo me. But his nervous tension prevented tenderness between us, and soon his kisses grew strained and cold. He could not hide from me his bitter shame.

"I was more tired than I thought, Lola," he told me, drawing away. "I composed almost all day, and I always give more to it than anyone can know."

"Everyone knows that," I answered.

"I shouldn't have invited you at this particular time—just after a long, hard tour, worn out by it in truth, and at the same time trying to compose a new rhapsody."

"Countess Von der Hellen thought I might be able to help you."

"You already have—more than you know. Just being with you—seeing your beauty—delighting in your wonderful *élan*—and by those moments just now on the balcony. I think I'll do a better job if it stops here. I mean—I'll still have an unfulfilled longing that may express itself in the wild passion of the Gypsy. It may be some fundamental instinct, you can call it my daemon if you like, that prevents me tonight—"

"You haven't seen my beauty yet," I broke in.

"I must see it! I've an artist friend in Bonn—I'll invite him tomorrow—"

Before he could protest any more—before the protests he had already made could mass against me and weigh down my heart—I sprang out of bed, walked rapidly to the lamp, and turned its wick full height.

He made a quick movement to draw closer his royal-looking robe of black silk brocade.

"I called you Aphrodite the first time I saw you," he began, with well-simulated ardor of connoisseurship. "But she was a fair Greek, and you go back to the aborigines of the islands—to Cytherea—perhaps to the Minoan counterpart of Artemis—"

I looked him in the eyes and smiled.

"You're not now the maestro at the piano, made up like a soul from purgatory. You can't pass yourself off now as another Paganini. You're either my lover—or an intruder in my room."

THIRTY-FOUR

AFTER twelve happy and sometimes glorious days with Liszt, the time of our parting neared. He had finished his composition and must give concerts in Prague; I had engagements to dance at Cologne and on down the Rhine into Holland. I thought that the adventure had enriched his life as much as mine; by the same token, I would have been as loath to enter a prolonged relationship as he. Our ways lay far apart.

The fact remained that he took a deep, fond interest in my career; and at our last dinner on the island, he gave me some advice that might have great bearing on its outcome.

"What does success mean, Lola?" he asked. "Isn't it the most complete and happy expression of one's energies and talents? I'm wondering where you could do the most and the best—through brief, shallow contact with thousands of people, or long, profound impact on one."

"What do you think?"

"Your beauty has great power. I think it is symbolic of the power of woman. How would you like to test that power further and help someone else who needs you?"

"Who?"

"A king. A mediocre king who might become great by your inspiration. There's no love in his life any more. He reigns over a rich and populous kingdom, one of the oldest in Europe, but he is tired—bored—lonely. He has a deep feeling for beauty, and I think you could restore his *joie de vivre*."

"Do you think he might make me a countess?"

"That would be quite a coup for the daughter of a self-made officer."

"Louis made Du Barry a countess—and I was once compared to her."

"Can that be your great ambition?"

I remembered the occasion of the comparison. It was the first time I had gone out with Rene—a shabby old officer had come up to speak to me at the Café de Provence. My memory that had settled on the scene took wing again, flew farther down the road, and showed me dressed to meet company in Grannam Ferguson's parlor. I could almost weep at the big-eyed girl I saw there, carefully uglified by her keeper. *"I am going to be created a countess by a king."* But Lady Kirk was not the least angry over the child's impertinent folly. She only felt sorry for her.

"It's a very great ambition," I answered Liszt.

"Lola, isn't that a little at odds with what I might call your republican principles?"

"It might be. I want it just the same."

"The king I spoke of is Ludwig of Bavaria. In my mind, Munich is one of the most beautiful capitals in Europe, but not very bright just now, and if you want to attempt the great adventure, don't wait too long. The king is past fifty."

Liszt promised to sing my praises to him, the next time he played in Munich. The subject, swiftly dropped, was picked up again in a curious way the following morning by a third member of our party. Both Liszt and I had taken for granted that it had consisted of only us two—we had sat alone in the big dining room. Actually another person had been at the table with us part of the time—standing by it, bending over it, filling glasses, moving dishes. He was called by the most common of German first names—Fritz. No doubt he had a surname, but I had not asked what it was. He was a middle-sized man of about forty, and I had only to look closely to see intelligence and character in his face. I had not done so, being occupied with other interests, although I could not remember what they were. We made our acquaintance when he came into the room to carry out a box.

"I heard what you and Meinherr were saying last night at dinner," he told me, in fluent, provincial-sounding French. "I hope you'll pardon me."

"It's nothing to be pardoned," I answered. "Herr Liszt did not hire a deaf-mute."

"I heard you speak of the possibility of going to Bavaria. As a servant, it was my duty to let it go in one ear and out the other. However, I've been thinking about it on and off ever since—and no matter the consequences, I resolved to speak of it."

"I'll thank you for any comment you wish to make. Will you shut the door and sit down?"

"No, madame. It will only take a minute. I want to say first that I saw you dance at Stuttgart. I could never again feel you were a complete stranger to me. I could never forget you—I was overjoyed when you came here to visit Meinherr, and I could look upon you several times every day. You give great joy to my eyes and to my heart. But you can do more than that for me—and for thousands and thousands like me—if you become the favorite of my king."

"Are you a Bavarian?"

"Yes, madame—from Ingolstadt."

"How could I help the people?"

"To bring us to Ludwig again. He is a good man at heart—but he has forgotten us. Our oppressors rule in his name, and crush us beneath their heels. If you should oppose them, you would go into great danger. Yet that is my prayer."

"What makes you think I could become the favorite of Ludwig?"

"I spoke of that to my friend Heinrich, and we both think there would be a likely chance. Ludwig is a great connoisseur and lover of all beauty."

Fritz lifted the heavy box on his shoulder as lightly as Lohar had picked up the iron. As he went out the door, I gave him a deep bow. Neither of us could have told what it meant, but I thought that we both knew.

I kept Liszt company on the river boat as far as Coblenz; and it was not his fault nor mine that our farewell fell short of what we both desired. We spoke glowingly of our joys shared; he would dedicate the new rhapsody to me; we would meet again before many moons; but our goodbye kiss was scanted because of the gaping crowd. Now a great margrave from Frankfurt was waiting to pay him honor. To Liszt's regret and relief, I went quickly to shore.

Passing the hours of waiting at an inn, I wanted to see Countess Von der Hellen, but feared I would not be welcome. We were not now in her salon electrified by Liszt. Perhaps she would be ashamed of the part she had played in the *affaire d'amour,* and then I would be likewise.

So I could not help but go and present my card. It was no longer a matter of choice but of harsh and often hateful inward law. It was a sign not of strength, in the true reckoning, but of weakness. The strong were always serene.

My expectations of being told that the countess was not at home failed gloriously. Instead, she received me literally with open arms and bustled me into a private chamber to give me beer and pretzels and to hear every detail I would confide of my visit with the master. When it was time for me to go to the boat, she asked me if my schedule would permit me to spend the night with her; as it did, I had my first sense of daughterhood since I had left Madame. Since then, it was my first stay at what seemed home.

When the house was quiet, I sat at the edge of her bed in my nightgown, and over milk and cake, told her many of my secrets.

"I know Ludwig quite well," she said. "You might be able to do a great deal for him—as he for you. But Lola, you're too young to shut yourself up in a great fortress as the mistress of an aging king. I wish you could go back to Rene."

"He told me not to come back unless I could stay."

"That was over five years ago and a great deal could have happened in the meantime. Why don't you dance in Paris? If he's happily married, you'll either not see him at all or else you can have a sentimental hour with him in a café and both go your ways. If he's free, stay with him as long as you can—as long as your fate permits. You've never had enough of that kind of love—the kind every young woman wants and needs—the everyday kind. Take it before it is too late."

Rising early the next morning, I wrote a letter to the manager of the *Opéra Comique,* requesting an answer at Rotterdam. When on the following night I danced in Cologne, I fancied my steps already Paris-bound, and they became unbelievably gay. At both Düsseldorf and Duisburg, whose names had an ominous sound in my ears, the crowds cheered themselves hoarse; and I did not begrudge a jog off my course to dance at Essen, where the roof all but fell down.

It behooved me to grow more sedate when I had crossed into the Netherlands. This was the law of the Medes and Persians of players; it had something to do with the Dutchman's strict religion; performers had trimmed their sails at the Dutch border since time immemorial, lest they go on the rocks. But I was to dance at s'Hertogenbosch, where the young Erasmus learned to hate the subjugation of the spirit and hence became the greatest Humanist of them all; and I decided to honor his noble ghost if I fetched up in jail.

So I performed my harvest dance, based on the corn maiden ritual of which Rene had told me. I was greatly proud of this composition, expressive of the people's love of life and hate of death and of the continuity of the seed, but I dared perform it under only the most favorable conditions, since almost always it was either a notable success or a dismal failure. More than once I had spoiled the effect by wearing too many clothes; tonight I stripped to a diaphanous robe that revealed every curve and molding of my body, for the female form itself is the most beautiful of all representations of fertility. Mine was not matronly and snow-white; it was small and almost ale-brown, but I thought it might fulfill an atavistic image of a corn spirit in the folk mind. As I danced, I thought of the young Erasmus, tormented as much by the flesh as by the spirit, and how I would like to tell him what no book could—though every woman could tell him if she would.

The cause of the wrought-up emotions of the audience·I found in my own feelings. This particular dance had never moved me as deeply as tonight, and very rarely had I experienced such exaltation on any stage. I had long known that this was Rene's dance—he had led me to the fountain of its inspiration—and now I had gone in search of him to cast the account. At every mysterious step I had felt closer to him.

After two nights in Rotterdam, I had intended to strike out straight for Paris. Instead, the warmed throngs demanded I stay twenty nights, the theater hushed long before the curtain, and the gathering suspense like that I had felt preceding the entrance of Liszt. Thereafter the manager engaged me for two weeks more to perform all the rest of my repertoire, at which I never caviled despite my haste.

Antwerp would not let me go short of a fortnight. Ghent and Ostend bade me tarry on the road, and I was too much of a trouper to pass by milk and honey in search of mead. At sea-washed Dunkirk, Calais, and Boulogne, the dance of the corn goddess still moved the crowds to exalted wonder. But ten leagues inland, at Amiens, the spectators were merely pleased. I kissed my hand to them in happiness and took the stage for Paris.

I went lightly, talking to the people and admiring the sights. I was in no way troubled about Rene—nine chances out of ten he was a sound paterfamilias, passionate in politics, proud of his pen, and with only a friendly smile for the poetic follies of his youth. If he were free I could spend a few days with him—even weeks I thought with a swelling heart—but more likely he would bring his wife to see me dance! Perhaps they were so deeply wedded that they could come in shared curiosity, make honest and fair comments to each other, discuss whether to speak to me but decide against it, go out to a pleasant café and then home to bed.

Six years! Dogs that had been young were now old. Probably the younker had set up for himself, by now; and the Gaffer had been put off by himself. The lingam still stood in the yoni in the mouth of the holy circle—that was Goodwife's business and mine—and the fires of the ghats burned with insatiable hunger. Above and beyond that, I knew nothing. I did not know why I was so sad.

I watched through a peephole in the curtain the theater swiftly fill. Rene did not take a seat up front, but in the rear of the galleries there were several tall, lean men, mostly with women, two or three alone, one of whom might be he. Wherever he might be, I danced to him. . . . I bade him remember the gifts I had given him, soft and warm, richer than pearls of the Rajah, sweeter than honeydew, white as the milk of paradise, and rose red, fragrant as frankincense and myrrh, smoother than Samarkand silk. . . . You swore you would never part with them. You told me you would prize them above all measure. With that I have kept faith; to your oaths I have been true. Is it women's dreadful lot not only to hold to our own troths but to live and die for those plighted by our lovers? Now that they have taken away our priestesshood and overthrown our power, will they deny us our beauty? Are we dust beneath their feet?

Pretenders, usurpers, what is your divine right? Hypocrites, where is the faith that was to supplant ours? What are the gains to the tribe since you thrust us to our knees? Half of the young men dead in war, half of the remainder in bloody feud. Worse yet, you feign to kill one another for our favors, when we could supply you all, our gifts to you endlessly renewed while yours to us grow scant? While you fight, our children starve, and they who were free wear chains.

Will we not lock our doors at last and laugh as you knock in vain? Will we not together roll a great rock in the mouth of the Circle of Stones, one that all of your frantic thrustings cannot remove? Then when we, too, are laid in the barrows, when the last-born babe is a gray ghost beside the dying fire, there will no longer be any good or any evil. There will be no longer any joy or any sorrow. There will be no death for lack of anyone to die. We will defeat you at last.

Nay, do not groan. We can bear pain but cannot stand its sight. Yes, we will again let you into our bowers, bare our beauty to you, lie supine. We will be bringers of delight until you so quickly tire. Once you were at our beck and call; now we are at yours. But never believe that we are defeated by you; instead, by our own greatness. You take advantage of it to enslave us.

Take it, if you must, only do not make us lie alone. Beckon to me, Rene. Call me, my lover. . . .

The music stopped, and in its place rose a great roar of applause.

THIRTY-FIVE

SURROUNDED by a throng of courtiers, I saw Rene the instant he appeared backstage. Almost before I could be aware of happiness, I felt deep pride.

He was a man of impressive stature. That should be obvious to all the people here, I thought. I wished they could know that he and I had been lovers. I wanted them to suspect we might be again.

He gave no sign of it yet. When I threw him a glance, he would not meet it, and finally I had to let it fall. Instead of joining the pleasant, happy court about me, in which my pride would double if he would only take notice of it, he stood alone, gazing at the scenery and apparently completely absorbed in its mechanism. Slowly it dawned on me that the other people were as unaware of him as he appeared to be of them. I could hardly believe that they were not impressed by his presence—I marveled further that they did not realize his distinction. Suddenly I knew why—he did not know it either. In his own opinion he was still the gauche, provincial Frenchman who had humbled himself before Jeffery.

Yet it did not cross my mind that I had been mistaken. Although he dressed hardly better than before and stood awkwardly, there had been wonderful developments in his countenance. I caught the eye of a stagehand and beckoned him into the press.

"The man in the wings there is Monsieur Saint-Denis, the great journalist," I told him. "Please ask him to come and speak to me."

At the invitation, Rene came to the edge of the group, only to stop, flush, and start to turn away. I dived through it and caught his hand.

"Will you wait for me and take me to supper?" I asked.

"If you've nothing better to do," he answered.

He disappeared behind a cloth flat. For the first time in my life I tried to give short shrift to an ovation, with the curious result that my well-wishers seemed all the more determined to prolong it. My efforts to leave appeared to excite some people only mildly interested in me until then; and their joining my court attracted more.

Beginning to feel a frightening pressure of bodies, I called "Rene!" The utter lack of response, with no positive awareness of my own voice, gave me a creepy feeling of having imagined the outcry. As had happened to me many times before, one eerie experience was quickly followed by another. My scalp suddenly tightened with an effect of crawling. I had been snatched back six years to a street scene in Bath and heard Jeffery speaking to Rene at the first meeting of us three. Rene had just splashed mud on the lord's clothes. *"You clumsy oaf!"* We doomed three, I thought with horror. . . . But the mental image was hardly formed before I realized that it was a hallucination. My mind and heart had been occupied with Rene at that instant, and my imagination stirred by his coming and then by his disappearance among the painted walls, hills, woods, and palaces in weird lights and shadows.

I realized the words were not the same as Jeffery had used, and when resounded in my ear, the voice was slightly different. Only the tone was identical. *"Vous tous en arrière!"*

A slice of bread thrown into the Seine could not have dissolved more quickly than the crowd about me. At one instant it had seemed a solid body. In a matter of seconds it resolved into about thirty commonplace men and women, distinct from each other without being distinguished, looking and feeling alone and afraid and cheap. Through them, somehow managing neither to touch nor to look at them, marched a small, pale man with childlike features. Behind him, briskly bustling despite the slow pace enforced on him by the leader—with the effect of a pig on ice—followed Monsieur Barteau, the manager. The little man stopped in front of me with a genuinely majestic air. Monsieur Barteau spoke in ceremonial tones.

"Miss Montero, it is my great honor to present *le duc* d'Antremont."

The duke kissed my hand; I bowed low. Perhaps because Rene was waiting for me, slowness seemed the dominant quality of the interchange that followed—the great nobleman's complimenting my dance, my thanks in return; his recalling a youthful acquaintance with Celeste Renalt, who he had just learned had been my teacher, my expressed pleasure in that fact; an invitation to supper and my voluble regrets that I had made another engagement. At that point Monsieur Barteau asked permission to interrupt. He waited in patience until it was formally granted; then he spoke with carefully chosen words.

"Lola, it occurs to me that the gentleman who has invited you to supper would be honored to yield to *le duc* d'Antremont."

"He would indeed be so, if it were possible," I replied. "As it happens, the engagement is of long standing and involves others. If *monsieur le duc* would pay me the great compliment of naming some other date—"

"It is only by happy chance that *monsieur le duc* is at leisure tonight. Obviously his great affairs—"

"Pray say no more, Monsieur Barteau. I yield to my fortunate rival and trust him worthy of the victory. Miss Montero, I hope to communicate with you again."

He gave me a wonderfully graceful bow and turned on his heel. Not to the manner born himself, but as between great lords and strolling players knowing what side his bread was buttered on, Monsieur Barteau added an unsubtle sneer. I could hear their departing steps on the wooden floor as I waited for time to move on to the next event. Its pace too was slow.

My courtiers did not return to me. They moved in front and behind and on each side of me, going their different ways, giving me glances that I knew must be simply curious, no matter how mocking or malign they might seem. I looked at the cloth wall behind which Rene had disappeared. I gave him time to emerge— twice as long as he needed—three times as long—then walked quickly there, as though it were the rendezvous we had arranged. I, too, went behind it, to find nothing but a chill passage leading to a dimly lighted street. This I ran through, suddenly emerging on a busy sidewalk under drizzling rain. People came and went under the lamp, each blurred-looking, and with changing highlights caused by wet faces or clothes.

I ran back and encountered an old man whose business it no doubt was to keep the door. I wanted to hit him for deserting his post until I saw his straggly mustache and pale eyes; he reminded me of a halt, half-blind, fumbling old *chokidar* of a dak bungalow in India, more at home with ghosts than with pukka sahibs on tour. He had become tired or lonely or hungry, and had wandered off to satisfy a need as great as mine to find Rene.

"*Grand-père,* did you see a tall man with a distinguished face and black hair go out this door?"

"No, little one."

"His name is Rene Saint-Denis, and he is a famous journalist. Do you know anyone who could tell me how to find him?"

"I know a cab driver who can find him for you, as a dog finds game for its master. Aye, he is an old dog. I call him *Vieux Chien.* His kennel is hardly a block from this door. Give me three sous for a messenger—"

He sent the boy off in breathless haste. The drizzling rain was boring in all its aspects. It seemed to be always starting to hum a song, dispiritedly sounding about three notes; but even on these it could not enlarge or improvise—even this dull tune it could not carry—and could only repeat itself with dismal persistence. The pattern of light and shadow under the flickering street lamp, at first suggesting mystery, soon showed trivial; the wet-looking people who passed were like damp, discouraged squirrels on a treadmill.

"Evidently *Vieux Chien* is not at his stand," I suggested, after a long silence.

The old man looked at me dreamily. "Pardon?"

I repeated the remark.

"Ah, yes. He no doubt has a fare. Behold it is a rainy night. Cabs are at a premium on such nights."

He grew empty-eyed again, and I was dreading the need of making some sort of decision, when horse's hoofs clattered on the cobblestones and a dilapidated cab loomed in the broken light. Out of it tumbled the messenger boy. The aged door-keeper was instantly up from his stool, wide awake, spry, courtly, and efficient. I became the central figure of a sequence of dramatic action—tipping both assistants, being helped into the cab and tucked out of the rain, and then departing behind an immensely animated horse amid slapping leather, creaking wheels, and fond cries of farewell.

The excitement never quite died away. When I revealed my desire to find Rene Saint-Denis, whose address I did not know, but one who was a leader writer for *La Républicaine,* my fear that *Vieux Chien* would become glum proved groundless. Instead he undertook the adventure with high esprit and became a jocund Oliver to my Roland. The quest took us first to the offices of the newspaper, from where a late-working clerk directed us to a café on the Rue des Scribes. Here the maître d'hôtel gave us an address in Montmartre which of a certainty had been late as last month Monsier Saint-Denis' abode. Unless he had died or moved. . . .

"Huzza!" cried the driver, cracking his whip.

It was now two hours past midnight, and our Argo sailed a lonely, forlorn sea. The rain neither increased nor diminished; and the people dimly seen in vaguely measured space and time told me stories of boundless sorrow ere they disappeared; the old man and his old horse became in my imagination tragic symbols of a meaningless existence, a huge and hideous joke played by the gods on mankind.

We seemed to come close to its point when he had reached a hotel in a walled court, witless and blind-looking save for square, dim, scattered yellow eyes. We could not find a driveway to the foyer, and since there was no place to tie the nag, I got out and ran through the rain to inquire of the concierge; and she, a sour-faced woman, would not let me in.

"Do you deny that Monsieur Saint-Denis lives here?" I asked.

"I neither affirm nor deny it."

"Will you let me go upstairs and see?"

"Certainly not. If he does live here, he has given me no instructions to admit a visitor this late at night."

"Has he given you instructions to turn away a visitor?"

"I decline to say."

She ought to be doing something with her hands, I thought—knitting, perhaps, like the women harpies on watch by the guillotine. Instead, they reposed calmly in her lap.

"Will you inquire of Monsieur whether he will receive me?"

"If Monsieur is here, he has given me no authority to disturb him."

"Do I look like a person whose visit would disturb Monsieur?"

"How you look or do not look is a matter not of my concern."

"Does Monsieur have other female company whom my visit might embarrass?"

"On that matter, being Monsieur's business and not yours, I decline to speak."

She was not a woman, I thought. She was a talking gargoyle—I could account for her quite reasonably if, standing barely out of the rain, I let my fancies roam. Perhaps she had been a woman only a few minutes ago but a shocking metamorphosis had taken place. Fate, never dreaming *Vieux Chien* and I would get here, paying us no whit of attention and suddenly faced with an emergency, had deputized the creature. She still looked like a woman with soft flesh, but underneath her clothes she was stone. . . . It was a habit of my mind to take flights of fancy when balked by a hard fact. The fact in this case was that an old termagant in petty authority had wrecked my venture.

I started to turn away, then stopped and looked at her again in wild surmise.

"If you let me go up to see Monsieur Saint-Denis, I'll give you two francs," I told her.

She rose from her chair, held out her hand, closed it over the coins, then unlocked the inner door.

"The fourth door on the left at the head of the stairs, mademoiselle," she told me cheerfully.

When I went out to pay the driver, the drops on my face felt as warm as the summer sea rain on the moor. I handed him twice his tariff and then ran back as joyfully as when Rene and I had raced with the storm.

"Don't stub your toe, *ma chérie,* on the broken step," the old woman warned me as I started up the stairs. So I went grandly and serene, unworried whether Rene's door was locked. But I wished for a jug of mead.

I laid my knuckles noiselessly on the door in a pooja knock, then turned the knob. It opened lightly with only a little creak; still I did not assume he was expecting and would welcome me: Rene would rarely bother to set the key. However, I need no longer be afraid that I had mistaken the apartment. The small tobacco-scented room I entered, identifiable by the wan glimmer of an all-but-extinguished lamp as a sparely furnished studio, smacked of Rene. There was the same disorderly pattern, although on a much more extensive scale, of books, papers, pens and inkwells, I had seen in the cottage in Cornwall. If he had a wife or a mistress, there was no evidence of her.

A dark curtain indicated an inner room. My eyes discerned nothing but vague variations of darkness, but my ears took in slow, quiet breathing. It was the same I had heard before wakening Rene in the dawn of our bridal night, instinct with his identity. Now the steady warmth of my body began to be varied with a cool, contrary

trembling. I went and got the lamp and placed it on a table beside
Rene's bed. It gave forth the merest mist of light, more like a pallor
of the dark, but this appeared to increase as I stood waiting, and
soon I could make out the shape of Rene's head and body. He had
gone to bed naked this warm night, but the rain had slacked the
heat of the brick walls, and he had drawn a sheet over his hips.

As I looked at the cloth, it began to suggest the fall of draperies
seen in the pictures and sculpture of otherwise nude subjects: wind
or gravity's unfailing respect for modesty. Suddenly I was certain of
what before had been the merest suspicion—that Rene was only
pretending to be asleep.

The effect on me of that discovery was a high surge of passion.
I felt myself being made inviting, easy of access, exquisitely perfumed. I was able to control my deep, aching breathing, turn up the
lamp a little, then with every aspect of stealth, lift the sheet. This
was the man I loved. The wan light revealed to me my treasure.
Beloved by me was his every substance and form, the brain and
spirit his body housed, and now I was anxious and in pain. I had
wanted Rene back, and suddenly, after six years, I had discovered
the necessity. It was necessary not only to my happiness, but to my
growth and it seemed to my very survival.

Without Rene, I must go—

It was not a real thought that started thus, only a fragment of
imagery which sudden wonder or terror left uncompleted.

It was as when a sleeper hears a sound in a quiet house that he
knows is not of worldly cause, but to which his wonder and terror
closes first his mind, then his ears. I had only to open a little door
of imagination to complete the sentence, to know what it had
started to tell me; but I put it by for now, lest I be too frightened.

Ready now, I pressed my lips to his.

"Lola!"

"Do you want me back, Rene?"

"If I needn't lose you again. I couldn't stand that."

"Would that be the only obstacle against taking me back?"

"Yes, I lost Guitera. I couldn't keep her because of you."

"I've found out we need each other. Have you?"

"All that you gave me, only made me want more."

"When I go from you, it will be only for a little while, and then I'll return. You'll be my only lover. Say yes, Rene."

"Yes, Lola."

I could complete now, without quailing from it, the image that had started to form in my fancy.

"Without Rene, I must go with Jeffery down into the mine."

THIRTY-SIX

I WAS united with Rene in the late summer of 1842. In the next two years, perhaps because of harmony with myself and with Rene, I was more in love with life than ever in my days.

The days themselves rejoiced my heart by their rhythms, sweet and sublime. . . . Cool, quiet dawns, timid in approach, then gloriously rushing. . . . Trees green and nobly shaped again, flowers displaying multicolors, rivers blue and bright, all nature's forms delightful . . . the ascending sun and high, bold morning . . . noon with its sense of pause, the shadows sharp and almost still . . . afternoons long-drawn and rich, the sun moving with royal leisure, then growing late . . . the intimation of divine transactions all about the heavens just before dusk . . . the failing light concealing nearer wonders only to reveal these farther off, such as stars that have burned invisibly all day or the moon that sailed unseen or perhaps ghosts to the quieted eyes of the mind, for it is the law of God that the turning down of any lamp discloses another's burning . . . the deepening tide of darkness . . . midnight solemn without being sad, an infinite solemnity perhaps, not imposed by God but caused by His most nearness . . . stars in long, holy vigil . . . another intimation of His raised hand just before dawn.

I was involved with the moon in all her comings and goings, her waxings and wanings. She was ever signaling to me of her great affairs and was never too busy to look at my little ones. Because I wondered at the tides' ebb and flow, they had communion with me that I surmised but did not understand. The running of the sap, the swelling of the seed, the revival of the grass, the nest-building in the trees, the ewes dropping of their lambs, the return of the swallows and their flight more lovely every day, and the fish following the warm currents of the rivers and seas, all were tokens to me of divine design, of which I was a part, with which my eating, sleeping, love-making, dancing, all that I thought and felt and spoke, every incident of sleep or waking, was forever intricately bound. It did not seem to me a fated, fixed design but one forever weaving. I could find no evil in it except what man put there. Not evil was the red-eyed weasel wantonly killing little birds; blackly evil was man who borrowed his pitiless heart. Blessed were the bees who raped the swooning flowers of their aromatic juice, for thereby these bore young; and blessed was I in borrowing their passion, warming my heart.

I was part and parcel with the summer and all who lived by it. I was in the earth where the weed grew, in its stalk and leaf, in the hoe that cut it down to make room for the cabbage, and in the hoeman. I rode the wains with the harvesters and was kin to the harvest; I was fragrant with the ripening fruit while I was greedy with its gatherers, satisfied with its eaters. With the wild geese I fled southward from winter's cold and ache, honking at my fellows, rejoicing in the warm, reedy ponds; yet I could not disclaim the hoarfrost snarling the grass, the petrified waters, and the dead-white drifts. I suppose we are all part-god.

Rene was but dimly conscious of these outdoor affairs. He was obsessed by the sharper, nearer conflicts of good and evil, as manifest in the doings of kings and crowds, councils, and armies. By that measurement this was a bad time in Europe; the age of Metternich was drawing to a troubled close; the poor were in dreadful plight; the human spirit had lost its bearings and was cast adrift in a sea of cynicism. In this war, Rene was truly a white knight. His pen was hated and feared by both the nobility, dreaming of the restoration of the ancient regime, and the money-mad *bourgeoisie*. He stood up for such as Tom Riley; with my support, he increased in stature. He had always been brave before the massed foe, dogged in defense of what he held right, ferocious in attack; and with me he gained a poise, perhaps a clearer sense of his own powers, whereby he saw more clearly, held more steady, and aimed more true.

Again I had a Happy Isle of joyous returnings. At first it was two rooms in a bleak hotel, later a flat in the *Quartier Latin*, finally a modest villa near Pont d'ena. In various seasons I toured all France, Belgium, Holland, Northern Italy, Switzerland, and Germany as far east as Nuremberg and as far north as Hanover; but journeyed no more to Vienna, Warsaw, and Berlin, because of the setting in of homesickness amid those distant scenes. I danced better than before, I suppose because I was happier than before. I danced to Rene, who was also Martin Nelson, and Papa and Chevalier Camille and Señor Professor and General Judson, and who all were avatars of Krishna the Joyous. Thereby I defied Kali and her ministers and manifestations in earth and hell.

There was rarely a month in which I did not spend a few days with my lover. Our friends were mainly journalists, painters, sculptors, poets, and musicians, most of them obscure but a few of great fame; among them we were honored and sometimes beloved. We pooled our money and many other gains and interests.

A curious exception was Rene's Sunday rides in and about Boulogne Forest in which I persisted in declining any part. I told him I did not want to break into his fellowship with the dozen or so Bohemians who called themselves *Les Chasseurs de Renard Rose*. He knew there was more to my refusal than met the eye.

"True, the girls who sometimes come to our meets are usually grisettes," he said. "But that is not the reason you refuse."

"I think not."

"Also, you learned to ride the same summer that you learned to walk, and you fear you'll put me to shame. But I'm not the riding jackanapes that you think. While many who took up the sport with me six years ago have dropped it, I have stuck to it and studied it assiduously and improved in it steadily. I am easily the best of our band. That is not saying much, I know; but Monsieur Jarat, the liveryman, proclaims me the equal of many a chevalier. A horse trader who came there only a fortnight past—Monsieur

Eugene, he is called—saw me ride and expressed a wish to ride with me on some future visit. Will you believe that he declared I would not attract unfavorable comment at a good hunt in England? And, Lola—if you should surpass me, don't you know I'd be proud? I would rejoice to have my fellows see you—beautiful as you are, yet the sweetheart of a mere scribbler, small and dainty but of no high birth—outride a marquise."

"My Rene!" I came to him and kissed him long, partly in tenderness and passion, and partly to stop his lips.

"I know why you won't come," he went on, his eyes darkening. "You are ashamed of what you think is my weak and foolish vanity. No, you think it something worse—servile aping of the rich and highborn. Why do not I ride a plowhorse into the fields? What has a *petit bourgeois* to do with jumping fences and shouts of tallyho! Why do not I keep faith with the poor, of whom I am a champion? Lola, my goddess, every man is a welsher. If he holds true once out of ten times, he should be counted a hero. We are not women, formed of Adam's most wiry bone, bending but rarely breaking, pliable to his breath but bars of steel over his heart —no, we are soft, as God made us ere He realized the devil would covet us. You he made not for our service—what a grim jest is that!—but for our protection. No, do not come with me to the paddock. Do not behold me dashing off, showing off, playing that I am an aristocratic sportsman. Then I would see myself through your eyes and pity myself."

In the early summer of 1844, Rene and I journeyed by boat to Rouen, so that he could report on a matter dear to the heart of all France—the building of the western façade of the Church of St. Ouen. On the late afternoon of our last day there, I wandered alone into its ancient cemetery. I did not quite know what had drawn me among the dark trees and the white tombs. There was some association in my mind with Joan of Arc, but I was sure that her despised ashes had not been buried in this ground; in fact, I was under an impression that they had been cast into the Seine. A cherry tree bearing blood-red fruit had somehow been planted or taken root among the funereal cypress, and I was musing over it, thinking of it as a kind of ghoul, when another lonely visitor saw me and to my great pleasure went out of her way to speak to me.

At my first clear glimpse of her I toyed with the pleasant fancy of her being Joan herself, leaving her heart-broken hauntings of the Market Square to keep rendezvous with me. She had an extraordinary beauty, and the design of her rich garments as well as her type of countenance suggested some of the beauties portrayed in Renaissance paintings. Indeed, I thought that she antedated these, representing a far more remote period, as though she had given a rose to Roland when he rode against the infidel. The word that came to my mind to describe her dreamy, somehow saintly beauty was "Gothic"—suddenly it struck me as curiously like the Botticelli Venus whom I fancied I, too, resembled. Yet this young woman and I had no superficial likeness. If there was any at all, it lay very deep.

"Aren't you Lola Montero?" she asked.

"Yes."

"I saw you dance in Calais. It was beautiful."

I was pleased with the notion that while I might have been a street-girl model for "Little Barrel's" painting, the finished work more nearly resembled my new acquaintance. She had the same golden hues of hair and skin, swanlike neck, and other-worldly smile.

But I could dispense with the pleasant fancy of her being Joan of Arc. It came to me that Joan had been a hearty girl, with peasant vigor and humor, tough as a filly, liking a vulgar joke—all in all far more like me than her. Indeed she was the farthest removed from a peasant of any woman I had ever seen. No duchess to whom I had ever curtsied had that delicate molding of flesh and bone. I had never heard French spoken more beautifully, but I was quite certain she was not French. The unindented line from the top of the forehead to the point of the nose suggested Greece. . . .

"Thank you for telling me," I answered.

"Are you going to dance here? I'd love to see you again."

"No, I'm here on a holiday."

"My name is Europa Demitros. I'm in Rouen with my brother

trying to buy an arras that once belonged to Richard de Beauchamp, Earl of Warwick. It's said to be concealed in a warehouse and shown to prospective buyers with the proper entrée."

She told me this with what I felt was high courtesy—to remove my disadvantage of knowing nothing about her while she knew what was commonly related about me. Her voice was lovely and rather childlike without having a child's eagerness; in fact her tone was so casual that I might suppose she was thinking of something else. But she had given me more to think about than I could deal with simultaneously. Demitros was one of the most common Greek surnames—Europa, to whom great Zeus came wooing in the form of a bull, was a decidedly uncommon given name. To meet a woman of this cognomen was interesting; that she was a rare beauty made the meeting a memorable adventure; to encounter her in an old cemetery added spice; that she was in Rouen on such a romantic errand was truly thrilling. Even so the main cause of my excitement was her mention of the Earl of Warwick. Evidently he had been a man of varied as well as rich possessions. This was the first time I had heard of him owning a priceless tapestry, although Señor Professor had told me of his once having an important prisoner named Joan of Arc.

"I suppose the arras is worth a tremendous sum," I said, as a showgirl could be expected to say.

"I've let it be known that I'd pay a hundred thousand francs, but no brokers have approached me yet."

"Was the Earl of Warwick you mentioned the same that governed Rouen four hundred years ago?"

"Yes, of course."

"The tapestry must have an interesting history—"

"Nothing is known of it before the Earl's ownership—probably he got it in Arras itself. He disposed of it to Jean de Luxembourg, head of the Burgundian army. Later it hung in the archepiscopal palace. But let us sit down on the grass and enjoy this beautiful late sunlight."

My memory was beginning to clear. The story of Joan of Arc had been close to the heart of Señor Professor and me, and I remembered now that she had been captured by Luxembourg's forces. Later she had been bought by the earl and turned over to the French inquisition to be burned.

"Could it be," I asked, when I was seated, "that Warwick bought Joan with that very tapestry?"

"You are very shrewd, Miss Montero."

"Joan was burned, but the tapestry still exists?"

"There is good reason to think so."

"In that case, a hundred thousand francs would be a cheap price for what was once the blood price of Joan of Arc."

"That isn't quite correct, you know—especially the term blood price. One of the reasons why blasphemers were burned instead of beheaded was to prevent the sin of shedding one little drop of blood."

The ripe cherries, almost in reach of my hand, looked like big drops of blood. The branches were a light, pleasant green in contrast with the somber pendulous boughs of the funereal cypress. The late sunlight found its perfect match in Europa's hair. But now I looked in vain for her resemblance to the Botticelli Venus; she merely reminded me of her, quite a different thing. She suggested the picture as it might be distorted by being seen through imperfect glass.

"You spoke of blasphemers," I said. "Would you say Joan was one?"

The lady laughed childishly. "Do I seem such a fool? She was a beautiful peasant girl, completely feminine, with the sweetest heart that ever beat in a French breast. Twenty-five years after her burning, the grand inquisitor of France annulled the edict of her heresy and declared her orthodoxy. I dare say that in time she'll be canonized. But that reveals the tapestry in an even more interesting light. It is said that Jean de Luxembourg wanted to spare Joan and refused ten thousand livres for her, but could not resist such a magnificent work of art. Who would imagine the old soldier being such an epicure!"

"Not I," I replied, not knowing what I was saying.

"You see, the masterpiece was in her fate from the first. It hung over her, as did her voices, when she was a little milkmaid in the village of Domremy. When the voices were silenced in the crackle of flame its colors were said to become brighter and its figures more beautiful. According to legend, it has continued to grow more beautiful ever since."

"I would think it might be unlucky."

"On the contrary, the great majority of its owners seem to have been unusually fortunate in all their undertakings. The story is that all bad luck that would have been their ordinary portion in life was put on the head of Joan. True, the last owner was not worthy to own it—I am repeating the legend, you understand—and was burned to death in the fire that consumed his château. According to report, the tapestry was likewise burned. Actually it was the only object saved from the fire."

A question rose on my lips that I was reluctant to put. To do so might carry me farther down a path of imagination I was most anxious to leave. Yet it was such a natural question. . . .

"Was the tapestry more beautiful than ever?"

The beautiful woman's laughter was like that which sometimes welled up to me from a delighted audience—warm and fond.

"How wonderful that you should guess that!" she cried. "There wasn't a smudge of smoke—a burned thread. Indeed the red colors were said to be a little brighter, enhancing its beauty. The action of heat could do that, you know, in the case of certain dyes."

"About the color of these cherries?"

"I couldn't say for sure. I've never seen it, you know. But I have heard the red tints described as cherry-red." She looked up at the fruit, her eyes bright and happy as a child's.

"It's such a pleasure to talk to you," she went on. "Your mind is so quick. I think you perceive that the burning to death of a pretty, visionary peasant girl saved for the epicures of the world a superb work of art. I mean—this is hypothetical—the very fact it was her purchase price made its owners prize it and hence preserve it—otherwise it would likely have gone the way of most of the great tapestries in the last four hundred years. Whether she became scapegoat for its owners—bearing their bad luck—is at least an interesting legend. But you know, Lola, she needn't have done so. It was her own pigheadedness, you might say. She could have lived and perhaps been restored to favor in the French court."

"Will you please straighten me out on that? I have a dim memory in connection with this cemetery—"

"Why my dear, we're sitting almost in the exact place."

"What place?"

"According to the legend handed down in the town, the cherry tree marks the spot she knelt, when before the inquisitors she abjured her voices and admitted she was a blasphemer, whereby she was to be saved from the stake. But a few days later she withdrew her confession and paid the penalty."

"I'm glad she was true to herself."

"What an odd way to put it. You mean, I suppose, you're glad that she was so stubborn. I don't think that's very kind of you, Lola, considering what it got her. I'm quite sure she herself wasn't glad when the flames had licked off her clothes and reached her skin. It was too late to recant then."

"I don't think she tried."

"I, too, am glad she withdrew her confession—but for a more rational reason. Had she recanted, she might have lived twenty—thirty—perhaps fifty more years; but her story would have lacked its dramatic climax, and the tapestry would not have become famous by her burning. It might have been hung on a damp wall—decayed—eaten by rats."

I knew now what she was.

"If her voices were real, wouldn't you expect them to speak up for her in her hour of need?" the monster went on. "One can't help but compare her fate with that of her judge, Pierre Cauchon. He became immensely rich and died full of years and honors and lies in state in the beautiful Chapel of the Virgin at Lisieux."

"You're very well informed on her story, Mademoiselle Demitros."

"I've always found it very interesting, and lately I've begun to feel that I understand it. Perhaps that will be a factor in the great good fortune—if it comes to me—of being able to obtain the tapestry. Mere money can't begin to pay for it. There has to be faith."

"Are you a collector?"

She laughed happily. "How charming of you, Lola! I should have told you I'm only an agent. I'm trying to get it for Monseigneur."

The title was proper in France for a prince of royal blood, and her using it without the article or the name indicated that her status was not that of a representative but a vassal.

"What does the tapestry show? The finest I ever saw presented a Biblical scene." But I did not know what path my mind was taking.

"This one is a hunting scene—far finer than 'The Boar Hunt in the Forest' although possibly by the same artist. It is called 'The Fowlers.'"

"Are they hunting with falcons?"

"Of course." The lady glanced at the long shadows and rose in sudden haste.

"I hope if you get the tapestry, it will remain in France," I said.

She shook her head, smiling as to a child. "Monseigneur is an Englishman," she said. "It will be hung in his castle on the moors."

As she started away her lovely hand caught a twig overhead and stripped off about half a dozen cherries. These she crammed into her mouth, and they were almost more than she could manage. As she looked back to me, laughing, some red juice ran down her chin.

THIRTY-SEVEN

I HAD two main paths of memory back to Madame, Chevalier Camille, and Monsieur Lavelle. One, of course, was by way of my own dancing. I never danced badly without finding consolation in their absence, nor well without wishing for their applause. The other path was through the skyrocketing fame of a ballerina calling herself St. John, pronounced in the English fashion. On reading of her debut in London, "a pupil of the well-remembered Celeste Renalt," I had realized that she was the Jones; and my delight over the fiend in human form calmly assuming sainthood knew no bounds.

Perhaps because I had been its victim in my tender years, I did not often descend to the passion of jealousy. The pangs that I felt at my fellow pupil's blazing star were tempered by a kind of family pride in her; also I suspected she had paid an awesome price for her fame. Going out of my way neither to meet her nor dodge her, I did not cross her path until shortly after Rene's and my return from Rouen; then, on going to Versailles to dance for the crowd, I discovered that she was on a half-secret visit there to dance for the court.

My act was over before hers began, and, on hearing about it in advance, she sent me a pass to the royal theater signed by the Master of Revels. Even so, I was grateful for a second invitation from an all-but-royal marquis to escort me there, for which no pass need be mentioned. So it chanced I sat only two boxes from the king, of which fact the Jones became immediately aware. It seemed to me she looked daggers at first, but she was too great a dancer to let pique mar her performance; and the adoration of the audience soon put her in sweet temper. There was no doubt in my mind that she was the peer if not the superior of Fanny Elssler.

After the show she kissed me with great exuberance, and we arranged to lunch together the following day. While a happy occasion, it was inconsequential except in one particular. I found that I was no longer in the least jealous of her career and suddenly more satisfied with my own. One reason was that mine did not preclude Rene. I found myself more a woman than an artist. I had so much to tell him when I saw him again. . . .

"The last time I saw you, Jones, you said your only lover was Agamemnon, and you expressed no flattering opinion of him," I reminded her. "I trust the situation is different now."

"The devil it is," she answered. "Lola, have you read an American poet named Poe?"

"I read a story—"

"This is a poem. It goes something like this: 'They are neither man nor woman—They are neither beast nor human . . .' He's talking about ghouls, but he might as well apply it to artists in general and ballet dancers in particular. I've passed a few nights in bed with some agreeable men, but, except for my reputation, they'd much rather have had barmaids. My body isn't a woman's body any more. It's just the set of tools of a damned ballerina."

It came to pass that when I returned to Paris after a brief tour through the pleasant provincial capitals of northern France, Rene and I went on a picnic. The wood lot of a farmer barely beyond sight of the spire of Notre Dame appeared a little lost remnant of the primeval forest from whence came fair-haired Clovis to kneel before a cross. The brook traversing it was old even then, I thought, despite its infantile gurglings; the boiled eggs we ate were laid but yesterday, although their like, with a little salt and pepper, were relished by the Roman soldiers likewise picnicking here, perhaps with high-smelling daughters of the Parisii who preferred their eggs pregnant and raw. We spoke of our first picnic on the moors of Cornwall.

"Do you know how long ago it was?" I asked.

"Eight years," he answered.

"We parted a few days later—so your pen could be free, and I could become a great adventuress."

He gave me a quick, uneasy glance that became instantly satisfied. "I think we did wisely. My pen did stay free in the years it would have been in the most danger. You gave me inspiration but no burden. When you came back at last, we were both independent. If not your fill of adventures, you'd had a good many—"

"Not nearly my fill. It's been more than twelve years since I told Lady Kirk that I was going to be created a countess in my own name—I'm no nearer it now than I was then. It's time I abandoned the notion, isn't it, Rene?"

"I dare say it's a little painful to put by a childhood dream—"

"Oddly enough, it wouldn't be the least painful. Instead it would be a very happy occasion. Do you know why?"

He shook his head.

"I've dreamed of being a countess more nights than I can count.

I know that it's a Cinderella wish but it's become for me a symbol of victory. Now I want to give it up—and I can't. I want to deny that it could come true, but I keep on believing that it will."

"Lola! What a strange illusion. I suppose it's an illusion—"

"I hope it is. I mean, there's something I want so much worse."

"What?"

"You."

"By the good God!"

"Yes, by the good God. It's the greatest good He's ever done me, as far as I know—His letting me want you more than anything. Perhaps I should say it this way—His great favor to me was letting me choose you instead of anything or anyone else. Well, you see now why I want to give up the dream."

"If it comes true, it's because you've discarded me?"

"But I won't discard you. It would be because I've lost you."

He started to say something—thought better of it—said it anyway. "By death?"

"I don't believe that would be the means."

"What could be the means?"

"I don't know."

"Lola, do you believe you'll become a countess?"

"Señor Professor told me—I wonder if you ever heard it—that in the days of Achilles the people believed what would seem to us an utterly senseless thing. It was that even the gods could not take back their gifts. I can't think it through—I have only a mist of feeling that somehow it's true. It seems to me I asked them to let me become a countess, and they said they would."

He was quiet a long time, and I felt closer to him than ever before. No, it was not a matter of relative position—somehow I had arrived at a new relationship to him, through some change in me, or one which had changed me. I could find no more precise description of it than that I seemed a part of him and he a part of me. I had no need of anything that this sharing did not bring. By this reality I had broken with my dreams.

"It would be a great prize," he went on at last. "I'd be sorry to think I stood in your way."

"I think you've helped me obtain something better than great prizes," I answered. "I would call it fulfillment, and I think that means the realization of a person's highest potentialities. To find out what 'highest' means we've got to measure according to our ideals—they may be a false standard, but they are the best we have. I think my highest potentialities were of a corn goddess. You told me, you know, I had the makings of one—a goddess of fertility just as real as those who served the shepherd tribes thousands of years ago. I serve my tribe by demonstrating the beauty of women. The more the people realize that, the better off they are. Perhaps I can't make it plain although I know it's true. Realizing the beauty of women makes men fertile—not alone in begetting children but in ideas and deeds. They honor their mothers, from whom nine times out of ten their ideals spring. At the same time they become more deeply male in their relations with women. They can't help but love life and try to make it better. They become more sensitive to all other beauty. There may be a higher inspiration than the beauty of women, but it doesn't come most men's way."

"*Précisément!*" Rene exclaimed—as any good Frenchman would.

"I'll tell you another way the expression of female beauty makes the world better. Although it's even harder to prove, I haven't the least doubt of its truth. It causes other women to want to be beautiful, and, by trying to, they become so. Lots of women won't try. To justify themselves, they deny beauty's power—it amounts to denying their own sex. Well, they'll never be anything but ugly, by that method. Are you interested in knowing how any woman of any age can become beautiful?"

"Academically," Rene answered, smiling.

"Simply by being completely and honestly female all the time. That's the whole secret. She cannot be what somebody has told her is female, what she chooses to think is female, but rather she must be in her inmost heart what she *knows* is female."

"It sounds easy. But I suspect it may not be."

"It's not only difficult but dangerous. All full living is extremely dangerous. Being truly female imposes terrifying obligations. She can give her favors only to those who deserve them, which means those who appreciate them and will thus benefit by them. She can't turn away from those who need her help. She's got to be the mother of Good."

"I don't know what you mean."

"In remembrance of the Mother of God. The great opponent of evil."

"Can she win?"

"I don't know."

"Why have you turned white?"

"I'm afraid that evil has the last laugh. It seems an inkling—it may be only a superstition." I moved closer to him, and pressed his head to my breast. "Anyway I've found happiness," I went on. "I dance for the people—and hearts leap up—and I look and see their shining eyes—and I know I am Woman. I come back to you, and know it most surely of all. Knowing that, I know more—that woman's heart still beats, and as long as it does, Good won't die."

"You *are* a corn goddess. That vision I had was true. Perhaps it's only to say you're a truly beautiful woman."

"Remind me of it, Rene."

"How?"

"You know. By the way every woman finds out her womanhood. At least, the most common way."

"Common," he said thoughtfully.

"Common as the air we breathe. Common without a sneer in it. Common as grass. Common as love itself."

"In the name of our love will you make me one promise?"

"I'll promise you anything."

"Only that you won't let me stand in the way of your being created a countess."

I hardly knew what he was saying.

"Oh, I promise—"

In a moment I had forgotten what I had said.

Our picnic in the woods was Sunday, a few days following my twenty-sixth birthday. For this he had missed his usual Sunday outing with *Les Chasseurs de Renard Rose*. He thanked *le bon Dieu* that he did, he said—it had brought about a growth in our relationship of great promise to our future happiness—and the hunt would have been dull anyway compared to that planned for the following Sunday. Monsieur Jarat, the liveryman, was going to borrow some hounds and Monsieur Eugene, making his horse-trading rounds, would liberate a live fox. Every Jacques Bonhomme had sworn to be in at the death.

"Won't you come out and watch?" Rene asked, his eyes bright as a child's. "We've agreed to rent red coats."

I thought of that troupe of hunters, vying with one another, lustily shouting tallyho, remembering it was unsporting to ride over crop or to leave gates open, careful not to thrust at their master of hounds, the good liveryman Monsieur Jarat or perhaps the ex-jockey, Monsieur Eugene. Don't be so proud. . . .

"Rene, I can't go."

Rene worked late on Saturday night; but I had not gone to sleep when he came in with a precious bundle under his arm. When he came to bed with me, I thought to hold him in my arms awhile as I loved to do before I slept; but in my first soothing by his warmth I drifted off. I had only napped, it seemed, when I felt him stealthily arise.

"Must you go so soon?" I murmured.

"Yes, darling. We've planned a very early breakfast at a café near Alma, and I must shave first."

He lighted a lamp, turned it very low, and carried it into our *cabinet de toilette*. The windows were still midnight black when, after comings and goings and noises he had tried in vain to stifle, he suddenly turned up the lamp with a proud cry of *"Voilà!"* His riding boots were newly polished, his buck breeches flared fine as the fox hunters' in Romney's paintings, and for crowning effect he wore a badly fitted, but lordly pink coat.

"What do you think of it?" he asked.

"I love you, Rene."

"I am being very silly," he told me. His face had fallen, to my shame. "I think I'll give up the whole business. If I had not promised my friends . . . but it will be the last time."

"Will you be careful?"

"My dear, we can hardly get those retired plowhorses into a gallop!"

I spent most of the morning at *Comédie Italienne* trying to work out a new encore; but my head was thick and my legs heavy, and at first I would not or could not think why. The truth broke upon me with stunning effect. I was deeply uneasy about Rene.

Once involved in a contest, he was an earnest and extremely hard competitor. The game planned for today was not a rowdy ramble through the lanes and bridle paths of the Boulogne Forest in the pursuit of an alcoholic fox. If the hunters tried to be in at the death of a real fox pursued by energetic hounds of whatever breed, some rough riding was in store. That Rene was undoubtedly a good horseman failed to comfort me. In the excitement of the chase, he might become overconfident.

There was no possibility of overtaking him. Impulse after impulse rose in me to take the river boat to the usual starting place, only to be blocked by the hard fact that it would be useless to do so and by my refusal to admit I was that much alarmed.

Then I hit upon a perfectly good reason to make the trip. Rene had been hurt by my refusal to watch the show. Truly I should have had more consideration for him and less for my own squeamishness. I would go out to Monsieur Jarat's livery stables and join him on his return from the field.

The decision made, I began to make great haste. In case I should want to ride to meet my lover, I put my old, but still pretty, habit in a bag, along with a bottle of wine to toast the victor. My haste continued until I boarded the crowded ship, then perforce stopped. She dawdled from dock to dock. I became quite sure that the hunters were back at the paddock if not on their way home. The river made a long loop to the Île de Puteaux, and the shadows were shooting out when I disembarked. I made the short distance to the livery stable in an excursion cart.

Several red-coated customers were idling about the paddock, enjoying coffee. Among them I recognized Pierre Vacassy, one of Rene's best friends. Suddenly I did not feel equal to the amenities.

"Where's Rene?" I asked.

"He's not in yet, but I dare say—"

"Are a good many still out?"

"Four, I believe. We had a late start and then more of a chase than we bargained for. Some of our merry band fell by the wayside."

His voice and countenance appeared calm; however, he was watching me more closely than he wanted me to know. I, too, wished to appear calm. I did not know what to say that would give that impression and still discover what I wanted to know.

"Were you in at the death?" I asked.

"There wasn't any death. The fox earthed. Monsieur Villette was the first there after Monsieur Jarat. I was second—"

"Ahead of Monsieur Eugene?"

"Oddly enough, he was one of the strays. The last I saw of him and Rene—"

"Rene?"

"Yes, the two of them were making it around a fence, while the rest of us stopped to open a gate. Evidently they encountered some rough ground—"

"You said four hadn't come in."

"Two others went to look for them, while the rest of us ambled in."

"How long ago was that?"

He paused barely perceptibly. "About two hours ago, I should say."

"Where can I go to put on my habit?"

"There's a ladies' dressing room—I'll show you. I don't think there's anything to worry about, but—I'll go with you."

My riding habit, though quite serviceable, was a rich green, beautifully cut. I usually felt festive when wearing it; snatching it on, I was sickened by how well it became me.

An image began to form in my brain which, although I did not recognize it yet, I found myself trying to dismember and destroy. My awareness of the effort made it break vividly out of the mist— it was of my mother, dressing to go to the shafakhana, when word had come that Papa had taken ill. *"Why aren't you crying, too, you heartless little wretch?"* The remembered voice appeared to have resonance: I recaptured every accent. *"If I was crying, I couldn't see to find your bonnet."*

When I returned to the paddock, Pierre and all his companions were ready to ride. A plain-looking man, plainly dressed with a worried face, was in the van—I took him to be Monsieur Jarat, the liveryman—and one of his hostlers was holding a trim-looking mare, bearing a sidesaddle.

"She's mettlesome," Monsieur Jarat told me, "but Monsieur Saint-Denis has said you are a good horsewoman."

"She'll do very well."

The sun had appeared well aloft when I had looked at it last; now it was a fiery orange, sinking into its glare upon the river. When we had cantered to the fence where Pierre had last seen Rene and Monsieur Eugene, not one red wink remained and the light had the illusion of clarity, caused I suppose by nearby objects appearing farther away and larger than life, which marks the first failing of the light. Monsieur Jarat put a horn to his lips and blew loudly.

"You see, Lola, the dogs bayed all about here," Pierre explained. "We don't know which way Rene and Monsieur Eugene may have gone."

At the third blast of the horn we heard a distant shout in reply. The men looked excited rather than relieved, as we turned our horses in that direction. Soon we caught a glimpse of a party of riders through a break in the woods. I was certain I had seen four horses—I could not be sure of four riders. But I need not remain long in doubt. One of the band spurred away from the rest and came cantering toward us.

He pulled up at sight of me. He was a very small man, with delicate features, who reminded me of *le duc* d'Antremont who had asked me to supper on the night of my return to Rene. I had an impression that he was riding a very fine horse of which he was in perfect control.

"This is Madame Saint-Denis," Pierre told him.

"Then I have bad news for you, madame," the little rider answered.

"What is it, please?"

"I am Monsieur Eugene. Monsieur Saint-Denis and I went around the fence, losing touch with the rest of the party. Later we attempted a short cut toward the cry, and Saint-Denis took the lead. When he came to a stone wall he did not know—".

He stopped, because the remainder of his party had now come into the clear. There were three animals, and in the saddles of two of them red-coated riders sat straight. Across the third saddle lay what had been a rider but was now only a load on a led horse.

I rode up and looked at what remained of my lover. I noted his head's lop on his neck and his dark hair matted with blood. I touched his face, then turned to Monsieur Eugene.

"You said you came to a stone wall?"

"Yes, madame, and monsieur did not stop to reconnoiter. He should have done so, but seeing that it was only three feet high, he decided to run up to it and jump it. He did not know that beyond was a very deep, steep-walled watercourse. He was thrown and killed instantly."

"The horse was not hurt?"

"He fell hard but was only cut and bruised."

"You said, didn't you—you must pardon me—that Rene, not you, was in the lead?"

"That is correct. To get to his body I had to work my way around. If I had been in the lead, I would have reconnoitered the jump—but then I am a former jockey—I rode for neither glory nor sport but for purses, which were no good to a dead man. Monsieur Saint-Denis rode like many gentlemen I have known, hell-for-leather. He ran a great race, Madame Saint-Denis, and died with his boots on. I grieve for him, but I salute him!"

Monsieur Eugene lifted his cap and looked at the other riders. All of these save Monsieur Jarat lifted or touched their hats—the old liveryman appeared too stunned. I was not in the least stunned. . . .

Rene had died with his boots on, true, but he also was wearing an ill-fitting pink coat, rented from a costumier. But it was not a case of "a peasant stand up thus." The Duke of Cornwall himself would not run a servant through for dressing up like a fox hunter.

He would only have a hard time controlling his mirth. Anything that happened to the fellow when so ridiculously arrayed would be hard to take seriously.

True, Rene had been in the lead when he and I had crossed the sand-covered peat bog in Cornwall. But I wondered who had been in the lead when Jeffery and an older man—a silly fellow who for a few minutes' pleasure in bed had created a rival for his wife and his barony—had started up a mountain in the French Alps. The latter, too, had been a keen sportsman, Jeffery told me.

The web was being woven, and I could not yet discern its design.

BOOK V

The Dark Mother

*T*HE weaving returned again and again to my mind during the hours that had to pass before I could start home with my dead. A hearse had to be sent for, an agent of police must ask questions and make out reports—the matter was complicated by my not being the deceased's legal wife. What none of Rene's friends or the officials knew was that I welcomed the delays. If they had not occurred naturally, I would have had to occasion them. I was not nearly ready to leave this scene.

Most of the time I sat in the parlor of Monsieur Jarat's villa behind the stables, where he saw I was disturbed as little as possible. Here I would have liked to give way to grief. Since to do so would hurt almost as much as to contain it, I would have liked more to let a little cloud on the horizon of my brain spread across it and envelop it, the resulting condition being called shock. Instead I was impelled, by needs greater than either of these, to think as hard and ably as I could. That necessity kept my emotions under control and my mind clear. I had no reason to believe I could thus serve my love for Rene or anyone living or dead by inquiries, but I was certain that if my questions were ever to be answered, I must make them now.

I asked if I might speak to Monsieur Jarat, alone. He came in awkwardly, and I hardly knew how to begin.

"Even if the truth about something is not important, one sometimes wants it," I said.

"Yes, madame." He considered briefly. "No doubt that's so."

"Suppose that instead of Monsieur Saint-Denis taking the lead, Monsieur Eugene had taken it. Perhaps in his excitement he did not stop to reconnoiter the jump, but luck being with him, he made it. Saint-Denis did not make it and was killed. I think if he were once a jockey, he might feel ashamed of leading an amateur to his death and would tell the story he did."

"It is possible that he would. But, madame, it is highly unlikely that a former jockey would attempt a blind jump without reconnoitering it. I do not know Monsieur Eugene well—this is only his second visit here—but he does not strike me as excitable. If he did reconnoiter it, he would not dream of attempting it. I know the place well—it would be next to an impossible jump for the best jumper in France. To run up to it and take it blind would be suicidal."

"Would the tracks show if a horse had jumped it?"

"Not after other horses had been ridden all over the ground in taking up Monsieur's body."

"What kind of a horse did Saint-Denis ride today?"

"A bay gelding, belonging to Monsieur Eugene."

"A better horse than usual, would you say?"

"Much better. Not blooded, you understand, but a sound animal worth five hundred francs. You see, madame, I can't afford to keep for rental horses of even that value. I can't charge enough to pay."

This mundane statement brought Monsieur Jarat and me into better rapport; also he appeared more alert and shrewd. He would be a good informant now, I thought; and, after all, he knew more about human nature than most *conseillers* of the high court. He was constantly on guard against it—otherwise he would be robbed blind—but remained tolerant and even fond of it. The frequenters of the great salons of Paris, heirs to the culture of the ages, would hardly pick him as an example of a highly civilized man; but I would like to see the civilization of one of them after handling the Sunday crowd at his livery stable. His good but modest clothes, his formal, well-kept but inconspicuous beard, and his shrewd but unembittered countenance, all proclaimed his genuine urbanity.

"Between the fence, where Monsieurs Saint-Denis and Eugene left the party, and the wall where Saint-Denis was killed, are there any jumps?" I asked.

"Now that I stop to think of it, there is a hedge of about three feet."

"If Monsieur followed the leader over that jump, he would not hesitate to follow him over another which, although a stone wall, was of the same height."

"Yes, madame, but as I told you, it's an all but impossible jump."

"What kind of horse did Monsieur Eugene ride?"

"A gray stallion of about fifteen hands." That was all that he said with his mouth. His eyes let slip something—a wish that I would not ask any further questions about the horse. He had nothing to hide from me, but his mind had something to hide from him. My silence served as a curiously insistent question. When it grew long, he spoke.

"He struck me as an extra-fine animal."

"How fine?" I asked.

"Just to look at him, the shape of his head and his legs, I would say he's a thoroughbred hunter. But I could easily be mistaken."

"What would a common horse trader be doing with such a horse?"

"He may have picked him up somewhere. He may be nothing exceptional."

"Has Monsieur Eugene good standing as a trader?"

"The agent went into that. He's new to the business but appears bona fide. He came from Hungary. That's a great place for raising horses. He's made his way here, buying, selling, trading."

"He speaks excellent French. Does he strike you as a typical jockey?"

"Foreigners often speak better French than Frenchmen of their class. Monsieur Eugene strikes me as a gentleman—I was going to say one who'd come down in the world. It stands to reason that would be true if he were once a gentleman rider who's now a traveling horse trader. Yet I don't find myself feeling he's come down any. He says what's proper to a horse trader, is respectful to his betters, all such as that; but seems to be enjoying every minute of it. As though it were all a great joke that nobody knows but him."

Monsieur Jarat was a little startled and perhaps embarrassed by his own flight of imagination.

"What did you think of his tribute to Monsieur Saint-Denis's sportsmanship?" I asked.

Monsieur Jarat's gaze shifted a little under mine.

"Since you ask—and I must say the question takes me by surprise—I didn't like it."

"Why not?"

"I find it hard to say. It doesn't stand to reason."

"Please say it anyway. Even if the truth is painful, I want to know it."

"I felt as if he was mocking all those men in their pink coats."

"Including one who could not hear him?"

"Him most of all. And I entreat your pardon for saying so."

Jarat's face was darkly flushed. No doubt he was relieved to be called to the door. He returned to tell me that the agent of police, Sergeant Postif, wished to speak to me again. Evidently my conversation with the liveryman had jogged his official conscience. He came in as Monsieur Jarat went out—a ruddy, tight-skinned, efficient man of natural good manners.

He told me that he was about to complete his report, and although it was a mere form, he must ask if Monsieur Saint-Denis had any previous acquaintance with Monsieur Eugene.

"He met him once before—during Monsieur Eugene's previous visit here."

"Very well. Please understand the department requires such information whenever there is only one witness to an accidental death. In this case the facts are clear. You will not be bothered again."

"There will be no inquest?"

"Certainly not."

"Suppose Monsieur Eugene was found to be formerly employed by or in some close connection with a gentleman who had once been a rival of Monsieur Saint-Denis in an *affaire d'amour*. Would an inquest be called for in that case?"

"In all due respect to romance, it would make the police a laughingstock. I have examined the scene by torchlight, and closely questioned the two men who arrived there shortly after the accident. I will not go into the details, but there can not be the slightest doubt that monsieur fell from his horse while essaying a difficult jump, struck headfirst upon a deeply embedded rock, and suffered a broken neck. His horse fell also into the ditch, but by merest chance, escaped with only cuts and bruises. If Monsieur Eugene was himself proven a deadly rival or a sworn avenger upon Monsieur Saint-Denis, no charge could be made against him. This would be true even if Monsieur Eugene had led the way over a jump that he could make, and had reason to believe that his rival could not. We can't bring men to the dock for malicious suggestion. If we could, he would still be acquitted of the charge. I myself am a former hussar. If Monsieur Eugene had attempted that jump, he, too, would have fallen."

He paused, then repeated firmly,

"The laying of any charge upon Monsieur Eugene would make the police a laughingstock."

Far be it from me, I thought, to attempt to bring the department to such a low condition. I had been brought there once by an absurd statement I had made to Lady Kirk. Suddenly the room cramped me, and since I had at least an hour more to wait, I went out of the house into the silvery night. There I found the full moon purposefully climbing the sky, although she knew well that when she reached the zenith, she must fall sick and waste away. To have forgotten that this was her night of nights gave me an eerie feeling. It was a recurrence of the night I had whipped Kali. It invoked the night I had said farewell to Rene as he had set out for France. Lately I had promised Rene not ever to let him stand in the way of my being a countess. Only on this rememorant night would I wish, with a shiver, I had not done so. Always the diwani came close to me on the night of the full moon.

I walked along the paddock fence looking at the horses. Most of them stood still, so inured to slavery that they had forgotten their ancient alliance with the moon, but a few of the mares flicked their tails and tossed their heads, promising a mighty skittishness when again they would be in heat; and a gray stallion, not very tall but wonderfully compact, stood with his neck arched and his legs flexed as though posing with a great captain on his back for a parade.

The moonlight was peculiarly lucid and my eyes felt very sharp. I had never seen a more beautiful animal, I thought, letting my fancies roam despite the rigid self-control I had maintained ever since sundown. . . . I could not understand his beauty, considering he was a slave. A tiger that Manu and I had seen in a pit, and a baffled, bewildered tigress driven from her haunts by beaters at a royal hunt in India could not compare with him. I had never caught a clear view of a tiger free in the jungle. . . . I wondered if the stallion had known what was to happen when his master saddled him today—what sensations came over him as, answering the pull of the rein, he found himself on ground that he had paced yesterday, on the way to the scene of great trial? If a falcon can be jealous of her master's passion, why can't a great stallion share it? Had he looked back, wanting to laugh at the nag that followed him —of obscure birth, his potency cut out of him when a colt, not a "he" now but an "it," never making a mare whinny with desire. Yes, "it" could sail over the three-foot hedge in his wake. Now it counted itself a real jumper, with its lank peasant up. But farther on was a brick wall behind which lay a death trap for horse and rider. Yesterday he had come up to the place, smelled, and looked well, made ready to jump, only to be checked the last instant. Now he was drawing near it in a collected canter. He felt his rider lower his hands. . . . Changing step, he tucked his legs under him for the greatest jump of his life. "Will you follow me on, April Gentleman?" A peasant stand up thus!

My eyes were sinking in my head. I looked at the moon, my old confidante, and tried to be reasonable. The horrid story I had told myself might not be true. Unless the gray stallion was one of the great jumpers of the world, it was manifestly untrue. By one bold stroke I could find out. I was still in my riding habit, my whip in my hand; I had only to tell a plausible story to one of the hostlers. . . .

There was a light step behind me, followed instantly, lest I be startled, by a quiet voice.

"Miss Montero?"

My mind hesitated briefly before it would identify my visitor as Monsieur Eugene. It perceived his small size and his clothes suggestive of a gentleman's groom, but for an instant was puzzled by his countenance. In the moonlight it seemed more delicately carven than in the dusk. It did not now remind me of the *le duc* d'Antremont's—instead, of some other that I could not at present place. His walk suggested bow legs, although actually they were perfectly straight.

"If I'm intruding, will you be so kind as to tell me?" he asked. "I'm well aware that you may want to be alone—and if not, I may yet be the last person in the world—" He paused as if embarrassed. I knew well he was not.

"Why should the fact that you were with my lover when he met a fatal accident prejudice me against your company? I've been told that you did everything for him that you could."

"I did nothing for him to mention." He seemed to mean "nothing worth mentioning," the ambiguous wording being caused by an imperfect knowledge of French. "May I ask if you admire Ixion?" he went on. "I saw you looking at him."

"If you mean the gray stallion, I admire him very much. But I'm unacquainted with his name."

"Ixion is one of the minor figures in Greek mythology. Zeus played a practical joke on him—sending a cloud in the form of the goddess Hera to make amorous advances to him. Deceived, he responded—and later, when he boasted of embracing the Queen of Heaven, Zeus had him bound to a wheel of fire in Hades. It was rather highhanded treatment under the circumstances, I thought, but divine law is not based on justice. It has nothing to do with justice, a purely human concept. Its sole purpose is to uphold the lawgiver's divinity. There can be no extenuating circumstances in sacrilege—no more than divinity itself can be extenuated. It is absolute or nothing."

"I didn't know that."

"You are not aware of seeing it strike today?"

"I know of no offense my lover had committed against the gods, for which he was struck down."

"Nor I. But perhaps you have committed one, for which your lover had to answer. However, Ixion had certain consolation in the infernal regions. The cloud was made female by Zeus's trick and she conceived and bore a whole race of centaurs. It was a fancy of mine that my stallion, if mated with a woman, could also be the father of centaurs. Hence the conceit of his name."

"You are very well educated, Monsieur Eugene, for an ex-jockey."

"Happily both my sister and I were well taught before hard times knocked on our door. In fact I hold the degree of Doctor of Letters from Pazmany University. If I did not like horses more than books—"

"I was told that you dealt in them, so I suppose Ixion is for sale."

"Oh, no. While my excuse for keeping him is for the siring of colts, I enjoy his custody. Would you care to know why?"

"Indeed I would."

"Then I'll give you a little demonstration. Please stand back from the fence."

Monsieur Eugene drew back about a hundred feet. Then he called in a low voice, "Ixion?"

The stallion threw up his head, a movement eloquent with what seemed pride.

"*Ella!*"

The stallion began to canter toward his master. I expected him to stop as he neared the barricade, for its rails were six feet high. Then I started to cry out, for apparently he was blind. At the last second before colliding with it he changed step, raised his forefeet, kicked gravity away with his rear, and sailed over the fence like Pegasus.

Monsieur Eugene rewarded him with a pat on the nose, meanwhile smiling with high sociability at me. Suddenly I knew of whom he reminded me. He was the male counterpart of that beautiful lady, Europa Demitros.

THIRTY-NINE

ON the following afternoon, I wrote a letter to Manu in formal Hindustani. It read:

My beloved,

The life of the great sahib of whom I spoke to thee, Rene Saint-Denis, a benefactor of mankind, a scribe of renown, and my lover and beloved, has been seized by Kali, and his remains put in the ground in the custom of the sahib-log.

Some days before then, in seeking complete freedom for his soul, he had asked me no longer to keep him under my protection, making the request at a moment when I most strongly craved his embrace of love. Lest by argument he delay the satisfaction of my desire, I granted his petition. Thou hast said, and sometimes I have believed, that since the night I defied and put Kali to shame, that she is powerless to destroy me and limited in power to destroy those I love and will be so until I make offering to her. Thou hast told me that had I grappled with her when she came for the old General Sahib instead of standing by with folded hands, he would yet be alive. Thou hast written me that a small dog, running wild in the jungle, seen by the wood gatherers for more than fifteen rains, is in truth my beagle, Shikra, who followed me on that night, and barked at Kali as I whipped her, and was the first of us two to give her contumely.

I know not whether all this be truth or seeming. Truly it is no more strange than many wonders thou and I have seen. If it is true, I have lost my lover in a manner like that of the great hunter, Esau, losing his birthright unto his brother Jacob, as told in the Sahibs' Bible.

Be it so, I feel no shame. God made us subject to great hungers, in the pangs of which we become as little children. It is a common thing for sahibs who have never missed a meal to speak scornfully of a mess of pottage, but it comes to me that Esau felt no shame for the bartering thereof, for God so made him and us all that sometimes a mess of pottage is more dear than all earth and heaven.

In any case, the Dark Mother has taken my lover from me. Thereby she brought joy to many who hated and feared his noble mind and bold hand, and perhaps caused a glint upon the eyes of the great lord who coveted me and of whom I told thee. But to me she has brought sorrow I cannot tell and tears I cannot count. Lightly thou didst speak of how I must walk alone. Didst thou know, Manu, thou who hast many kinsmen and friends, how lonely is that walking? How silent is the house, how motionless the curtains, how cold the meats on the table, how wide the bed, how empty the heart?

But I will not go early to sleep and slumber long, so that in dreams I may hear his voice and see his face. Manu, there are great works toward. I know not how to go about them, hardly what they are, and least of all I know their consequence; but full well I know they must be performed. And it is meet that I, Lola, call upon my servant, Manu, to follow me in these ventures, and to lend me his great strength in their accomplishment.

Thou wilt remember that on my departure from Hind, I could not let thee come with me. I had been cast forth from my husband's house, and I lost great izzat, and had neither fortune nor name, therefore I would be shamed to be served by a man of thy parts. But lo, I have again become a burra memsahib. My name is known and honored in many cities, and I am paid much silver and even gold for my nautch dancing, and for two rains I have shared the couch of the great sahib, Rene. It is true I have not yet been made a countess by a king, and perhaps this and other mead must be won ere I am strong enough to undertake my great task, but thou mayest follow me even now and from now until the last hour of requital without shame to either of us.

Monies I have left with thee to pay thy way to the port, and then under the deck of a great ship to the meeting place. So when this letter comes to thy hand, thou shalt call thy loved ones about thee and for one moon take leave of them with many embracings and weepings, as one whose horoscope has been cast and whose near moment of death is known. Then thou shalt part with them as one who goes to the burning ghats, never more to busy thyself in their affairs, and whose returnings in the twilight are no more than a shadow falling and fading, a tapping on the window, a fumbling of the latch, a vision in the dream of a sleeper. Thou shalt make haste on the journey and thou shalt not fear the loss of caste by crossing the black waters, for such caste as thou hast is of no worth in England, and the izzat that thou shalt gain as the follower of Lola will restore thy loss thrice over.

If by delaying no longer than one moon, thou mayest journey on the ship Lord Clive, I bid thee do so, and there seek what news thou canst of her once boatswain, Martin Nelson, once too my lover. When thou shalt come unto London, be not dismayed if I am not waiting on the dock, for although thy spirit will run ahead of thee and try to tell me in a dream what ship thou art on, it may be I will not understand. So thou shalt make thy way to a part of the city called Soho, and to an inn called The Far Eastern, where many journeyers from Hind take lodgings and where thy food and lodgings will be paid for, until such time as I can come to thee. Wait for me there, Manu, my beloved.

I do not know what will befall. But I will tell thee of the vision that came to me, when I mused upon the days spent with my lover Rene. "It is the law of God that the turning down of any lamp reveals another's burning."

thine own,
Lola.

FORTY

I MAILED the letter in Paris and fancied it passed from hand to hand, boat to boat, down the Seine, out upon the ocean, through the Straits of Gibraltar into the Mediterranean, making eastward more slowly but almost as sure as a robin flying southward. Unless gone astray, it had surely reached India and perhaps was being borne down the mother river when at Christmas I went to Coblenz to pay a holiday visit to the Countess Von der Hellen.

She had invited me when I had written her of Rene's death. To judge from my share in the love and *liebesträum,* a visitor could hardly tell me from her daughter-in-law or even her daughter. I still had her, I thought with joy when I lay in bed—and Manu, soon to set his face toward the setting sun—and, at their last writing, my three Happy Islanders in Bath. Somewhere on the road was Mab de Lille, my sister of some metaphysical womb. Somewhere on the sea, or perhaps in port with his blue-eyed Ingar, was my lover Martin Nelson. To Manu I had called him a former lover, but that had been only a convenience of expression. His love for me had lighted an unextinguishable lamp in his brain. As long as he lived, it would pour a stream of joy, however small, into his heart.

I still had Jeffery, but I did not know the nature of the possession. On New Year's night, when I brought a cup of hot punch to the countess's bedside, her good, big face was troubled.

"Lola, two or three times you've mentioned an acquaintance with Baron Lundy of Blackmoor. You never told me how far it went, yet I have always surmised a relationship between you of great depth. When I heard news of him today from Baroness Rothschild of Frankfurt, I decided—with some misgivings—to pass it on to you."

"Why with misgivings, Countess?"

"I don't know. I met him only once—on his way home from the French Alps, where his father had just been killed. He was a youth of nineteen. I was dismayed by him, although I never knew why."

"What is he doing now?"

"He's at Frankfurt, to talk with a philosopher—so he calls himself —who lives there. His name is Schopenietz the baroness told me. She says he is a horrid old man who thinks he will reshape civilization. Lord Lundy is the guest of her cousin, Prince Otto of Thurn and Taxis. If you like, you could invite him here."

"That's awfully kind, but since I'm going to dance at Mainz, I'll try to meet him in Frankfurt."

The countess nodded at what appeared a prosaic, sensible statement. Frankfurt was only a morning's boat ride from Mainz, barely an overnight journey from Coblenz; "trying to meet" Lord Lundy there did not sound in the least exciting to her; perhaps because it could mean so much that it meant almost nothing. She did not know that it was one of the least casual utterances I had ever made and even now I could hardly believe my ears.

Hours passed—light ebbed and flowed—the waters of the Rhine and then of the Main washed along a ship's hull. I took a room in a hotel in Neustadt—I wrote and dispatched a note—I read a reply. I put on a pretty dress and topped it off with a sable jacket and cap. I went downstairs and into the parlor. Still all of these items did not begin to add up to the overpowering sum of finding there a tall man with an acquiline countenance and golden hair—Jeffery, Lord Lundy of Blackmoor.

We exchanged greetings, talked a moment, and went to take a carriage. Bright out-of-doors reminded me that I had not seen him for four years except through the eyes of Mab de Lille and, vaguely at a distance, through those of Europa Demitros and her brother Eugene.

His hair seemed a brighter gold, which could be an effect of the golden day such as frequently broke the cold spells in the Rhineland winter. He looked no older, as though the materials of his composition were not subject to wear and tear, like a Renaissance painting by a master of technique as well as of art. On my first acquaintance with him his countenance appeared barely to miss being beautiful. It had had a flaw, I thought, but this had become increasingly hard to find. I saw him now as the most beautiful male being I had ever laid eyes on, not excepting the gray stallion Ixion.

Lie still, Rene. Don't speak. I will be true to you in some way neither of us know.

"Let us drive into Old Town, see some of the fine sights, then circle back to the Anlagen," Jeffery said. "The light is marvelously lucid, as it must be in heaven. You'll never see old Frankfurt in better weather."

Beside me in the carriage, I could picture him as a gigantic golden eagle, with a captive he had carried off as a baby and raised in his eyrie. He could still lift her in his talons and carry her, swooning, to the top of the mountain crags; they could make love in wicked ways but could never be mates; in the end he must devour her or she would destroy him.

"In my opinion Frankfurt is the noblest of all German cities," he told me, when we had passed the site of the old city wall, marking fourteenth-century Neustadt from first-century Alstadt. "The name means, you know, the fort of the Franks—blond barbarians with golden braids fought for it and perhaps held it against the Huns. Three centuries after Attila—what do you think?"

He was looking at me with luminous eyes. "What?"

"I'll show you the exact spot in a moment. It is now occupied by the Leonhardskirche—a pile begun early in the twelve hundreds. The cathedral is about the same age—so are some of the palaces. . . . Here's the place. The time is the deepest midnight of the Dark Ages—the last half of the eighth century—Rome had fallen only three centuries before. Then up out of murk of barbarism rose a truly great king—one of the greatest of all time."

"Did Charlemagne live here?"

"This is the site of one of his palaces. Eleven hundred years ago he held a great court here, and proclaimed himself ruler of all Europe west of the Adriatic. But, Lola, eleven centuries from now visitors to Frankfurt may not look at this spot. They may never have heard of Charlemagne. Instead the guide will take them to a building in Neustadt. It's the site, he'll tell them solemnly, of the home of Schopenietz, who lived here in the middle decades of the nineteenth century."

"Will he have conquered half of Europe?"

"Captains who can put his philosophy into practice may have conquered the whole world."

"What is his philosophy?"

"It's hard to put in a few words. The will to conquer, as opposed to mercy on the weak. The dominance of the male principle in life— the beauty of maleness. For instance, Lola, he wouldn't think your dancing nearly as beautiful as a squad of soldiers drilling. They drill as a result of their own and their captain's will to power—when they go into battle, their good discipline results in power. And, of course—so he believes—the female form is greatly inferior in beauty to that of the male."

I had never seen Jeffery more buoyant. Evidently Herr Schopenietz's teachings had not only fascinated but elated him. I had a feeling that he was less bound to me, less influenced by me, than any time since our meeting—as though the new doctrine had tended to set him free. . . .

"This is what he said about the female body," he went on. "It's intended for bearing and nursing babies, involuntary acts like the pulsations of digestion instead of positive acts of power. He said women's only other use is as playthings of soldiers. However, they often caused young men to behave foolishly, weakly, and shamefully. They forget they are the superior, dominant sex. They idealize their mothers and wives—"

"Behudgi!" I broke in.

Some of his high color dimmed. "What does that mean?"

"It means fool's talk. Is any man's body as beautiful as Vivian's? I don't mean the second one. I mean the first one."

A long time ago I had struck Jeffery's shin with a lead-weighted cane, dealing him heavy pain. That pain was only a twinge compared to what I had dealt him now. He was made helpless by it—I saw fury try to rise in his eyes only to be washed down by waves of pain. Its dew came out on his white face—minute globules bright as oil. Except for his helplessness he might try to kill me, I thought. I did not speak to him and, after swiftly perceiving I was in no immediate danger, did not look at him. I looked at the towers and the walls and the gates and thought upon the people who had come, had dealings with them, and gone. There had been so many. It was so easy for a little man named Schopenietz to speak of them as never had great Shakespeare; to put them into the pens of his prejudices; to pretend to know more about them than did Jesus or Buddha. Yet it might be quite true that those who made his base rantings their religion might conquer the world. All that was necessary was to make enough people believe that a squad of soldiers drilling was a more beautiful sight than a pretty young girl dancing.

"I'm glad you said that," Jeffery told me after a long silence. "I was drunk, and it sobered me up."

"I don't know what you mean."

"I fancied I had escaped from Vivian—I, too, mean the first one—and so from you. I'd caught delusions of grandeur from that specious fool. I thought I could forget her and let you go your way."

"If I said something to stop you from letting me go my way, I wish I'd cut my tongue out."

"What a lie! You know our bondage to each other is inevitable. Moreover, it's the greatest thing in your life."

"Is it?" I was not asking him, so perhaps I was asking myself.

"It seems a tremendous joke—my following that Pied Piper. Actually, though, it must be a marvelous sort of flimflam to addle a head as hard as mine. It's pathological lying, of course—the old man believes it himself. Also, it's wonderfully appealing to those who hate or fear women. I see now that it's part and parcel of the sex war—it's nothing but a new declaration of that war—but that makes it all the better as a tool. Lola, what I told you before was perfectly true. Millions of men can be trapped with it. They'll live in barracks and sing marching songs and worship shibboleths and use one another's bodies, and after a while they'll kill any people their leaders tell them to. Lola, I was born a century too soon, and too well born. I have neither the stage nor the incentive for great emprize. If I had, I would use Schopenietz. He can be the greatest windfall the forces of evil ever had."

"Do you know what you're saying?"

"What?"

"That woman is the greatest enemy the forces of evil ever had."

"I'm inclined to think she's their only enemy. The men who oppose evil are inspired by their mothers. But she's lost faith in herself—"

"You once spoke of the Evil principle in life, as opposed to the Good. Could that be the Male principle as opposed to the Female?"

"What an absurd notion!"

"Is it? True, I've never known any philosopher to put it forward —starting with Plato they've been looking the other direction. Out of the Female principle comes love for the helpless and the sick, care for the old, compassion on the weak, mercy for all. Out of those come beauty and honor, nobility, life as opposed to death. Out of the Male principle comes cruelty, selfishness, hate, revenge, murder, war. There's the answer to the real riddle of the Sphinx —it's human life itself. Part lion, part woman means part beast, part goddess. That's what mankind is."

"I have an idea how Schopenietz would answer that. Why love the helpless or care for the sick and old? What is compassion but self-pity seen in a mirror? He would say that beauty and honor are empty words—nobility an illusion when it is not a pretension. The reward of life is death."

The winter sun warmed the driver on his high perch and he smacked the horses into a vivacious trot. I thought of the night I had searched Paris with my stout comrade Vieux Chien. Then I had searched for, and perhaps found, the fountain of life—his old, dulled ears had heard it splashing. What was I seeking now?

FORTY-ONE

JEFFERY and I got out of the carriage at the Anlagen, a landscaped park, with gardens and walks and pavilions where the burghers were wont to gather on bright, warm afternoons in the milder seasons. We saw the platform where a band played, benches for sweathearts, swings for children, *Biergartens* for the placid middle-aged—all deserted now despite the sunlight like yellow wine. We found a stone seat bathed in it under a naked tree.

"You know, then, who is your great enemy," I said.

"Yes. You."

"Not personally, of course—just as a representative of Woman."

"The champion of women, I should say."

"As the champion of Old Berkeley, you have to conquer me or destroy me."

"I suppose that's as clear as we can ever put it."

"But you're not willing that I keep out of your way."

"It's unworthy of you, Lola. I was willing to let you go for a year—for two years—longer than that, to attend to your private affairs. I spoke wildly on the moor, but when I'd thought it over, I had no objection to your lesser projects—marrying Colonel Reeve, for instance—going on the stage—even living with and loving Saint-Denis, provided it didn't make you break troth with me. I was very patient in his case. Except for Europa's report—"

"What was it? But first tell me a little about her. I was greatly impressed with her."

"To be impressed with her is a tribute to your discernment. When I found her and her brother in Thrace, they were dying from spiritual starvation. They were children of a high but impoverished nobleman and brought up in the mysteries of Dionysus—once the main cult of the northern shore of the Aegean and still flourishing among the so-called 'red'—blond—Thracians. Indeed Europa was chosen as the bride of the Goat-Man in the midsummer rites—a licentious orgy according to Greek Christians but very interesting to students of religion. However, lovely Europa was in love with Dionysus only in lieu of his father Zeus. It had worked itself out as love for her brother in lieu of me—at least she immediately identified me with both the father-god of the lightning and the bull-lover of her namesake. Her brother wanted to return to safety in Zeus's thigh, if you know the story and understand what I mean. Both found complete happiness—perhaps I should say self-realization—at Blackmoor."

"Do you employ them both?" My voice shook without cause.

"They are in the nature of vassals, subject to my call. I often commission Europa to buy for me rare works of art—usually associated with historical events in which I am interested. She's quite a zealot in the chase, and amazingly successful. Although her main purpose in going to Rouen concerned you—I thought you'd gone there with Saint-Denis—she hoped to kill two birds with one stone. As it happened, she failed in both projects."

322

"I knew what one of them was. To get the tapestry—"

"She didn't bid enough for it. Somehow you made her believe it would bring me bad luck. She was greatly remorseful and asked me to use a cattle whip on her. Of course, I didn't—knowing how she was outmatched in you."

"What was her other project?"

"She thought she could persuade you to come and live with me at Blackmoor. But in a very few minutes she saw the hopelessness of even proposing it."

"She wouldn't object to my living with you?"

"Lola, I sometimes think you are deliberately obtuse. I told you how my miners stone to death any one of their number that breaks one of my rules."

"Who'd stone her to death?"

"Her brother, I believe, if she actually broke faith with me."

"Isn't she your mistress?"

"She spends occasional nights with me, to our mutual pleasure. She's a very beautiful woman."

"Is her skin hairless, like mine? I have a feeling that it may be covered with golden down." I was visioning two forms as beautiful as the serpent-entwined sons of Laocoon.

"She is not a female faun, if that's what you mean."

"What tasks do you find for her brother?" I asked, when I had gotten rid of the image.

"Not very many. He has gone into a business that interests him, and carries him all over Europe."

I drew a deep breath. "You said a while ago it was unworthy of me to keep out of your way, and while you were very tolerant of my attending to private affairs—"

"As long as they did not threaten our ultimate union. For instance, I was rather charmed with your adventure with Liszt. As he might have known, he played and composed marvelously for the following few weeks. But I doubt if he ever gave you the credit. He's pathologically vain."

He paused and I waited, thinking he might speak of Martin Nelson. He would not be charmed by what he thought was my adventure with him; but would not likely suspect it was more than that. He did not mention my Norseman, and I dared not, lest my voice tell too much.

"But finally your patience was exhausted," I said.

"You are referring to the death of Monsieur Saint-Denis?"

Jeffery asked the question in a meditative tone, and I could answer it with a nod.

"I can say that I was relieved to hear it. My patience with your absence from me wasn't exhausted—I take no such imperious attitudes with you, Lola—but my dismay over it had become acute."

I was grateful for the winter sunlight pouring unrestrained through the leafless tree. In high summer this seat would be deeply shaded at this time of day; people would sit here to enjoy the cool; but now the naked boughs, passing almost free the tepid shine, could be called a providence on my chilled veins. If Rene's soul had not perished, I wondered what providence had been made for it in Kali's courts or wherever it might be. In the winter of death, was it grateful for the pale remnants of the too great abundances of the summer of life? I wanted it to sleep. . . . Go to sleep, Rene. Pay no attention to these affairs. I will look after everything. . . .

"You say, Jeffery, you were relieved to hear of his death. Doesn't that suggest that you'd been in doubt as to whether it would occur?"

"Of course."

"When Europa's brother Eugene took his horses to the outskirts of Paris, you were still doubtful?"

"Eugene had written me that he expected to ride with your lover, who fancied himself quite a horseman. . . . Look, Lola, at that jackdaw. Someone's been feeding him here. Look at his bright lecherous eyes—"

I did look at the creature. He hopped about with a vivacity somehow revolting; as though his every aim and appetite had the nature of lechery. He could not pick up a crumb of bread with decency; of all God's creatures I knew none that so mocked Him. A vulture, accursed aforetime, did the same hideous hopping to his dreadful feast, but otherwise had a somber, perhaps a tragic dignity of doom; his cousin the big carrion crow whom the daw so reviled had horrid habits that he could not help, but a fellow feeling for others afflicted, the potentiality of grace. A jackdaw could be taught to talk, but always in a tone of raucous contempt for his teachers. Saved from the Flood by the Ark, he had since joined the enemy camp. Every move and sound he made was in gloating over his apostasy—flaunting his assurance that the enemy camp would win.

My brain reeled, then went back to what Jeffery had just said.

"When Monsieur Eugene wrote you about Rene—his fancying himself a horseman—didn't it remind you of your father, fancying himself quite a mountaineer?"

"He didn't, as a matter of fact. He considered himself a true sportsman and a never-say-die Englishman. I can't help but smile to remember how he looked down his nose the same time he was blustering agreement to my suggestion that we needn't rope up."

"I suppose Monsieur Eugene had to smile when he saw Rene in his pink coat. Such a fine fox hunter couldn't possibly refuse to follow him over a three-foot wall."

"We all have our little vanities. Saint-Denis was an admirable fellow—he deserved a better end. I mean, Lola, fate dealt rather meanly toward him, to have him break his neck in that ridiculous attire. It was different with my father. He fell clean nearly two hundred feet, howling like a Comanche Indian. It wasn't altogether from terror, either—it was partly fury, I think, and partly a last bravado taking that quite magnificent form. The effect was even more magnificent. I suppose you know that the vibrations of the human voice often dislodge loose rock on steep slopes. His howls loosed some stones that came bounding after him, knocking down others, some of them jumping fifty feet in the air. There was a fine clatter and then a rumble and finally a deep-toned roar as the stuff crashed into the ravine a thousand feet below."

"Could you still hear your father?"

"His shouts were cut off in about three seconds, I should say, at the foot of the sheer cliff. When the last echo had died, the silence was sublime. I'd expected to come in only to the barony and to Vivian—now I felt as though I had inherited the whole world."

"You suggested that his shouting was partly from fury. Did you mean—at you?"

"Oh, no. At what he thought was his bad luck—or at his folly in getting in such a fix—or even at what he called God. We hear of a good many people, knowing they are going to die, calling on God for mercy, but I dare say a great many hate Him worse than hell. This is when they can no longer speak—when they're dropping faster and faster down a bottomless cliff. . . . To get back to your question, it couldn't cross my father's mind to blame me in the least. He had persuaded himself that I loved him—I dare say most fathers are similarly persuaded about their sons. Possibly a glimmer of the idea might have struck him just before he struck the rock —I've often wondered about that. Isn't it strange, Lola, that although truth sticks out like a sore thumb, nine times out of ten people will believe the lie? Any old lie, just so it's a little more pleasant than the truth. That's especially true in regard to evil. 'Good' people can't bear to look at it, even to admit it exists. They'll admit crime committed by strangers—they're quick to believe 'the worst' of anybody they know—meaning that he sleeps with his neighbor's wife— but evil out of hell is intolerable to their minds—unless, as I say, at the very last, when they've got nothing left to lose, they see the light."

"The light," I echoed.

"What's wrong with that figure of speech? Do you think that good is bright and evil is dark? The best place to do evil is under the lamp. And if they do catch a glimpse at the very last, is it too late?"

I could not keep my eyes off Jeffery's face. His eyes were alive and glowing with his thoughts; nothing less than grandeur was in its acquiline molding; I knew him for an illustrious prince. The movements of his nobly formed lips in shaping words made my lips burn. . . . At a distance, we would be taken for innocent young wooers. The living and the dead would be no wiser. The best place to do evil is under the lamp.

"Too late for what?" I asked.

"An interesting thought occurs to me. If what we call the spirit survives after the body's death, it must be by some unity with the spirit of the living. At least it would attempt such a union—its naked existence in a material world would be a poor dish—it would want flesh and senses whereby to realize life. If it couldn't do any better it might employ the body of an animal. The whole cult of lycanthropy—still alive in southern Germany and thriving vigorously all the way to the China Sea—is, of course, based on that supposition. For instance, a Bulgarian peasant might suspect that jackdaw of harboring the spirit of the preceding Lord Lundy. He's got enough life for two and seems very interested in our conversation. Or, say, that of your lover, Saint-Denis. Personally, I regard it as one of the most childish and empty of the superstitions."

"That isn't what you were starting to say."

"No, I was going to say that if a spirit could, it would unite with one with whom it had a strong tie in life, and who would promise it as much renewed life—as many thrills—as possible. It would look for the strongest partner obtainable. Then why not with its own dispatcher?"

"What do you mean, Jeffery?"

"I mean, my dear, King Hamlet's ghost not uniting himself with his weak son, but with his strong brother. Isn't it a great deal more likely? He'd found out that evil wins. That it happened to be practiced against himself makes the fact only more plain. If my father's soul ever realized that my taking him mountain-climbing wasn't entirely for the pleasure of his company, it would lose no time in uniting with mine. Do you think it would go searching for some boresome heaven resounding with hosannas? It would jump at the chance, of course."

"And become another Young Berkeley in your service?"

"To carry on the conceit—yes."

"Was that why you didn't worry as to whether Rene or I led the way into the aisle of poles?"

"I could argue—for the sport of it—that your spirit would certainly join my camp, if not come in to mine."

"You don't say things like that for the sport of it, such awful things. Why do you say them?"

"You forget, Lola, that I'm something of a theologist." He tapped the stem of his watch, then held it to his ear. "The afternoon has passed very swiftly."

Truly it had passed and the evening shadows were long and cold.

"Our further business will have to be postponed," I said.

"I'm sorry to hear that."

"I have a few other private affairs that must be attended to. But they ought not to take very long."

"You'll hurry, won't you? Remember that I've been faithful to you from the day we met. The other women in my life have been only shadows of you. You can't say the same of yourself."

"No, I can't. My lovers have been the antithesis of you."

"Yet that is proof of the power of our bond. I know that finally it can't be denied by either of us—that our bodies and spirits will be united. The day it happens is the day that I live for, and in the end I would never be content with less. Yet I've been a most ardent lover, never remiss in my attentions, and perhaps you are now ready to give me a first reward."

"What reward would you like?"

"One night's possession of your beautiful body, without any yielding of your spirit, before we separate for the last time."

"I'd like to give it to you. A few minutes ago, I came close to offering it to you. Not as a reward for your devotions, but from desire. But I'm afraid I couldn't give it without my spirit, which I'm not yet ready to surrender."

"Will you try and see?"

"Not now. Not until I've settled some other affairs."

"Then let me know when you're ready to settle ours, and we'll arrange a rendezvous anywhere in the world you wish."

"I want to meet you on the moor."

He turned white from suspense. When he spoke, he held his voice low to try to hide its tremor.

"I'm not certain what you mean. Until now you've insisted that we meet on neutral ground. I hardly dare speak what I hope you mean—"

"I'll meet you on the moors of Blackmoor—where you went with Mab de Lille—where you lost Vivian."

"Where I lost both Vivians."

His pupils spread until they filled the irises brimful and turned into mirrors of intense blackness, in which the darkest image would look white. I was afraid to look into them until the blue rims again emerged and slowly widened.

"And where," he went on, with a dim beautiful smile, "I will find both of them again in you."

FORTY-TWO

A TOUR of eastern Germany in the breaking spring took longer than I thought, and I headed for London in great haste. Then horses went lame, trains ran late, and ships encountered head winds, all to stay me from seeing Thames mouth until almost summer. The deposit I had made at the Far Eastern Hotel was calculated to board Manu a bare month. If both my letter to him and his voyage to me had sped, he might be come and gone.

But the host, an affable Levantine, greeted me with a smile too bright to screen bad news. The old Celestial, as he called him, had arrived a fortnight before; except for some astonishment at the amount of water in the world, his aplomb had been perfect; able to speak only a hundred or so English words, he had already explored a good part of London. Where was he this minute? This minute he was making his way to Regent Park to visit the zoo, his favorite resort.

I went there and stalked the bypaths until I caught sight of a turban. At this distance its wearer did not give away his age, but his bearing was proud, and on working nearer I saw that his costume was most proper. It would not be for Manu, servant of Lola Memsahib, to show meanly before the alien, even while he was waiting for her summons. His loincloth was formally fastened, his chadar as sedately wrapped as a Brahman's, his coat blue silk, and, despite the warm weather, his shoulders were draped in Cashmere shawls. He swam before my eyes, and I hid in a crowd until I could steady myself.

Manu was standing close to the elephant pen, his nose not three feet from the dangling, dejected-looking trunk of an old cow. Not far away stood a high hedge planted when the Prince Regent had laid out the grounds for a palace; and I thought to my great joy that by crossing the grass I could take him by surprise. While sneaking up on him, my heart's tom-tom beat out a little tune I had not heard since we had knelt together in the rain.

Then I must weep again, for, on the assumption that he was out of hearing of the outlanders, he was in conversation with the elephant. It was a correct assumption, I thought, with a surge of my soul. No human being but me was in sound of his voice, and I, too, was of the Hind-log. So were the other elephants who might give ear. Probably all of them had been born in the Indian jungle, amid the silence and dimness, and the still, green-tinted air, then taken prisoner in *kheda* operations; for very rarely would the grave giants breed in captivity where their pigmy masters could watch their mountainous passions, and where the calves must wear chains.

I could not hear what he was saying, but could imagine him remarking on the differences, which Hathi was bound to notice, between London and India. The rain here, for instance, unworthy of the name, being a miserable cold drizzle by which the rice and melons at home would scorn to sprout. The moon and stars were smaller and less bright, because they were either a different set altogether, or much farther away. The food was manifestly inferior for man and beast. He felt for Hathi, having to eat dry hay instead of juicy grass and delectable sugar cane; but he himself had not had a passable curry since his arrival.

"Badzat!" I called from behind the hedge. By cupping my hands over my mouth I tried to disguise my voice.

Manu whirled, his eyes round with awe.

"Barnshoot!" I shouted, the most comprehensive insult in Hindustani.

But there was too much joy in my voice to fool him any longer.

His *"Lola!"* in reply sounded like the wind in the chimney of the cottage on the moors ere my bridal adventure. He came running toward me as I clawed through the hedge.

It had happened that about a dozen people, collecting to watch some action in the next pen, had moved in our direction only the second before. When I thought of them again, they were standing about ten steps distant, most of them gawking in lively pleasure. Near them, but managing not to be among them, were two blond young men whose walk and Malacca walking sticks indicated that they might be army officers in mufti, and whose sun-browned faces suggested they were lately home from a tropic clime. These might be pleasant faces in their native haunts, but in India they had had practice in expressions of cold contempt, into which they readily fell. Into such they had fallen now.

"The most disgraceful exhibition I've ever seen," one remarked to the other loudly enough to be heard by the whole assembly.

I felt hardly any surprise at this interlude and no dismay. Surely only a rare chance had brought two sahibs to catch a young memsahib and her Indian servant in a tearful embrace, and, even if painfully pukka, as Englishmen they could be expected only to raise their eyebrows and stalk past; but this was a great moment in Manu's and my life, deserving of some notice by the gods.

"To look at her, one would think she was a pukka memsahib," the other officer replied in a tone of lordly scorn. "But fine feathers don't mean fine birds."

It was going to be all right. . . . The gods were in high good humor. . . . I could not guess what . . .

"So ye gentlemen don't like it?"

It was a big male voice rising from the cluster of gawkers. I had noticed there a hulking countryman, but until now I had not realized that he was taller than his brawn made him appear and that he stood lightly on his feet.

"If you're addressing me, I do not," one of the officers replied.

"Nor do I," his friend added—the conversation seeming as formalized as that of a Punch-and-Judy show.

"Well, how would ye gentlemen like it if I snatched ye by the backs of your dirty necks, and kicked your arses from 'ere to Piccadilly?"

The two officers stared haughtily, then swung their sticks and walked on.

"And ye, Chris, come with me," a skinny little cockney girl told the giant, clutching him by the arm. "Ye've no call to use such 'orrid language in front of the lady."

"The 'orrider the better, Chris," I cried, streaming tears, "and God bless you."

In a moment Manu and I were again alone. He turned to me, a high flush on his face.

"Think you it was Krishna?" he asked.

"Why not?"

"Aye, I believe it was very Krishna, but I did not know he could speak English."

"He speaks in all languages, and all lands."

Manu was eager for me to see the Hind-log in the zoo—following me properly to the pens and cages when people were in view, at other times holding my hand. His own odyssey had stirred his imagination in regard to his compatriot's captivity in a far-off land.

"What in our tongue is this writing?" he asked, indicating a sign on iron bars.

" 'The common panther of India,' " I answered.

"And that one?"

" 'The black panther of India.' "

"The black and spotted ones are in different cages, as though they are the Hind-log and the sahib-log. Doesn't the keeper know they are full brothers of the womb?"

"I didn't know it either."

"Aye, often the spotted mother drops a black cub as a white ewe a black lamb. But mark you, Lola, although the cubs start life even save for the color of their skins, they do not end up even. All hunters know that a full-grown black panther is more to be feared than his spotted brother. Why is that?"

"I don't know, Manu."

"Nor do I. But it comes to me that the black panther can't hide in the spotted light and shadow of the jungle as does his sibling, and hence must more often do battle. Also the villagers say he belongs to Shaitan, and tie out goats for him to curry his favor. They say so only because he's black, as they picture the devil. But it comes to me that the children of evil don't declare themselves so by their color."

"I'm of the same opinion."

"Now here's the pen of his great kinsman, the royal tiger. Truly he's a prince in his own jungle, turning from his path only for a raging elephant. Behold the pride with which he paces, gazing at us with sleepy yellow eyes. Does he feel cast down? Does he think his princehood has been taken away from him? Nay, every day meat is put before him, without his lifting a paw. Clean straw is provided for his bed. What is that but tribute to his majesty? Does he think the people have come to see him? Why not that they are brought here, for him to see?

"Hard by is the den of bears. . . . Many of these I know not, but he with the white chevron on his breast comes from the highlands of India. He lives on wild fruit and grubs and honey, but if men come upon him suddenly in the thickets he will charge and kill. Then as he gazes at his slain, he must say to himself, 'What a fool I was to be startled half out of my wits by these big rabbits!' Even so, no qualm of regret touches his brute heart. How did Brahm come to dream such a dream as he!"

"How did he come to dream of these wicked ones?" I asked, when we had come to the snake pits.

"Are they wicked? It's true that if you are bitten by this long one"—Manu pointed to a twelve-foot king cobra—"you will live but the fourth part of an hour. If you're bitten by this short one,"—he indicated a two-foot krait—"you'll live a full hour. If you are bitten by yonder rat snake, bigger than both put together, you'll live to old age, unless otherwise stricken down. In the mouths of two, Brahm dreamed poison; in the other he dreamed only teeth. Is it fair that the first two should be sent to hell on that account, and the third spared the punishment?"

"If the cobra bites his own kind, will the bitten die?"

"Nay."

"Do any of those jungle folk slay their own kind?"

"Almost never. They fight for the best food and the best wives, but the vanquished one makes off, limping and ashamed. Only man slays his own kind as a common thing."

"Man is more bloodthirsty than a tiger, more pitiless than a bear, more venomous than a snake."

"Brahm dreamed him so, the priests say. Truly, man is the only evil in the world, and I think he is the only ugliness and the only beauty, the only truth and the only lie—but my head swims. Let us go and look at the innocent deer. Once my smell would have given them a great fright, but they are used to it now, and one—an old hind—will put her nose through the bars to be scratched. Then by your leave we will see a buffalo, feigning to be a wild bull from the jungle, but who is only a tame plow beast, shirking work in a pen as fine as a giraffe's. Finally we will laugh like little children at the monkey-log."

When all this was behind us, I bought a bottle of spiced wine at a vintner's, and we drank it in a secluded corner of the park.

"Didn't you tell me, when I was a chota memsahib, that I must surpass the other memsahibs of Hind and become a great shahzady?" I asked.

"Aye, I said it would come to pass."

"The time is now near for your word to be made good. As soon as we can get ready, we'll go to the court of a great maharajah, where I shall seek to be made a countess. Now that's the same rank as though I were the wife of the earl who long ago kissed my hand at the levee in Dinapore."

"Would you then march ahead of most all the memsahibs?"

"Only wives and daughters of kings, and duchesses and marchionesses, would precede me through a door and sit ahead of me at table. I would precede and sit ahead of viscountesses, baronesses, the wives of baronets and knights, and all without title. At great levees I could wear a small crown, called a coronet. This would be blazoned on my carriage, if I have one, and even on the paper on which I write letters."

"That would be an excellent thing." Manu's eyes gleamed.

"To be created a countess by a king would be a great triumph. Thus it is well that we put aside all future affairs until the prize is either won or lost. Mark, that we needn't make haste. One year—two—three—wouldn't be too many to spend in the keeping of a vow great as this. Thereby a last wish of my father will come true, and in the quest I'll obey his last command. Thereby I will pay a large debt to my mother and a small one—though it doesn't seem small in my heart—to Lady Kirk and her like. Thus I may prove myself before the gods. And besides all that, Manu, you and I will be happy as the day is long."

Manu took my hand and kissed it, his eyes bright with tears. "Aye, we will be happy as in long ago, before you looked upon the evil pooja in Chota Nagpur."

"In the many moons and perchance suns of our joyous adventure, we won't speak of what may lay beyond, so if anything need be said in that regard, it's best we say it now."

"That also is true."

"Have you any news for me, Manu, ere we set forth?"

"In your letter, you bade me inquire of Nelson Sahib, the boatswain who was your lover. It so chanced that with only a fortnight's wait at the port, I, too, sailed upon the *Lord Clive* to Suez. Nelson Sahib was not then aboard, but the lascars spoke of him freely when, after their speaking of him on their own account, I led them on."

"Did the lascars speak highly of him?"

"They said he was the best of the sahib-log they'd ever known."

"Did they tell you of his fortunes?" I was braiding grass blades and did not look at Manu.

"They said that having wedded a memsahib of the North, he was now a mate on a ship of his own nation."

"That's good news. Did the lascars tell of how he came to my stateroom on the ship?"

"Only near the journey's end, when I had made fast friends with one of them, did he tell me. It had never been spoken of on the ship, but a sahib passenger had told Reeve Sahib of seeing Nelson

Sahib go there and Hosain heard of it only through a babu in the employ of a lawyer, who came to make inquiries. Nelson Sahib beat him with a frayed rope and sent him shrieking away."

"That was in Bombay?"

"Yes, memsahib." Manu, whose hands were almost always under good control, began to braid grass blades.

"Is it meet, Manu, that you should hide your thoughts from me?"

"Nay, Lola, by my soul! After beating the babu, Nelson Sahib sailed the next day with his shipmates. At Suez, when he went ashore, he was set upon at night by *badzats* and terribly beaten, so that for half a year he could not sail on any ship, and his face was changed, and he will limp a little to the day he dies. It was thought that the babu somehow sent word to his evil friends in Suez on that very sailing."

After a long time—not half a year, perhaps only half a minute whose passing was as unfelt as centuries by the dead—my blood warmed and thinned again, and was again thrust by the pump of my heart, and my slack vocal cords tightened to make sound.

"If so, it was fast work. What did you think, Manu?"

"I was glad of a folly, perhaps a wickedness, I had committed before leaving Patna."

"Is it to be revealed?"

"Aye. When I learned from your letter of the death of the great sahib, I trembled with fear. So with five rupees I bought from a Nepalese what is known as a kukri. When my chadar is correctly folded, I may wear it flat upon my chest, well-concealed, but easy of access."

"Show it to me."

Manu did so by one smooth movement of his hand. However, I had seen kukris before—curved knives with heavy convex blades which, striking with an overhead sweep, will cleave a man's skull and sometimes split his breastbone. Usually they are carried in bulky wooden scabbards. This one was in a loose sheath of dried deerskin. Its hilt was of beautiful worked teakwood and its edge was razor sharp.

"It is made for killing people, and I hate it," I said.

"But it is also used for chopping wood and many other things."

"It belongs to Kali, not to Krishna the Joyous."

"Aye, Krishna carries only a pipe on which to play to the cow-herdesses ere he frolics with them. But Krishna can be wrathful, as we have seen."

"No matter what wrath is upon you, you shall not take it from its sheath. If I'm slain in your plain sight, you shall not draw it in revenge. For my life taken from me there is no blood price, and that is the word gone forth from me that I shall not recall and you shall not disobey. Only in defense of our lives or of what is dearer or of some other in mortal danger may it be wielded, in hope of God's mercy upon us."

"If I should see you slain, I could not hold my hand—"

"If you can't hold your hand in that pass, take it now from off my heart, and go your way."

"Wah! And this is the chota memsahib I carried in my arms from the great pooja of Chota Nagpur! Truly you are Lola, who before now was Râdhâ, beloved of Krishna, named for Lohar of the Great Iron. Nay, I will not draw the knife save by your consent or at your command, and if I break that word, may you be parted from me in this life and all lives to come, and may I wail outside your door through all eternity in vain! The steel shall lie inert against my breast. I shall not speak of it if you will but remember it is there. Remember, too, that I am only an old gardener of little wit, but I love you until earth and heaven shall pass away. Now will you arise that I may kneel and kiss your feet in token of our bond? If you will not, give me leave to die!"

"Nay, but in great joy thereof, I will kiss your mouth."

FORTY-THREE

*N*EXT to Prussia, Bavaria was the greatest of the German lands. Like the third of his kingdom which King Lear gave Goneril, it was a populous domain "with shadowy forests and with champains rich'd, with plenteous rivers and wide-skirted meads," only on a much grander scale. Indeed the great Danube swept two hundred miles through its lovely hills and dales, and the Main drained its fertile plains to pour into the Rhine. Its capital, Munich, was not the equal of Paris or Vienna, but compared favorably with Brussels, Buda-Pest, and Prague, and in my opinion beat Berlin hollow.

Manu and I did not arrive there as soon as we had intended. I had danced very little since losing Rene and was short of money and clothes, both of which I needed in good store for what might be a long siege of Ludwig's palace. But we had forsworn haste, and our year together on the road was itself a joyous adventure. I performed at most of the big cities west of Warsaw, eschewing Munich only to enhance the novelty and I hoped the sensation of its future storming. In the way of fame and fortune, it was my most successful year upon the boards.

Near its end, I wrote the Countess Von der Hellen, telling her of my proposed adventure. I made plain that I did not expect from her a letter of introduction to Ludwig, which would embroil her, however slightly, in what might become an *affaire célèbre,* but would be grateful if she wrote him confidentially about a visitor coming soon to his kingdom. She replied with a warmhearted note that the situation was far more complicated than I realized, but she would attempt to do a great favor for her old friend the king, hoping that it would turn out the like for me. To Herr Freys, manager of the Hof Theater in Munich, I addressed a request for an engagement. Encouraged by his enthusiastic reply, Manu and I set happily forth, arrived at the capital in an auspicious rainstorm, and put up grandly at the Hotel Maulick.

From that moment the pleasant, leisurely movement of events began to quicken as though the short hands of the big clocks looking down on us were bustling to overtake the long hands.

When I called at the office of Herr Freys, he sent word out by a henchman that he was engaged, and anyhow he had decided against my appearance at his theater. I had no choice but to retire with all the dignity I could muster. Before I could catch my breath, a card bearing the name of Count Rechberg was sent up to my room. Ten minutes later my hand was being kissed by one of the most romantic-looking young noblemen I had ever seen. He had the honor, he told me, clicking his heels, to be equerry to Ludwig, King of Bavaria.

"I am sensible, Count Rechberg, of the honor of your visit."

When we were seated at a coffee table, he laid aside formality with his gloves and walking stick and spoke frankly and earnestly.

"Miss Montero, I didn't come here at His Majesty's command. Always I try to save him making commands which, for one reason or another, he would find embarrassing to acknowledge. But he's aware of my visit to you, and it's in accordance with his wishes."

"I'm most grateful."

"It happens that two friends in whom he puts great confidence have spoken to him of you. He intended to honor the theater with his presence and summon you to his box. But because he had expressed this interest in you, some very powerful people in the kingdom took steps to prevent his meeting you."

"I don't understand how they could cross the king."

"Alas, the king is subject to public and official pressures. I could say much more, but this is neither the time or place. The two persons who prevailed upon Herr Freys to cancel your engagement are Herr Senfft, the agent of the king's sister Queen Caroline-Augusta in Vienna, and Von Abel, the prime minister. The reason given was that you are a divorced woman of notorious character. The real reason—but I'll say only that the high praise the countess gave you defeated its purpose. By stopping your performance, they were quite certain that they had prevented the presentation."

"If he considered the countess's recommendation valid, couldn't he summon me to court?"

"He could—but he won't. In the first place, religious hypocrisy has reached the point in Munich whereby his inviting to court a divorced woman would be shouted in the press. In the second place— and I'm compelled to be frank—of late His Majesty has been constantly less assertive. Indeed, I may say that the Austrian queen and Von Abel are the real rulers of Bavaria."

Count Rechberg was about twenty-six, handsome, dashing, and debonair. One might, therefore, make the mistake of underestimating his powers and passions. Suddenly I perceived that he was capable of great affairs. The finest thing about him, I thought, was his loyalty to the king, blazing through every word and expression. Part and parcel with it was the courageous statement he had just made.

"Then how may I go about meeting King Ludwig?" I asked.

"Present yourself at the palace, on the excuse of bearing a personal message from Countess Von der Hellen. I will see that friendly gentlemen-in-waiting are at the doors."

"That is very kind, Count Rechberg."

"Pray do not give me credit I don't deserve. Having seen you dance in Vienna, and hearing such pleasant reports of you from the old countess and from Liszt, I was resolved that His Majesty be not deprived of what pleasure he might derive from a few hours in your company. He is one of the loneliest men on earth, and his pleasures these days are like angel visits, brief and far between. Since meeting you, I find myself thrilled by a new hope. Have I your permission to speak with utmost frankness?"

"I wish you would."

"Reading between the lines of the countess's letter, I took it you might be amenable to a prolonged association with the king, provided he desired it."

"That's quite true."

"Some of the best in the world, both men and women, have sought preferment in the courts of monarchs. In this case every true well-wisher of the king and of his people would be overjoyed if he could make a romantic friendship that would revive, even briefly, his joy in life and his interest in the living world. In his younger years he set much store on the beauty of woman. Now he's lost all that, and there seemed no hope of its being restored. Even if the king dared defy the Austrian party and the Hypocrites by having a favorite, the girl's position would be one of utmost difficulty. They know that their power lies in separating him from the people—in letting him wither away in his gloomy palaces—and they would hound her in the press and have her mobbed in the streets. Knowing what they were in for, few young women of real worth would accept the post. Yet since meeting you, I've had the strangest inkling that you might take up the challenge, and win! If I ever laid eyes on a beautiful adventuress who might turn the tide of the king's debility and decline, you are the one."

"It's a very great compliment," I answered, my spine tingling in a joyous way I had forgotten. I had not expected an adventure of this scope.

"Will you try it, Lola?"

"I'd love to!"

"Then listen to me and believe me. Victory can't be won in one meeting with His Majesty, but it can be hopelessly lost. It's not enough to please him, or even to delight him: while he might have the inclination to invite you again, he wouldn't have the spirit. You must capture his imagination powerfully and at once. Are you reasonably well informed on the fine arts?"

"I've had instruction in them," I said, thinking of Señor Professor.

"He's had no other real interest in years. His greatest and indeed only pride is his beautification of Munich, and no doubt that will be your best avenue of approach to him." The nobleman reflected, then his face fell. "At best it's a frail chance—"

"If I'm to attempt it, Count Rechberg, I ask that you be completely frank as to the obstacles."

"The greatest is the ingrown isolation of the king. It's a vicious circle—the more he withdraws, the greater his suspicion of those who attempt to approach him. He is quick to uncover their hidden motives. Courtiers get short shrift."

"I may get short shrift, but he won't uncover any hidden motives in me."

"What do you mean, Miss Montero?"

"I haven't any."

He looked curious, then decided not to prolong the interview. "I suggest that you present yourself at five."

I presented myself in a brown velvet frock remarkably quaint and demure. Passed along from door to door by courteous gentlemen-in-waiting, I was brought finally to one in charge of the palace guard. Count Rechberg announced me and went out; I walked on foamy rugs toward a rosewood desk as big as Liszt's piano, behind which sat a gray-haired man in a long black coat. I had glanced at the pictures and statuary as I passed; but at him I looked long and intently. Thereby I knew that the long chance I meant to play was my only chance.

Ludwig was a tired and troubled king. But a king he was—a thing rare and mysterious. My mind was telling me that while some men sat on thrones with all the outward show of kingship, they were not kings; they had not entered into the mysteries of the appointment and emerged majestic. Majesty was something like grace, I thought—it permeated the body, mind, and soul; it was also comparable to genius. That was one reason the character of King Lear was such a magnificent creation. Dethroned, naked, and mad, he remained a king.

The man who had become King of Bavaria was a sensitive, imaginative, good man, without much strength of character. His face had lighted up at sight of me, then dimmed, and he looked only weary. When after my curtsy he had invited me to sit down, his direct gaze avoided me and instead moved among the wonders in paint, ivory, wood, bronze, and stone. Was it my first visit to Munich? How did I like the Konigsbau? I must visit the Englischer Garden and the Nymphenburg Woods . . .

"I'm sorry that I won't have the honor of dancing for you," I broke in.

"We were sorry to miss the pleasure," he answered, a little startled. "We were told you're a great artist—"

"I'm not, sire. I'm a popular performer. But the plain people like me, and even the connoisseurs are glad to get down to earth now and then."

"To earth—" Again his eyes rested fully upon me. "Yes, I should think they would." For the first time he used "I" instead of the royal "we."

"I dare say even a king would like to, occasionally," I suggested.

"Some rulers do so. I envy them but don't appear able to emulate them. All strength comes from God's earth. Tell me, Miss Montero, are you Spanish?"

"No, sire, I was born in Ireland."

"You must be of high birth, to have such delicate beauty."

"It's delicate, perhaps, but it, too, comes from the earth. I'm well born on my father's side only."

"Then Lola Montero is only a stage name?"

"No, sire. I adopted Montero from the name of a Spanish savant with whom I was once in love. I chose Lola when I was a little girl in India, in admiration of Lohar, the blacksmith."

"A blacksmith?"

"I was thrilled to see him lift and pound the iron."

"I can understand that. I was once thrilled to see a groom master a vicious stallion. By the way, my old friend Gertrude, Countess Von der Hellen, wrote glowingly of you. I assumed she wanted royal favor on your performance. But she went to considerable lengths—"

Ludwig paused and looked at me with a startled question.

"She hoped for more than that, sire," I said.

"Can you—will you tell me what?"

"She hoped that you would favor me."

He held his breath a second or two and then asked, "In what way?"

"In a relationship like that of Louis XV to Du Barry."

"*Gott im Himmel!* I must confess that possibility crossed my mind. She's a romantic old soul and often tells me that I am ceasing to be human—" He stopped, his brows knitted. "Pardon me, Miss Montero, but I'm still puzzled. You no doubt wanted some fanfare to further your career—perhaps an invitation to dance at the palace. But you must have permitted Gertrude to think—"

He stopped because he was embarrassed. It was there that I had an advantage of him, for I was not.

"I was perfectly frank with her, sire."

"Does that mean you confess—" He stopped.

"If you mean by confession an admission of guilt, I do not. I feel no guilt. I was told years ago that you would be happier and therefore a better king if you had a beautiful young woman to be your companion. I hoped you would choose me."

He rose, went to a window, then resumed his seat.

"What did you mean, Miss Montero, by the word 'companion'?"

"I mean someone to be with you day and night, whose mind and body you could enjoy."

"But I don't understand. You have every mark of a lady—unless it is your frank speech, for which I'm very grateful. You are beautiful and young, able to charm young men or to make an advantageous marriage. How, when you had never laid eyes on me, could you assume that you could tolerate such a relationship with me?"

"I assumed that I could. I'd never heard anything about you that would make me assume otherwise."

I began to speak slowly, feeling my way—I had never before been forced to put the matter in words. "I think I make the same assumption about most men with whom I have a good deal in common. But for me to feel that I would not merely tolerate but enjoy such a relationship, there must be a strong appeal to my senses or emotions. I must want to make a man happy—give him a great gift, perhaps—pay him a great tribute. In that case I feel thrills that I know could grow into passion. I think all normal women respond so, unless deeply in love with someone or thwarted by guilt or fear, although a very great number may deny it to themselves. Also many women are ashamed of their sex and hence don't regard the gift of their beauties as a great gift. Differing from so many, yet I can't feel guilty about what my woman's heart tells me is good. I mustn't be afraid, because even as a child I was committed to become an adventuress. When I heard about you, my imagination was strongly stirred. It would be a wonderful adventure, I thought, to become a favorite of a king. I could imagine myself talking over with him his great affairs—comforting him when he's tired—trying to help him be a good king. I've seen only a few kings in my life, and have never been kissed by one. I thought how wonderful it would be to have him choose me for his sweetheart and take me to his bed. Understand that in this I was assuming he would appeal to my senses or my emotions. My emotions were already touched by what I heard about you—living utterly alone; giving over your power to others; trying to make a life out of pictures and statuary. Imagining myself your rescuer gave me a romantic thrill that I felt sure could lead to other thrills. Any doubt I had in my mind as to wanting to be your sweetheart was relieved at my first sight of you. You were gray and tired-looking, but you filled my ideal of a real king."

While I was speaking at this length, I had tried not to be influenced by his responses. There had been a conflict of emotions in his face, and some of the things I was saying had hurt or angered him. I had to go on with it, though. It was very doubtful that the complete truth would win for me, but I was perfectly sure that any departure from it would defeat me. To capture his imagination I had to trust it.

"Do you realize you're the first person who has dared say to me that I've given my power to others?" he asked, as though he could hardly believe his ears. There was anger in his face, but wonder, too.

"It's said whenever your name is mentioned, sire. About four years ago one of your subjects, a waiter, told me so. He said that others rule in your name and oppress the people. He wished the people could be brought back to you."

"The people can't eat their cake and have it. This is a limited monarchy. The so-called Austrian party wins at the ballot box— Abel heads the cabinet. But why I should explain to a dancing girl—"

"You needn't explain, sire. I only answered your question."

"Since I've gone this far, I'll ask another. Why do the people want to be brought back to me? I've never shown any great capacity as a ruler. Aren't a dozen heads better than one?"

"They believe, sire, that you care for them and will try to help them. They feel that they belong to you and you to them. They know that as a prince, you helped Greece win liberty from the Turks. You've never wanted to lead them to wars of conquest. You are already the king—so you have no ambitions to be served at their cost. That isn't true of politicians."

"All this is to imply that if I make you my mistress, I'll again take power into my hands—curb the Austrian party and Von Abel—stop withering away in art galleries—have closer ties with the people. Isn't that the implication? It seems to me perfectly plain."

"I think you'd love me more than any picture, and be more likely to love the people."

"This is the most extraordinary proposal ever made to me. The reason that I continue to listen—and not have you put out of the palace—is the feeling that you're perfectly sincere. No, that's not the only reason, if I, too, must be honest. However, it's time I tested your sincerity. What profit are you seeking—of a material sort, I mean—in this adventure?"

"If you came to love and prize me enough, I hoped you'd make me a countess."

"You said you were well born on your father's side. Did he bear arms?"

"He bore weapons, sire, at Waterloo. Wellington promoted him from the ranks to a lieutenancy on the field."

"That too is an astonishing reply. I must tell you to start with that the chances of my elevating to the nobility the daughter of a self-made officer wouldn't be one in ten, even if—but before I consider 'ifs' please come with me."

He led the way through a hall to a magnificent room hung with female portraits. This was "Die Schonheitengalerie"—the Gallery of Beauties—famous all over Europe. The subjects were all notably beautiful women whom the king had known. I recognized several, including the gorgeous Lady Milbanke, wife of a British ambassador, and Charlotte de Hagn, the great ballerina.

"I confess, Lola, you're a joy to my eyes," the king told me. "But perhaps they have been dazzled by your wonderful esprit. Does your portrait deserve to hang here?"

His voice was warm, now, and there were color and light in his face.

"That will be for you to decide."

"I'll make the decision here and now. You shall join the company —that much, at least, I'll have to commemorate a delightful adventure."

"It's a great honor, sire."

But it was not the honor I had sought. The delightful adventure that the king could thus commemorate was not the one I had hoped to share with him. He was taking this door to escape from me, this way to reject the renewal of life, its thrill and its love, which I could give him but which he did not crave enough to grasp. Some paint cleverly laid on a cloth would do in my stead—then he could go on dwelling in a dream. The cup of defeat was bitter at my lips.

But I did not drink it yet. My heart flamed. . . .

"May I propose an artist who I believe would do me justice?" I asked.

"Yes, and if he's available—"

"It's Ingres in Paris. He suggested I sit for him not long ago. He wants to paint me in the nude in a harvest field."

"That would be very beautiful. The setting would be perfect for you. The thought of it makes my blood flow warm. I would name it Demeter, I think—or Pocohontas. It might be the most beautiful in the gallery."

"Still—when you put your hand on the lovely-looking flesh, it will feel cold. Even Ingres can't make it glow with life."

"Life," he said in a low voice as he put his hand in mine to do with what I liked. "Wonderful life!"

FORTY-FOUR

$\mathcal{M}$ANY a story that I had told myself came true in the next year.

Like Du Barry, like Pompadour, I was the mistress of a king. He built a little palace for me on beautiful Barerstrasse, one of the gates of which no coach but his could enter. There I, Lola, who once had been Lucy Riley whom my step-grandam threatened to whip, had a salon wherein the *beaux esprits* of all Bavaria delighted to foregather, often to meet great men from beyond our borders. Neither seen nor heard frequently at the Residenzschlosse, I reigned supreme over Ludwig's country palace in Fulda Forest. Besides his darling, his joy, and his pride, I was becoming recognized, not only throughout the kingdom, but in council halls all over Europe, as his inspiration, whereby he was changing from a royal recluse to a reigning monarch.

A storm was surely brewing. I was in the way of the Austrian party and the Hypocrites led by Von Abel. There was beginning to be broad innuendo in the press regarding a modern Circe and her Indian magician practicing deviltry at the palace; but there was no open attack on me as yet, because the people were pleased with their king's emergence, and they must be courted before they could be inflamed. Indeed when the Abel-owned Palatia Corps of students at the university demonstrated against "foreign influence" in the court, a new corps called the Alemannia was formed in my defense. I was "honorary sister" to the dashing young men and I could not appear in the streets without them gathering about me with usually courtly but sometimes noisy homage.

When Herr Senfft, confidential agent of Queen Caroline-Augusta in Vienna, hired Manu to arrange a tête-à-tête, I was pleasantly excited. After making sure there was no one in hearing, he came to business quickly. If I would go to Paris and stay there, I could take with me the round sum of two hundred thousand francs.

"You're in a bed of roses now, Miss Montero," he told me, "but how long will it last? The people support you now, but we control the press, and they can be easily persuaded that you're debauching the king and betraying the country."

"I think it may last"—and in respect to my distinguished visitor I spoke my true opinion—"as long as two years."

"Possibly. What will happen then?"

"The tide will turn as it always does."

"Will Ludwig stand by you?"

"He can't, if the peace of the kingdom is at stake."

"Miss Montero, we have much in common. Both of us are adventurers—we've both come up a rough road. I can't tell you how much I respect your abilities and your spirit. In respect to your common sense, I'll ask another question. The Austrian party and those who are only too well described as the Hypocrites don't want and won't have a real reigning king. The stake is enormous—the guns they will unlimber are many and heavy—and you are their natural target. When you're forced to flee Munich a year or two from now, how much treasure can you carry away?"

"I may be lucky to escape with my life."

"Precisely."

"But you see, Meinherr, you've misjudged me. I'm an adventuress, but I'm also beloved by and loyal to the king."

He sat quietly a moment, a winning and I thought fine expression on his face.

"Is it true, Miss Montero," he asked thoughtfully, "that you desire to be raised to the nobility?"

"Yes, Meinherr."

"Don't be alarmed—I'm neither fool nor knave enough to offer you another bribe. I was only going to say that I hope you win the prize before too late. It won't affect the outcome in the least, and I've never met anyone more deserving."

He kissed my hand and departed.

When I told Ludwig what had been said, his eyes filled with tears.

"You would be safe here—I need never let you go—if you'll let me forget I'm the king," he told me.

"No, because I remember I'm the favorite of the king."

That night he told me he would create me the Countess of Landsfeld. In the morning he took great joy in devising my shield. The first of the four fields was to be red, bearing a white sword with a golden hilt, emblematic, he thought, of the power of beauty. In the second field, blue, was a gold-crowned lion rampant, as in the arms of his great ancestor Henry the Lion. A blue dolphin in a green field was an ancient emblem of humanitarianism, he said, as well as signifying constant changes in color, each more beautiful than the last. The fourth field, white, was to be charged with a single red rose. He did not know what it meant. It was only a sign that he loved me.

"And now I must go from you on business of my own," I told him three months later.

"Is that the way you reward me for making a peasant's daughter a great margravine?" He stamped about the room in mock wrath, then asked wistfully, "For how long?"

"I can make no promises, sire."

"You don't even promise to return?"

"I'll return if I may."

"What does this mean, Lola?"

"You've made me a countess, and it marks the end of a great adventure. I'll leave you with nothing owed between us, without bond save the bond of love, for such time as I must. If then you want me to return, and I'm able, I will do so in the pursuit of another great adventure, this time to keep a promise made to my father many years ago. I must go anyway, sire, but I will go with greater happiness and hope if you give me leave."

"Where is your forelock?" he asked with the dim smile that of all his expressions I was most fond.

"My head is thick today—"

"Aren't you Morgan le Fay? You remember that if a mortal could catch her by the forelock, she must perforce grant him his wish. But when Roland could have caught her thus, she threw an enchantment over him and floated away, so he never won the armor of Achilles. By what forelock can I hold you?"

FORTY-FIVE

NOTHING held or stayed Manu and me, as we made for Blackmoor. We set sail at Rotterdam and disembarked at Topsham. From hence we took stage to a village on the Teign; because a letter had gone ahead of us, we were met here by a two-horse carriage in the care of a venerable driver. Lodging had been engaged for us at the inn, the coachman told us; and we would start for Blackmoor soon after sunrise.

During our brief conversation he kept giving me troubled glances, after which he seemed to have difficulty collecting his thoughts. However, this appeared his only infirmity. He helped the porters with my baggage and his high-held head and independent manner indicated a vigorous old age. Oddly enough, he wore plain clothes instead of the impressive livery one would expect to go with the handsome horses, emblazoned harness, and baronial crest on the finely appointed rig.

"What is your name, Gramper?" I asked.

" 'Tis Owain, ma'am." His Devonshire accent had overlaid a richer dialect, I thought.

"It's a Welsh name, I believe."

"Aye, and I'm a Welshman born and bred."

In the morning we took down the ancient road that made to Two Bridges on the Dart, but soon stopped at the cut of a grassy lane.

"Here be one of the two roads to Blackmoor," Owain told me. "Lord Lundy bade me take ye up t'other, a league farther on, but I'll take ye this'n, if ye gi' me the word."

I felt surprise and pleasure that he would disobey Jeffery. It was not what I had expected from any of his minions—even this hardy old Taffy.

"What's to choose between them, Owain?"

"T'other's half a league shorter, but 'tis rougher, too, on account of the ore carts plying back and fore."

"Then let's take this one." I was quite sure that was what the old man wanted me to say.

"They be some fords and mudholes on this road, but naught to bother us. And it be true—this one's a heap more lonely."

Owain sat holding his reins tight, his whip lifted, and with what seemed deep anxiety on his worn but manly face.

"I don't mind the loneliness. We'll get to see more animals and birds."

Owain turned into it with every sign of relief. I could not imagine why, since most drivers like to keep to busy roads, where they may meet their fellows and now and then stop for a word or a nip in friendly courtyards. "A heap more lonely" probably did not half fill the bill. Ahead of us wound two wheel tracks, all but grown to grass, through the green wilderness. I had the sense of being suddenly deep on the moor, much farther out under the open sky.

"I wouldn't think that Lord Lundy's coach could travel this road," I remarked, when two wheels of our carriage went in and out of a pool of quagmire.

"That she can't," he answered cheerfully. "When he has great folk coom to visit him, lords and the like, they coom by t'other road."

"Who has come by this one in the past year?"

"A farmer, now and then, making a short cut to his cot."

"How long since you brought anyone over this road?"

He was not beholden to answer. I could see that in his face, but a kinder, better, perhaps braver impulse prevailed.

"Just when, I couldn't rightly say. But she was a young French lady who looked a little like ye."

"Was her name Mab de Lille?"

"Something like that, I warrant."

"Was her coming in over this road lucky for her—or unlucky?"

The old man got out a white-dotted blue handkerchief called a belcher—named in honor of a pugilist of fifty years before—and mopped his brow.

"Ter'ble hot, it is," he remarked.

"I'd call it very pleasant."

"That French lady—she didn't stay here very long, if ye'd call that unlucky. And if I ever dreamt that comin' this way was bad luck, I'd not brought ye."

Owain had no more to say for a long way. Time was streaming behind us, but we could not measure it as well as the curves and reaches of the road, the brooks we crossed, the great granite tors in whose blue shadows we sometimes passed, ducks and cranes flying overhead, and once a magnificent falcon that made me think of Vivian.

"Ye favor another lady who I knowed," Owain suddenly broke out. I had the curious impression that he had been thinking about this ever since he had fallen silent. Perhaps he had debated long with himself before deciding to speak of it.

"Miss Europa?"

He had his back to me, and I was a little excited, without knowing why, as I waited for his response. He held his head perfectly still.

" 'Twant her I was thinking of," he replied at last. "If you and she favor each other, I ne'er noticed it. No matter. 'Twas someone long ago."

Under his cap I saw Owain's gray hair. He had been alive on the earth, a definite and unique being, for perhaps seventy years; and suddenly a presentiment quickened my pulse.

"Did she live in Wales?" I asked.

"Aye, until she was sixteen."

"You raised her?"

"In a way of speaking."

"At sixteen she came to Blackmoor, to be the bride of a young lord?"

"Aye, and I coom wi' her."

"Her name was Lady Vivian Rhys, and she was Jeffery's mother."

"That be true. And ye favor her as she looked then almost beyond my wit to believe." He looked off across the moor, and the strange fancy came to me that if I could peer closely into his eyes, I would see her images.

"How old was she when you saw her last, if you care to tell me?"

"Why, she was seven and thirty. She'd dwelt at Blackmoor twenty-one years."

"So few?"

" 'Twas fair many, when ye count 'em up."

"Her husband was killed when her son was nineteen. She must not have outlived him very long."

"Only a year, 'twas."

"When she died, was she still beautiful?"

"Beautiful's no word for her, first to last. I know no word that's equal to making you see her."

"Has your master got a good portrait of her?"

"If ye mean Lord Lundy, he has none that I know of. They was two in the hall, both of 'em fit to talk, but they was took down one night, and I never seen 'em again. I'd give a pretty for a glance at one of 'em. And ye'll pardon me, for catching ye up when ye called his lordship my master."

"I thought you were his carriage-driver, Owain."

"I drive his carriages and his coach when he bids me, but I have no master, nor mistress either, now my lady's gone." He paused, and said slowly, "On any road I please."

"Did your lady and you first come by this road?"

"Aye; and now I'll show ye why I coom this way today wi' ye. 'Twill be a little way to walk, but on firm ground."

He tied the reins to a wheel, then led the way over the heath to two rows of big stones forming an aisle. Rene had told me of such monuments, found frequently on the moors, and usually in connection with a funeral barrow. At the end of the aisle was a ten-foot cross of hewn granite.

"'Tis a sight ye don't see no where for miles about," Owain told me. "Folk say that Saint Patrick himself raised it here when he passed this way from Glamorganshire—to beat off the devil them heathens worshipped 'mongst their rows of stones. He beat him so bad, folk say, that he won't come nigh this place."

It would have been a familiar story to Rene. He had told me of several stone crosses amid ancient monuments, their raising always attributed to some saint and wreathed with legend. Actually the cross was a pagan emblem before it was a Christian one, and was apparently associated with nature worship: hundreds had been found in the oldest reliquaries in India. This did not in the least dull the attention I was paying Owain. Instead I was intensely alert, fearful of missing the least nuance of his expressions.

"Then it must be a lucky cross," I suggested.

"Folk say the devil's hard put to it, to snatch the souls of 'em who's kissed it."

"Did the French lady kiss the cross?" I asked.

"Aye."

"Did Miss Europa?"

"Nay. She and her brother coom by the other road."

I had one more question to ask but this was not the time. Instead I pressed my lips to the rough stone and signaled to Manu to do the same. Owain had the air of having done what he could in a difficult and dangerous situation: from henceforth it was out of his hands.

We were a league farther on before it dawned on me that the clue I should follow up was Owain's declaration of his freedom. Freedom was a mysterious word, perhaps the most significant in all human relationships with the Seen and Unseen. It could apply to trivial things or it might describe the condition of a soul.

"I should have known you're a free man, Owain, by your not wearing livery," I said.

"Aye, but 'tis not always a sure thing," he answered. "Some what wears a lord's livery are free. Some that don't are bonded."

"Are you the only freeman at Blackmoor?"

"I'll not say yes or no. Ye can judge for yourself, if ye stay there long enough."

"Lord Lundy told me that if any one of his miners break his rules, the others stone him to death." But I hated the sound of this in the quiet noonday, under the summer sun among endless green things growing.

"Aye." The long-drawn word indicated thoughtfulness, but no affirmation or denial.

"If you should break one of his rules—"

"The miners wouldn't lay hand on me, much less a stone. They know I'm free. Lord Lundy would either take no notice, or bid me go my way."

"How did you come to be free, Owain? Can you tell me?"

"Why, 'tis a simple thing. I coom here with my lady, and since she was free, the like was I. She was never bound to stay, so I'm not. She was never aught but free, and when she chose to depart by a dark road, I could have gone wi' her. I would've if she'd told me she was going, and would take my hand."

Manu could not understand English, but a quality in Owain's voice made him reach and clutch my hand. Owain spoke quietly as might a king, whose words no man could challenge or rebuke.

"Lord Lundy didn't have much luck with his Vivians, did he?"

"I'll not answer that, miss, if ye please."

"Owain, did you and Lady Vivian come here by this road?"

"Aye."

"Did she kiss the cross?"

"Aye, and the like did I."

"How then could you believe in its good fortune?"

"The folk say so. My lady was fair happy for middling long; whether it helped her be, I'd not know. But I knowed she stayed free—free to come or to go, to live or to die. Now we be cooming to a deep ford. Ye'd best lift 'ee feet a mite."

We crossed the ford and began the ascent of a long down overhanging the stream. It was at least an hour past noon—we had come about twenty miles, I thought—and I had begun to wish we had put up a lunch. Lately Owain had been peering ahead, I thought for the first glimpse of Blackmoor Keep. I had dreaded it, a while ago —so little I knew what was waiting for me there—but suddenly weary and a little faint, I, too, watched for its towers. I had been fated to go there, perhaps the edict made on a moonlit night of long ago, when Manu had prophesied that I would look fate in the face. Perhaps the first law of my life was not to make Manu a false prophet.

When, near the top of the hill, Owain showed me the castle crowning a distant hill, my first feeling was of a contract kept, a pilgrimage all but completed. That was strengthened by my seeing that the distant pile was not really a castle in the sense of the great half-ruined fortresses on the Rhine, instead a many-towered mansion, differing greatly only in its setting from many lordly seats in England. It overlooked what appeared to be a wooded park and a good-sized village at the foot of the down. Smoke rose from what must be a mill of some sort nearby.

We were half the remaining distance and had turned from the lane into a hard-packed road when Manu spoke in a calm tone.

"Memsahib, there are two horsemen at the edge of the woods yonder."

I saw them in a moment. One, standing by a bay horse, was much shorter than the other, mounted on a gray. Then Owain, whose old eyes were still keen, saw them, too.

"There be Lord Lundy coom to meet ye," he said.

"Very well."

At that moment Jeffery waved, then cantered toward us. I had never seen him ride and my heart leaped with this new and unique joy. Grace is tranquility achieved through power. His happiness and beauty were as tranquil as his mastery of the beast that sped him to his desire. The whole scene had such deep meaning to my soul that at first my gaze did not differentiate horse and rider—their harmony gave the effect of my seeing a centaur. But soon I noticed what a magnificent horse this was. A gray stallion, not very tall, he was the finest I had ever seen with the possible exception . . .

No, there was no exception. He was even finer than when I had seen him last, from having a finer rider.

Jeffery stopped close by the cart with the tranquility of an eagle lighting. His eyes said so much I almost missed what his lips were saying.

"You told me, Lola, to meet you on the moor."

FORTY-SIX

THE moment became filled with small event to which I did not seem to pay attention . . . Jeffery's groom trotting up in what proved to be a sidesaddle—his light spring to the ground and removal of a saddlebag from which he took a small traveling case—his setting the case on the ground and then fastening the still bulging bag behind Jeffery's saddle. . . . Meanwhile, Jeffery was asking me about my journey, as he smiled into my eyes.

The groom was ready now. He stood waiting to give me his arm to help me down. Jeffery spoke in an easy tone to Owain.

"You can take Thad back with you. The countess and I will have lunch on the moor and then ride in."

I started to get out of the carriage only to be arrested by Manu's quiet but powerful glance.

"What is your command, memsahib?" he asked.

For only an instant did I fear his interference. What a foolish fear it was!

"Truly, Manu, the great sahib and I made a rendezvous on the moor which we must keep."

"Do you want me to remain with you and the sahib, for such service as I may do?"

"It isn't needful. Go with Owain and the groom in the carriage and, when you've eaten, wait for me outside the village on the road. I will return before dark."

His eyes filled with illimitable love for me, then he touched his forehead with both hands. I almost tripped getting down, and was afraid the watchers would think it was caused by undue haste. I spoke at some length to Owain, so he would see I was in no hurry for him to drive on. I had every air of calmness.

"I suppose there's a riding skirt and jacket in the bag?" I asked Jeffery, calmly for all to hear.

"I thought you might like to slip them over your dress, in case we go through a mudhole."

"That's very thoughtful of you, Jeffery. I'm surprised that a man could think of such things."

"You may put them on in the woods there. Change your dress for them, if you think they'd be too hot." He turned and spoke to Owain. "You may go in now."

I smiled at him and at Manu as I turned to go the short distance into the woods. Owain called to the horses; their hoofs clumped the hard road and the carriage wheels made their characteristic sound. I would get hold of myself now, I thought. I would get rid of this excitement that made me feel guilty—or of the guilt that had excited me. Putting on a riding habit would calm me. It would be an assurance that I had no other prospect this afternoon than riding in with Jeffery after a picnic lunch in the shade. Tonight Manu would sleep in my dressing room. Tomorrow I would attend to the business I had come on, the shape of which I did not know—not till tomorrow.

I opened the bag and found a green habit, about the shade of my own. It had been rained on to judge from its slight mottling, and was a style of ten or fifteen years before, but it should fit me perfectly and become me beautifully. Also there were a comb and brush in case my hair became disarranged, and a hand-mirror. Therein my eyes showed very bright and I quickly turned them away. In the brief glimpse my face appeared as clean as on leaving the inn, and, I thought, suddenly more beautiful. . . . If a flower started to open at sunrise, it might appear at full bloom at ten o'clock. But a very close observer would see that its perfect fullness was not attained until noon. Perhaps I had never been as beautiful as today. . . .

The habit was too small to put over my dress, and the day too warm to wear both with comfort. When I had changed, I still felt cramped, so I took it off again, removed my heavy petticoat, and on donning it over only my shift I could commend myself for my common sense, for I felt much more free. As I emerged from the copse, the feeling had the effect of a high elation. I had come to such a wonderful place to give freedom rein. There were no walls on the moor, no treacherous gates and doors. There were places where, by raising your head for an occasional survey, you could see for miles, while yourself remained unseen. You could do what you pleased without danger of being taken by surprise. Full under the great lamp in the sky you could obey any prompting. You could dare yield to the long-thwarted most hidden craving. . . .

"How charming," Jeffery said, when he saw me in the quaint riding habit. He spoke with emphasis, indicating a good deal of enthusiasm, but again he was hiding something under the lamp. I looked into his darkened eyes and felt that he had expressed pleasure in order to conceal a great, however poignant, ecstasy.

The gray stallion was grazing without restraint of any kind; even his reins were fastened out of his way. Jeffery was holding the mare, and groomlike had me put my foot in his hand to mount, instead of lifting me into the saddle as so lightly he could have done.

"I left the bag in the woods. Will it be safe?"

"If you look toward Blackmoor Keep, you can see the carriage. The men in it are our closest companions, and they'll soon be out of sight. There'll be no other traffic on the road today. So you can understand how safe it is."

"Does all this belong to you, Jeffery?" I gestured to the immense landscape.

"As Alexander Selkirk was supposed to say—as Robinson Crusoe did say in the book—I'm monarch of all I survey. Actually the land itself is not worth much more than Crusoe's island. But the tin under the ground—and the game above it—are priceless."

He turned and called in a low voice,

"Ixion?"

The gray stallion raised his head, arched his neck, fluffed his tail, and lifted one foot in a pose of alert vivacity wonderful to see.

"Come."

The animal broke into a handsome collected canter, then stopped still at Jeffery's side.

"I was a little afraid that show wouldn't come off," Jeffery told me, when he had mounted. "For quite a while Ixion answered to *Ella* instead of come, and I've had trouble getting him back on English."

The remark started two trains of thought, one of which I resolutely checked as not pertinent to the day. It was pertinent to yesterday and to tomorrow; all it could do now was dull my sharp, ecstatic sense of freedom. The other dealt with freedom in connection with Ixion. He had not run away as his instinct would have once commanded. He had been set free from its domination whereby to live twice as richly and dynamically as Jeffery's slave. That meant there was no such thing as perfect freedom. You traded one master for another. The trick was to pick the best . . . the one that paid the best wages. . . .

Jeffery led the way into what looked like a forsaken footpath. His silence and the glances he sometimes gave me—as though he could not quite believe I was close behind him—made me expect an exciting surprise. It proved to be a bewitching scene of water and greenery. What I first thought was a long narrow pond was really one reach of a large brook, indeed a small river, flowing slowly as a lovely dream. The shadow that the high bank flung across it caused the waters to look black in contrast with the vivid green of its banks and the rushes and grasses growing in its shallows. Curling around a blind bend with what seemed ineffable grace, it flowed gently as sweet Afton for nearly a furlong, then appeared to debouch into a verdant bed of waterplants. Probably this was only a shelving bank, I thought, the main current taking a sharp curve out of sight.

"I thought this was a good place to have a bite of lunch," Jeffery told me.

The words were mild and their tone casual despite the almost magical charm of the scene. Yet that alone did not fully explain their impact upon me.

"I'm not as hungry as I was." This was quite true.

"It's a good thing. I brought only a little, so as not to spoil your appetite for a trencherman's dinner tonight."

We made ourselves comfortable in the shade of the high bank. The saddlebag produced a white cloth, shelled eggs bright as porcelain, sandwiches, glasses, and a well-wrapped bottle of champagne chill from a cold cellar or icy spring. I thought of another lunch I had eaten on the moors. I had sat with my lover in the Circle of Stones emblematic of fertility. We had been alone as Jeffery and I at this moment—as far from any one—as unwatched, unguarded.

The grass had been avid green, the moss-beds rich. The air had felt balmy and the sky had been serene. In that wonderfully limpid light, every tint and hue of color would become distinct, and the least detail of form beautifully revealed. We had been alone as never were Adam and Eve on the day of their strange discovery, for here was no serpent and no sword. Yet if it had not been for the swiftly gathering storm, Rene's pride and fears and instilled guilts might have divided and conquered us.

But now there are barriers greater than those, Rene, between us, and someone is sitting in your place.

Lie still, Rene! But need I ask it? What other choice do you have?

FORTY-SEVEN

"E'VE had it quite lively at Blackmoor throughout the spring," Jeffery was saying.

The remark broke into my revery—it was extraneous to the thoughts and fancies inspired by the scene. Why shouldn't Blackmoor be lively when Lord Lundy wished it so, it being a great country seat with every luxury, staffed no doubt with scores of expert servants? People came there on his invitation to hunt on the moors and fish in the rivers. . . . The aristocratic sportsmen could bring their beautiful young wives, slim ladies with fair hair and thin, high-bridged noses and delicate mouths in which butter, to look at them, would not melt. . . . But at the magnificent board sometimes a lord grew tipsy and must be taken to bed. Perhaps the hand of Jeffery's trusty butler had been heavy over the tippler's glass. Perhaps his lovely bride had noticed, but she could not be sure it was not accidental; and later she lost her way in the long, dimly lighted corridor. Her husband lay snoring and what he would never know would never hurt him. . . .

There was a deeper sleep than that . . . Even Manu was miles away, and what he did not know . . . Miles could not measure the distances of some who had loved me. If ghosts exist they have no hearts and are impervious to pain.

I wished I didn't love myself. I wished I could hate myself.

"Some of my guests were interesting people," Jeffery went on, when I had made a comment. "A few were statesmen—a good many brilliant politicians. Their problem was revolt growing throughout Europe against the system set up by Metternich. I suppose you felt it in Bavaria."

I was listening intently now. "Yes, I did."

"A rather big blowup is expected next year. So, of course, some of my friends were put out with me, for refusing to take active part in suppressing it. I couldn't bring myself to do it, Lola. I'd become reluctant to leave Blackmoor even for a few days. Almost everything I wanted in life was here. I think I can say now that everything I want in life *is* here?"

"By the way—is Europa here now?" I asked.

"Much to her disappointment, she had to miss welcoming you. She's in San Casciano, searching for the manuscript of a very great book about an ideal prince. Eugene is away also on one of his ventures."

"How did you happen to find such unusual—"

"It was a good piece of luck. You may not realize it, Lola, but I'm a serious student of religion. On my way back from India I went into Thrace, with the idea of looking into the Dionysiac mysteries still practiced there, and I got to see the fertility rites at Bizye. Europa and her brother thought that they, too, were studying the cult, while actually they were involved in it head over heels. Highbred, imaginative people are likely to get lost in erotic esoterics of that sort."

"Jeffery?"

"My beautiful Lola!"

"You speak so sanely sometimes—"

"Sometimes! I've told you I'm the most completely sane—"

"If you are, why did you come to meet me on the horse that Eugene rode in a race with Rene—a race that Rene lost?"

"If you could want proof of my perfect sanity—I should say my super-sanity, compared to most people who count themselves sane— you need look no farther. True, it gave you a shock at first sight of him. That shock has been diminishing ever since—you'd have a hard time now experiencing more than its semblance. But its fading brought into a relief a fact that until now you've had a hard time admitting. I mean, of course, Rene's death. He isn't here any more, Lola. All bonds between you and he are severed by the hardest and coldest of all facts. For the first time—I venture this is true—you are today finding yourself reconciled to it."

I looked for the stallion but for the moment could see only my mare, fastened to an iron ring set in a big stone. This startled me a little—in looking at the river I had not observed how Jeffery had tied the animal and had assumed he had slipped the reins over a natural projection. Evidently this has been a favorite retreat for some lordly rider, who, not wishing the company of a groom, had ordered the convenience. The mare had gnawed the grass almost to its roots for a radius of perhaps four feet. Only by standing up did I locate the stallion, picking and choosing his fare half a furlong distant . . . There is no such thing as perfect freedom. The trick was to pick a master that paid the best wages. The mare was still mastered by her inclinations to run away and assert herself. The stallion had made a profitable surrender.

But it was quite true that I looked at him without the least shock.

"You see, Lola, romantic attitudes don't get very far compared to realities," Jeffery told me while my eyes devoured his beautiful face. "What does it matter if this is the same horse? He jumped a ditch where Rene's horse fell—perhaps Eugene knew he would fall— perhaps he was serving me on that occasion as might Young Berkeley. You remember the fun we had over him, don't you?"

"Perfectly," I said. It sounded so pat, almost so funny, that I said it again. "Perfectly."

"Thereby you suffered a real loss, a sharp grief. But you knew all the time, as I did, that the loss could be made up a hundred times, and the grief changed into—rapture."

"I wonder if I did!"

"Rene died in the same way my father did, trying to keep up with someone better than he was in that particular game. You re- member my thoughts about the spirit of the dead linking itself with the living—the strongest and most vital it could find, that would promise the most thrills—so you can imagine Rene's taking up with Eugene's. Mine would be too much for him. He wouldn't be equal to it. But if all that is just a pleasant fancy, the fact of his departure remains. The only facts that a person should concern himself with are those important to his living triumph and joy. Isn't that sane?"

"Terribly sane."

"Of our kinsmen and 'loved ones' who've been dead a year, how many would we recall? If every one had the secret privilege, believing that it was his alone and no one but God himself would ever know, the jump in population would be negligible."

"I don't believe it."

"Hardly anybody would believe it of himself, until he searches his soul."

"Even his unwillingness to believe it shows idealism—"

"That's thin gruel, Lola. You can have it, if you like, and the feast, too. Your potentialities for joy and triumph aren't half realized. You *will* realize them through complete union with me."

"For how long?"

"Forever."

"That's a frightening word."

"I know it is. I wonder how so many people dare bandy it about."

I wiped the sweat from my face.

"But it's not cold sweat," I said, controlling my breathing well. "I'm not that frightened. I'm just hot."

"It's been an hour since we've eaten. We can go in now."

Only for one shattering second did I think he meant to go to Blackmoor Keep. Then I could not believe it of him, my great lover; and in a second more perceived his real meaning. He had not brought me to this beautiful place with a weak or trivial intent.

"If the water's cold, I won't do it."

"No, it flows from a warm spring and is almost exactly blood heat."

"I'm not much of a swimmer."

"I swim very well. You needn't have the least fear. We'll hold hands and float."

"Then let's not look at each other until we're in the water, because—"

"I know. The grass is so green and soft. But you'll be glad we waited when our moment comes. I, too, will be glad—even for waiting all these years."

I went close to the brink, let down my hair, and began to take off my clothes. I was in no hurry; my movements appeared serene. I watched the increasing whiteness of my reflection in the water; by looking closely, I saw where it was not white. I had never known what lechery meant before, but now I wanted it for my companion always. I wanted it to live in my body and brain, ever ready to draw in my eyes and harden my heart. I had thought it was part of passion, but it was a different, a softer, a more unearthly thing.

Beside me I was aware of whiteness moving in a faint, golden haze. Jeffery and I slipped into the water at almost the same instant, and we looked at each other for the first time. His countenance was still hawklike, and his floating in the crystal-clear flood gave an illusion of soaring in the air, but his body was too beautiful for that comparison; I thought it was the most beautiful on earth. Why had I ever been content with any other? Had I been so, or only told myself so? My eyes drew in and my heart felt hard because I need never be again. As the shadow of the high bank dropped behind us, the deep-searching sunlight found us and put us on display, each of us made more beautiful by the other's reflection. The waters did not appear to magnify Jeffery's male beauty as much as disclose its multiple aspects, as though they were bathed in the whiter, clearer light of another sun. All his dimensions seemed simultaneously revealed, and his gentle movements as he glided toward me divulged every detail of his form in repeated rhythmic turn.

He had caught my hand and now I could lie motionless, only my face above the warm, soft, slowly moving tide. At first Jeffery paddled with his free hand, but now, turning on his side to face me and sculling indolently with one leg, he laid his hand on my breast. It was only resting there, and the impalpable pressure of the water bore it slowly back along my body.

As the channel made a sharp turn, Jeffery and I drifted on into ever shoaling water. Again we were in the shadow, and soon floating into a heavy growth of moss and water grasses.

I came to rest on a bed of undreamed-of luxury. The dense waterplants were softer than feathers between me and the shelving bank, smoother than my own silk-smooth skin, and wet.

I lay on my back, with one hand, palm up, over my eyes as though to shield them from the light. . . . Do what you like with me, my inertness told him. I will yield my body and all that you desire.

Let me know the taste of the fruit of evil, that will fall into my hands when my soul is lost.

See, I lie low in the rank, wet weed.

"You're asleep, my own, but I'll waken you, and have you always," I heard him murmur.

Peering between my fingers, I saw his pupils fill the irises but I dared not look into the black mirrors. There came creeping a golden faun.

FORTY-EIGHT

AN hour had passed since my lover and I had come to shore and I was drying my hair in the late-afternoon sunlight. We had not yet dressed, but had talked of many things, and laughed; and neither our voices nor our faces were now strange. Presently he went to his clothes, took his watch from his waistcoat pocket, touched its stem, and held it to his ear. Then he spoke without any apparent change of tone.

"We've still plenty of time to go down into the mine."

"I don't know what that means."

"More than you might think, but on the face of it only a rather thrilling experience. It's not a part of the mine where the miners work—instead a very old part, the ore having been dug out centuries ago. It's reached by a separate shaft that I have a good excuse to keep open, since it helps in ventilating."

"On the face of it a thrilling experience, but what lies underneath?"

"I should say not a mysterious but a mystical experience, mainly, I suppose, because of the legends connected with it. I feel sure it will mean a great deal to you. You can call it a ceremony, if you like. Our marriage ceremony will be before the world, but this between us alone."

He saw perplexity in my face and paused.

"You forget I can't marry as long as Anthony lives," I said.

"No, I haven't forgotten. But perhaps you forget the famous line from Horace, *'Dulce et Decorum est pro Patria Mori.'*"

"It is sweet and becoming to die for one's country—"

"The Colonel is a model officer, and I'm sure he would subscribe to the sentiment."

Jeffery spoke simply without change of expression. The perplexity went out of my face and out of my mind and soul; the meaning and the law of life appeared perfectly clear. I wondered why I had ever been confused. It was only a matter of what master paid the best wages . . .

"Even the others who went down with me got quite a lot out of it, although I doubt if they could tell you why," he went on. "I believe they've felt a kind of linkage with me ever since."

"I want to be united with you—forever."

"That's what I want. Foolish as it may seem, I feel this journey together can be the real consummation of our marriage. But you may not want to go, after I tell you what it is. Neither of my parents ever went there—neither did my mother's old servant Owain. The shaft goes straight down for nearly a thousand feet. The car is lowered perfectly safely against a friction-checked cable and lands where oil lamps are kept burning. From this light, you would go with me through a passage of total darkness into the light again—to a part of the mine being worked and from where we'd be drawn up in the steam-powered ore lifts. It's the path that the blind miners used to follow in their worship of the Erlking—even today the men take pride in going through it at least once. It winds between two chasms—the slightest misstep means death—but the journeyer only has to keep hold of my hand to be perfectly safe."

"Has anyone ever fallen?"

"Not if he put his trust in the guide."

"Who was the guide before you?"

"An old miner. Ordinarily he would have picked a young miner as his successor when he became infirm, but I asked for the office when I was eighteen, and got it."

"Is the place warm?"

"That part of the mine is very warm."

"Pitch dark?"

"You've never imagined such darkness."

My lip twitched and I could hardly speak. "In what way will my journey be different from the others?"

"At one point on the path a wide shelf of rock juts out over the chasm. It was once the altar of the Erlking—the miners still believe it's sacred to Old Berkeley. I've been out on it—in fact the former guide took me there—but I've never taken anyone there. That's where I'm going to take my bride."

"There used to be—sacrifices made there?"

"According to legend. I suppose it's true."

"Is an idol there?"

"There's a stone carving of some kind. To play the game according to tradition, I've never struck a light and looked at it. I felt it that day—it's rather roughly worked and wet from drippings. I couldn't recognize its form."

Looking straight at it in the open day, I still could not quite recognize Jeffery's form. Its sheer beauty had until now captivated my senses to the mazing of my mind. Its flat muscles suggested Greek statuary—particularly the Hermes of Praxiteles, I thought. Certainly it was such a body as a great sculptor would give a god he was carving. A man with such a body could easily become godlike in his thoughts and feelings, especially if it accompanied an intelligence of great power and brilliance.

What did godlike mean? With a surge of my will, I recalled what Monsieur Eugene had told me. He had given me a hint of the nature of godhead, as he saw it—and he, too, must have been a profound student of religion to have become involved in the Dionysiac mysteries in Thrace. His words did not apply to simple tribal gods and goddesses chosen by the people for their courage or beauty. The gods he referred to were much less human, more divine. They derived their divinity from being worshipped—worship was the food that made them gods, the real ambrosia. The laws of such a god had nothing to do with justice, their sole purpose being to support his godhead. There could be no palliation in the enforcement of his law, because the least breach was a sacrilege. Divinity was absolute or nothing.

In that respect, Jeffery was godlike. There could be no palliation in the enforcement of his law. But after perceiving that, I could not treat with it rationally or morally: I remembered the golden faun's stealthy advance on a water nymph in feigned slumber. The echo of it was on me, all over me and through me, now. His beautiful hands were superbly strong. When they were not caressing me, I wanted them to be remorseless in their works. I knew now why Europa had asked to be whipped for looking back to her childhood gods. Even on me there must be no mercy—for my least doubts I must bear the allotted punishment. The thought still frightened me as a first hallucination might frighten a man of breaking mind, but the time would come . . .

All my bearings lost, dizzy as though from a witch's brew, yet I still sought some reasonable explanation for his victory all but complete.

"I want to ask you something, Jeffery. You told me that Europa regarded you not only as Dionysus but his father Zeus. How do you regard yourself?"

"Only as Jeffery, Lord Lundy."

"For how long have you wanted to take me down into the mine?"

"Ever since I met you."

"You wanted to take me more than anyone?"

"Anyone then alive."

"Was there some sort of symbolism connected with the god of the underworld taking Persephone every year down into Hades?"

"I don't know. There might have been. Those old allegories have enormous impact on the racial mind."

"When we go down, will you hold my hand?"

"No, you must hold mine in token of complete trust in me. As long as you have that trust, you are absolutely safe. But if it falters for one second—if in panic you try to go your own way—you'll never see the light of day again."

"Then it's a religious ceremony, isn't it? It's a kind of confirmation in your religion. It signifies the complete surrender of my body and soul."

"Lola, isn't that what you've always craved?"

"With one part of me, yes. Now that part has grown. If you want me to, I'll go down with you into the mine."

"Then we'll go at once."

We dressed quickly and in silence. With my hair still flowing, I mounted the mare; Jeffery sprang on the gray stallion and swept ahead of me at full gallop. Up the dim path I rode as fearlessly behind him as I had ridden ahead of Manu to join the waiting Rajputs, but in a different cause, with a different love. He sped up the road toward the village, the stallion's hoofs clumping the packed clay, and I wanted him to turn off soon, lest Manu should have come searching for me and his eyes meet mine. But luck was with me—it could not fail me from now on. Jeffery turned off into a bridle path far short of the houses.

The sun was glowering above a granite tor as we came up to what looked a little like an immense well. It was enclosed in a stone wall about five feet tall; and over it could be seen the top of an iron car hanging in the well mouth from a four-inch cable of rope. This hawser ran over a pulley suspended from a derrick to a huge iron drum at one side on which it was wound with countless coils. A gap in the wall permitted access to the car.

Jeffery dismounted leisurely, not aware of my desire for haste. He was starting to explain the mechanism when he could well understand that desire.

A strong shout rolled swiftly up our path.

"Wait for me, memsahib!"

Jeffery gave a little start, glanced back at our pursuer, then his eyes wheeled slowly to mine.

"It's your servant."

"Yes."

"What does he want?"

"I don't know."

"Must we wait for him? It takes only a second to get in the car—"

"Yes, I must wait for him."

Manu knew I would wait, for now he stopped running, perhaps to save his breath for something he had to tell me.

"Would he like to go down with us?" Jeffery asked.

"No, he won't go down."

"Then give him short shrift, will you, Lola? I can't wait."

"He'll be here in a moment."

Manu came up, a little paler than his wont, his eyes as I had always known them. But I would not look at them.

"Memsahib, do not go down into the mine," he told me.

"I desire to go with my lover."

"In the name of my love for you and yours for me, I pray you not to go."

"It is foolish talk. The great sahib desires me to go. Am I to balk his desire because of the prayer of an old gardener in second childhood?"

"Aye, I am an old gardener, but if your heart were not already hardened—"

"What do you fear? I will walk along a narrow path, holding the sahib's hand. Do you think he plots to slay me?"

"He does not plot against your life, but against your soul. Onto this he has already grappled, when he lay with you in the weed."

"How do you know, unless you did spy on me, badzat that you are?"

"Aye, I spied on you. More than that, I have spoken—"

"You have spoken behudgi. Go from me quickly, lest I dismiss you from my service for ever."

"Nay, I will not go until I have spoken, though I never lay my eyes on you again. Nor do I speak behudgi, as you yourself would know if you will return to the true seeing of your childhood, and of all your years until this day. Many a soul he has destroyed. But there were two that he could not, both of the same name, and one of them was the poor sort, barely fledged, that is found in our lesser brethren, the beasts and the birds."

"Can't you tell the old fellow—" It was Jeffery's voice, good-humored sounding now, but there was a darkness on his face. Presently I saw it was only the long shadow of one of the posts of the derrick.

"Not yet," I answered, and turned again to Manu.

"What of the other?"

"Hers was the soul of a woman as beautiful as you are. She never lost her freedom to come and go, no matter her awful fate. When there was only one road left whereby she might depart, a dark and dreadful road, she took it, and her soul was saved."

"What was that road? Speak quickly."

"You laved in it today, but when she floated down to the bed of moss and grass, she was beneath the flood. When the great sahib went in search of her, it was on that bed that he found her."

After a brief pause, I turned to Jeffery.

"The old fool has heard that there are evil spirits in the mine, and fears for my life," I said.

Jeffery gave a little sigh. "I hope you were able to reassure him."

"Not altogether. In fact he's made me a little nervous. Are you sure the lift is safe?"

"Perfectly. Look at that rope. There's a friction device against its running out—"

"Will you get in first?"

"Of course."

"If it shakes very much—" Then I looked into Manu's eyes. "Draw back a few steps," I told him in a harsh tone.

"Aye, memsahib." He withdrew close to the drum.

"Look at it," Jeffery was saying as he stepped through the arch and down into the lift. "It's steady as a rock."

"Manu, it comes to me that we must make offering unto Kali. Our lives will then be at her mercy, but our souls will be saved."

"I cannot act save at your command."

Once more I addressed Jeffery. "I've had to take a firm tone with the old man, but he'll behave himself now. I'll get in with you—"

I moved into the opening. Jeffery stepped back a little in the car to give me room and was raising his hand to catch mine. But I paused and spoke over my shoulder to Manu.

"If you love me, Manu, strike."

His hand moved swiftly as a mongoose leaps when the cobra lashes out too far. His big curved kukri concealed under his carefully folded chadar flashed over his head and down in a swift wheeling stroke like the sweep of an ax in the hands of a giant woodman.

But although the edge was razor-sharp, only the superhuman strength of love could have driven it clean through the great cable of new hemp.

The part of the rope attached to the car shrieked as it sped over the pulley, then lashed the wall of the well. At the same instant Jeffery made a gigantic attempt to leap through the arch. I saw his face when he saw he was too late. In the same fraction of a second it dropped out of sight.

There followed a brief interval of silence before we heard from him again. Then out of the well rose a sound that at first I did not recognize—that I thought must be a scream of terror until my mind could leap to the truth. Instead it was a howl of laughter. It rocketed up, eloquent of deathless mirth here and hereafter. It must have hurt the ears of God upon His throne.

It was growing fainter but no less terrible as I beheld its terrifying answer. Down the well, the swiftly dimming light revealed a great slab of stone part from the wall, appearing to hang suspended for an instant in mid-air, then fall out of sight. At once other sections splintered off, and far, far below us there rose a deep-throated rumble that swiftly swelled. The rim of the shaft began to crumble, and I stepped back just in time. The wall enclosing it began to fall apart, many of the stones tumbling down, revealed for an instant, then disappearing. The rumble rose to a roar as of an avalanche heard by frightened woodcutters in the high snows of the Carpathians. It transcended sound—the ears could no longer cope with it—it was a dreadful possession of the whole brain that would soon shake it into madness.

The sides of the shaft leaned slowly inward and pitched down. The derrick gave way and fell in twisted ruin. And my soul went from me, listening over the well, and it thought it could still hear piercing these thousand thunders a wild exultant peal.

I thought it was the last laugh, and no one ever born could ever laugh again.